Royal Rush: 75 Days to Fall in Love

Royal Rush: 75 Days to Fall in Love

by

Lissandra Rowe

2026

ROYAL RUSH: 75 DAYS TO FALL IN LOVE

ISBN 13: 978-1-63679-965-0

This Trade Paperback Original Is Published By
Bold Strokes Books, Inc.
P.O. Box 249
Valley Falls, NY 12185

First Edition: February 2026

Credits
Editor: Cindy Cresap
Production Design: Susan Ramundo
Cover Design By Tammy Seidick

Dedication

To the Spanish culture, art, music, language, food, and love that is so beautifully inspiring.

Thank you to my loved ones for always giving me grace and encouraging me to finish what I'm writing and being my hype squad when I'm certain I will never.

This book is a love letter to so many amazing things ingrained in my heart, and I hope all of you love it too.

CHAPTER ONE

"Earth to Mikaela." The unmistakable teasing filtered into Mikaela de Medreno Soliz's consciousness as she blinked slowly. She sat up, smoothed her black linen pants, and met the cheerful gaze of Dayanara Diaz, her longtime best friend, across the sleek polished table between them.

"God, I didn't even realize I fell asleep," Mikaela said. She stretched her arms and then ran a hand through her hair.

"Don't worry, you look flawless," Dayanara teased her, reading Mikaela's mind. "As always. You're the only person I know who can wake up from a nap looking like you strolled off the set of a *Vogue* cover shoot."

Mikaela laughed. "I love you, Daya," she replied. "But you're so full of it."

Dayanara shrugged. "Okay, maybe you were drooling a little."

Mikaela shook her head as she glanced out the small round windows of the de Medreno family's private plane. Her shoulders relaxed as the jet began gently descending over the emerald-blue waters of Cayo Azul.

Home. The world beyond these shores—Paris, Tokyo, London, New York City, Dubai—had always dazzled Mikaela with its bright lights, prestige, and promises of fun and temptation, but nothing compared to the quiet majesty of Cayo Azul's small island kingdom.

"Nearly there," Dayanara said, her voice quieter now. "What's on your schedule for this evening? God knows there was no time to rest during the Venice Film Festival."

Mikaela nodded. "My mom must have told the stupid PR agency to RSVP us for every event there. I'll speak with her about that. I understand the importance of strategic appearances for the family, whether on the film festival circuit or for other events, but she has always been more enamored by the society stuff than I ever have."

Mikaela glanced down at the thin white-gold Cartier watch draped loosely around her right wrist. *Right on time.* She watched as the outline of Castillo Blanco grew closer. The royal estate, perched high atop a rolling hill, nearly blinded in the late afternoon sun. Its imposing white brick and polished marble was comforting as it sparkled against the sun, a quiet paradise away from the chaos and expectations of the rest of the world. Here, just a stone's throw off the east coast of Spain and nestled in the vast crystal-blue waters of the Mediterranean Sea, Cayo Azul was Mikaela's sanctuary. For generations, her family guarded it fiercely and guided the million or so inhabitants honorably.

Mikaela straightened in her seat, as she checked her phone and pulled a compact from the black leather Louis Vuitton tote next to her. Even now, returning from the glamour and excitement of the Venice Film Festival, she felt the weight of responsibility settle back into her soul. Though her family's name was not as well-known outside their shores as royals in other countries, Mikaela understood her place as the only child of Cayo Azul's king and queen. She took a deep breath as she dotted a nude pink gloss over her lips and blended light streaks of concealer along her cheekbones. Venice had been good to her and Dayanara, despite the nonstop slate of commitments. Their skin was still sun-kissed after a few days in Sorrento between film festival appearances that Mikaela had insisted upon after seeing the packed eight-day agenda from the family's London-based PR agency. Now, however, it was time to return to Cayo Azul duties. Her father would see that she was brought up to speed on all royal business.

Dayanara pocketed her phone as the jet slowed to a stop on the tarmac at the island's only airport and glided to the luxurious hangar exclusive to the de Medreno royal family and associates. The familiar de Medreno family crest was paved boldly into the smooth concrete of the hangar floor, claiming the private hangar as their own and off-limits to the rest of the island. As the jet's door opened with a gentle hiss, Mikaela and Dayanara stood as their assigned security officer took the metal steps down first. The familiar blend of ocean salt, sultry jasmine, and fresh citrus filled the air. It wrapped Mikaela in the scent of home as she took a deep breath before stepping onto the stairs. The warm island breeze tousled her hair over her shoulder.

"Sorrento really brought out your natural blond," Dayanara said, fixing Mikaela's wind-blown hair.

"Mmm," Mikaela said. "The break in southern Italy was probably the best part of the trip, if I do say so myself. If I have to put on another designer gown and make small talk with an endless parade of socialites and self-important entertainment industry people, it's going to be *way* too soon."

"It's good to be home, isn't it?" Dayanara said as they paused for a brief moment on the stairs. The security guard gave them a quick nod, signaling that the hangar was clear and one of the discreet black Escalades from the royal fleet was waiting nearby to return them to Castillo Blanco.

Mikaela nodded, the distant sound of waves crashing against the shore a comforting hum, and looked around in satisfaction. The deep green rolling hills went on for miles around them. "It's good to be home," she said.

Even if the outside world tries to claim me. Cayo Azul is mine. And I, in turn, belong to it.

Chapter Two

As the Escalade entered the grounds of Castillo Blanco, passing through tall, wrought-iron gates after being waved through by two security guards in a small booth, Mikaela glanced longingly at the modest home just visible behind the imposing and brightly lit castle.

That home was Mikaela's private residence, and she longed to pour a glass of wine and crash onto one of the lush sofas on its large, semicircular deck overlooking the ocean, with part of Cayo Azul's bustling, well-heeled City Center province in the distance.

"You should at least say hello to your parents," Dayanara said, as if reading Mikaela's mind.

She wrinkled her nose. "I know," she sighed. "I'll check in with my father. See if there's anything urgent I need to know before tomorrow's meetings."

The Escalade slowed to a gentle stop at the end of a long driveway, opposite a sapphire-blue pool with a large marble fountain at its center and surrounded by expertly manicured greenery. As their uniformed driver carefully swung the vehicle door open, Mikaela glanced up the twin staircases at the other end of the pool. The staircases wound up to a wide, wraparound front patio and large double doors.

"Have you spoken to Alejandro recently?" Dayanara asked, waiting patiently as their driver carefully stacked their luggage onto a dolly.

Mikaela shook her head. The only son of her father's younger brother, Alejandro had long been more of a brother than a cousin. "He's in Vienna until tomorrow, I think," she said. "The DACH region was hosting some diplomatic meetings this week with some of the smaller European island nations. I would have much rather been in Vienna as well, but you know my mother. She seems more determined to see me in the society pages of the international papers rather than preparing to take on more royal responsibilities from my father."

Dayanara laughed. "I *do* know your mother."

They fell into step together as they walked up the staircase, their driver dutifully wheeling their luggage to Mikaela's private residence.

"I think she's just worried about you," Dayanara said. "After all, the king is nearly sixty years old. It's quite a lot of responsibility to take on from him, even if he's gradually easing you in. Perhaps she just wants you to have some fun."

"She's always had a *unique* way of showing her worry," Mikaela scoffed. "And besides, her idea of fun is sitting runway-side at Fashion Week and being photographed at weddings for socialites she barely knows. Mine is serving my father and the country that runs through my blood. I've understood the importance of my role since I was small. I've been prepared for it practically every day since I was born. The *queen* needs to understand…"

A brief look of panic washed over Dayanara's face.

"…That I'm ready. I was born ready. Even if she's not."

Mikaela turned toward the front doors at the light sound of someone clearing her throat gently.

"Good evening, Mikaela," her mother said. "I see you've returned safely from Italy."

"Of course I have, Mother," Mikaela replied. "With the schedule that you and the agency committed me to, it was difficult to have even a moment to breathe let alone find any trouble."

Mikaela's mother arched an eyebrow. "Good evening, Dayanara. Thank you for accompanying my daughter on the trip. Though I know she can be a bit…*difficult* at times."

"Mikaela? Never, Your Highness," Dayanara replied good-naturedly. "Well, I'll grab my luggage from your place and head home. Get some rest, Mikaela."

Mikaela nodded as Dayanara hurried away. They had been friends for years, ever since Dayanara's mother was hired as Mikaela's private tutor when she was just four years old, and Dayanara had become quite adept at reading the royal family's dynamics over the years.

"Terese's new chef prepared a gazpacho earlier," her mother said. "I'll have her serve you with some fresh bread. I'm sure you're terribly hungry after traveling today."

Mikaela followed her into the eat-in kitchen area, dropping her tote into a chair with a thud. "Is Papa here?"

"I believe he and Eduardo are wrapping up a call with the Spanish health minister," her mother replied, referring to Cayo Azul's trusted prime minister. "I will let him know that you've arrived safely."

"Thank you," Mikaela said. "We have several meetings tomorrow and I want to make sure I haven't missed any details while I've been away."

"Alejandro is covering the diplomacy functions in the DACH region," her mother went on smoothly. "Quite impressively, I may add. The Germans are very taken with him, his knowledge of the area, and how well he speaks the language."

Mikaela took a long spoonful of the gazpacho, savoring the silky-sweet tomatoes and velvet richness of the olive oil. *This new chef is good.* "Interesting that I was not sent to Vienna and Alejandro to Venice," she said. "Papa and I have been strategically ramping up my responsibilities as a working royal over the last four years, and I'm not certain that the film festival should have taken precedence. Even if I do not speak German," Mikaela said pointedly.

Her mother smiled tightly. "I'll check on your father."

Mikaela sighed, feeling the tension ease from her shoulders as her mother left the kitchen. She glanced at her hand, still gripping the large silver soup spoon, and then at her reflection in the ornate decorative mirror on the opposite wall.

Damn. I just got this manicure three days ago and my nails are already chipped. I haven't even had a chance to take Luna out for a ride yet. Luna was a beautiful Clydesdale horse and one of Mikaela's most cherished possessions. The sleek chocolate-brown mare had been a gift for her sixteenth birthday, and Mikaela had won many elite show jumping and dressage prizes throughout Europe with her. These days, Luna enjoyed her personal stable on Castillo Blanco's grounds and Mikaela saw to it that she was spoiled rotten.

Mikaela took another bite of the gazpacho, but her relaxed reverie was broken as she heard two familiar voices in the distance. *Was that my name? Are they talking about...me?*

The rest of the gazpacho forgotten, Mikaela strode out of the kitchen and across an Oriental rug sprawled over the dark hardwood of a long hallway that led to three conference centers that doubled as meeting chambers for the Royal Council. Her father often worked in the first one, the largest, and Mikaela paused outside the door to listen.

"How do you know it's not just an experimental phase?" her mother said. "You know this younger generation, Bartolo. They're much more open than ours was."

"An experimental phase?" her father responded. "Cristina, this experimental phase you speak of has been Mikaela's whole life. Do I need to remind you of the playdate with Dayanara and her cousin when she was visiting from Spain? Mikaela was *six* and the first thing she did was run up to Olivia and kiss her cheek. And that night, she told Dayanara's mother that she loved Olivia and wanted to be her husband."

Mikaela felt her face heat as the long-forgotten memory floated to the surface of her mind's eye. The rare occasions when she was allowed to be around children her own age growing up had been exciting. Dayanara and Alejandro were great friends and trusted allies, so they were usually the only ones allowed to be close. Mikaela shifted uncomfortably as she recalled her unabashed crush on Dayanara's cousin, long before she somehow realized it was considered wrong and something to be ashamed of. *Fuck that.*

"She was a little girl!" her mother said. "She was young. She did not know what was wrong or what was right. How do you know she won't meet a man tomorrow and fall deeply in love?"

Her father sighed. "Love, you cannot tell me that you don't realize our daughter loves women. When has she ever, in thirty years, met a man and fallen in love? I've thought long and hard about this for many years now. I know my daughter. I see the way she looks at beautiful women. It is not something she can control, Cristina."

"And what do we do, Bartolo?" her mother replied. "She wants to take on more responsibility. I can't keep committing her to these functions and events while having Alejandro step in to cover royal duties."

"I told you not to do that," he said with a chuckle. "Mikaela is ready. You know as well as I do that Cayo Azul has a longstanding tradition of kings and queens abdicating around sixty years of age, and then winding down duties in an official royal capacity over the following few years. This is an important generational tradition that infuses our island with new ideas, leadership with strength and stamina, and someone to represent the times we are in. And honestly, Cristina, I am tired. Cayo Azul is my life, my blood, my country. But no king is meant to rule forever. New generations require new leadership and someone who understands them because she *is* them."

Her mother sighed. "Mikaela is not like the rest of the Cayo Azuleans, and you know that. She is royalty and we've raised her as such."

"Yes, and she is *good* with our people," her father said. "Don't you see it? Cayo Azuleans like her. She has been prepared to take over as my heir since she was born, and she has handled the duty and responsibilities with grace, intelligence, and compassion. Cayo Azul is in a beautiful place, literally and figuratively. Tourism and travel are flourishing. The value of our land skyrockets every year. Our university's foreign student enrollment went up a hundred and twenty percent last year."

Mikaela felt a rush of pride as she listened to her father's praise. While he had taught her much over the years, it was rare to hear him speak so candidly about her. Her belly warmed with satisfaction at the wide-ranging accomplishments their small island nation had achieved in recent years.

"We have so much in motion to ensure our people see and know they can trust their leaders, but it can take time to see the benefits," he said. "Eduardo's team has been carefully monitoring the restlessness in Este."

Mikaela frowned. *Restlessness?*

"There's also one thing…" his voice trailed off. "Something befitting of an incoming leader to strengthen her legitimacy, something representing unity and hope."

Her mother sighed. "Yes. We will have to speak to her together, because I know she won't like it coming from me."

Mikaela's ears perked up as a strange gnawing feeling began low in her belly. *Now what?*

Her father chuckled and Mikaela could hear him pull her mother onto his lap. "Come here, you beautiful lady," he said. Mikaela wrinkled her nose as she heard them kiss. "I know you try with her, love. But are you trying to reach her where she is? Or where you are?"

What does that mean? Her mother vocalized the same question behind the heavy door.

"It means," her father went on, pausing for a moment. "What are you going to do when Mikaela refuses to marry a man? We both agree that she needs a partner. But we both understand how love works, meaning there is *no* rhyme or reason to how love works. I am willing to support her in having a wife. Are you?"

Mikaela didn't hear her mother's response through the blood pounding in her ears. She walked backward, away from the cool frosted glass of the conference center door, and nearly stumbled in her white stiletto ankle boots over a corner of the thick rug.

She glanced up as the door to the conference center opened, and she straightened as her mother startled and blinked at her.

"Mikaela," she said. "I'm glad you're here. There's something your father and I need to discuss with you. Please, join us in the chamber."

Mikaela cursed inwardly as she followed her mother into the elegant space, its long, polished table illuminated by the bright white moonlight streaming through tall, arched windows. A chandelier overhead cast warm yellow light across the table and her father sat at the head, before his laptop and a stack of glossy folders bearing the de Medreno family crest.

Her father smiled at her as she sat. "It's good to see you, my daughter," he said gently. "I trust Venice treated you well?"

Mikaela nodded once. "Yes, Papa," she replied. "It was quite a long day of travel. Unless there is something urgent, I may return to my—"

Her father cleared his throat gently. "There is an important matter to discuss, Mikaela," he said. "Your mother and I have arranged a more formal meeting about this with the rest of the family, but I'd like to speak to you first. As you know, Cayo Azul has a longstanding tradition of royalty abdicating around the age of sixty. You understand this is an important tradition that makes way for fresh leadership, new ideas, and trust in the next generation. I have no intention of breaking this tradition that has worked so well through the last several generations of royalty. Time is no longer a luxury on our side."

Mikaela's breath caught, but she ensured her carefully neutral expression didn't waver. She knew the time for a leadership transition would be soon, but it was still jarring to hear her father discuss it so frankly. "You're really stepping down?"

He folded his hands. "Not immediately," he replied. "There are things that should be firmly in place first and things that will take time to wind down. But I have every intention of following this tradition with dignity."

"I understand," she replied. "And what things must be firmly in place to prepare?"

She noted the brief glance exchanged between her parents as the pit in her stomach deepened.

"A royal consort would portray strength and stability," her mother chimed in smoothly. "A symbol of unity and excitement. Love, partnership, and a brand-new legacy for our island to usher in the next generations."

Mikaela sat back in her chair for a moment, willing her face not to give away how hard her heart hammered against her ribcage. The tides of expectation crashed around her as she blinked.

"Is that truly necessary?" she finally asked. "A partner in order to most effectively rule Cayo Azul? How old-fashioned, Mother." She took a deep breath. "Besides, how can I get married when I'm not even dating anyone?"

Her father's gaze sharpened. "You are not being asked to marry a stranger," he said.

Mikaela threw up a hand helplessly. "Oh, thank you for that."

"Mikaela," her father went on, quieter this time. "There is documented intelligence of growing discontent in Este. A widening in the financial gap between the residents there and elsewhere on Cayo Azul. This is something we knew was a bit of a risk when we began entertaining foreign development twenty-odd years ago. Unfortunately, Este has not caught up to the rest of the island for several reasons and their struggles have led to restlessness. I am working closely with Eduardo to devise solutions that provide a more immediate impact for the people of Este, but a royal wedding? A celebration of new leadership in time with the traditionally expected transition? This is how we show proactivity and strength while promoting unity."

Mikaela blinked at her father, who regarded her kindly and expectantly. She crossed her arms tightly across her chest as the warm air felt sharp in her lungs. *Get married. Not if.* When. *And soon.*

Frustration filled her chest. "With all due respect, Papa, marriage is not a strategy on a larger political chessboard," she said tightly. "Cayo Azul has always been a firm proponent of the marriage bond. If and when I choose to marry, I want the choice to be *mine*. And *hers*," she added pointedly. "Something culminating from deep love, not an exciting event to calm unrest and strengthen the Crown."

"Mikaela," her father said gently. "I understand you're tired after a long day of travel. We will have another discussion about the marriage strategy and succession plan soon. I know you understand the importance of the de Medreno legacy, the expectations, and our generational traditions. Let's reconvene once you've had a chance to settle back in."

Without another word, Mikaela walked stiffly down the long hallway. Her footsteps echoed in a quick, angry rhythm as she headed toward the front doors.

"I am *not* getting married," she muttered as she threw open the door, her knuckles white from the tight fists she didn't realize she'd balled her hands into, and stalked into the evening air toward her personal residence. "They can't make me."

CHAPTER THREE

The tomatoes are done, Mother!" Isabella Acosta Ramon called across the tiny kitchen of their home in Cayo Azul's Este province. The last rays of sunlight filtered through smudged windows and danced across the burnt orange clay tile floor. "Should I start cooking the prawns?"

Isabella listened for a response and pulled a jug of olive oil from the cabinet. "Mami?" She tried again.

It had been a long, hot day on the east end of Cayo Azul, a wild, open, and rural area filled with miles of working-class farms and modest, ramshackle homes that dotted the unkempt green landscape. Though the day was long, Isabella had been dutiful in assisting her mother with the seemingly endless housework. Her father had left two nights before to have a drink at the local tavern and they hadn't seen him since.

Par for the course for Papa. Isabella grabbed a small frying pan. *Who knows when he'll show up and when he'll leave. And who knows if he'll be lucid or if he'll eventually pass out somewhere with a glass of water.* She was certain her mother had finished her double nursing shift at the island's large hospital hours ago and wondered if she was still sleeping or perhaps taking a shower.

Isabella gently knocked on the bathroom door. There was only one bathroom in her family's small home, but she always let her mother shower first and for however long she wanted. *She deserves it, with all she has to put up with from Papa.*

"Mami?" she called. "Are you hungry?"

Isabella whirled around in surprise as the front door of their home flew open, and her mother stepped inside as she held up her father. His right arm was slung loosely around her neck and his eyes were glassy and half-shut. Her mother took a deep breath, the small but noticeable show of fatigue enough to spring Isabella into the same commonplace routine that she and her mother had perfected over the years of her father's alcoholism.

"Isabella, my love, help me get your papa to bed, yes?" Her mother winced as she pulled his heavy arm off her shoulders.

Isabella nodded and nearly toppled over as she ducked under his left arm. With a heave, they half-dragged him into the bedroom where he landed with a soft thump onto a faded quilt spread neatly across the bed. His head rolled across a thin pillow and his unfocused eyes fell closed.

That was easy. Easier than some of the other times he's arrived home drunk.

As she turned, she nearly gasped at the sight of her mother in the doorway. "*Mami!*" She carefully pulled her mother's left hand away from her face. "What happened? Where did this bruise come from?"

A large purple half-circle was already forming at the corner of her left eye. It was only then that Isabella noticed the tear tracks that skated down her worn face, too wrinkled and tired to be someone just forty-four years old.

"It's nothing, my daughter," her mother said. "Please, go make dinner. I'll be fine."

"Absolutely not," Isabella said. "What happened to you?" She froze and swallowed. "Did…Did Papa do this?"

They both straightened as her father groaned from the bed. "*Ay*, Isabella," he called mockingly. "Always so concerned about your mama. You two have always worked against me, you know that?"

Isabella knew better than to engage with her father when he was in this state. She threw him a sidelong glance and then stepped out of the bedroom, gently closing the door behind her. "Tell me, Mami," she said as she glanced back at her bruise. "Did he do this?"

Her mother's mouth thinned into a single line, but she didn't answer. "I was called to pick him up by the police. He was wandering around the outskirts of City Center, up to God knows what. How he got all the way there, I'll never know. Smelled like he spent the day swimming in tequila. In fact, he probably did."

"City Center?" Isabella repeated, wrinkling her nose.

Her mother nodded. "He must have been drinking the entire time," she muttered. "He knows they already don't like the looks of him over there, and if he's drunk and making trouble…well, he's an easy target for the police. That doesn't fit the fancy image they want to portray, with all those European vacationers and their money. He's looking for trouble and, well, trouble found him. He's lucky he wasn't arrested and thrown into jail."

"He should know better," Isabella said. "You've deserved better for too long, Mami."

They walked into the kitchen, but Isabella stopped her mother as she automatically went to the stove. "Go sit down," she said. "Rest. I'll get you some ice and then finish dinner."

Her mother threw her a grateful glance as she sank into the threadbare sofa. "Thank you, my daughter."

As Isabella reached into the freezer for a handful of ice cubes, she stiffened as a muted crash came from the bedroom. She glanced at her mother, who placed a finger over her lips and shook her head silently.

"I drink because that's the only way I can deal with you women," her father shouted. "That's the only way I can tolerate this miserable life. Maybe you two should care about me for once and all that I've done for you instead of protecting each other like I'm some monster! You want a monster, I'll give you one…"

Isabella remained perfectly still as her heartbeat pounded in her ears and his shouting faded, a telltale sign she had learned meant he would be passing out soon. Relief flooded her veins. *I wish he'd just stay away for good. But who wishes their father away forever? I was taught to honor and love my parents. But how can I honor and love someone who honors and loves alcohol more than his wife and daughter? And himself?*

Isabella ran a hand through her hair and blinked away the sudden tears that blurred her vision as she regarded the dinner that still needed to be made. "We should make a police report," she said firmly. "Papa shouldn't do these things. He shouldn't…" she glanced back at her mother's bruised face. "… be allowed to get away with how he treats you."

She sighed. "And what? Send your papa to jail? He'll lose his job, Isabella. The job he can barely keep as it is. Working as a groundskeeper for Cayo Azul is hard work, but the kingdom does pay a little above average. We need his income too. There are only so many hours of the day I can be at the hospital and only so many odd jobs you can do without your university education."

"Mami, we don't have the money for me to attend university," Isabella replied. The olive oil sizzled in the frying pan as she carefully added the prawns. "I'm okay with that. I would rather stay here in Este and help you."

Her mother clucked her tongue. "You're too smart to stay here, Isabella," she said. "Graduated secondary school at the top of your class. You should have already finished at the university, but you've been stuck here instead. You're much too good for this place."

Isabella's throat involuntarily closed up, but she refused to turn away from the stove. "So are you, Mami."

"I've learned to let your papa go in one ear and out the other, Isabella. The words used to hurt more than his occasional hands, but I've numbed myself to it all. I enjoy being a nurse at the hospital. Helping people. Healing them. Watching beautiful babies being born into this world, and seeing the joy those parents feel when they meet their newborn. Which reminds me often that the highlight of my life was when you arrived in this world."

Isabella took a deep breath. "You were only nineteen," she said. "And now you've been stuck with Papa ever since."

"The best thing that ever happened to me was when you were born," her mother said firmly. "Regardless of how life has turned out, it has been good because you're in it. And I will find a way to get you somewhere better or to the university, even if it's later, so you can use that smart brain of yours and not be stuck here taking care of your mami and drunk papa in Este forever."

Isabella turned from the stove and regarded her mother. She leaned back and rested her head against the back of the sofa. Fatigue and defeat deepened the lines across her face as she held the ice against her eye. A dull gray had started to streak like ash through her once-dark curls and the long eyelashes that framed dark brown eyes had thinned, blending with the crow's feet and wrinkles.

"I love you, Mami," Isabella murmured.

"I love you too," she said. After a moment, her mother stood and placed the remaining ice in the sink. "Finish the prawns, please. And don't forget to add garlic and chili leaves, I just bought fresh cloves from the market yesterday. I'm going to sit outside for a moment and feel the sun setting on my arms. I'll help you plate dinner in a few moments. We'll make one for your papa just in case he wakes up later, yes?"

Isabella watched her mother for a moment as she wearily slipped outside onto the modest front porch and nodded. "Yes."

CHAPTER FOUR

City Center was Cayo Azul's gleaming heart that pulsed with energy from affluent tourists and stylish new-money residents who had benefitted greatly from the island's economic investment into capitalism.

No City Center building is older than me. Mikaela gazed from the tinted windows of the Escalade at the bright, twinkling lights illuminating luxury apartment buildings, boutique waterfront hotels, and sleek, ultra-modern cafés, bars, and shops neatly set back across wide sparkling sidewalks from the palm-lined boulevards. *A testament to our catapulting growth over the last thirty or forty years.*

Scores of shiny German luxury vehicles were parked along the streets, their flashy logos as ubiquitous as the mouthwatering scents of fresh seafood and expertly prepared paella that filled the cool night air. *No wonder Germany adores Alejandro so.* Mikaela felt a flash of pride as she considered her younger cousin's brilliant business mind. *His knack for trade agreements is unparalleled. He's incredibly adept when it comes to economics.*

At night, City Center still took Mikaela's breath away and filled her with wonder at the knowledge that *this* was hers. The island, its success, its people. They depended on her to be the trusted leader that protected their interests and the nation of Cayo Azul.

Two crisply-uniformed police officers stood at the corner. As the Escalade passed, Mikaela could catch what the one with the dark mustache was muttering to his partner.

"Drunk asshole." He shook his head in disgust. "All the time, that guy. I don't know how his wife does it."

The police force and first responders in Cayo Azul laddered up to their small but mighty military—her uncle Juan's domain. Mikaela considered her uncle. Juan de Medreno Soliz ran a tight ship, so it was no wonder the Cayo Azul police force didn't tolerate even the slightest bit of public debauchery, and certainly not in City Center.

As the Escalade pulled around the back of Tryst, one of City Center's most cosmopolitan nightclubs, Mikaela took a deep, steadying breath, hoping to inhale the vibrancy of the district as the glowing sun gradually descended to the horizon. Splashes of light pink, deep red, and purple streaked off the tall glass windows of the immaculately maintained buildings around them, giving way to the neon lights of City Center's rooftop lounges. The unmistakable rhythm of flamenco and the fast, lively beats of reggaeton pulsed through the air as fashionable residents and well-heeled tourists mingled casually under the twinkling string lights of trendy restaurant patios.

"Shall we try to find your future wife tonight?" Dayanara said, as her light teasing brought Mikaela back to the present.

Mikaela pulled her gaze from the lively City Center atmosphere and swallowed hard, trying to ignore the pull of *something* she hadn't felt before so deeply.

What if? The thought flashed through her mind before she could tamp it down. *What if it works out and I meet someone amazing?*

A twinge of heat deep in her belly flushed Mikaela with warmth before she shook the fantasy away.

"Not likely," she answered with a resolute shift against the black leather seats. They suddenly felt sticky and suffocating. "They're out of their minds if they think they can arrange a marriage for me," Mikaela took a deep breath, smoothing her white minidress across her lap. "That's not how love works. That's not how marriage works. It's not how *anything* works. And I don't see what it has to do with me being named the next leader of Cayo Azul." She gestured vaguely at the base of her throat. "As soon as they confirmed what was expected, I felt like…like I couldn't breathe or something."

Dayanara raised an eyebrow. "You're freaked out," she replied matter-of-factly. "If I didn't know you as well as I do, Mika, I'd even venture to say you're a little bit scared."

Mikaela scoffed. "Scared? Of this? No, Daya, I'm livid. My parents have some nerve, thinking I need to be married off to be fully effective as the eventual leader of this beautiful island. Forget my master's degree with honors or that I've been gradually taking responsibility from my father for four years now. You'd think those things would matter much more."

Dayanara shrugged one shoulder as the Escalade pulled up gently to the private back entrance of Tryst. She glanced at Mikaela with something akin to sympathy.

"Nope," Mikaela said as she shook her head once. "Don't look at me like that. No way. I'm not going out like that. I am Mikaela de Medreno Soliz, for God's sake. They can't make me get married just because they think I should get married."

Dayanara regarded Mikaela knowingly. "Is it because it's something out of your control?" She paused. "You don't have to answer that. You know you love to be in charge. *Much* more than others." She grinned wickedly. "Maybe you've avoided love because it scares you a little bit. You thrive when you're in your element, we all see that easily. But love? That's something *way* out of your comfort zone. And I do know you well, Mika. When you fall in love, it's going to be deep. After all, marriage is forever."

Mikaela opened and then closed her mouth, saved by their driver politely opening her door as he waited for her to exit the Escalade.

"Just think about what I said," Dayanara said as she gently patted Mikaela's hand. "Come on, princess. First round of martinis is on me."

The neon lights and thumping bass pulsated inside Tryst like a wildly beating heart, electrifying throngs of partygoers already sliding close together on the large dance floor, expertly controlled by the forty-something queer Canadian expat resident DJ.

Inside the coveted VIP area of the nightclub, Mikaela and Dayanara sipped frosty martinis in the darkened relative obscurity of Mikaela's preferred corner booth. Tryst's exclusive VIP section was closely guarded by muscular security, and Mikaela's booth had already been cordoned off with black velvet rope in anticipation of her arrival. With a view of the sprawling, multilevel interior, including the main dance floor below, and easy access around the corner to the private VIP-only rooftop terrace, Mikaela could people-watch and move with ease.

"*Salut*." Dayanara gently clinked the wide lip of her martini glass against Mikaela's, careful not to spill the icy pink liquid of her cosmopolitan. "To growth and happiness, my friend."

Mikaela raised her glass and brought it to her lips for a slow sip of smooth imported vodka infused with Chambord and freshly squeezed pineapple juice.

"You know, it's encouraging that your father is willing to allow a same-sex partnership because he understands that will be true to who you are," Dayanara said. "And that your mother is in agreement."

Mikaela rolled her eyes. "Oh, perhaps I should grovel at his feet and thank him for that crumb of compassion," she replied. "Look, I know my sexuality is unconventional. I've never tried to hide it from my parents. But just because I am who I am doesn't mean you can put some random woman in front of me and…"

"It's a good step for your parents, that's all I'm saying," Dayanara said pointedly. "And besides, it sounds like they'll let you choose someone rather than make it an arranged marriage."

"I'm not even dating anyone." Mikaela took a slow sip of her martini. "I'm not even remotely interested in anyone at the moment. Shall I just pluck someone out of the sea?"

Dayanara shrugged. "You know, you probably could. Any woman-loving-woman would *love* to be with you."

Mikaela fixed her with a look. "That's not true."

Dayanara swallowed the last of her martini in one gulp. "That Russian socialite…" She snapped her fingers. "Alina? All you had to do was look at her and she was practically in your lap all night."

Mikaela thought back to the wedding in Croatia she had been forced to attend for someone she'd only met a handful of times throughout the years. "Sure, but…"

"And the daughter of that billionaire tech guy, she made her interest *very* obvious last time we were in New York City, if memory serves. She was sweet. A lot sweeter to *you*, I bet…"

Mikaela sighed as the bass thumped louder around them. "Okay, I get your point," she said. "But I don't know if I've ever been in love, truly. Is it so awful if I want to marry someone I'm madly in love with rather than for convenience or to someone who is only interested because of things like titles or influence?"

"No," Dayanara replied thoughtfully. "Maybe you're just looking at this all wrong. Maybe instead of focusing so much on taking more responsibility, you should also consider opening yourself up to, I don't know, *love*. The idea of finding a partner, the love of your life."

Mikaela shook her head and tossed her hair off her shoulders confidently. "I don't know," she finally said. It felt like it was time for a change of subject. "Do you suppose Ian is working tonight?"

"Oh, what if he is?" Dayanara's dark eyes lit up as she twirled the stem of her glass between her thumb and index finger nervously. "Do you think he's here?"

Mikaela glanced at her with bemusement. Ian McCarty was the bar manager at Tryst. His parents, Irish expats who had since returned to Dublin for retirement, had headed Castillo Blanco's grounds and housekeeping crew for many years. Ian had grown up within the walls of Castillo Blanco and had opted to stay even after his parents' return to Ireland.

"You know, I don't think you ever told me exactly why you two broke up," Mikaela said casually. "You seemed happy together."

Dayanara chewed her lower lip. "I…We…" She sighed. "It's, um, complicated."

Mikaela threw a confused glance at her. *We've never had secrets.* "Wait, Ian didn't hurt you, did he? Or cheat or do something crazy, right?"

Dayanara shook her head. "No, nothing like that," she replied. "He was a perfect gentleman. It was more so me, really."

Mikaela sat back against the smooth leather of the booth. "Good," she said after a moment. "He seemed distraught when you two parted ways. It was what, a year ago now?"

Dayanara nodded. "Do you think he kept his hair longer? I always liked those curls on him."

Mikaela shook her head good-naturedly as she glanced at the circular main bar and spotted Ian. He nodded up at her from afar, his affable grin crinkling the corners of his hazel eyes.

"Oh shit," Mikaela said as she held her hand up in a quick wave.

"What?" Dayanara sounded panicked. "He's working tonight, isn't he?"

Mikaela watched, frozen, as Ian excused himself and took the narrow stairs two at a time up to the VIP section. "Yup," she replied. "You've got about a minute until he's at our booth."

Dayanara groaned and gratefully accepted a second martini from a passing waitress.

"Ladies!" Ian's friendly Irish brogue boomed over the thump of the house music as he grinned at them. "Lovely to see you lot out tonight. Staying out of trouble?"

"As always, Ian," Mikaela replied warmly. "How has Tryst been treating you?"

Ian shrugged one shoulder. "Can't complain," he said. "I've got two new bartenders and they've been rather good so far. Summer season has been busy. Loads of tourists this year, I know you love to hear it." He cleared his throat slightly and shoved his hands into the pockets of his nondescript black work pants. "Hey, Daya."

Dayanara took a deep breath. *She still cares for him.*

"Hi, Ian," Dayanara said.

Everything was still for a beat before Mikaela spoke as she glanced between them and then at Ian. "Why don't you sit and catch up with us for a few minutes?"

Ian clambered into the booth next to Dayanara as she scooted over to make room. "I know you girls have been staying clear of trouble, but what kind of trouble has been finding you? Anything fun? Remember when one of the pipes broke and flooded the entire kitchen prep area the evening that your father and uncle were hosting the police and first responder annual awards ceremony?" Ian chuckled to himself. "I'd never heard Chef Terese string together so many Spanish curse words and make them sound so eloquent."

Mikaela and Dayanara laughed at the shared memory. "Our Mikaela here may be getting married soon," Dayanara said. "We're not sure yet to whom, but I'm sure you'll receive an invitation soon enough."

Ian's mouth fell open as Mikaela rolled her eyes. "Wait, I'm confused," he replied. "Mikaela, have you finally found the one?"

Mikaela shook her head. "Sadly, not even."

Ian looked between them in amusement. "Okay, one of you will have to elaborate because I'm lost here."

Mikaela took a deep breath. "My parents seem to think that before I can fully and officially be embraced into Cayo Azul leadership, I should have a romantic partner," she said. She glared at her martini glass. "They would like me to get married, which is ridiculous for a multitude of reasons including the fact that my ability to lead has nothing to do with my romantic life, the fact that I highly doubt they've had a similar conversation about Alejandro because, well, he's a man, oh and I have been working closely with my father and Eduardo for years now taking on every challenge, everything they've asked of me…" Mikaela ticked off the reasons on her fingers as Dayanara giggled.

"Well, except for settling down and getting married." She cut in teasingly.

Ian whistled low as the strobe lights danced across his face. "Wow, Mikaela," he said. "I never thought I'd see the day. Whatever woman you choose will be incredibly lucky. But I get it. Love is…is not easy."

Ian and Dayanara both glanced down at the table and refused to look at one another.

"It means she has to be vulnerable," Dayanara said as she glanced pointedly at her friend.

Mikaela sighed. "You're right, Daya," she said as she gazed across the nightclub. Ensconced in the dark privacy of the booth, she felt strangely comfortable reflecting on the churning emotion just below the steady surface. "I've always prioritized responsibility and duty over emotion. That's what good leaders must do to ensure their land and their people are secure and well. You become accustomed to not reacting every time a tough emotion comes up."

"Plus you might put your heart out there and risk it getting broken," Ian supplied.

"I might make the wrong choice," Mikaela said with a nod. "Love is a huge risk. I mean, what if I'm not enough for someone? Love has always been elusive to me, so maybe it's something I'm not meant for. But I'd rather not find out and get my heart crushed under the weight of failing. I would never forgive myself if I failed my future wife *or* my duties as a leader."

"You? Not being enough for someone?" Ian's eyebrows practically rose to his hairline. "I find that rather impossible. And remember, Mikaela, love might be a huge risk, but consider the reward too. You deserve to find the love of your life. I hope you do." He shrugged. "And I hope I get invited to the bash, because royal parties are the best."

Mikaela laughed and swatted his strong forearm. "Of course you'll be there."

"You don't give yourself enough credit, Mikaela," Dayanara said. "I think you're, like, *made* to be someone's love. You're so protective of those you care about. She's out there. I know it. We just have to find her sooner than later."

Mikaela raised her nearly-empty glass. "Salut. At the very least, I'm grateful to be blessed with wonderful friends. That's more than some have. As for the rest? To be determined."

Ian cleared his throat awkwardly. "Speaking of friends, can I ask for a few minutes between us?"

Mikaela glanced between Ian and Dayanara in surprise, but she nodded. "Sure," she replied hesitantly. "Let's step onto the terrace."

Ian nodded and stood, waiting politely for Mikaela to exit the booth first. She glanced back once more at Dayanara, who looked equally confused.

As they stepped onto the tiled open-air oasis, its sleek white lounge furniture scattered in a loose semi-circle and glass railing providing a panoramic view of City Center and the moonlit ocean just beyond, it dawned on Mikaela that perhaps Ian wanted to find out how Dayanara was doing.

"Um, so I…I've been hearing some things." Ian's voice was low and uncharacteristically serious. "You know, working the bar here and more so at some of the taverns outside City Center in my off time. I don't know if it's cause for any real concern, but the chatter has gotten louder lately so I wanted to bring it to your attention."

Mikaela frowned. "What chatter?"

Ian shrugged uncomfortably. "You and me, we go way back, Mikaela. Not many people these days know I grew up mostly at Castillo Blanco too. That my parents worked for the royal family for years and they loved it. Your family was wonderful to us, to them. We were treated like extensions of your family and we all speak so fondly of our time there together."

Mikaela nodded. "I'm glad, Ian. Your parents are wonderful, hardworking people. I've always considered you a trusted friend. But help me understand what you mean."

Ian took a deep breath and glanced back at the door to Tryst's VIP section. "People on the island…They're talking a lot. At first, it started as just the usual complaints from people upset about their own shitty lot in life, you know? Looking to blame someone. Guys blowing off steam after some beers at the taverns."

Mikaela nodded again, cautiously.

"It's getting louder now," Ian said. "More pronounced. People are getting…agitated. I overhear a lot. They're starting to organize, mostly over in Este. A lot of the guys there travel to Santa Julianna for work and they connect there. There's a committee forming in Este. They're looking to make some noise now, *real* noise. I just wanted you to know."

Mikaela arched an eyebrow as the night breeze ruffled her hair over her shoulder. “A committee for what?”

Ian sighed. “Opposition, Mikaela.”

The understanding dawned on her just as the slow, creeping discomfort seeped into her belly. “You can’t be serious, Ian,” Mikaela said. She recalled her father’s mention of strife in Este earlier that evening. “My father is well-loved by his people. He would never want any Cayo Azulean to be left behind. The decisions being made are for all our benefits. I know because I’ve been part of these strategy meetings for four years now. Besides, you said it yourself. Tourism is through the roof. Our education minister just won an award for our school curriculums.”

Ian looked down at his hands. “I just want you to be careful and aware, Mikaela,” he said. “I know you and your family, but something somewhere is getting lost. People outside City Center are growing resentful and there’s this us versus them feeling that’s spreading fast, almost like a poison. Your father is a kind, astute leader and I’m sure your family can find a way to proactively counter these sentiments.”

Mikaela took a deep breath as the knot of discomfort ate at her insides. “Thank you, Ian,” she said finally. “I appreciate your insight. I’ll bring this to my father’s attention right away.”

As they returned to the booth, the humidity inside the nightclub instantly warming Mikaela’s face and neck, she exchanged a glance with Dayanara.

Ian ran a hand through his sandy-colored curls. “I’ve got to go and make sure the newbie bartenders aren’t pouring all my expensive stuff out in one night.” He cleared his throat once more. “Good night, Daya. You two, uh, take care of each other. Good luck with the wife search,” he called over his shoulder with a laugh.

As Ian walked away, Mikaela felt Dayanara’s attention shift back onto her. “What the hell was that? Was he digging for information about me on the terrace?” She flipped her dark hair over her shoulder. “I mean, I’m just curious what he said.”

Mikaela smiled brightly as she tried to tamp down the uncertainty about everything, as unfamiliar phrases like “love,” “opposition,” “wife,” “uprising,” and “marriage” floated through the back of her mind. She was loathe to express the swirling uncertainty growing inside her, even in the presence of her longtime friend and closest confidante. “Anyone can see that man is still crazy about you,” she said finally, satisfied that it was a truthful response. “I’m ready to call it a night. The longer today continues, the stranger it gets.” Mikaela stood, reassuring herself. “I’ll figure everything out.”

Chapter Five

The next morning, Isabella woke to an oddly still house. After the chaos of the evening before, she and her mother had eaten quietly and then headed to their respective bedrooms early. Though they didn't speak any more about her father, Isabella had learned the anxious, avoidant energy between them meant the same thing: *Stay quiet, walk on eggshells if you must—anything to keep him passed out so he doesn't wake until he's sober.*

The morning sun was white-hot and practically blinding as Isabella gently opened the front door. She knew exactly where to find her mother and, without a word, sat on the worn wooden porch swing next to her. She took a deep breath as her mother raised her coffee mug to her lips. The salty breeze carried the light scent of the sea, and it filled Isabella's lungs as the sun warmed her face.

"How are you, Mami?" Isabella asked after a moment.

"Doing better, my daughter," her mother said gently. "Your papa was gone when I woke up. He had an early start at work today. As for me, I'm enjoying a few moments of peace."

Isabella nodded. "I don't know how he can drink like that and then make it to work the next day."

"He's on such thin ice with that job," her mother said as worry flashed across her face. "I hope he can keep it."

Isabella chewed her bottom lip for a moment as she gazed across the wild green fields before them. "It's the longest he's kept a steady job since the fish processing factory closed," she said. "Surely his tenure means something."

Her mother gazed across the front yard. "I wish you could have known him, remembered him, before," she said wistfully. "Before the dishonorable discharge from the armed forces and the anger and the decision to turn to alcohol as his crutch in this world."

Isabella took a breath. "I know he was removed from the armed forces under complicated circumstances, and he's harbored resentment…"

Her mother nodded. "He always felt like he was set up to fail," she replied thoughtfully. "And it was an impossible situation, but the kingdom has never taken well to trouble in its ranks. Your father may have been forced to bear the brunt of his choices, but not everything is so black and white. As you get older, you'll see that there's so much more gray in every situation than most realize."

Isabella considered this for a moment. "I should start looking for a more permanent job," she said. "The odd jobs, they don't provide enough stability for us. I may not have my university education, but surely there's *something* I can do here. They're building resort after resort in City Center. I can clean rooms. Serve food—"

She was cut off as their neighbor, Roberto Jimenez, nodded in greeting as he ambled up the winding gravel walkway to their front porch.

"Good morning, Roberto," her mother called with a polite wave.

Roberto tipped his wide-brimmed fedora at them as he reached the porch. As the mayor of Este, he was well-respected among their neighbors and often acted as a critical liaison between those living and working in Este and the ruling class in City Center.

"Beautiful morning," he replied with a smile. He leaned casually against one of the stucco beams holding the roof over their porch. "I couldn't help but hear you mention all the new construction happening in City Center, Isabella."

Isabella nodded. "Yes," she said. "I'm hoping to find more permanent employment soon, and with all the new resorts and hotels being developed, I want to find something well-paying there."

Roberto snorted and shook his head as he glanced into the distance. His sun-weathered skin had started to thin and wrinkle, and his face was hardened by years of island politics. "So many in Este want the same thing," he said. "A fair shot to work, to earn a living for their family. You deserve it. Everyone deserves that." Roberto frowned. "Do you know what the geniuses in City Center are doing instead? Bringing in cheap labor to run and work the new resorts from outside Cayo Azul. They think bringing in those from other areas of the world on temporary visas will be more cost-effective than employing their own people who desperately need jobs. Surely you've seen that they've broken ground for another new resort where the old fish processing factory used to be. Even the contractors there now are with some fancy new company out of City Center, meanwhile there are at least half a dozen construction companies right here that are starving for work."

Her mother placed a hand over her chest. "Roberto, are you sure? The royal family would approve this?"

Roberto nodded. "I asked about the job forecast and Este unemployment rate at the last mayoral council meeting," he said. "I was told they expect the new City Center resorts to bring in approximately five thousand jobs. Do you know how many they told me they have earmarked for those here? Sixty, Araceli. *Sixty* out of five thousand. The rest will be divided among those in City Center and those they want to bring in on temporary visas. They want to keep us poor, Araceli. They want to keep us struggling. We're easier to control that way."

She shook her head. "The de Medreno family has always been fair and kind," she said. "I can't believe they would make a decision like this."

Roberto shrugged. "Money talks, you know? So does power." He leaned in closer. "And I think it's time we take some of it back. Remind the royal family that they are meant to serve us, the people of Cayo Azul. Not the other way around."

Isabella frowned as her hands tightened in her lap. "The royal family has always ruled, Roberto," she said. "And you know our armed forces don't take dissent lightly. What can possibly be done?"

Roberto crossed his arms. "That's what they want you to think. Our armed forces have never had a *real* rebellion to contend with. Trust me, ladies. People are waking up. The fishermen, the dock workers, even our farmers. They're tired of being ignored while the ruling class sits in their palace, in their luxury apartments, drinking wine and dancing to music while we break our backs and fight over crumbs."

Her mother fixed Roberto with a look. "What are you saying? As the mayor of Este, you are the one with the most influence when it comes to the ruling class."

Roberto nodded. "We're organizing, Araceli," he said. "We've asked for the basics for too long. We will now start demanding a voice, equal opportunities, and the same *respect*."

Her mother looked out at the horizon as the sun cast a bright white glow over the fields. "And what happens when you begin demanding?" she asked. "What do you think will happen to those who challenge the Crown?"

Roberto looked grim. "I know the risks involved. We all do. I've been meeting quietly with others influential here in Este. We're building a formal opposition, something the ruling class will not be able to ignore. It's early now, but it's spreading fast and we're making contact with some *very* influential people. We need to be thoughtful and strike when the timing is right. Think, Araceli. Do you want Isabella and the children she'll one day have to continue in a world like this, where the wealthy few decide everything?"

They fell silent for a long moment as the distant sound of waves crashing against the shore offered gentle background noise.

"No," she finally said. Her voice was steady but tinged with an uncertainty that Isabella rarely heard. "No, of course I don't."

Roberto tipped his hat once more as he straightened. "The tides will turn, ladies. We will not be left behind."

Isabella and her mother watched as he turned back down the winding gravel path, the weight of his words sitting heavily between them.

Roberto turned once more. "Oh, Isabella," he called. "I meant to tell you that Javi will be on break from university next week. He was asking about you."

Isabella forced a smile. "Oh, that's nice of him," she said politely. "I haven't seen Javier in some time…"

She stopped short as her mother elbowed her in her ribs. "…I mean, I'd love to see him when he's home. I'm glad he's doing well. It will be nice to catch up."

Roberto grinned and waved once more. "I'll let him know. Ciao, ladies."

As he disappeared from sight, Isabella turned with a glare. "Really, Mami?"

Her mother sighed and fixed her with a knowing look. "Javier is a wonderful young man, Isabella," she said as she sipped her coffee. "And he's had interest in you for years. These other young women in Este would love to date him."

Isabella rolled her eyes. "I see," she said evenly. "So just because every other woman my age in Este thinks Javi is hot, I should too?"

Her mother shrugged. "You're too stubborn for your own good," she replied amusedly. "Javier is a good man. He's your age and he's polite, helps his family, and works hard at the university. He'll be finishing his master's degree in some kind of engineering. He'll get a good job and be successful. Wouldn't you want someone like that? He'd be so easy to be married to, Isabella. Especially with the way he looks at you when he comes around."

Isabella wasn't sure why, but a bubble of raw frustration rose in her chest. She had known Javier since they were children. She grudgingly admitted to herself that he *had* grown into everything a woman could supposedly want: tall, charming, and a bright, attractive smile that made all the other local women blush a deep shade of crimson and stumble over their words. He worked hard alongside his father, Roberto, and at a university in Spain, where his brain and education would catapult him to success wherever he chose to settle.

"I suppose I should give him more of a chance," Isabella murmured. She ignored her mother's eager nod of agreement and wondered about the faint unease she felt instead. *It's not the first time I'll go out with him.* Isabella resigned herself to Javier's temporary return. *Every time he's touched my hand or leaned in close, I've felt…nothing. No desire, no nerves, no spark.*

"Eventually, if he senses your disinterest, he'll move on," her mother replied gently. "All the young women around here would love to date Javier."

"I know." Isabella sighed. *That's the problem. I* do *know. I know how wonderful he is, how he checks every box I should have for a partner, and yet I don't feel anything beyond friendship with him.*

After a moment, Isabella felt her mother glance at her. "You're the best one, though," she said proudly. "And Javier knows it too. It doesn't hurt to go on a few dates, my daughter. You're young and you should make time for fun too. Besides, it might take your mind off of...*here*." She stood and gestured at the peeling white paint of the doorframe before them.

"You're right, Mami," Isabella said. "I'll go out with Javi when he's back for his visit." She stood as her mother slipped back into the house and tried to ignore the impending sense of resignation and frustration pressing against her chest.

CHAPTER SIX

Mikaela sat patiently at the long mahogany table that had been polished to such perfection that she could see her distorted reflection when she glanced down. Despite the high, arched stained glass windows in the palace's largest conference room—known as the unofficial Royal Council chamber—she felt on edge. It had been a little over a week since she'd been brought in to discuss her future with her parents, and she had been decisively avoiding the conversation since. She had dutifully shown up for her endless slates of meetings, project management, and other royal business, but had otherwise steered clear of her parents.

I'm just delaying the inevitable. She straightened her spine as she listened to Eduardo carefully mentioning reports of unrest in Este.

Her father listened, his presence commanding even while in thought. "And who's decision was it to earmark only sixty jobs for the residents of Este?"

Eduardo cleared his throat. "What we need the people to understand, Your Highness, is that this is an investment into Cayo Azul's future," he said. "The developer of three of the five resorts is based in Bangkok and they have shown great interest in further development, dependent of course on how these initial plans go. They have since made clear that they would like to have the majority of the businesses run by Thai nationals. If we acquiesce a little to them now, the possibilities are endless for further investment in partnership with this developer. And then we can *all* reap the benefits."

Her father stroked his chin thoughtfully. "I understand what you're saying, Eduardo," he replied after a moment. "But I don't like it. The optics are bad. It looks like we're selling out our island to foreign developers. The average household income in Este is one-eighth of that in City Center. *One-eighth.* When the fish processing factory shut its doors twelve years ago, many of the nearby restaurants and shops that the workers frequented were also forced to close. Those in Este need opportunities too, and urgently."

Eduardo nodded. "Understood, Your Highness. I have been in touch regularly with Roberto Jimenez, but he has been…uneasy lately. I'm sure he's feeling the heat from Este. After all, he represents them as their mayor. But I should mention that when we had that conversation at the mayoral council meeting about the new resorts, he was *very* angry. He blew up during the discussion and had to be forcibly removed from the meeting. Since then, he has been distant."

Her father sighed. "A little care can go a long way, Eduardo," he said. "I would suggest taking your aides and doing a trip to Este. Meet Roberto where he is. Take a look around the area. Hold a town hall, listen to the people, and find out what we can do to assist them right now. I don't want to lose this developer partner, certainly not if the indication is they will invest further after these resort projects are complete. But we must show our own people they are important too. Have we revisited the Este scholarship program? What about increasing funding for their schools and developing a job training and certification program for those interested in being teachers to ensure Este's schools have the same student to teacher ratio as the newer ones in Santa Julianna and City Center? Education and communication are the keys here that we need to unlock a new sense of unity. Let's figure out ways we can show investment in our people as well as our island."

Eduardo glanced down at his hands. "I agree, Your Highness," he said. "I will, uh, revisit the Este scholarship program. It did fall down the priority list as these external partnerships have become very, uh, lucrative for Cayo Azul."

Her father sighed. "Not lucrative for everybody though, eh? We must tread carefully here. The next decade or so will be very important for our island and our people, especially as I begin my plans for abdication and transition to Mikaela. We must stress unity while continuing to strategically invest in the partnerships that have changed our island's fortunes so drastically over the last decades."

As the meeting adjourned, the Royal Council filtered out of the room one by one until her father, Alejandro, and her uncle Juan were the only ones left. She glanced at Alejandro as her father cleared his throat once more.

Uh-oh. Her cousin's smile wasn't his usual playful grin; instead, it was one filled with warm sympathy for what Mikaela realized was to come.

As Mikaela took two strides toward the door, she was met by her mother quietly entering the cavernous room. "Not yet, Mikaela," she said. "We need to speak with you. A few minutes for the de Medreno family only."

Mikaela took a deep breath and feigned annoyance. "What is it now?"

Her father's expression softened into one of mild amusement as he regarded her. "Sit, Mikaela." His tone was firm but not unkind.

Reluctantly, she took her seat once more and sighed. *Here we go.*

Alejandro squeezed her hand comfortingly. "Easy, cousin," he whispered. "I promise this won't be that bad."

Mikaela fought the urge to storm out of the room anyway. *He's not the one being forced to marry.* "If you say so," she whispered back resignedly.

"I am concerned by the growing number of reports of unrest, primarily in Este," her father said as he sat back against his opulent leather chair and folded his hands across his middle. "We must be proactive. The people need to see that the Crown is strong, united, and committed to every Cayo Azulean."

Juan nodded. "Our armed services are stronger than ever," he said. "There will be no protests or organized dissent of any kind, you have my word."

Her father fixed his younger brother with a stern look. "While I am appreciative and forever grateful for the might and strength of our armed services, fighting is not always the correct answer. It can often be the *easy* answer, but bringing the armed services in now will only fuel distrust and resentment. Particularly when we don't know how deep or organized this unrest is just yet. Instead, it is time for hope and harmony."

Mikaela nodded. "I understand and I agree," she said. "We should bring in Roberto and his team to collaborate on a panel designed to invest specifically in Este. Surely if not jobs, then we can take some of the developer's hefty financial investments and find other ways to repurpose a percentage of that in Este so they see the benefits and an improved quality of life."

Her parents exchanged a glance before her father leaned forward. "That is excellent, Mikaela, and I do have Eduardo and his team on it. However, your mother and I know that you can help in another, more indirect way. You recall our conversation the evening you returned from Italy, yes?"

Mikaela's stomach lurched. "You can't possibly still be serious about that."

Her mother took a deep breath. "We're throwing a gala in two weeks," she said. Mikaela knew that the bright expression pasted across her impossibly smooth, recently Botoxed face was not quite genuine. "It will be quite exciting, Mikaela. A grand celebration like we haven't hosted in many years. This celebration will remind the people of our stability, our leadership, and our love for Cayo Azul."

"That's great," Mikaela replied tightly as her chest constricted. "You want me to help you plan a party? Isn't that what you have the whole event planning team at the PR agency for, Mother?"

Her mother's gaze softened, though Mikaela recognized the steel in her spine. "Prior to the gala, we will release a statement announcing your intention to marry," she said. "By the end of the evening, you will choose your future wife. This should not come as a great shock to you based on last week's discussion. You understand the why. Now we will strategize the *how*."

Mikaela blinked, stunned. Even though she knew this was coming, the reality still hit like a cold slap. "Excuse me?"

"I like it," Juan mused, as though Mikaela hadn't spoken. "A royal wedding will show the people that the Crown is committed to the island, strong and powerful, as generations continue and Bartolo begins the leadership transition." He finally nodded at Mikaela. "Besides, wouldn't you like to have a future queen by your side?"

Mikaela's first instinct was to respond sarcastically, but she knew Juan didn't take kindly to those who ribbed him. *I'll never understand how he had such an even-keeled, opposite son.*

"This...This is an insane idea," Mikaela sputtered. She looked around the table, but the expressions on their faces confirmed that this wasn't all some strange joke. "You expect me to select a wife out of thin air? Marriage isn't..." She struggled to find the words. "...A political move or...or a power play."

"This is about more than you, Mikaela," her father replied. "It's about Cayo Azul. Our people. A royal wedding will be a beacon of stability and a symbol of love."

Mikaela threw a glance at her cousin. "What about him?" she asked. "Can't Alejandro find a wife instead?"

Alejandro laughed good-naturedly. "I get it, cousin, but you are next in line for the crown," he replied gently. "That is what people want to see. I'll have a royal wedding one day, but no one will be as engaged and invested in mine as they will yours."

"And what about what *I* want?" Mikaela shot back at her father. "What if I'm not ready?"

"You are ready," her father said. "You've been raised for this your entire life. And you will not be choosing out of thin air, as you may assume. Your mother has personally invited several prominent Cayo Azulean families and even some from beyond the island, from Spain, Portugal, the UK. They all have eligible daughters around your age and will be in attendance."

"Oh great, *Mother* oversaw the guest list?" Mikaela retorted. "I can only imagine the eligible women she'd select for me..."

"Mikaela, *enough*," her father's voice was firm. "Your duty is to this family and our island. I know it feels sudden and perhaps even unfair, but we must protect the Crown and each other."

Alejandro reached for her hand again. "I know you, Mika," he said. His tone was surprisingly thoughtful. "I know this isn't what you want right now. As our fathers get older, the responsibilities will continue to transition onto us. Sometimes that means putting the greater good over our own desires."

Mikaela deflated against her chair at her cousin's soft words of understanding. "I know, Alejandro."

"Who knows?" he went on confidently. "Perhaps you'll run into someone who surprises you. You deserve the best. And I know the best will find you."

Mikaela glanced down at his hand on hers as the invisible weight of familial expectations pressed against her. "Fine," she said at last. "I'll do it. I'll play along. But if I am married to someone I don't love, it will *only* be a political marriage of convenience and appearances. Love can't be forced."

Her father gave her a small, approving nod. "That's fair. That's all we ask."

"We should decide on a timeline," her mother said. "How long is necessary to court someone before making a decision?"

Mikaela bit her lip. "I must be able to choose a partner with thought and genuine connection," she said. "Isn't that what you want for me? Someone who can support me and who I trust?" Mikaela glanced pointedly at her mother as she pursed her lips but didn't argue.

"As far as a required timeframe, I don't know," Mikaela went on. "I'll need to get to know her. Sixty days? Ninety days?"

Her father nodded encouragingly. "It must feel right," he agreed.

"Time isn't unlimited, Mikaela," her mother said. "Not anymore. We'll meet you in the middle and agree to seventy-five days. By then, the public will expect an announcement after the gala. A royal wedding will give us the trust and unity our people need as we work to resolve and transition."

Mikaela rose stiffly from the chair and unclenched her fists long enough to run a hand through her hair. "If you'll excuse me, I have a lot to think about and ready myself for."

As she strode through the long, tiled corridor, the weight of what was to come settled heavily across her shoulders. *Two weeks to prepare for a decision that could shape the rest of my life. No big deal.*

She turned as she heard Alejandro walking quickly to catch up with her.

"Cousin," he called as he fell into stride with her. "How are you feeling?"

"As positive as can be expected," Mikaela said. "I'll do what I can and play my role. Though I think it's silly that I am having a spouse forced onto me to be taken seriously as the future queen and provide some sort of unified comfort to the island."

Alejandro wrapped a casual, protective arm across her shoulders. "I know, Mika," he said. "I'll be there every step of the way with you. No way you're going to end up with some woman who doesn't treat you exactly right. Besides," he laughed. "Maybe there will be someone interesting in your leftovers."

Mikaela playfully smacked Alejandro's shoulder. "Only you would think that. Maybe you ought to get serious about finding a wife too."

Alejandro's dark eyes twinkled. "Maybe," he said. "Good, you're smiling again. Meet by the pool in thirty? I think *you* need an afternoon to relax and *I* have a bottle of the best Obstler from Vienna that I've been dying to crack open."

Mikaela considered this. It was a tempting offer. "I can't," she said with a sigh. "I'm hosting that women in leadership dinner tonight in City Center. I need to run through my speech and the slide deck a few more times."

As Mikaela continued toward her private residence, she knew time was ticking. *I officially can't avoid this forever anymore. But maybe I can focus on my other duties, the ones that truly matter, before all this silly gala and wife stuff takes precedence.*

In the quiet calm of her home, a small, stubborn part of Mikaela couldn't help but wonder if perhaps Alejandro was right. *What if, amidst the politics and pretenses, I do find someone who makes my heart beat so much faster?*

Mikaela shook the dangerously enticing thought away. Love—real, aching love—was increasingly seeming like one of the few luxuries she would not be afforded in this lifetime, certainly not when her family and the island were counting on her.

Chapter Seven

Isabella removed the plastic lid from her white cardboard cup and stirred her macchiato. The steaming liquid lightened as the fresh cream blended seamlessly with the hot coffee. The coffeehouse had been there as long as Isabella remembered, a small, nondescript building along the main street of Este. Its sun-washed bricks with faded, hand-painted sunflowers and deep green ivy along the windows lent to its reputation as a relaxed local haven. The heavy glass door was propped open with a single brick most days, welcoming the warm, salty breeze and friendly chatter from the street outside.

She glanced at Javier as he pulled out the chair across the wooden table from her and sat. He had been home for several days now and this was the first time Isabella had agreed to meet him for a casual, one-on-one date. Earlier during his university break, they had gone to dinner with a group of old friends from school and, on a separate occasion, joined a casual afternoon seafood boil hosted by one of Javier's friends along a quieter stretch of beach in Santa Julianna. For reasons she couldn't quite put her finger on, Isabella preferred having the buffer of a larger group with them when they went out.

"Here you are," Javier said as he bit into a croissant sandwich with what Isabella could see was some sort of bacon and pesto. "I was catching up with Vanessa," he said as he nodded toward the register, where the coffeehouse's longtime owner moved expertly between cabinets and an industrial-sized refrigerator. "Her natural gas and electric bills for this place have tripled over the last year. Another small business on the island hurting because of decisions from those so out of touch." He sighed.

"That's terrible," Isabella replied. "Vanessa has poured so much love into this place for so many years."

Javier nodded at her cup. "How's your coffee?"

She took a long sip of her coffee, savoring the rich, sweet warmth. "Very good, thanks."

A brief silence stretched between them and then Javier sighed. "My croissant is good also, thank you for asking," he said pointedly.

Isabella straightened her spine. "My apologies, Javi," she replied, hoping a smile would ease the sudden tension. "I must've been off in space."

Javier took a deep breath and studied her for a moment. "No, it's okay," he finally said. "I…I do like you a lot, Isabella. I can't help but notice, though, that I always ask you questions. You know, how you're doing, what you're thinking and feeling, how your coffee tastes. You never ask me any questions in return."

Isabella swallowed hard as she realized he was right. "Oh, Javi, I'm sorry," she replied. "I'll try to be more—"

He shook his head. "It's fine, Isabella," he cut her off. "Don't apologize. I don't want you to *try* anything, I just want you to be interested too. But of course, that can't be forced…"

Isabella took a deep breath and glanced furtively around the cozy, unpretentious coffeehouse. A long counter ran along the wall opposite their table, where a large espresso machine hissed and steamed as it filled the air with the rich aroma of freshly brewed coffee. Behind it, scarred wooden shelves were stacked with tins of cacao and glass jars filled with looseleaf teas. She blinked as her gaze fell on a new flyer in a plastic frame next to the register. A single fist pumped into the air above bold words stating to *Make Your Voices Heard!* Below the words, smaller print using charged language invited residents to join a new, local Este committee and demand change from the Crown.

As Isabella refocused her attention on Javier's words, she couldn't ignore the nervous pounding of her heart. He was finally catching on closer to the truth.

"Let's enjoy our morning together," she finally said. She forced what she hoped was brightness into her tone. "After all, I'm going to miss you when you return to the university."

It's a half-truth. It's been nice having more of a social life and catching up with friends. And Javier isn't the worst person to spend time with.

As Javier grinned back at her, seemingly satisfied, Isabella wondered if "not the worst person to spend time with" was an exceptionally low bar for a potential partner. Deep down, she knew the truth.

"I almost forgot," Javier said as he fished around in his leather messenger bag. "Check this out."

He smirked as he tossed a large envelope onto the table between them. "The king and queen themselves are summoning us peasants to their castle, as though we should feel so lucky."

Isabella stared down at the ornately detailed envelope, sealed with the de Medreno royal crest in thick gold wax. "What is it?"

"I was invited to the royal gala this weekend," Javier said dismissively. "As the son of the mayor of Este, apparently, I'm distinguished enough to merit an invitation to the princess's glorified speed dating event or whatever they're trying to do. Marry her off or something since King Bartolo is getting older every day."

Isabella ran a finger along the edge of the thick, heavy paper as she recalled Javier's friend who had hosted the seafood boil joking about some sort of upcoming royal event. "It sounds like a once-in-a-lifetime invitation," she replied with a shrug. "Perhaps you should bring your friend. He had quite a bit to say about Princess Mikaela." She grinned teasingly as Javier snorted with laughter.

"Normally, I'd agree," he said. "But you do know the princess is seeking a wife, right?"

Isabella's heart kicked up a notch, though she wasn't sure why. Despite not knowing much about Princess Mikaela, she had seen plenty of photos throughout the years—enough to know that she was drop-dead gorgeous, all long, dark blond hair, piercing dark eyes, soft, full lips, and a natural golden tan that was typical of nearly all Cayo Azul residents, a proud sign of their shared Spanish heritage. "I'd heard occasional rumors," she replied evenly. "I didn't know there was truth to them."

Javier raised a thick eyebrow as he swallowed another bite of his croissant. "Where there's smoke, there's always fire, Isabella," he said. "Anyway, I *am* bringing a plus-one because there's no way I could stand to rub elbows with royalty without someone to spend the evening with. What color dress do you suppose you'll wear?"

Isabella nearly choked on her coffee. "I'm sorry, what?"

"Come on," Javier said as he leaned back and slung a casual arm over the back of the chair next to him. "You and me, dressed to the nines. You said it yourself. It's a once-in-a-lifetime invitation. Let's enjoy the food, the free booze, and let loose on the de Medrenos' tab."

Isabella shook her head. "Javi, I don't know," she said uncertainly. "This sounds like a serious event. The royal family—"

"Couldn't care less about people like us," he interrupted her bluntly. "This whole thing is a joke, Isabella, come on. They're trying to distract everyone from the real issues by throwing a party. It's ridiculous, because when has relating to your people by throwing obscene amounts of money around *ever* worked? My father sees right through it and so do I."

Isabella chewed her bottom lip. It was true that Javier's disdain for Cayo Azul leadership had sharpened as his father's influence over him became apparent. *The last thing I want is to be dragged into whatever rebellion they're planning.*

“I don’t know if being your plus-one while you mock the royal family to their faces is my idea of a good time,” Isabella said pointedly. She set her nearly empty cup down decisively.

Javier laughed, unbothered. “You wound me, Isabella. But if it helps, I promise I’ll behave. Like my father has said, drawing too much attention to ourselves too early will result in our cause being nipped before it has a chance to really take off.”

Isabella considered the growing curiosity she felt. It wasn’t so much about the grandeur of it all, but more so about the world that had always felt so distant despite being just thirty kilometers away. She wondered what it would be like to step into the castle and be in the same room as Mikaela de Medreno Soliz. An unconscious shiver ran down her spine at the thought of the enigmatic princess. The king and queen had so far kept her life mostly private and shielded from the world, aside from standard announcements and precisely planned public relations fare over the years. Even her official social media accounts were rarely updated and clearly run by someone hired to oversee her public persona. Isabella hadn’t been paying attention lately to realize the princess had been taking on more of a public-facing role or that the king’s traditional abdication was sooner than later.

“Okay.” The word slipped from her lips before she could stop herself as the image of Mikaela burned brightly in her mind’s eye. “I’ll go with you, Javi.”

Javier leaned forward. “That’s my girl!” he exclaimed. “Don’t worry, Isabella. It’ll be a night to remember.”

As they stood to leave the small coffeehouse, Isabella fought the urge to roll her eyes at Javier calling her “his girl.” Still, as they fell into step in the blinding late morning sun, she couldn’t shake the strange excitement deep in her belly that he might be right about one thing: It’d be a night to remember.

Chapter Eight

Mikaela took a deep breath as she gazed into the large gilded mirror framing the dressing table in the sitting room just outside her bedroom. Her reflection stared back at her, composed and regal, but her stomach flip-flopped nervously beneath her polished exterior. In the distance, she could hear Dayanara and Alejandro chatting about something downstairs. The entire day had been a parade of people in and out of her private home—chefs, tailors, event planners, estheticians, hairstylists, and makeup artists, to name a few. Most of them had since left, as the clock ticked closer to the evening's gala.

Her hair fell around her shoulders and down her back in shiny, loose curls that highlighted her natural streaks of blond and her lips had been glossed to perfection. Her expertly tweezed eyebrows and dark, carefully curled lashes framed a gaze that still held a hint of angst at what was to come, while the makeup artist's seemingly magical combination of powder, bronzer, highlighter, and soft blush accentuated the natural angles and curves of her face. Mikaela took a deep breath and blinked once, hoping the guarded coolness she felt disappeared. *No such luck.*

She smoothed the front of her satin dress and adjusted its thin straps over her tanned shoulders. "This is unbelievable," she muttered under her breath.

"Unbelievable?" Alejandro said, as he strode into the sitting room. Mikaela gritted her teeth as he met her eyes in the mirror and flopped casually across the chaise in the corner. "I mean, what better way to choose a wife than the biggest party we've had in years with *all* the prominent, eligible women around?"

Mikaela opened her mouth to retort but closed it as Dayanara entered the room. She bent to adjust the strap on her black Manolo Blahnik heels. "I'm just saying, if you pick someone solely based on how hot she is but she can't have a conversation to save her life, I'll never let you live it down. How am I supposed to *pretend* I like someone forever?"

Mikaela rolled her eyes, though she couldn't help her small smile. "And therein precisely is the issue, but no one wanted to listen to me," she replied. "But yes, Daya, I'll make sure it's someone you can stand too."

"Thank goodness," Dayanara said dramatically as she sat heavily on the chaise next to Alejandro.

"Listen, if it gets too overwhelming, just pick Daya," he said, feigning seriousness. "She'd make an excellent wife. She keeps you accountable and doesn't take your shit. Oh, and you guys are already best friends."

Dayanara giggled. "I mean, we *might* need to have an open arrangement because as much as I *love* our princess, she's missing some important equipment I'd need."

Mikaela laughed, grateful for her best friends and the distraction from her growing nerves. "Thank you both for the overwhelming support. Really inspiring. Besides, a certain Irish countryman will be in attendance tonight that I don't think I'll be able to compete with."

Dayanara squealed so loudly that Alejandro covered his ears. "I knew it!" She appeared to think. "But what if someone approaches him? He *is* single, after all."

Alejandro and Mikaela exchanged a knowing look. After a beat, the door to the sitting room creaked gently as Mikaela's mother stepped inside, her movements precise and deliberate. The light-hearted energy of the room shifted and was quickly replaced by an impending sense of obligation as they watched the queen, tall and regal in her glittering midnight-blue gown, smooth her elegant dark blond chignon.

Dayanara and Alejandro stood and filed out of the room as Mikaela's mother paused behind her.

"Mikaela," she said quietly but firmly. "It's time." Her dark eyes flicked over Mikaela's dress with approval. "You look…*stunning*. You are *beautiful*, my daughter."

Mikaela swallowed. She wasn't sure if the sudden lump in her throat was a result of all the nerves, the rare display of maternal tenderness, or a combination of everything. "Thank you, Mami," Mikaela replied.

"Remember, tonight is about so much more than you think. I know you're unhappy, but this is truly about the future of the Crown."

"I understand," Mikaela replied automatically, straightening her posture instinctively.

Mikaela's mother placed a gentle hand on her shoulder. "You are representing the de Medreno family. Our legacy. Our *future*. Show them who we are. Strong, graceful, intelligent, and resolved. I pray you will find someone who will stand beside you through it all. And I pray that *she* will be as strong and wonderful as you."

Mikaela nodded, refusing to betray her stoic expression at her mother's indirect acknowledgement—and was that a resigned acceptance she'd heard?—of her desire. "I'll do my best."

Her mother lingered for a moment and then bent to sweep a kiss across the top of her head before turning to leave the sitting room. "I'll see you downstairs in ten minutes. Do be on time, please."

Exactly one minute after she had left, Dayanara and Alejandro tumbled over one another back into the room.

"How is she so intimidating without even trying?" Dayanara hissed.

Alejandro crossed his muscular arms confidently over his tuxedo and leaned against the doorframe. "It's a royal gift, passed down through generations," he said with mock solemnity. "And I think Mikaela has already perfected it."

She shot her cousin a look. "I am *so* not intimidating."

Dayanara and Alejandro exchanged a glance before Dayanara cleared her throat.

"As a heads up, several reporters and news crews are outside the palace now," she said. "I know she's your mom, but the queen sure knows how to generate an audience."

Mikaela fought the urge to groan loudly. "Great, paparazzi too."

"They will not be allowed inside the event," Dayanara assured her.

Mikaela took a deep breath. "I guess it's now or never." The weight of responsibility felt impossibly large. "I just need…a second."

Mikaela stood and walked through her adjoining bedroom to the large, semicircular marble balcony. The evening air had cooled considerably but still smelled of jasmine and sea breeze. She gazed at the island below as a gentle gust teased strands of hair around her face, City Center aglow in the immediate distance with its colorful lights while the vast ocean stretched endlessly just beyond. A large Cayo Azul flag fluttered from its perch on Castillo Blanco's tall entry gates in her peripheral. The deep navy blue and bold burnt orange stripes were meant to represent twilight and sunrise, endings and new beginnings, the cyclical nature of life, and the natural order of the universe.

Fitting for tonight. Mikaela turned her attention back to the pristine view before her.

Though it was a view Mikaela had gazed at countless times before, tonight it felt…anticipatory and unknown.

Like the entire island is holding its breath with me. Mikaela bit her lip. There was something exciting and intriguing about the unknown, a growing buzz of electricity in the air that gave her the smallest spark of hope.

"It's beautiful, isn't it?" Dayanara's soft voice broke Mikaela's dreamy reverie as her friend leaned against the thick, smooth railing.

"It is," Mikaela said. As the hazy blue twilight of the evening deepened, she tried to steel herself against everything she knew was right outside—her mother, the gaggle of event planners and PR people, bright flashbulbs, prominent families from near and far, the thumping nighttime energy of Cayo Azul, the noise, lights, music, cameras, and action.

She turned as Alejandro stepped onto the balcony with a small silver tray. "It's all yours, Princess," he said warmly as he nodded at the majestic view before them. "This island, this life, it belongs to you. And you were made for it."

Mikaela took one last sweeping look around the beautiful island visible from her balcony and filled her lungs with the scent of *home*. *I'm ready. Let's do this.*

She turned toward her friends one more time. "Shall we?"

"Before we do," Alejandro gestured at the tray. "I brought something for us."

Mikaela glanced at the three shot glasses on the tray, each filled with a clear liquid, and raised an eyebrow. "You're kidding."

"Absolutely not," Alejandro said as he handed out the shot glasses. "A pre-gala toast, if you will. For courage, clarity and, most importantly, fun."

"Come on, Princess," Dayanara teased her good-naturedly. "You've got the whole night ahead of you. Let's start with a toast."

Mikaela hesitated and then relented. "Fine. What shall we toast to?"

Dayanara pretended to think and then lifted her shot glass to the glittering stars. "To surviving the madness."

Alejandro laughed and raised his own glass as tall palm trees rustled in the distance. "To keeping Mikaela sane."

"Remember, you've got this," Dayanara said after a moment. "Just be yourself, okay? The *real* Mikaela, the one Alejandro and I have known for so long and love so much. Not the cool, polished princess. I promise if someone tonight is worth your love and commitment, they'll immediately see what we do every day."

Mikaela laughed despite herself and hugged her longtime friend as the ocean breeze brushed her bare shoulders. "I think that's the sweetest thing you've ever said to me."

"What she said," Alejandro added. "And if they're all insufferable, I'll handle the rejection letters. Very diplomatic, I promise. After all, that's what I do. Oh, and to Mikaela maybe, just maybe, finding someone worth all this drama." He winked slyly and tipped his shot back.

The knot of tension dissipated just slightly. "Thank you both. For everything. Here's to the future, starting now." She took a deep breath and then tilted her head back. The sharp burn of the vodka on her throat was startling but strangely grounding. "And whatever comes next."

With one last wistful glance at the island below, Mikaela reluctantly followed her friends to her home's short, curved staircase.

I don't know exactly what the night will bring, but at least I know I'm not walking into it alone.

Isabella swallowed hard, her arm tucked neatly into Javier's elbow, and tried to appear unimpressed as they waited patiently in a line of partygoers as sharply-dressed security officials in all black suits patted, waved their wands, and barked out occasional questions before gruffly waving people through.

She smoothed her emerald-green off-the-shoulder dress, made from a faux silk that Isabella was secretly grateful for. *At least it's not clinging to me in this humidity like real silk would.* She ruefully adjusted the thin silver belt around her middle. It cinched the dress in a flattering way that showed off her figure—or she at least assumed it flattered her, judging by the way Javier looked at her when he picked her up earlier that evening. The dress fell to just above her knees and Isabella had paired it with a simple pair of borrowed black stilettos that buckled around her ankles and had been dug from the corner of her mother's closet.

"All phones and mobile devices have been turned in?" A deep voice interrupted Isabella's thoughts as she realized with a start that they had made it to the head of the security line. She glanced at Javier, who sighed heavily and nodded.

The security guard quickly waved the wand across Javier's tuxedoed chest and down each leg. Javier shot him a look.

"Hey, careful there, bud," he said. "Any closer, and you'll be up close and personal with the Jimenez family jewels. And I hate to tell you, but those jewels are for the women only."

The security guard straightened, as he stood tall and towered over Javier. He fixed him with a long look that Isabella knew was meant to relay that if he was not on the job right now, Javier would be regretting his smarmy remarks.

"Javi!" Isabella admonished him with a whisper as they were pointed through to Castillo Blanco's grounds. "You shouldn't talk to the security guard like that. He's just doing his job."

Javier glanced around. "Look at this shit," he said in a low voice as he gestured sharply. "It's ostentatious, Isabella. I was hoping to keep my phone with me to take some photos and video to pass along to my father and his organizers, so they could share them with our people and show them exactly how out of touch and tone-deaf the ruling class is."

Isabella's stomach sank. So that's why Javier was so hell-bent on going. It was a political plan to bolster their cause and further agitate. "I see," she replied evenly and then took a deep breath. "Can we try to enjoy the evening then? After all, we're already here. We got all dressed up for this."

Javier shrugged as he glanced around with practiced indifference at the enchanting grandeur of it all. A wide marble terrace with circular double staircases curving down into the sprawling gardens before them held groups of mingling guests. The wide walkways of the gardens were bordered by fragrant, colorful blooms and symmetrically designed around a long, shallow rectangular pool that stretched along the main pathway. Isabella glanced at the blue water as she absent-mindedly searched for her distorted reflection. The pool's surface was still, reflecting the soft glow of paper lanterns and sparkling string lights that crisscrossed above their heads.

"I need a drink," Javier said loudly as he grabbed Isabella's hand and guided her purposefully toward an outdoor bar beneath an elegant canopy. A few nearby heads turned in curiosity at his brazen declaration, and Isabella felt the first burn of embarrassment as she refused to glance back. Guests stood casually around the bar's polished wood counter as professional mixologists made drinks with exciting flair. Nearby, high pub tables were scattered across an open terrace adjacent to the bar. Isabella spied an open table and pulled at Javier's tight grip on her hand.

"I'm going to grab a table," Isabella told him as she gestured at the open space. Javier nodded and then turned his attention back to the sparkling line of bottles behind the bar. "Good," he said. "I'll get you something to drink too."

Isabella fought the urge to decline before reaching the table, realizing that he hadn't even asked her what she drank. With a moment to herself, Isabella looked around as she took in the grandeur of it all.

And then she saw *her*.

Isabella's stomach dropped and her senses narrowed, as the din of small talk around her faded to a low buzz. The strange pull that had fixed her gaze on Mikaela de Medreno Soliz brought a wave of something Isabella wasn't sure she had felt this strongly before: *yearning*.

Mikaela stood at the top of the staircase nearest her, the picture of elegance and defiance. Her posture was poised and regal—after a lifetime of practice, Isabella supposed—but there was something in the way she held herself with a quiet intensity that seemed almost determined and even rebellious. Isabella watched as Mikaela scanned the crowd below and realized too late that the princess's gaze had landed on her. Isabella froze as her brain screamed at her to glance away, but they held each other's eyes for a long, steady moment. The air felt electric as a shiver shot down Isabella's spine, and for a moment she forgot how to breathe. She couldn't look away even if she wanted to, and she knew deep down that she didn't want to.

God, she's beautiful.

It was then that she realized she was smiling as Mikaela arched an eyebrow and returned the tentative smile with unbridled curiosity.

"You'd think they would've sprung for something a little higher end than Cuervo." Javier's complaining was jarring and unwelcome as he sat and handed Isabella a paloma. "But it's free drinks for us, right? I guess we should enjoy it while we can."

He studied her for a moment. "You okay? You look like you've seen a ghost."

Isabella blinked and forced a shaky shrug. "I'm fine," she replied. Her voice sounded foreign even to her own ears. "Just taking it all in."

Javier nodded as he took a swig from his ranch water. "Quite the show, huh?"

Isabella opened her mouth to respond, but the loud tinkling of a bell interrupted her. "Cocktail hour will be over in ten minutes," a pre-recorded voice sounded over speakers hidden within the greenery. "Please begin making your way into the grand ballroom. I repeat, cocktail hour will be over in ten minutes. Please begin making your way into the grand ballroom."

Isabella glanced at Javier. He grinned once more as he held up his drink. "Well, bottoms up. Let's see how the rest of this night goes."

Chapter Nine

Mikaela felt the buzz of anticipation throughout the grand ballroom as event planners discreetly began shepherding guests inside for dinner. Round tables with thick white tablecloths had been scattered in a loose semicircle around a polished marble dance floor. The ballroom's high ceilings were adorned with familiar frescoes showcasing Cayo Azul's history, with each panel serving as a vibrant homage to the island's triumphs. Massive crystal chandeliers illuminated the vast space with warm, golden light that reflected off the gilded moldings and smooth floor.

"You have to admit, your mother outdid herself," Dayanara whispered.

Mikaela nodded. It was true. Through the doorways leading to a service kitchen, Mikaela could see scores of uniformed waiters with trays of champagne flutes and hors d'oeuvres waiting for the signal to begin serving. "The queen knows how to throw a party, that's for sure," she grudgingly admitted.

After a few moments, the lead event planner held open the doors from a separate corridor where Mikaela stood with her family and friends and gestured them through.

Mikaela carefully measured her steps as she trailed just behind her parents. Her uncle Juan, Alejandro, Dayanara, and Eduardo and his family flanked her from behind. She could feel the weight of her parents' presence as they walked hand in hand, a vision of elegance and power, and led the rest of the royal family to a long, rectangular table at the other side of the ballroom. The sounds of applause as guests gave them a standing ovation faded to the back of Mikaela's mind as her thoughts wandered to the mysterious woman she had seen outside. The woman appeared guarded at first, gazing at her with a mixture of curiosity and appraisal, and then had appeared to relax as the subconscious smile that lit her face seemed aimed directly at her.

Or is that just the right thing to do when you realize your gaze collided with the princess's? As she sat at the center of the table, she hoped she wouldn't be asked to say a few words. For whatever reason, she kept revisiting those fleeting moments on the terrace.

"See anyone you like?" Alejandro leaned over with a whisper. "Anyone lucky enough to catch your eye yet?"

Mikaela thought of the woman outside. *Gorgeous.* The word slipped through her mind before she had a chance to stop it. Her long, dark hair fell straight over her shoulders and her dark brown eyes were framed by long lashes, high cheekbones, and deep dimples on either side of her full lips, something Mikaela had noticed almost immediately.

Instead, she cleared her throat and refused to scan the tables across the dance floor before her. "No."

Alejandro fixed her with a look that said he didn't believe her and opened his mouth. He closed it as a string quartet in the corner struck up a new melody. Mikaela was grateful for the familiar rich, sultry bolero.

"Ladies and gentlemen, your King Bartolo and Queen Cristina," a voice sounded over the speaker system. A hush fell over the ballroom as all attention was drawn to the center of the dance floor. Her parents, dressed in their royal best, stepped gracefully onto the dance floor and exchanged a brief, loving glance. Her father confidently took her mother's hand and guided her effortlessly into the first few steps of the bolero, their movements fluid and magnetic. His strong frame balanced her delicate, precise femininity as they danced and spun slowly to the music.

Gasps and soft applause rippled through the crowd as her father gently tilted her mother toward the floor, then lifted her back up seamlessly as she kicked a leg out and spun around him, their hands never breaking contact. The bolero was a sensual, intimate dance punctuated by their perfectly timed turns and dips.

Mikaela watched her parents thoughtfully. *They truly love each other. And my mother certainly knows how to put on a show.*

As the bolero came to its breathtaking conclusion, her father dipped her mother low once more and held her there for a beat before lifting her back to her feet. The room erupted into applause as her father gently raised her mother's hand to his lips and kissed it tenderly. They waved and bowed to the seated partygoers before exiting the dance floor arm in arm.

"That's one way to set the tone and remind everyone of the strength and unity of our family," Alejandro murmured.

"You know my mother has a unique flair for the dramatic," Mikaela replied with a laugh. She was going to say more, joke with her cousin again, but the words died on her lips as her gaze settled on the woman at one of the far tables near the terrace. *Shit.*

"Earth to Mikaela," Alejandro said. "What, losing your touch? Can't think of a witty response?"

"I…" Mikaela tried to glance away, but there was something about the woman that she couldn't look away from. "I…" She tried again. Her pulse was thumping in her throat.

Alejandro glanced at her. "Are you okay?"

"Who is that?" she asked. Without a word, Alejandro studied her for a moment and then followed her gaze.

"Wow, good choice, cousin," he said. "She's beautiful."

Mikaela flushed as she forced nonchalance. "I'm just wondering," she said stubbornly. "I haven't seen her at any events or functions."

Alejandro studied the woman for a moment and then nodded. "I don't know who she is off the top of my head either. I know she's the plus-one of Javier Jimenez, but I don't know her name."

A rush of disappointment settled deep in Mikaela's belly. "Javier Jimenez? Who is that?"

Alejandro thought for a moment. "I believe he's Roberto Jimenez's son. Mayor of Este. Someone Eduardo is keeping an eye on as of late. In fact, it may make sense to say hello to Javier. Get a read on him. That could be your in. I'll even go with you. I'm curious myself how his father has been doing since expressing such discontent and pulling away from the Mayoral Council."

Mikaela glanced between Alejandro and the woman. The disappointment, surprisingly bitter, rose again as she watched who she presumed to be Javier sit down next to the woman and hand her a crystal tumbler from the bar. The woman glanced up at him, her dimples on full display, as he sat and leaned over slightly so he could speak into her ear. *That's enough.* Mikaela tore her gaze away.

"You never know, they may just be friends," Alejandro said. "Only one way to find out."

Mikaela glanced back at the woman, a brief shock tingling through her chest as she met her dark eyes across the ballroom. Again, the woman's lips curved into the faintest hint of a smile and Mikaela melted. Just a little bit.

She glanced down at the delicate china set before her by a gloved waiter. "Okay," Mikaela said after a moment. "After dinner."

I'm a psychopath. Isabella's inner voice of reason spiraled. *A well-dressed one, but a psychopath nonetheless.* The speed with which Mikaela had averted her gaze after they saw each other across the ballroom made Isabella cringe. She picked up a silver fork and stabbed at a sliced carrot on her plate. Again, Isabella realized that she was smiling at the princess, something she couldn't seem to help subconsciously doing each time she glanced at her. It felt natural under her warm gaze, as if her body knew something that her brain hadn't caught up to—or refused to acknowledge.

As Javier drained his second bottle of Modelo, Isabella wondered how she was going to keep up with him. He was three drinks in to her one, and her second paloma sat barely touched before her. She tried to ignore the nagging alert and chalked it up to unresolved trauma thanks to her papa.

I've never seen Javi unable to handle his alcohol before. He's just extra on edge being at this gala that he was so adamant on attending.

As if reading her mind, Javier clinked his empty bottle down and held up his hands in a conciliatory gesture. "Okay, okay," he said. "I'll hold off for now until I get another. I can tell you're bothered."

Isabella wasn't sure *what* she was bothered by, but she had a sneaking suspicion it had more to do with the princess across the ballroom than Javier's drinking. "I just want you to be careful," she replied diplomatically.

Javier snorted. "Yeah, yeah," he said off-handedly. "I always am. Besides, I'll be heading back to Spain for the rest of the semester tomorrow evening. I should be allowed one more fun night, especially on the de Medrenos' tab, before it's back to university, right?"

Isabella shrugged. "I understand."

Javier shook his head after a moment. "They work us really hard in my engineering program," he said thoughtfully. "There's little time for fun, but I remind myself that it's all for a better future. So many of us just end up stuck in Este forever. I know you don't fully understand as someone who hasn't taken the next step to attend university, but it's a tough workload…"

Isabella's mouth fell open and she was briefly unsure if she'd heard Javier correctly. "Don't belittle me," she snapped, the sharpness of her words surprising even herself. "I'm well aware I haven't attended university and if I had I would in fact already have graduated. This is not for my lack of wanting or lack of drive or intelligence or—"

Javier leaned over and patted her back. It felt condescending and Isabella bit her lip to keep from publicly shrugging him off. "Isabella, I didn't mean it that way," he interrupted her. "Look, the reason I even brought it up was because I wanted to speak to you. About *us*."

Isabella froze. *Uh-oh.* The sound of glasses clinking and the small talk of their tablemates drowned in her ears as she caught the weight of Javier's gaze. He scooted his chair closer to her.

"Isabella," he started, his voice sounding oddly vulnerable. The faux bravado had been replaced by something softer that made Isabella swallow hard. "I've been thinking about us a lot. I know we've occasionally spent time together in the past and we've spent more together during this break than we have in a long time. I've enjoyed every minute of it."

Isabella's hands gripped her paloma. *Please don't. I'm not ready for this conversation.*

"I don't want to be just friends," Javier said as he placed an arm across the back of her chair. "We've done this back-and-forth thing for so long. But we're older now, ready to settle. You and I, we make perfect sense together." His jaw tightened. "I've always liked you, Isabella. You know that. I've been patient, but I don't want to wait forever. Not as I start to plan my future and where I'll intern this summer. Barcelona has a firm I'd love to get into. Wouldn't you like to join me there? Get a fresh start out of Este?"

Isabella gazed at him and her heart sank under his offer. She hated the hurt in his expression as her silence stretched longer.

God, this would be so much easier if he was just another asshole. She thought back to her conversation with her mother and her promise to give Javier a chance. Frustration bubbled inside her because it didn't make sense. Javier was right; on paper they were perfect together.

So why can't I feel anything *for him? Why can't I feel for him what I feel for...* Isabella glanced toward Mikaela's table and her heart sank further to her stilettos. *...What I feel for* her *in just a few stolen glances?*

"Wow," Javier muttered. He pulled back, as if he'd been stung. "You can't even respond."

Isabella cleared her throat. "Javi," she said. The lump in her throat was unexpected. "I...I can't give you what you want. You're amazing, and you deserve someone who loves you so much..."

Her voice trailed off as Javier scoffed. Isabella realized with a start that Mikaela and her cousin, who she recognized as Alejandro de Medreno Soliz, had stepped away from the long, rectangular table across the ballroom. She hoped she appeared furtive as she glanced around, finally spotting them along the edge of the dance floor.

"How can you not?" Javier replied, frustrated. "I haven't even told you my expectations yet for a relationship or an engagement. You're not even giving us a real chance. Everyone sees how good we are together, Isabella. My papa. Your mother. All our friends. Why are you so against giving this a chance? And who do you keep looking at?"

With that, Javier craned his neck to follow where Isabella had been looking just moments before. He stilled as his gaze landed on the princess.

"I just don't feel the way that you do," Isabella replied lamely. "How... How can I explain something I don't even entirely understand myself?"

Javier stared at her for a long moment, and Isabella shrank under his darkening stare. "It's the princess," he said. His voice was barely audible, but Isabella could hear the clarity. "That's who you keep getting distracted by. It all makes sense now. Why you've never shown real interest in me or any other man in Este. I thought...I thought you were just holding out for the right one."

"I am," Isabella said, knowing that part was true at least.

"But it's not me," Javier finished flatly. "Or any man, Isabella."

Isabella looked at him pleadingly, but stayed silent. "I…I don't know how to respond to that."

Javier scoffed and took a long swig from the frosty Modelo that appeared at the table. He pushed back his chair and yanked the beer off the table.

"Don't bother," he said as he stood abruptly. "That alone is response enough. Enjoy the rest of your night. Good luck finding your way back to Este."

Isabella opened her mouth to call after him but snapped it shut at the last second. He stormed out of the ballroom and out to the terrace, where she assumed he would leave without her. Her heart pounded as waves of guilt, shock, and melancholy coursed through her. As vulnerable as Isabella felt, no one else in the ballroom seemed to pay them any mind and appeared wrapped in their own mingling. After a moment and a long sip of her paloma, Isabella recognized one more feeling that crept up deep in her chest beneath the stinging embarrassment: Relief.

At least it's all over. No more pretending. But what now?

CHAPTER TEN

The ballroom was alive with revelers, music, and conversation that echoed off the high ceilings. At the edge of the dance floor, Mikaela tried her best to subtly scan the room, but the sea of faces around her was becoming increasingly difficult to navigate.

"Who exactly are we looking for?" Alejandro asked, as his gaze also swept the cavernous ballroom.

"You know who," Mikaela replied shortly. "I just…want to find out more."

Alejandro grinned. "It's your party, Mika. You can do whatever you want."

Just then, Mikaela spotted Javier and his mysterious date. Her heartbeat kicked up a notch as she understood from afar that they were deep in what appeared to be a serious conversation. Javier looked positively upset and his date appeared thoughtful and melancholy.

I would never let her look so sad. Mikaela bit her lip as the thought zoomed across her mind.

Before Mikaela could point them out to her cousin, a woman about her age in a slinky red dress approached expectantly. "Your Highness," she said as she stepped closer, her London accent unmistakable. "I was hoping to steal a moment of your time."

Alejandro deftly stepped away and shot Mikaela a knowing look. "I'll leave you to it."

As Mikaela forced a polite smile and shook the woman's hand, she spotted Dayanara across the dance floor. As expected, Ian had found her. They both looked flushed and excited as they leaned closer to hear one another over the din of the gala. Mikaela felt a slight pang in her chest as she half-listened to the woman in the red dress gush over her hair and half-wondered if she'd ever find someone who made her glow like that.

"I don't know if you'd heard, but I left my husband," the woman went on, raising a suggestive eyebrow.

Mikaela snapped back to attention. "I'm sorry, what?"

The woman chuckled. "I know, we tried to keep it very hush-hush," she said. "I did get the art galleries in London, New York, and Paris out of it, so it wasn't a total loss." She waved her hand dismissively. "I have missed…" she took a deep breath, "the intimacy though. Especially that of being with a woman. That was something Carl could never satisfy for me, of course."

It dawned on Mikaela that this was the woman who had been married to the son of the chairman of London's top law firm and promptly birthed three of his children. There was something that had happened though…

"Wasn't Carl in a motorbike accident?" Mikaela blurted out, then remembered her poise. "I mean, how is he doing? Much better, I hope."

The woman flushed uncomfortably. "He is paralyzed from the waist down, unfortunately," she said. "He's been in near-nonstop physical therapy and had an extensive spinal surgery, but the doctors don't seem to have much hope of him regaining use of his legs." She stepped closer and dropped her voice to a whisper. "I mean, that's why I left and took the kids. How on earth could I take care of this wheelchair-bound man *and* three young children? I'm only thirty-one. I don't think it's fair to spend my life playing nursemaid and giving up so much at such a young age. So, I *am* single in *every* way, Your Highness." The woman finished suggestively as Mikaela stared at her.

Opportunist the word flashed through Mikaela's mind as she clamped her mouth shut. They were everywhere, and running into them wasn't new. Mikaela had been warned about opportunistic people since she was a child, whether they tried to ingratiate themselves with her through the false pretenses of friendship or something more.

Over the woman's shoulder, Mikaela caught an approving glance from her mother. Mikaela knew she was simply happy to see her playing along and making nice with all the important people who had shown up…for what? *For an opportunity to be married to a princess? To pretend they know anything about Cayo Azul or* me*?*

"I have to go," Mikaela said abruptly as she turned. "You should check on Carl. At least give him a call or let him spend time with his kids once in a while. It's the right thing to do."

Mikaela finished excusing herself as politely as she could. Frustration flared in her chest as she saw that Javier and his mysterious plus-one had disappeared. Neither were still seated at their table and Mikaela couldn't spot them anywhere along the dance floor or bar.

As she stepped onto the marble terrace and took a deep breath of the warm, jasmine-scented breeze, she looked down at where she'd first locked gazes with the woman much earlier in the evening. The gardens were quiet now, with most of the party inside the ballroom and a few throngs of guests chatting closer to the outdoor bar.

"Mikaela!" Her mother's stern voice could be heard above the sounds of the gala. She turned long enough to see her cutting an imposing path across the ballroom while searching the revelers for her.

Shit. Surely the woman in the red dress had stormed away, embarrassed and perhaps chastened after being rejected so sorely. Mikaela knew her mother wanted an update, *stat*, and to probably re-emphasize the importance of making nice with everyone.

Mikaela took one last look across the twin staircases and then hurried down the one nearer the shallow pool. Looking once over her shoulder, she slipped her stilettos off and hurried across the manicured lawns, a heel in each hand. After a few moments, the sounds of the gala faded further away as Mikaela reached the stables behind Castillo Blanco. Luna whinnied, her long tail swishing in anticipation as Mikaela approached.

"Hey, girl," Mikaela murmured as she stroked her mare's sleek neck. "You miss me, huh?"

She glanced over her shoulder once more as she dropped her stilettos next to Luna's oversized stall. An extra pair of her olive-green breeches were folded neatly in a cabinet nearby.

"Who says we can't take a quick ride even if I'm in a dress?" Mikaela said as she finished buttoning the breeches under her gown and patted Luna's nose affectionately. "Nothing wrong with needing to clear my head."

Luna neighed approvingly as Mikaela slipped a worn leather bridle over the mare's head. She swung herself onto Luna's back. She knew her mother would have a nuclear meltdown if she saw her now, wearing riding breeches, a wrinkled dress, and no helmet.

But she'd have a nuclear meltdown if she knew I left the gala anyway. Might as well make it worth the drama.

"Let's get out of here for a little bit," Mikaela said to Luna as she prodded her into an easy trot across the far back of the castle grounds. The rhythmic sound of Luna's hooves on the soft grass were balm to Mikaela's frayed nerves. She took another deep breath of the warm night air, reveling in the dark privacy and dense quiet.

As Mikaela urged Luna farther from Castillo Blanco, her heart skipped a beat when she caught sight of a figure in the distance. Though it was too dark to make out the color of her dress, Mikaela sat up as she recognized tendrils of dark hair brushing over slender shoulders in the breeze. She slowed Luna to a stop as they approached, and she drank in the sight of the woman she had been seeking earlier. She stood near a low stone wall, her arms crossed protectively over herself, and gazed out at the darkened landscape.

She's lost, Mikaela realized as she dismounted Luna. Her steps were tentative as she approached the woman, and she felt strangely shy without the glitter and grandeur of the gala surrounding her. "Are you okay?" Mikaela asked. "You look like you could use some company."

The woman turned in surprise and then her expression softened as her gaze collided once more with Mikaela's.

"Your Highness!" Her voice was a mixture of shock and shyness. "I'm so sorry. I just got a little lost. I promise. I was trying to exit the gala, but I left from a side door of the ballroom and thought I knew my way back around to the terrace. Apparently not. My deepest apologies."

The woman held her gaze but continued to stammer apologies. Mikaela tilted her head, fighting the urge to step closer, to brush the hair from her shoulders and ask her who she was. Instead, she took a deep, steadying breath.

"It's okay," she said at last. "The grounds of Castillo Blanco are expansive and can be especially hard to navigate at night. We have an excellent security team. I'm sure they would've located you and helped right away."

The woman nodded as a small smile tugged at her lips. "I appreciate that, Your Highness."

Mikaela hesitated and then finally took a step closer. She probably looked strange, bare feet and breeches under her now-wrinkled-beyond-comprehension dress.

"We can skip the formalities," she replied gently. "Can I ask why you were leaving the gala so early? Did your, um, boyfriend need to leave?"

The woman searched her face with a mixture of warmth and mirth, pausing for a beat before responding. "Javier is not my boyfriend," she finally said. She glanced down and brushed a strand of hair behind her ear. "In fact, right now I'm not even sure we can be friends again."

Mikaela fought to keep her face poised and devoid of the surging relief coursing through her veins.

"Sorry," the woman said after a hesitant sigh. "It's been a complicated night."

"I can relate," Mikaela replied with a soft laugh. "Mind if I join you?"

The woman shook her head emphatically as Mikaela leaned beside her against the cool stone wall, acutely aware that their shoulders were mere centimeters from brushing.

"I'm Isabella Acosta Ramon," Isabella said. Her expression was genuine now, gentle and inviting, as the dimples on either side of her lush mouth deepened. Though it wasn't necessarily royal protocol to shake hands with those she didn't know, Mikaela knew that *none* of the last few minutes were royal protocol, so she took Isabella's warm, outstretched hand and lingered just a moment as she shook it.

The distant sounds of the gala were barely audible now and the world felt hushed and still as an invisible electric current seemed to crackle between them. For the first time that evening, Mikaela could breathe—and there was just one name repeating itself in her head until she burnt it to memory: *Isabella Acosta Ramon.*

❖

Though the silence lingered for another slow moment, Isabella's heart was pulsing in double time. One-on-one time with Princess Mikaela de Medreno Soliz was the last thing she had expected as she stumbled around the darkened castle grounds looking for the way back to the terrace so she could get a rideshare. Distracted by the tangles of thoughts fighting for her attention, Isabella had turned the wrong way at some point and was hopelessly lost on Castillo Blanco's grounds.

"You know, *Isabella Acosta Ramon,*" Mikaela began, her voice low and steady as she teased out her name. Isabella felt herself melt a little, though she wasn't sure if it was Mikaela's cool confidence or the way she teasingly emphasized her name. "I've found that sometimes stepping away from all the noise is the only way to keep your sanity intact."

She's the princess. She's gorgeous and smiling and inches away, but she's the princess. Get it together.

Isabella exhaled. "I didn't mean to step *this* far away," she replied lightly. "I'm not even sure where I am anymore."

"You're on the quieter side of Castillo Blanco," Mikaela said. "Maybe this was the right place to land anyway." She glanced down at the grass before leveling her gaze and straightening her shoulders.

To Isabella, it looked like a rare display of shyness before she caught herself. "It's easy to lose your way out here if you're not familiar with the grounds," Mikaela said, all business again. "But please know our security team would have quickly found and assisted you."

Isabella tilted her head as she glanced at Mikaela. *But you found me instead.* The words were so close to falling from her lips, but instead Isabella fought to meet Mikaela's poise with what she hoped was her own semblance of unbothered detachment. "Thank you," she said. "I didn't mean to wander so far, but I was a bit distracted. Tonight has been…a *lot*."

Mikaela's expression softened. "I'm sorry that your evening didn't go as planned," she said. "I understand more than you know. A gala full of expectations and opinions you never asked for? A duty to put the greater good over your own goals and desires? Trust me, you're not alone in feeling that tonight is a lot."

Isabella studied Mikaela for a moment and her defenses lowered just a fraction. Sure, Mikaela was the princess of Cayo Azul, but right now she just seemed…human. "You make it look easy," Isabella said. Perhaps it was the dark privacy or the quiet away from the gala, but she felt oddly comfortable talking to Mikaela even as the fluttering deep in her belly seemed to intensify each time she met her gaze. "All of this. The pressure, the attention, the splendor and prestige of it all. I don't know how you do it."

Mikaela laughed, the sound warm and surprisingly self-deprecating. "Easy? I wish. It's all smoke and mirrors, really. Half the time, I'm just trying to make it through without tripping over my own feet or giving someone something to write about."

Isabella stepped closer as Mikaela ducked her gaze. *She's not as cool and detached as she wants to be*. For some reason, the revelation made her wonder what it would be like to tangle her fingers in Mikaela's long hair and meet her soft lips with her own. She blinked the fantasy away as Mikaela continued.

"Seriously," she said. "It's not as effortless as it seems. But I suppose you learn some tricks through a lifetime of expectations and civic duty. Moments like this, though? Away from the crowd, where I can feel the breeze and soak in the quiet moments…" Mikaela stole a glance at Isabella and then looked out into the darkness. "They make it bearable."

Isabella felt her cheeks flush and her pulse quicken as she soaked in her closeness to the princess. The heat, the dominance of her presence, the steadiness of her gaze that seemed to see more than she was ready to share; they were all things that made Isabella realize she wanted to stay right there, rooted in place, all night.

"You're very good at this," she said.

Mikaela raised an eyebrow. "Good at what?"

"Making people feel seen," Isabella said with a deep breath. "Even when they aren't sure they want to be. Thank you. For talking to me, even when you have an entire gala in your honor." Isabella gestured in what she hoped was the general direction of Castillo Blanco.

Mikaela's expression softened as a flicker of vulnerability flashed across her face. "Maybe it's because I know what it's like to not feel seen. But I'm glad if I can make you feel that way." Her gaze drifted toward the darkness again before returning to Isabella. "You don't need to thank me. This has been the highlight of my night."

Isabella was sure her heart stopped mid-beat. For a moment, it was just the two of them in the stillness of the island night, the air seeming to buzz with electricity and anticipation, and the distant hum of the gala forgotten. *I want to live in this moment forever.* Isabella surprised herself with the intensity of her immediate attraction to Mikaela.

Mikaela cleared her throat gently. "You shouldn't stay out here alone," she said. "I'll help you back to the castle. One of our security people will personally escort you home."

Isabella hesitated as she glanced toward the area she had wandered from. "Are you sure? Este is a bit of a drive."

Mikaela touched her arm reassuringly. "I will see to it that you are safely driven back to your home. Someone on our security team will be happy to help."

Isabella nodded, unsure what to say.

Mikaela gestured toward Luna, who stood a few yards away calmly grazing on the thick grass. "Can I give you a ride back to the entrance? It'll be quicker than following us and I promise Luna is a sweetheart."

Isabella blinked in surprise as her gaze darted at the tall, sleek mare before returning to Mikaela. "You're serious?"

"Totally," Mikaela replied, already striding to Luna and giving her a gentle pat on the neck. "It's the least I can do after finding you all the way out here."

Isabella hesitated for only a moment before following Mikaela. "I've never ridden a horse before." Her breath caught as she felt Mikaela's gentle fingers along her sides as she helped her climb onto Luna's back.

"Don't worry," Mikaela said confidently as she mounted Luna in front of her. "You'll be in good hands."

The current of warm tenderness just below Mikaela's self-assured surface was enough to ease Isabella's nerves, though she felt more exhilarated than fearful. She followed Mikaela's lead and allowed the princess to reach behind and guide her hands just above her hips.

"Hold on," Mikaela said. "We'll take it slow. Are you ready?"

Mikaela's dress was soft and buttery beneath Isabella's fingers, and her skin was warm under the thin fabric. "I'm ready," she said, glad that her own voice sounded equally confident.

As Luna started forward with a smooth, steady gait, Isabella's arms unconsciously tightened around Mikaela's middle. They moved through the grounds of Castillo Blanco in silence, the quiet intimacy of the moment lingering even as the castle's bright lights came into view and the noise of the gala sharpened around them. Still, for the first time that evening, Isabella could breathe.

Chapter Eleven

The drive back to Este in the sleek black Escalade was silent except for the faint hum of the engine and the occasional sound of thick tires on the winding roads to Isabella's home. *Back to reality*.

She sat against the leather back seat and stared out the window as the landscape blurred before her. Her mind was far from still. She thought of Mikaela and the way her voice was both soft and authoritative as she introduced Isabella to the security officer who would drive her home. The way she placed her hand protectively over Isabella's arms wrapped around her waist for a long moment as she slowed Luna to a stop. Mikaela hadn't seemed fazed by the openly curious glances—including a few jealous ones shot Isabella's way—from a few guests lingering outside. In fact, Mikaela hadn't seemed to notice anyone else at all as she helped her dismount Luna.

Isabella leaned her head against the cool window and took a deep breath. Mikaela carried herself with a steady confidence and cool poise for sure, but there was something else she discovered too—an undercurrent of sincerity and a few flashes of shy vulnerability that made her feel comfortable and open before she even knew it. The way Mikaela had looked at her, spoken to her, and made her feel seen had peeled back carefully guarded layers that Isabella didn't know she had. The quickness with which those walls fell around Mikaela was alarming.

As the Escalade pulled into the cracked concrete driveway, she straightened in her seat. Despite not knowing if or when she would see Mikaela again, Isabella felt an unexpected surge of confidence and joy.

"Thank you," she said to the security officer as he opened her door.

"Of course," he replied. "Have a wonderful night, *señorita.*"

Isabella stepped into the familiarity of her family's modest home as her gaze landed on her mother. She sat at the kitchen table, as the soft glow of a nearby lamp illuminated her hands while she stirred a cup of hot tea.

"You're home late," her mother said. She looked concerned but curious.

Isabella grinned. "You don't have to wait up for me, Mami," she replied. She dropped a quick kiss on her head before settling into a kitchen chair next to her. "I'm twenty-five, after all."

Her mother shot her a tired look. "Of course I do, my daughter. You'll understand one day when you have your own children."

Isabella swallowed hard. *Right. Kids.* She knew it was possible, but perhaps more difficult. *What does that even mean?* The thoughts started bubbling up again, but Isabella was acutely aware of her mother studying her closely.

"It was…an eventful night," Isabella said as she sat forward and rested her chin on her hand.

Her mother raised an eyebrow. "I take it Javier wasn't good company? The car that dropped you off was not his."

Isabella sighed as she ran a hand through her hair. She hadn't even contemplated what to tell her mother. "He wasn't the problem," she said carefully. "Or maybe he was. Or we both are. I don't know. He wants more from me than what I can give, Mami. I know I should like him. I know he has everything going for him and any woman would be lucky to have his affections. I just…I tried, Mami, I swear. I just don't see him that way. He didn't take it well."

Her mother's expression softened as she studied Isabella's face. "I see."

"I don't know," Isabella mused. "Maybe there's something wrong with me. Maybe I don't know how to love. Javier is as close to perfect as someone can get, right? Yet when I imagine myself in his arms or sharing a kiss, it feels hollow."

Mikaela's face flashed in Isabella's mind and she swallowed hard. Something deep inside her rebelled against the idea that she was incapable of love. Inside, she knew it was instead that Javier could never give her the all-encompassing type of love that left her breathless and begging to be consumed by the blazing fire. Again, the memory of her arms wrapped around Mikaela's waist flashed in her mind and warmed her belly.

Her mother's hand on hers broke Isabella's reverie. "I know your heart," her mother said. "You know how to love, harder and more fully than most. Your heart is one of the best things about you. I've always worried that you would fall for the wrong ones, give your heart away and have it returned tattered and bruised until there was nothing left of it. I was proud to see you keep it guarded safely until I realized that wasn't the answer either. I didn't want you to miss out on something wonderful because you've guarded your heart too closely and you're scared to unlock it. You know how to love and you deserve only the best, most fulfilling love. If Javier is not that, then so be it, my daughter."

Relief washed over her at her mother's trust and easy acceptance of her choice not to force things with Javier. "Thank you, Mami," she replied. She hesitated before continuing. "That's not all. I…I did meet someone."

Her mother's thin eyebrows shot up. "At the gala?"

"Yes," Isabella said. She craned her neck, sure that she didn't want her father to overhear the rest of their conversation. "Where is Papa?"

Her mother frowned. "He didn't return after work. That usually means he's out at the taverns."

Isabella took a deep breath as a sense of relief flooded her at her father not being home. She ignored the sense of foreboding reserved for when he did decide to make his return. "It's complicated, Mami. The person I met at the gala. I…They're not like anyone I've ever met. I felt so secure and so…"

"Seen?"

Isabella blinked, surprised by that word following her all the way home. "Yes," she said simply. "Exactly that."

Her mother took a long sip of tea and then patted Isabella's hand. "That does sound eventful. Though perhaps tonight wasn't so terrible after all. Does this person have a name?"

Isabella briefly recalled the moment she locked eyes with Mikaela on the terrace. Everything she had been waiting for came crashing out of the deepest parts of her and into bright, undeniable focus. The quiet stirring in her chest, the sparks and thrill, the intrinsic pull as though her body and the whole world around her screamed for her to follow her instincts.

For the first time, Isabella understood with absolute clarity why her heart had never opened to Javier. It had been saving itself for someone who could set it alight. The joy and calm anticipation of knowing that everything would be okay—even if she never saw Mikaela again—finally spilled over as Isabella responded.

"Mikaela de Medreno Soliz."

The white-hot morning sun rose over the island, casting a soft pink and golden glow over the rounded balcony outside Mikaela's home. In the bright morning light, she could see the shimmering expanse of ocean in the distance as gentle waves lapped against rocky cliffs. Mikaela took a long, steadying sip of fresh peppermint tea. Her gaze remained unfocused as her mind lingered on Isabella Acosta Ramon.

She exhaled and leaned back in her chaise as she ran a hand through her hair. Mikaela wasn't sure what bothered her more: the fact that she couldn't stop thinking about Isabella from the moment she woke this morning or the fact that she didn't *want* to stop. For the first time, someone had managed to crack the polished exterior she had carefully constructed as her own personal royal armor. It was unsettling.

She recognized the quick rap of knuckles on her bedroom door. "Come in," Mikaela called absent-mindedly.

Alejandro stepped through Mikaela's bedroom carefully and plopped into the chaise next to her. He was already impeccably dressed. "You're up early. Couldn't sleep?"

Mikaela didn't look up. "Actually, I slept excellently." It was the truth. She had slept better than she could remember and woke up feeling energized and refreshed, even if Isabella was the first thought that flooded her mind.

"You seem…exhilarated," Alejandro said amusedly. "When are you going to spill about the girl?"

Mikaela glanced at the ceramic mug in her hands. "What girl?"

Alejandro snorted. "Oh, you know, just the one that you came riding out of the darkness with like some literal knight in shining armor who rescued the maiden. You know, the one you disappeared with for nearly an hour."

Mikaela shrugged. "It wasn't intentional," she said. "We just kind of… found each other."

"Oh, how romantic," Alejandro replied with a laugh. "I suppose you'll share at this morning's debrief?"

Mikaela rolled her eyes and took another sip of tea. "It's ridiculous that the gala even requires a debrief."

Alejandro sighed. "You know the purpose. And you understand your duty. I'm just trying to prepare you, because your mother has barely been able to contain herself and her questions all night."

Mikaela groaned as she stood. "You're really not selling this debrief meeting, cousin," she said and then paused in the bedroom. "It's been so quiet all morning. Where's Daya?"

Alejandro shrugged. "I saw her leave last night," he said casually. "I think she went back to her apartment. She and Ian wanted to continue their conversation somewhere more private, if you catch my drift."

Mikaela wrinkled her nose. "Oh," she responded. "She always takes the downstairs guest bedroom. I should text her and see when she'll be back today."

Alejandro sighed and fixed Mikaela with a knowing look. "Do you ever think you maybe…well, are a bit dependent on her, Mika?"

Mikaela bit her lip. "What do you mean? She's my best friend. I mean, besides you. But you don't really count since you're my cousin."

Alejandro scoffed good-naturedly. "Thanks a lot," he responded. "No one would ever dispute that you two are the best of friends. Daya has been there for you through thick and thin since we were children. But did you ever consider maybe she's ready to…I don't know, spread her wings a bit?"

Mikaela considered this. "She's my unofficial lady-in-waiting," she said. "We've always taken care of her. Do you think she wants us to increase her monthly stipend? I know her City Center apartment and utilities are on our books. I—"

Alejandro cleared his throat. "No, I don't think that at all," he responded carefully. "But I do think that, at some point, it's natural for people to have their own desires and goals in life. Good friends, especially longtime ones, read between the lines."

Mikaela was quiet for a moment as she pulled a pair of heeled calf-length boots over her navy-blue skinny pants. "Daya and Ian are perfect together."

Alejandro nodded. "A match made in heaven."

"I wonder why they ever broke up," Mikaela mused. She threw a fitted Ralph Lauren denim jacket over her navy blue and white striped top and considered this.

He shrugged. "Did you ever ask her?"

Mikaela fixed him with a look. "Of course I did. She never said much about it except that it didn't work out. I didn't push."

"Maybe it's time to encourage her," Alejandro said. "Because I know Dayanara loves our family and loves you most of all, Mika. Platonically, of course. Would she take a big leap, even if it was one she wanted, or stay where it's comfortable in fear of rocking the boat?"

After a long moment, Mikaela nodded once. "I understand."

Alejandro touched her forearm affectionately as they walked toward Castillo Blanco. "Sit with it, Mika," he said. "She may be your unofficial lady-in-waiting, but you said it yourself. She's also your best friend. But right now, it's time to talk about your next steps."

Mikaela straightened and brushed a stray hair from her face. She knew she'd have to face her family, their probing questions, and the endless planning for her so-called future. As the main entrance to Castillo Blanco grew closer, she allowed one last moment for her thoughts to wander over Isabella—the way her name felt on her lips, the way her smile deepened her dimples as their gazes met over and over again, and the way she looked at Mikaela as if she saw right through the pretense.

Mikaela and Alejandro walked through the heavy doors held open for them by the castle's security detail. "I'm ready to face whatever awaits," Mikaela replied confidently. "Let's do this."

Chapter Twelve

Streaks of sunlight streamed through the towering arched windows of the royal council chamber and danced over the polished mahogany table where Mikaela found herself facing her family once more. This time, her mother sat at the head of the table—normally reserved for the king—and her gaze was locked onto Mikaela. Her father sat to her left as he sipped from a steaming mug of coffee and scrolled through email on his tablet. Her uncle Juan sat to Cristina's right, and Alejandro, barely concealing his amusement, was next to his father.

"So," her mother said, her tone clipped. "Care to explain where you disappeared to last night or shall we add this to the growing list of reckless decisions you seem intent on making?"

Mikaela kept her face neutral. "I needed air," she replied truthfully. "The gala was becoming overwhelming and I thought a quiet moment outside would help."

Her mother's expression narrowed. "You missed dessert, the toast, and multiple opportunities to engage with guests who traveled across the island or from their home countries to meet you. And don't even get me started on whatever it was you said to Beatrice Smyth. She left the ballroom in tears, by the way."

Mikaela shifted uncomfortably. "My intent was not to make her cry," she said. "However, she was beyond insufferable. Did you know she left her husband after he was in a horrible accident and became paralyzed?"

Her mother shot her a glare. "We do not participate in gossip, Mikaela. That is none of our concern."

"Well, she *certainly* isn't someone I would be interested in," Mikaela responded evenly.

Alejandro held up a hand as he leaned back in his chair. "Okay," he interjected. "Mikaela was clearly otherwise occupied. Perhaps with the *mystery* girl she was seen escorting outside."

Mikaela glared at Alejandro. "She does have a name, but I don't even know—"

Alejandro threw a knowing look back at her. "Don't even know what? People notice these things, Mika. A beautiful stranger, a ride on your beloved Luna through the darkness, and then being personally escorted out by you? Practically the stuff of romance novels, if you ask me."

"I didn't," Mikaela replied flatly.

Her father hid a chuckle behind his coffee mug and then cleared his throat as they lapsed into expectant silence. "Let's stay focused, please. We need to align on a direction for what's next so I can update the Royal Council. The gala was excellent, but people across the island will want clarity soon after all the excitement and publicity around this event. We must continue showing unity with actionable progress."

Mikaela took a deep breath. "I am aware of my responsibilities," she said firmly. "But I'll need to get to know her. Isabella Acosta Ramon is her name. She lives in Este." She took a deep breath. "If I don't feel as though I love her after seventy-five days, I will not marry her. Likewise, if she doesn't love me, I will not force her to marry me. She can return to Este and resume her life."

Her mother opened her mouth but was interrupted as Juan cleared his throat and tossed his shaggy dark hair off his neck. He slung his tablet onto the table with a loud clatter.

"I've compiled a list of steps we should take moving forward," Juan said as he glanced around the table.

Her mother nodded and waved him on. "Thank you. Go ahead."

Juan squinted down at the tablet screen. "First is narrowing down the list of Mikaela's considerations." He glanced at Mikaela. "Though it appears one name stands out already."

Mikaela raised an eyebrow. "What do you mean?"

"Why, Isabella Acosta Ramon, of course," Juan said smoothly. "As general, I did a bit of research into the armed forces' population database while you were discussing."

Mikaela sighed. "That was quick."

Juan continued, unfazed. "As you mentioned, Mikaela, she's from Este," he read as he scanned the screen. "Twenty-five years old and the only child of Fernando Acosta and Araceli Ramon. Based on birthdates, it appears Araceli had her quite young at just nineteen years old. Araceli is a respected longtime nurse at the national hospital in Este." He paused. "Lots of service and professional achievement awards. And it looks like Isabella followed right in her footsteps. She graduated at the top of her high school class and received honor roll recognition each year, but I don't have any record of her attending university, either here or outside Cayo Azul."

Mikaela shifted uncomfortably as Juan continued to rattle off personal details about Isabella, her family, and her upbringing.

"As for Fernando, well, that's a different story." Juan's tone darkened as he continued to skim over the tablet. "He's an island groundskeeper employed by, oh look at that, the government of Cayo Azul. Works in all three provinces. Not a nice guy. Dishonorably discharged from the armed forces several years ago, when Isabella would have been just over a year old. Several petty arrests over the years, mainly due to alcohol. And it appears his struggles continue, because he's currently in jail on public intoxication charges."

Mikaela's stomach twisted, but she kept her expression neutral. "Uncle, you're taking all the fun out of getting to know her myself," she said lightly. "So, she has a problematic father." Mikaela bit her lip, already sensing her parents' reluctance. "I agree that's not ideal—"

"I'll handle it," Juan cut in before Mikaela could finish. He looked up from the screen around the table. "We don't need Fernando causing a large issue. If Isabella is who Mikaela wants to pursue most, then Isabella is who should join her at Castillo Blanco for the next seventy-five days."

There was a beat of surprised silence as her father studied his younger brother over his glasses with a mixture of curiosity and caution. "This level of involvement in my daughter's affairs is unusual for you, Juan."

Juan shrugged his broad shoulders. "Perhaps," he replied. "Though Isabella could be a compelling candidate. Her background is humble but respectable. Hers and her mother's, anyway. She's relatable. She's from Este. This could help strategically bridge the gap between the monarchy and the people of Este, where it appears there has been the most discontent as of late. It even looks as though her family is longtime neighbors with none other than Roberto Jimenez."

Her father nodded in understanding. "I see what you're saying," he said as he rubbed his chin in thought. "Mikaela has shown interest and Isabella has qualities that could help strengthen us. This connection could be more beneficial than anticipated."

Mikaela hated hearing her family discuss her and Isabella as though they were simply strategic pawns in a larger game of politics. "What's next?"

"The situation with Fernando Acosta will need to be addressed discreetly," Juan said. "I'll see to his release and ensure he remains out of the public eye. He will not be a problem."

Mikaela felt a strange mix of gratitude and unease. She knew enough about her uncle to know that he relished being brash and seemed to enjoy the power he found in aggression. His sudden enthusiasm for Isabella was unexpected, but she trusted he understood the importance of unity and royal progression. She couldn't deny the flicker of hope that sparked deep inside. *Could this really be happening?*

Alejandro leaned toward her. "Well, Mika, looks like you've already got everyone scheming for you. Better figure out how you feel about Isabella fast before a wedding is on the calendar. I can't wait to meet her. Bummer that she doesn't have a sister."

Mikaela laughed softly as her thoughts drifted once more to the evening before. She had no idea what was to come or if Isabella even *wanted* to spend the next seventy-five days at Castillo Blanco with her, but one thing was certain—Isabella was already much more than just another name on a list.

❖

Two days later, the front door slammed as it rattled the chipped wooden frame at Isabella's family home. The resounding shake was ominous and seemed to reverberate through the entire house as Isabella's head snapped up from the kitchen table.

She exchanged a quick look with her mother as they dropped the carrots they had been peeling and chopping for that evening's vegetable and white bean soup. Fernando stalked inside and stood with his hands on hips, his dark hair disheveled and a spray of five o'clock shadow darkening his thin face. Isabella's stomach dropped, a common reaction to never knowing which father she would encounter that day—the quiet and distant sober one or the aggressive, angry drunk. Though his work shirt was dirty and untucked and the stench of old alcohol clung to him, his expression was sharp and focused.

"I'm done," Fernando announced as he threw his dirty work backpack onto the floor. "Seems they've had enough of your old man at the government of Cayo Azul. I work my ass off, work my ass off, work my ass off, and what do I get? Fired. Those asshole City Center cops had it out for me. They've been seeking me out for months and they hassle me every time."

Her mother froze and her hands trembled as she shakily dropped the peeler with a soft *thump* onto the table. Isabella's stomach twisted as the gravity of her father's declaration hung over the room.

"Fired?" Isabella repeated incredulously. "Oh, Papa, what did you do?"

Fernando swallowed hard and glared at her. "I know, it's all my fault," he said sarcastically. "It always is, right? They took me in to the drunk tank a few days ago. Ridiculous. I wasn't even that drunk. I told you, those City Center cops are on a power trip lately and they've had it out for me. And this time our government that's always hated me decided they'd had enough. The cops hauled me out this morning, but delivered an official letter." Fernando ripped a wrinkled sheet of paper from his back pocket. "I've officially been let go." He sat heavily on the worn couch. "I don't know why you bothered to bail me out. Should've just left me there to rot since I'm such a disappointment to you both."

Isabella shot another look at her mother, but her head was in her hands and her elbows rested on the table under the weight of her sagging shoulders.

"I didn't..." Isabella started in confusion. "Mami worked twelve hours yesterday, I don't think she did either..."

Her voice trailed off as Fernando's face darkened again. "Well, someone had to!" His voice rose. "What's for dinner?"

Her mother pressed a hand to her forehead and stood from the table. Isabella could sense that her normally reserved, resigned mother was positively seething with rage.

"Fernando," she said as her voice shook. "What are we supposed to do? How will we survive? Do you suggest I just move into the hospital and become an indentured servant?" Her voice rose shrilly and Isabella recognized something she had never heard in her mother's tone before: desperation.

Her father stepped closer and opened his mouth to retort, but a sharp knock echoed from the front door.

"Are you expecting someone?" he said as he angrily gestured to the door. "Oh, I'm sorry I interrupted your evening plans. Forget about me and everything I've sacrificed for both of you ungrateful women!"

Isabella glanced between her parents and her heart sank at the tears gathered in her mother's eyes that threatened to spill over at any second. She couldn't remember the last time she had seen her cry, and the lump in her own throat nearly threatened to choke her as she moved to answer the door.

Please don't be Javier. Not now. Not after everything.

Isabella stopped short and blinked at the two men on their porch. They both wore crisp uniforms, one with the pressed dark blue of the Cayo Azul police and the other wearing the drab olive green of the military. Shining pins and seals hung proudly from his shirt pocket, catching glints of the setting sun, as he smiled warmly at her. Despite his friendly expression, a chill ran down Isabella's spine.

This can't be good. What the hell did Papa get into?

"Good evening," the police officer said, his tone formal. "We'd like to speak with you and your family. May we step inside?"

Isabella hesitated, but her mother stepped forward and nodded as she regained her composure. "Please, come in," she said tightly. "May I offer you something to drink?"

The men stepped inside as their polished boots clicked against the tile floor. Her father glanced between them nervously, but he remained silent. The men stood side by side, with their arms clasped behind their backs as they exchanged a brief look.

"We are here on behalf of the de Medreno family," the police officer spoke after a moment. "We understand you may not have been expecting us and that this may be unconventional. However, we have been personally sent by His Royal Highness King Bartolo and Queen Cristina."

Her mother blinked and grabbed at the wall to steady herself. "What?"

Isabella stood beside her mother as her mind raced. *Mikaela. Could it be?* She glanced at her father as he rubbed a weary hand over his stubbled chin. *No. He must've finally done something really awful.*

"I am Brigadier General Jose Barrientos," the military man introduced himself. "My troops and I work directly under the commandment of General Juan de Medreno Soliz. There is a proposal we would like to discuss with you regarding your daughter, Isabella."

Confusion was written all over her mother's face as she glanced at Isabella. "My daughter? What could the royal family possibly want with her?"

Jose stepped forward, his expression unreadable. "Her Highness, Princess Mikaela, has taken an interest in getting to know your daughter further after the recent gala. We have been personally authorized to offer your family a substantial financial arrangement in exchange for Isabella spending the next seventy-five days at Castillo Blanco. We expect that to be in the range of about six times your husband's monthly salary, paid each month for life."

The words hung in the air, strange and surreal, as her mother stiffened. "No," she replied. "Absolutely not. I don't care how much money you're offering. I will never sell my daughter to the royal family. I don't care who they are."

Isabella's heart lurched in her chest as she tried to keep up. Jose stepped back respectfully but remained steady. "This is not a demand, Señora Ramon," he said, his tone softer. "Isabella would not be a prisoner at Castillo Blanco. She would have complete freedom as she enjoys today. You are also welcome to visit her at Castillo Blanco. This arrangement is purely one of mutual consent."

"Arrangement?" Her mother scoffed. "You think this is consent? To uproot her life and dangle an obscene amount of money, as though we have no integrity—"

"Mami," Isabella cut in. She willed away the tremble in her voice. "Please, let me speak. This is, after all, my life and my choice we are talking about."

Her mother's expression blazed as she turned to Isabella. "I know you connected with the princess at the gala," she said. Tears traced down her cheeks and Isabella understood with a hard swallow that her mother was fearful. "And I accept that. But not like this. I cannot allow it."

Isabella's mind raced with surging emotion, each one fighting for dominance. Guilt tore at her as she took in her mother's weary face, her father's inability to keep a steady job, and the lack of employment that made finding her own work outside of odd jobs so difficult. The thought of her mother working herself to death at the hospital just to keep them barely afloat made her want to cry. And then there was Mikaela—her quiet strength and confidence, her gorgeous smile, and the way she so easily worked her way around the walls Isabella didn't even realize she had. The idea of seventy-five days at Castillo Blanco—at Mikaela's mercy—wasn't just tempting, it was incredibly intoxicating. As her thoughts spiraled into yearning and desire, Isabella nodded and faced Jose.

"If I agree, you promise my family will never have to struggle again?" Isabella asked. "My father was recently let go from his job and work is hard to find here. My parents will be taken care of?"

Jose nodded. "Correct. Fernando and Araceli will be provided for financially for the rest of their lives, even if the seventy-five days does not end in marriage."

Her mother put her hand on her forearm. "Please think about this, my daughter," she whispered. "I'll work a hundred hours a week if I must. You don't need to do this for their money."

Isabella nodded. "I know, Mami," she replied gently. "But what choice do we have, now that Papa has been fired? Besides, I'd like the opportunity to get to know the princess too. This will give us, you, a chance to finally breathe. I love you."

Her mother searched her face but said nothing. She wrapped Isabella into a tight hug. "I love you too."

"Is your final answer that you accept this proposal?" Jose asked after a respectful moment.

Isabella nodded. "I do."

He straightened as the two men prepared to leave. "That is excellent news," he replied. "The royal family will be ecstatic to learn of this outcome. I will be in touch with further details soon, though I expect to escort you to Castillo Blanco in the next three to five days."

Isabella nodded again as she walked with them to the front door. They stepped onto the porch and Jose turned once more.

"Ah, yes, and there is one last condition I must ensure you understand, Señorita Acosta Ramon," his voice was low and commanding, but not unkind. "You cannot, under any circumstances, make Princess Mikaela privy to the financial component around this arrangement. If you do, the agreement will be void immediately and your family will no longer receive the agreed-upon financial support. Understood?"

Isabella's chest tightened as she wondered why Mikaela wouldn't be aware of these key details. "Yes," she said with a nod.

Jose tipped his cap satisfactorily as they left. Isabella waited a beat and then closed the front door as she turned to face her family in stunned silence.

"How can…" her mother wiped away a tear. "How can I be sure you'll be okay?"

"I'll keep my phone with me at all times," Isabella reassured her. "I promise to check in with you regularly."

Her father looked between them, his expression blank, as he stood and ambled toward the bedroom. "Well, you will finally provide for your parents, eh? After all I've sacrificed and done for you, you will finally do something for me. At least now I don't have to listen to your mami jaw at me all day for being unemployed this time."

Isabella's jaw tightened as she shot daggers into her father's retreating back.

A few minutes later, she found herself alone with her thoughts on the front porch swing. Isabella stared at the jagged cracks in the concrete as her mind wandered to Mikaela. The memories of her striking silhouette against the clear white moonlight and the way her voice sounded both soothing and commanding when she spoke to her eased the tension in her body after the unexpected visit from the royal emissaries.

Seventy-five days at Castillo Blanco. Isabella blew out her breath. *Seventy-five days in Mikaela's orbit.* She shivered despite the warm evening air. The thought of being near Mikaela for that amount of time and spending entire days alongside her, getting inside her world and her mind, sent an electric thrill down her spine. Isabella recalled the soft vulnerability Mikaela had flashed and imagined what it would be like to be the focus of that magnetic intensity.

Isabella's cheeks burned as her mother joined her on the porch swing, as though she could read the tantalizing thoughts that made her pulse quicken. Still, questions swirled at the back of her mind as she considered the strict instruction around the financial arrangement. Isabella knew that any true connection with Mikaela couldn't be built on secrets and dishonesty, but she ignored the strangeness of it all and allowed herself to indulge in the fantasy.

"I can help you leave, you know," her mother said. "I have a little saved. Enough to get you to Spain. My aunt has a flat in Madrid and you can stay there until you get on your feet. Find a job, start earning. It's not impossible and I'll help you too." She cast a sidelong glance at Isabella. "But something tells me that's not what you want to do."

Isabella took a deep breath and shook her head. She couldn't help it. The likelihood of outrunning the reaches of the royal family was small, and Isabella understood deep down she didn't want to anyway.

"It'll be okay, Mami," she finally said. She put her arm around her mother's shoulders and tilted her head until it rested against hers. "You'll be okay. *We* will be okay."

Isabella knew she couldn't guarantee that, not right now, but the same wave of calm anticipation she had felt days before washed over her. Whatever awaited her at Castillo Blanco, she couldn't deny the excitement coiling inside her.

With a soft sigh, she enjoyed the tendrils of anticipation that curled around her and the magnetic pull every time Mikaela's face flashed in her mind. For the first time in a long time, Isabella felt something more than uncertainty. She felt *alive*.

Chapter Thirteen

Mikaela glanced anxiously at the heavy double doors of the opulent dining space. It was about a quarter of the size of the ballroom and designed for smaller, more intimate gatherings. She took a deep, steadying breath as she smoothed the clingy fabric of her black one-piece jumpsuit. The wide legs and thin spaghetti straps belied a cool casualty, though Mikaela chose to dress it up with a fitted dark denim jacket, open-toed black heels, and her hair blown out straight and smooth as it fell over her shoulders.

The intimate cocktail hour preceding the dinner reception had just begun. It was already filled with familiar faces, including family, trusted close friends, and members of the Royal Council. Mikaela gracefully accepted a champagne flute from the jacketed waiter's silver tray as he paused at her side.

Tonight was about power, elegance, and connection—namely with Isabella Acosta Ramon. Mikaela knew she had arrived at Castillo Blanco early that morning and, much to her chagrin, learned that Isabella had a full slate of introductory meetings that had already been set up. Though Mikaela understood the importance of ensuring Isabella had the lay of the land right away, she was annoyed at being made to wait for an official reintroduction at tonight's welcome reception.

No sign of Isabella yet. Mikaela carefully swirled the champagne in her glass as she tried not to focus on the double doors bathed in a warm glow from the crystal chandeliers above.

"You've been staring at those doors for a full minute." Dayanara's voice interrupted her thoughts. "I don't think looking at them any harder will make her appear."

Mikaela glanced back at her. "If Ximena Rodriguez wasn't so chatty, perhaps they'd be on time."

Dayanara shook her head. "Why am I not surprised that Ximena would want to get in front of her right away? Anything to involve herself." She chuckled at Prime Minister Eduardo Rodriguez's overeager wife. "What's your plan? Are you going to pounce the moment Isabella walks in or is the ice queen going to play it extra cool?"

Mikaela arched an eyebrow and took a slow sip of her champagne. "I don't pounce, Daya," she replied lightly. "That's far too obvious."

Dayanara fixed her with a long look. "Sure, because the Mikaela I know hasn't been walking around with her head in the clouds for over a week at the thought of Isabella. You practically light up like a wolf spotting prey every time Isabella's name is mentioned."

Mikaela smiled confidently. "It's not my fault there's this...*thing* between us," she insisted. "I don't know how to explain it."

Dayanara tilted her head. "Let me guess," she said teasingly. "The moment she walks in, you'll hit her with one of those devastating glances of yours and expect her to make a beeline for you and fall at your feet?"

"Something like that," Mikaela said. "We'll find out soon enough."

Before Dayanara could retort, the double doors finally opened with a flourish and a few guests around them turned to appraise Isabella and Ximena.

Mikaela straightened her spine and finished her champagne in one long swallow as her gaze locked onto Isabella, who appeared composed and radiant. Her dimples deepened as she was introduced to a few people Ximena pointed out, leaning over to whisper their names. Isabella's black midi-length wrap dress was one that Mikaela recognized as Armani, and the detailed stitching that gathered at the waist flattered her in all the right places. Her long, dark hair had been professionally curled into loose ringlets that hung down her back with the top layer pulled up and away from her face, save for a few strands framing her profile. For a moment, Mikaela was sure she had forgotten to breathe.

Dayanara leaned closer. "Here we go," she whispered. "Let the games begin."

Mikaela was quiet for a moment but straightened at Dayanara's words. "She certainly knows how to make an entrance already."

Her anticipation surged as she waited impatiently for Isabella's gaze to find hers, and that tantalizing wordless connection to spark between them. Instead, Isabella stayed rooted to her spot, glancing once or twice at Ximena for guidance, as a few people shook her hand.

A flicker of annoyance rose in Mikaela's chest as she strolled purposefully, unbothered and confident, to the expansive tapas platter elegantly set on a long buffet table as guests automatically stepped aside and out of her path. She felt a strange heat on her back as she immediately knew that Isabella had finally spotted her. Mikaela lingered at the table as she carefully filled a small ceramic plate with a dollop of fig and goat cheese spread, a few crackers, and a bite-sized shrimp empanada. Still, Isabella made no move to approach.

Oh, this is how we're playing it tonight? Bet. Mikaela swiftly plucked another glass of champagne from a different waiter and rejoined Dayanara. *She's in over her head if she thinks she'll beat me at this game. Isabella's first lesson starts now.*

❖

Isabella blew out her breath in frustration and resisted the urge to stamp her feet like a child. Her entire body was urging her to go to Mikaela from the moment she walked into the dining area, but her brain stubbornly warred against it and kept her rooted to her spot at Ximena's side.

Keep it cool. She gets everything she wants and she's expecting you to go to her right away. Questions swirled in Isabella's mind after the whirlwind day. She'd had barely one hour to get comfortable in her guest suite before she'd been whisked away by a small contingent consisting of Prime Minister Eduardo Rodriguez's chief of staff, his wife, and the royal family's executive assistant, Lucia. The chief of staff, a tall, no-nonsense woman, gave her a brief tour of Castillo Blanco and introduced her to everyone from the house manager, Terese, to the grounds manager, Carlos. Isabella was then ensconced into a small conference room, where she was given a brief overview of the royal family and a rapid-fire history of Cayo Azul. It went deeper than what Isabella remembered learning in school, and she had sat, dazed, as she tried to remember the official stances, positions, and political achievements that had been shared.

She was finally escorted back to her guest suite, where a seamstress, hairstylist, and esthetician awaited to help her get ready for this evening's official reception. Still, one exchange from earlier stuck out in Isabella's mind.

"Of course, you understand that Her Royal Highness Princess Mikaela shall lead this relationship and any marriage that may ensue," Eduardo's chief of staff had said. "Princess Mikaela is to be the final decision-maker and head of household, so to speak. Of course, make no mistake. You shall be a team and you will always have your own free will to pursue your own interests and any passion projects you may wish to take on."

Isabella hesitated for just a beat as the chief of staff shot her an empathetic look.

"Know that the princess understands her responsibilities well," she said, gentler this time. "I've known Mikaela for a long time. She doesn't let many into her close inner circle, but she's fiercely protective over those who are there. She understands that she will take care of you and I know she will protect you."

Isabella swallowed hard as she was brought back to the present by a classical guitarist in the corner gently plucking his strings as he began an upbeat song. Whether it was a desperate attempt at self-preservation or innate stubbornness that told her to cling to even the smallest measure of control, Isabella straightened as she finally looked at the gorgeous woman across the room.

As she fought against drinking in the sight of her slender form and warm confidence, Mikaela glanced over and met her gaze as her smile softened into a slow, teasing curve of her lips. Everything seemed to still around Isabella, but she couldn't look away.

God, wouldn't it be satisfying to submit to her? The thought fired across Isabella's mind, sending heat deep into her belly.

Isabella turned, giving Mikaela her shoulder, as she ignored the thought and joined the conversation that Ximena held with the three women around her. She gratefully accepted a glass of red wine from a circulating waiter and took a casual sip as she nodded along and pretended to keep up with their small talk. Inside, Isabella's nerves were on edge as her mind wandered over her strange, deep attraction to Mikaela and the building desire she felt for her. It was almost as though something that had always been inside her was now awakened, and the intensity of it alarmed her.

Isabella stole another furtive glance across the room. Mikaela's back was now to her as she held court and chatted casually with a small throng of people who orbited around her eagerly. Isabella was slightly annoyed at Mikaela's apparent unbothered attitude and the easy way she turned away from her, though she told herself that was crazy because she had turned from her and broken the connection first.

But maybe it would *be satisfying to throw myself off the deep end, cede all control to her, and submit.* The acknowledgement didn't seem as intimidating as she drank in the sight of Mikaela.

At that moment, Mikaela turned again and raised an eyebrow expectantly as she regarded Isabella staring at her with what was probably a dreamy grin. Flushed with embarrassment, Isabella turned once more, resolutely this time, as she reinjected herself into the conversation around her.

"You know, we should say hello to Mikaela," Ximena said after a moment. "Come, Isabella. I am quite sure Queen Cristina would be thrilled to facilitate the reintroduction."

Isabella's pulse quickened as she nodded and dutifully followed Ximena across the room, watching politely as the prime minister's wife clasped Cristina's hands and they air-kissed one another in a showy greeting. *It's now or never, I suppose.*

With the formalities out of the way, Cristina beckoned to her daughter. "Mikaela!" Her voice did not imply choice. "There is someone you should be reintroduced to."

Mikaela straightened and murmured something to the woman beside her, who Isabella recognized as Dayanara Diaz. Mikaela's dark eyes sparkled with intrigue and a surge of electricity seemed to fill the room as Isabella's heart fluttered wildly in her chest.

Cristina placed a hand on Mikaela's shoulder and gestured to Isabella. "Mikaela, you remember Isabella Acosta Ramon, of course. Señorita Acosta Ramon, you may already be acquainted with my daughter, Mikaela, from the gala."

Play it cool Isabella's brain warned her again. She took a deep breath. She couldn't help it; every time she was near Mikaela, she had the overwhelming urge to smile. "Thank you, Your Highness," Isabella said smoothly. "We've met. Though I didn't realize we'd be meeting again so soon."

Cristina shot a sharp glance at Mikaela, who appeared to be biting back amusement as she regarded Isabella. "And I didn't realize you'd be so unimpressed by the occasion."

"Mikaela!" Cristina admonished her before turning to Isabella. "My apologies, Señorita. My dear daughter appears to have forgotten her manners."

Mikaela didn't break her lingering gaze on Isabella. "Are you hungry?" she asked. "Terese's team makes excellent tapas. Come, get a plate before the best of it is gone."

Isabella nodded as she fell into step with Mikaela. She was acutely aware of Cristina and Ximena watching them curiously as they walked away. Her stomach growled at the sight and smell of the tapas before her.

Mikaela handed her a plate. "You know, for someone who has barely eaten today, it took you long enough to venture to this side of the room," she said smoothly, though Isabella zeroed in on the undercurrent of electricity in her tone.

"You were so busy stealing the room's attention," Isabella replied. Her tone belied her playful defiance, though her eyes remained purposely trained on the trays of food. "Though I must admit, you make it very difficult to look away."

Mikaela raised an eyebrow and Isabella was sure she saw a flash of pink splash across her cheeks. "I appreciate the sentiment. Here, I thought you were going to ignore me all evening."

"Ignore you?" Isabella said lightly. "Seventy-five days is a long time. What would be the fun in that?"

"No fun at all," Mikaela said. She leaned in slightly, her voice low enough so only Isabella could hear. "Especially when I haven't been able to take my eyes off you all night either."

Isabella blinked, momentarily caught off guard by Mikaela's nearness. "Touché," she said.

A single bell tinkled loudly over the casual conversation and gentle strums of guitar that swept the room. Isabella glanced up, sudden heat burning across her neck, as Ximena clinked a spoon against her champagne glass.

"Dinner is ready!" she called. "We appreciate you being here this evening and hope you're enjoying yourselves. On behalf of the de Medreno family and the Royal Council, we invite you to please join us in the next room over for a formal dinner."

Mikaela met her eyes. "I'm certain you'll be sitting with me."

Isabella nodded in response and fell into step with Mikaela again. The centimeters between them felt glaring, hot, and as though there was far too much distance. Isabella fought the urge to lean closer to Mikaela and instead regarded the smaller dining room. A long granite-topped table stood impeccably set with a crisp white tablecloth, illuminated by flickers of white tea candles floating in round, water-filled centerpieces. Her heart skipped a beat as fresh anticipation coursed through her. She couldn't help but feel like she was willingly striding further into the lion's den—and something deep inside her didn't want to stop.

Chapter Fourteen

Mikaela had to hand it to her mother. The queen was an expert host, especially when it came to small, intimate gatherings. Shadows danced along the mahogany-paneled walls from the elaborate candelabra above and silky white floral arrangements stood between the floating centerpieces, filling the room with the light scents of orchid and calla lily.

She and Isabella were seated next to each other near the middle of the table. Mikaela knew Isabella was trying to play it cool—*too* cool—and it only steeled her determination to work her way beyond those protective walls once again.

With a sigh, Mikaela picked up her heavy soup spoon and dipped it into the decadent lobster bisque before her as her mother fixed Isabella with a practiced smile.

"Have you given much thought to what a royal wedding might look like?" her mother said. "Any must-haves you've dreamed about? We have an excellent events team contracted through our public relations agency and they'll be happy to assist with each detail."

Mikaela's heart dropped as Isabella blinked in surprise. "I…I can't say I've had much time to think about it, Your Majesty," she replied diplomatically.

"Understood," her mother went on smoothly. "You've had quite a change and may need some time to settle in. Of course, you'll have plenty of time to consider the details, but we'll need to settle the basics soon. The guests we expect require ample notice for an event such as this." She took a delicate sip of wine. "The palace gardens would make a stunning setting for an end-of-summer ceremony, don't you think?"

"Mother," Mikaela interjected calmly. "Let's take things one step at a time. After all, Isabella has only just arrived."

"Of course," her mother replied. "But do remember it's important to plan ahead. These events take time, as you know. A royal wedding is a momentous occasion. Not only will it celebrate the soon-to-be queen of Cayo Azul," she paused as she regarded Isabella, "and her bride, but it will emphasize unity, progression, and strength to our people."

Mikaela shifted coolly and hoped her discomfort didn't show. "I'm certain we will have plenty of time to discuss these details later."

Her mother sighed. "Very well," she said, waving a hand. "You two must continue to connect and have these conversations. After all, the sanctity of marriage is one of the core tenets of Cayo Azul. After the wedding and the handfasting ceremony, you two are bound together. For life, forever."

Mikaela felt Isabella's wide eyes dart to her. She took a deep breath as her irritation softened. "When does Papa return from Spain?" she asked as she took a slow spoonful of her soup and tactfully changed the subject.

I'm sure Isabella is feeling the pressure. Mikaela barely registered her mother's response. *God, what if it's too much for her? Could she really decide that she'd rather return to Este?* The uncertainty was foreign to Mikaela, and the thought made her blood run cold with disappointment.

Thankfully, Alejandro cut in, charming as ever, as he flashed his million-watt smile at Isabella and kindly peppered her with softball questions about herself. Mikaela was grateful for her cousin's ability to sense and diffuse tension, and she listened as Isabella seemed to relax while reminiscing about being the captain of her high school's women's futbol team.

"An athlete!" Alejandro exclaimed. "How exciting."

Isabella blushed. "I don't know," she said ruefully. "Futbol was the only sport I excelled at."

As they continued chatting, Mikaela tried to picture a younger, teenaged Isabella racing across the field toward the black-and-white ball, as her dark hair streamed behind her and her toned, tanned legs glistened under the sun in those tiny futbol shorts… *Stop it.*

As dessert was served, the light conversation continued, and Mikaela could sense Isabella's guard lower just a little bit. After Alejandro politely excused himself from the meal early for a quarterly grants review with Cayo Azul's federal nonprofit arm, her mother eyed them once more over her lavender creme brûlée.

Oh God, what now? The queen appeared to be carefully considering her words.

"Have you two thought about children?" her mother finally asked and then paused as she looked between them. "Not *immediately*, of course. But let's be realistic and not overly dramatic. Children are still expected, despite what may be an unconventional marriage. It is of the utmost importance to keep the royal lineage progressing, which Mikaela knows well."

"Of course, Mother," Mikaela replied. "All in time."

"It would be lovely if you both welcomed a child," her mother said. "I understand there is even an option called reverse in vitro fertilization, though that may require a longer stay in the States. I hear they have exceptional clinics that do that. Isabella, that means you can be implanted with a fertilized egg from Mikaela. The advances in technology these days are stunning, aren't they? What a world we live in."

"Excuse me," Isabella said. Her voice sounded guarded and hoarse. "I need just a moment." She gently pushed back her chair and stood, refusing eye contact with Mikaela as she slipped out of the dining room.

Mikaela's chest tightened as she ignored her mother's pointed look.

"Please, Mother," Mikaela said in a low voice. "Give us room to breathe."

"Marriage is an imperative, Mikaela," her mother said firmly but not unkindly. "It's important to understand what it means, what it entails, and that you have selected the best person possible. There are many, *many* more expectations because of who we are. You must consider all of this and choose wisely."

Mikaela stood. "I'm trying," she replied tightly. "For all I know, Isabella is now packing her bags. I will fix this."

Her mother shrugged one shoulder. "If she is, then she's not the right one for you. This life? It *is* pressure, Mikaela. I have shielded you from as much as possible, but you will need someone who will stand strong at your side and encourage you when you're in doubt. Not shrink away when the lights get bright."

The words echoed in Mikaela's head as she stepped into the quiet halls of the castle and wondered which way Isabella may have gone. The gentle tap of stilettos pacing across marble led Mikaela to a small alcove. Moonlight poured through the floor-to-ceiling glass window, bathing Isabella in an ethereal glow despite the obvious tension in her shoulders.

As Mikaela blinked at the image and drank in the sight of her, her heart was practically in her throat. She didn't *want* Isabella to go anywhere but to her.

"You left in a hurry," Mikaela said. Her soft voice filled the quiet alcove as she took a cautious step closer.

As she regarded Isabella, Mikaela could feel the tension draining from her wary gaze, leaving them with only that magnetic desire wrapped in the calming sense that everything was going to be okay.

"What, were you worried I'd run away before your mother tried to impregnate me herself?" Isabella replied, her voice tinged with a guarded sass. "It's just…it's a lot."

Mikaela arched an eyebrow and took another careful step closer. "I *really* don't want that visual, thank you very much," she said. "I know it's a lot. My mother has a way of steamrolling people."

She recognized the sheen in Isabella's dark eyes that she tried to rapidly blink away. "It's fine," Isabella said, too quickly and too firmly. "I'm fine."

Mikaela studied her for a long moment. She didn't want to push and she didn't want to stay silent. "It's okay not to be," she said finally. "I'm on your side, Isabella. Always. Even if it doesn't feel that way right now."

There was a beat of stillness and Mikaela could sense that Isabella was warring with herself whether to push her away or let her in. It made her chest ache in the best and worst way.

"Do you always follow people when they leave the table?" Isabella finally asked teasingly.

"Only when I'm worried about them," Mikaela admitted and then sighed. "Not usually."

Isabella nodded as she appeared to consider that. "I didn't expect… any of this."

"Neither did I," Mikaela replied gently. "I'll give you some time. But I meant what I said. I'm on your side. If it ever feels like too much, you can tell me. I'll listen."

The tension seemed to dissipate as Isabella exhaled, and Mikaela could almost see the weight lift from her shoulders. "Thank you," she said. "I will do my best to, um, *adjust* to the royal expectations. Whatever those may be."

Mikaela felt a swell of relief at the diffused tension as an idea curled its way around her brain.

"I want to take you out," Mikaela said. The idea made her heart beat just a little faster than she cared to acknowledge.

Isabella blinked. "Take me out?"

"A real date," Mikaela said as she tried to keep her voice steady. "Or, as real as it can be given the circumstances. No friends or Royal Council around, no protocols to follow. Just the two of us."

Isabella studied her carefully as she chewed her bottom lip. *God, what I wouldn't give to nip at that mouth.* "Surely you have more important royal duties to attend to?"

Mikaela arched an eyebrow. "What if I told you this *is* my royal duty?"

Isabella's defenses cracked just enough for her face to light up. "You're very confident, Princess."

Mikaela shrugged. "I have my moments. Besides, if we're going to figure out the next seventy-four days, you deserve to see what it's *really* like to be with me. Beyond all the circumstance, the responsibilities, and, you know, the queen."

The air felt charged as Isabella paused for a beat before nodding. "I would love that."

"In a few days," Mikaela said, wondering if she imagined the slight fall of Isabella's face. She knew the anticipation would be tortuous. Patience wasn't Mikaela's strong suit, but she understood that Isabella had been through a massive, rapid life change.

I don't ever want to see those tears again. Isabella needs time to breathe. And then we'll see who each other really is.

"In a few days," Mikaela repeated. "I'll see to it that your schedule is cleared tomorrow. Take the day to rest, get settled in. Explore, if you'd like. Make yourself comfortable. We'll have the following time for just you and I, yes?"

Isabella nodded, her smile lingering as Mikaela walked her back to her suite. As they fell into step down the long hallway, Mikaela couldn't stop stealing glances at Isabella. Her glossy dark curls occasionally caught the faint glow from the stained-glass Tiffany wall sconces. There was a softness around her after her unexpected vulnerability, and it tore into Mikaela's protective instincts. She took a deep breath as she fought to keep from wrapping her arms around her.

Outside the suite door, Isabella turned to her as her hand hovered over the knob. Mikaela recognized the intrigue and heat as Isabella searched her face, questioning.

Focus on saying good night. Mikaela tried to ignore her quickening pulse. She could see the cracks forming in Isabella's resolve, the faintest glimmers of trust beginning to take root, and Mikaela surprised even herself with the intensity that replaced her practiced cool.

Wait. Let things unfold naturally. Don't rush. She's worth it.

Mikaela politely opened the door for Isabella. "Good night."

Her heart swelled at the faint smile that ghosted across Isabella's lips as she held her gaze for another moment. "Good night, Princess."

As Mikaela walked back down the hallway, she silently promised herself that when the time was right, when she was certain Isabella was ready, she wouldn't hesitate. She would show her exactly who Mikaela de Medreno Soliz was.

Chapter Fifteen

Exactly three packed days later, Mikaela stood glaring at the pristine kitchen she currently warred with. Her hands were perched resolutely on her hips as she considered the stainless-steel pan before her. It was the afternoon of her official date with Isabella, and Mikaela had chosen a casual get-together at her private pool. The luxurious in-ground pool was tucked away just behind her private residence, protected by tall, lush palm trees and vibrant bougainvillea draped across a tall wrought-iron fence. The bright splashes of magenta and orange alongside the temperature-controlled turquoise water looked like something out of a luxury tropical travel magazine. Sleek white linen chaises lined the stone patio, shaded by oversized white umbrellas, and the covered open-air kitchen and bar provided a relaxing escape.

Terese lingered nearby and watched politely as Mikaela's frown deepened at the shiny stove knobs. "You know, Your Highness," she said, "the appliances *can* seem a bit overwhelming at first. I'd be happy to—"

"I've got it, Terese," Mikaela cut in. She flashed a smile at Castillo Blanco's longtime house manager. "I'm perfectly capable of making lunch. Really, how hard can it be? It's just grilled cheese and tomato sandwiches."

Terese raised a skeptical brow but nodded. Mikaela twisted one of the knobs on the sleek stainless-steel oven and yelped in surprise as a blue flame shot up from a corner burner. The smell of gas hung in the warm air as Terese opened and then closed her mouth.

"Are you quite sure? I can whip those up and be out of your hair. Why don't you relax by the pool?"

Mikaela shot Terese a look as she threw a thick slice of wheat bread into the skillet and carefully topped it with a golden piece of aged cheddar. "See?" she said. "I'm doing it. I mean, surely I'm not so incapable that I can't even fix a casual lunch." She poked at the contents of the pan with a fork. "Um, how do I flip this?"

Terese pointed at a drawer hidden beneath the marble countertops of the nearby kitchen island. "Use the spatula. You may need to keep flipping to ensure even cooking."

With that, Terese wiped her palms on her crisp white apron and nodded. "I'll leave you to it then," she said. As she turned to leave, she couldn't resist adding, "Though I do wonder how you'll handle the blender for those green smoothies you mentioned. It's a bit…temperamental."

Mikaela fixed Terese with a look and held up the spatula triumphantly. "I've got this."

Exactly five minutes later, Mikaela stared woefully at the blackened bread crumbling in the pan. "I don't have this," she muttered as she wondered where she'd gone wrong. Just then, she noticed a text on her phone from Dayanara that had been sent ten minutes ago.

Incoming wife-to-be.

Mikaela knew Isabella had a get-to-know-you chat with her that morning but hadn't realized it was already lunchtime. *And yet, we have no lunch.* She blew out her breath in frustration.

"Are you…cooking?" Isabella's mildly incredulous voice from behind startled Mikaela.

She turned sharply from the stove to find Isabella leaning casually against a pillar that held up the kitchen's open-air roof. Her dark hair had been pulled back into a neat bun, though the light breeze had helped a few face-framing strands escape. Her loose white linen cover-up and black one-piece bathing suit had a plunging neckline that teased just enough of Isabella's golden skin. Mikaela had been utterly unprepared for the sight and her mouth dropped slightly.

"I…I didn't hear you come in," Mikaela said, as she tried to shake off the uncharacteristic fluster.

Isabella took a step closer. "I think, um…" she pointed delicately at the pan, "*that* might be a bit burnt." She sniffed the air. "Is that *smoking*?"

Mikaela turned and twisted the burner to its off position as she waved a hand over the light tendrils of gray smoke that curled up from the charcoal-like bread. "Shit," she muttered and then took a deep breath. "I was trying to make a poolside lunch for us, but clearly I'm not meant for the culinary arts."

Isabella laughed and peered into the pan. "Wait, did you not add olive oil or butter?" Mikaela knew she was trying to hide her incredulousness and was slightly annoyed that she could hear it in her voice anyway. "You were… you were cooking on a dry pan? Oh, Mikaela, you're lucky this didn't go up in flames."

Mikaela bit her lip but couldn't help smiling. "Well, I…I didn't realize."

Isabella looked closely at her. "How many times have you worked a stove and made a meal for yourself?"

Mikaela felt the flush creeping up her neck as she thought back. "I guess…" She sighed. "Well, I guess none that I can remember."

Isabella's eyebrows shot up, but her face softened as their gazes locked. As the banter fell away, the air between them shifted as Mikaela became acutely aware of how close Isabella was standing and how little clothing she was wearing. She fought the urge to glance at Isabella's full lips and close the small space between them.

Isabella cleared her throat, breaking the moment, though her cheeks flushed. "Okay, it's fine," she said with a nod as she surveyed the kitchen. "No problem. We'll stick to something simple. Surely there's enough here for a small charcuterie."

Mikaela exhaled. "Surely," she replied teasingly. "I'll stick to making drinks."

As Mikaela opened the large stainless-steel refrigerator, she spotted a silver tray wrapped in clear plastic. Thick slices of fresh tomato topped with Italian-imported mozzarella, a crisp dark green spinach leaf, and a drizzle of balsamic were neatly lined along the tray. *Terese*. Mikaela pulled out the tray gratefully and made a mental note to send a thank you text to her.

Focus, Mikaela. Her thoughts drifted back to Isabella's lean, smooth form. *Let's see where this leads.*

The pool water had been warmed by the sun, and its soothing heat was reminiscent of a relaxing bath. Isabella perched at the edge of the pool, dipping her legs in just up to her knees as she enjoyed the feeling of the sun across her shoulders. Mikaela gently hopped into the pool as the sun glinted brightly off the blond tones in her hair. It curled slightly at the ends where it touched the water, and Mikaela closed her eyes and swirled her hands beneath the surface.

She's so effortlessly gorgeous.

"You're staring," Mikaela said knowingly as she blinked.

"Am not," Isabella shot back, though her voice betrayed her.

Mikaela walked across the tiled pool floor with deliberate slowness to where Isabella sat. Droplets of water snaked down her toned shoulders as she rested her forearms on the pool ledge at either side of Isabella's legs. She tried to ignore the quickening of her pulse as Mikaela's wet skin brushed against her outer thighs.

"Maybe I should warn you," Mikaela said, her voice low and teasing. "Since we're on an official date and all. This is what being with me is *really* like. Some unexpected chaos, a little fire—"

"And burnt sandwiches," Isabella interrupted her with a smile. "I guess I'll be in charge of the cooking."

Mikaela laughed, a throaty, sexy sound that made Isabella want to wrap her arms and legs around her. "That too. But also…moments like this." Her gaze softened and lingered on Isabella in a way that made her wonder if the heat of the day had already arrived or if Mikaela truly had that effect on her.

Isabella gave in to the pull that seemed to electrify her. She leaned in slightly as she opened and then closed her mouth, biting her bottom lip instead. "You might be trouble," she said.

Mikaela was quiet for a moment. "That may be, but if you trust me and you are mine, I will always take care of you."

Isabella's heart was in her throat as she nodded. "Okay," she said. "Let's do this."

At that moment, the timer on the blender sounded, loud and unwelcome, and cut through the flirtatious tension. Isabella was determined to not get caught staring again as Mikaela carefully stepped out of the pool, water coursing down her long, toned legs, and padded to the kitchen.

"At least I can handle smoothies," she called playfully over her shoulder. "Though I'll let you decide if this is better than designer dresses and formal galas."

So. Much. Better. Isabella regarded Mikaela for a long, sweet moment as she flipped open cabinets searching for glasses. "This is really you, huh?"

Mikaela shook her head ruefully. "I don't know if I'm ever just one thing, but…yeah," she said as she poured the frozen green concoction into two tall glasses. "This is me too."

Mikaela handed her a frosty glass. "Banana, mango, spinach, pineapple, and crushed ice. Good for the immune system and the energy."

Isabella glanced at the glass, unsure. "I don't know," she replied. "Good old caffeine in the form of coffee is my go-to for energy."

"You don't have to drink it," Mikaela said. "There's always a pot of coffee or three brewing around the main castle. It keeps the Royal Council running, after all. I can have Terese send out a thermos."

Mikaela stepped back into the pool and trailed her fingertips lazily through the water. Isabella didn't want any interruptions. The one-on-one time with Mikaela was deliciously satisfying and if not breaking the connection meant holding her nose and drinking a green smoothie, so be it.

She held her glass up in a mock toast and then took a long sip. She blinked as she tried not to grimace at the bitter spinach. "Thank you, but this is fine."

Mikaela watched her with amusement as Isabella took another long swallow and kicked her feet beneath the water.

"So, Princess," she said, drawing out the word. "If we're going to do this date properly, I think it's only fair we get to know each other."

Mikaela smiled teasingly. "Oh? What would you like to know?"

Isabella playfully tapped her index finger against her lips. "Hmm, okay. Here's an easy one. What's your favorite thing to do when you're not busy being Her Royal Highness, the future queen of Cayo Azul?"

Mikaela groaned dramatically. "God, that sounds exhausting the way you say it."

"You *are* the one born into it," Isabella reminded her with a laugh.

"Tragically, yes," Mikaela replied with mock drama. "To answer your question, I love horseback riding. I spent much of my childhood and teenaged years traversing western Europe in professional competitions." She had a faraway expression as her tone grew more serious. "There's a beautiful sense of freedom when horseback riding, where it's just me with my thoughts and of course Luna, that I don't get many other places. No expectations, no responsibilities, just freedom."

Isabella wondered what it must be like to have grown up in such a regimented life, unable to go anywhere or do anything very freely. Though Isabella had her own hardships and traumas, one of the things she enjoyed most about growing up in Este was the wild freedom she and the local kids enjoyed. People were poor, but neighbors looked out for one another. Running through the lush green fields and screaming at the top of her lungs as the sun faded into the horizon while she and her friends played hide-and-seek or freeze tag were things that had shaped her childhood.

For all the financial freedom we never had, I suppose we enjoyed a different kind of freedom. And for all the wealth and privilege that Mikaela enjoys, she never really experienced that *type of freedom.*

"I wouldn't have guessed that. I figured you'd be more into City Center yacht parties and film festivals."

Mikaela groaned again. "Don't even get me started on film festivals," she said. "I mean, yacht parties are nice. But sometimes…sometimes I prefer to just breathe. What about you? What does *Isabella* love to do?"

Isabella blushed at the way Mikaela drew out her name teasingly. "I love reading and futbol of course, when there's a pickup game in the neighborhood. But I do love books the most. They've always been an escape, a way to open up the world a little more."

Mikaela nodded. "What's your favorite book?"

"That's impossible!" Isabella playfully splashed in Mikaela's direction. "I imagine it'd be like choosing between your children. I suppose if I *had* to pick…*The Shadow of the Wind*."

Mikaela looked impressed. "Excellent choice."

"You've read it?" Isabella asked, unsure why she was mildly surprised. *She's not some self-absorbed royal party girl. But I think I already knew that…*

"Of course!" Mikaela exclaimed with a laugh. "You're not the only one with great taste."

Isabella pursed her lips. "Well, you may have to school me on the *fashionista* side of things," she said. "Ximena and Daya have been so wonderful about helping me select a wardrobe, but I don't know if I'll ever make it to your level. You know, where you look like you stepped out of a runway magazine no matter what time it is."

Isabella felt her face flush with Mikaela's quiet gaze on her. "You seem to be doing just fine."

"Careful," Isabella said. "You're starting to sound as though you're flirting with me."

Mikaela's expression slipped into something softer before she appeared to recover. "Next question." Her voice was low and gentle, and Isabella wondered for a moment how deep she could dig.

"Okay." Isabella took a deep breath and tucked a strand of hair behind her ear. "If you weren't the princess, what would you be?"

Mikaela considered this for a moment. "In another life, I'd love to be a journalist. Spend my life traveling the globe. I mean, without the royal responsibilities and meetings and events and expectations. Write articles, take photographs, share content, help people understand one another. Really *share* the world."

"That sounds amazing."

Mikaela nudged her forearm gently and Isabella swallowed hard at the casual contact. "And you? If you could be anything?"

"I think…I'd love to own a small coffee shop somewhere."

Mikaela grinned. "You really do like your coffee."

Isabella laughed. "Yes, but it's truly about the vibe more than anything. I'd want it to be something intimate, a place where everyone belongs. Sort of like my favorite spot back home." She glanced down at her legs. They looked pale and distorted beneath the still water. "The owner, Vanessa, has been struggling with rising costs recently. I hope she'll be able to keep her place open. I'd love for it to be something like what she's built, where people can come in, drink coffee, get lost in a book or their thoughts or each other."

Mikaela nodded. "That suits you well."

Isabella glanced at her. "Why is that?"

"Because you *are* intimate," Mikaela replied. "And smart. And definitely stubborn."

Isabella rolled her eyes. "Wow, thank you."

Mikaela's expression was softer and more vulnerable now. "You want to create a place of belonging. You *care*. You know, with the amount of people I've met over the years, the ratio of those who truly care versus the entitled ones who don't care at all is so small. It's disappointing. The fact that you want just a tiny corner of the universe to shape into something *better*, somewhere safe and warm, says more than you think."

Isabella blinked, caught off-guard by her sincerity, and the warmth between them seemed to deepen as their playful flirting teased into something deeper.

"You surprise me, Mikaela. This whole date thing might not be so bad after all."

She felt Mikaela studying her with a faint softness. "Good," she finally replied. "I like getting to know you."

Isabella's gaze fell to Mikaela's soft, full lips and she marveled at how easy it would be to throw herself into the warm water and close the gap between them.

I don't want this date to ever end.

Her thoughts were no longer tangled in doubts, but instead consumed by the ever-growing pull she felt toward the princess who somehow always made her feel seen.

CHAPTER SIXTEEN

The moon illuminated the courtyard and reflected around the still, silvery puddles that gathered around the decorative pool's ornate Italian tile edges. Isabella breathed in deeply as she inhaled the familiar scents of salt and jasmine. The day with Mikaela had been amazing and she marveled at how quickly the hours seemed to tick by. Afternoon had turned into evening as Isabella wistfully noticed the sky darkening with streaks of bright red and deep orange that eventually gave way to a soft navy blue. Isabella hadn't expected how much fun she would have beyond the prestige and surface-level luxury, just her and Mikaela.

She's so beautiful. Isabella stole a glance at the sharp curves and soft angles of her profile. *Beyond beautiful.*

Isabella conceded to herself that the pressure she'd expected to feel on this date—especially after the welcome reception—hadn't been there at all. Perhaps because it was their first real day alone together or done under the pretense of *what if* and *let's just see what happens*, it felt like they were both able to relax and show up as themselves.

Mikaela slowed as they reached the bottom of the artfully curved left staircase to the main entrance of Castillo Blanco, now so familiar to Isabella, and guided them purposefully out of sight from the ever-present security guards posted just outside the expansive foyer. For a brief moment, only the sound of the trickling fountain behind them could be heard within the stillness.

Nobody gets to see this side of Mikaela. Isabella shivered a little at the thought. The feeling of privilege, like she had been made privy to the most beautiful secret, and a rush of affection for her raised goose bumps along her forearms.

"Are you cold?" Mikaela asked as she gazed at Isabella under the moonlight.

Isabella shook her head, even as she wrapped her arms around herself against the breeze. The casual zip-up sweatshirt and loose linen pants over her bathing suit didn't provide much protection from the cool night air. "It's okay."

Mikaela was quiet for a beat. "You look like you're cold," she said, a hint of vulnerability in her voice once more. "Are you so used to ignoring your own needs, your wants?"

Isabella knew the question was meant to be rhetorical but was surprised at how easily Mikaela read her. "The breeze is a little chillier tonight," she finally admitted.

A smile played at Mikaela's lips. "If you're cold, it's okay, Isabella," she said. "Always feel comfortable talking to me."

Isabella's pulse quickened as Mikaela stepped closer, the distance between them nearly nothing. Her heart and brain warred loudly in the background as she tried to make sense of what was real and whether the pretense had really dissipated into the twinkling night sky or if it was just wishful thinking.

Mikaela gently brushed a few strands of Isabella's hair behind her ear as her slender fingers lingered for a beat. The sweet, intimate touch sent another shiver through Isabella, but she knew they *both* knew it had nothing to do with the island breeze. Isabella *wanted* Mikaela like she had never wanted anyone in her life.

"You should go inside," Mikaela said, her voice low. "Get warmed up. Rest."

Just as Isabella was trying to ignore the crushing disappointment at the polite dismissal, she felt Mikaela touch her hand and intertwine her fingers with her own. Slowly but confidently, as if testing the waters, Mikaela leaned in. Isabella's heart pounded loudly in her ears as she felt the warmth of Mikaela's lips just millimeters from her own.

Mikaela hesitated for the briefest of moments, as if giving Isabella a chance to pull away.

No. Fucking. Way.

Isabella gave in to the electric energy around them and closed the space between their lips. Mikaela's mouth was warm, sweet, and sure, giving Isabella the certainty she needed as she deepened the kiss and tangled her hands in Mikaela's hair. Castillo Blanco, the quiet front courtyard, and the rest of the island beyond those tall iron gates fell away as fireworks dazzled behind Isabella's eyes and hot sparks coursed through her veins. Mikaela's hands commanded her waist as she drew her closer and held her tighter against her. The heat from Mikaela's body warmed Isabella, and she wanted *more.*

Perfect. The thought flashed across Isabella's mind as she crushed her lips against Mikaela's mouth again. *This is perfect.*

After a long moment, Mikaela gently pulled away, breathless and all swollen lips and flushed cheeks. Isabella rested her forehead against Mikaela's for another moment, loathe to let the evening end.

"Good night, *amor*," Mikaela said as her lips brushed Isabella's ear.

"Good night," Isabella echoed her. Mikaela turned and began down the path to her home. Isabella took a deep breath and disliked the feelings of cold and emptiness that seemed to settle around her without Mikaela nearby. Isabella's chest constricted as Mikaela disappeared into the night and she fought the overwhelming urge to throw off her shoes, sprint after her, jump into her arms, and kiss her over and over again until the sun began peeking over the horizon.

After a moment, Isabella climbed the stairs wearily and nodded in thanks to the security guard who held the door for her. The kisses had been sweet, intense, and filled with promises of an enticing future neither had fully dared acknowledge until now.

After closing the door of her guest suite behind her and kicking off her shoes, Isabella perched on the edge of the luxurious king-sized bed and pulled her hair down from its bun. As she shook out her hair, Isabella wondered how long she'd feel lightheaded and breathless from kissing Mikaela. With a deep exhale, she finally flopped back onto the satin sheets as she smiled at the ceiling.

Whatever comes next, it will be real. It already is.

As the first few days of Isabella's stay gently rolled into the first couple of weeks, Mikaela found herself disarmed by how easy and natural it felt to have Isabella as part of her life—as though they were always meant to somehow find and immerse themselves in one another. She enjoyed the delicious anticipation she'd wake with each morning, as her heartbeat quickened with the reminder that Isabella was nearby somewhere. The quiet early mornings, as the stifling sun stretched higher into the sky and curls of pink cotton candy clouds faded over the ocean, had become unspoken time together. Mikaela was surprised the first time she ventured into a quiet, open area of Castillo Blanco's grounds, adjacent to her private pool, for her daily morning cardio, only to find Isabella gliding through the water as she did determined laps.

Mikaela had an hour each morning with her personal trainer and found herself having more difficulty focusing than usual. As she'd suffer through deep squats, tight lunges, and quick sprints across the grassy space while trickles of perspiration dotted her temples, she could hear the perfectly timed splashes just beyond the tall palm trees surrounding the pool. Despite her best efforts to focus on her core strength or even the burning in her calves, Mikaela's mind would inevitably wander over stolen glimpses of Isabella's toned arms slicing through the turquoise water or the wet strands of hair, loose from her ponytail, that would drip down the back of her neck.

They quickly learned to end their dawn exercise routines around the same time, as they would shower and reconvene at the tall marble-topped island in the pool's kitchen area. Mikaela put in a personal request to Terese to ensure there was always a pot of fresh coffee brewing and a bottle of vanilla creamer in the refrigerator for Isabella after her swim. Isabella would try but fail to fully disguise the slight wrinkling of her nose as Mikaela would blend herself a green smoothie and then they would sit quietly together, eager to catch up on the day ahead over breakfast.

Mikaela took a deep breath as she reminded herself to focus on the meeting at hand. In the Royal Council chamber, there was little time for daydreaming as she glanced around the long table. Her father sat at the head, flanked by Eduardo on his other side. Alejandro sat next to Eduardo and across from Jorge Acevedo, a short, portly man who was also Cayo Azul's longtime transportation secretary.

They turned to Mikaela expectantly as she glanced at the screen of her laptop. Statistics, figures, and graphics supporting the development of a state-of-the-art public bus system across Cayo Azul glowed brightly at her from the neatly organized report Jorge had prepared.

"As you know, I've been a big proponent of developing a true public transportation option servicing all of Cayo Azul from the moment this project was first floated," Mikaela said. "Thank you, Jorge, for the research you've put into this study. After all, a public bus system isn't just about convenience. It's also about equity and sustainability. If we want to continue strengthening our economy and improving life for all Cayo Azuleans, we need reliable, accessible transit that reduces the reliance on taxis and expensive rideshares."

Eduardo listened as he stroked his chin. "The benefits are quite clear," he said.

"In the long run, this will help the people of Este," Mikaela went on as she skimmed the report she'd read several times already. "It will provide an economical, convenient option to get around the island. If we start small—say, sixteen or twenty buses with five or six strategic routes—for a year or two, we can use that as a case study and have metrics to fully understand its effect and where it can be improved prior to expanding into a full system."

Alejandro nodded. "Mikaela's recommendation is not only viable, but strategic," he said. "Her insight into the benefits and challenges aligns with my thoughts as well."

Mikaela's father studied her for a long moment before speaking. "Your grasp of this project is commendable," he said. "It's clear you understand the nuances and how to approach it from a strategic point of view."

Mikaela smiled. "One thing I did want to note, Jorge, is the importance of ensuring efficiency here," she said. "We must integrate environmentally-friendly practices wherever possible to minimize our carbon footprint. As you know, we provide an annual sustainability report to the UN in alignment with their Sustainable Development Goals. This supports the annual grant money we receive from them, so it's imperative this is implemented in a thoughtful way. Now, remind me. What is the price differential between the two hybrid bus options you mentioned?"

As Jorge scrolled through his report and launched into hybrid and electric bus prices versus gas-powered, confident satisfaction coursed through Mikaela. The years of preparation under her father had helped the transition from advisor to expert immensely. She sensed the shift over the last year, with the earned trust of the Royal Council as they flocked to her for guidance and to get her perspective on ideas and challenges.

As the meeting adjourned, Mikaela stood. She noticed her father and Eduardo exchange a quick glance before her father motioned to follow them into his private office. The air felt heavier as Mikaela sat in a leather chair before her father's wide mahogany desk. Antique tapestries adorned the walls, stretching nearly to the ornately carved crown molding, and the chandelier high above was set to low, warm lighting.

Eduardo spoke first as he crossed his arms. "Your Highness, my team has done additional research into Isabella's background as per protocol. There are some things I think are important to note here."

Her father nodded, his expression serious. "As you know, Isabella came to the gala at the invitation of Javier Jimenez. He is the son of Roberto Jimenez, Este's mayor. Roberto has served us for nearly a dozen years as Este's representative."

Mikaela felt a flicker of unease. "And?"

Eduardo sighed. "Based on my recent visits to Este, I suspect Roberto may be solidifying his power there by spearheading a formal resistance movement capitalizing on the growing unrest." He held up his hands. "Now I don't have anything concrete yet, but the overall atmosphere in Este is... different from the last time I visited."

Mikaela blinked. "And when *was* the last time you visited, Eduardo?"

He stiffened. "I have since discussed with your father the importance of maintaining a presence there," he said. "With the years of internal and external investment in City Center and even Santa Julianna, I do understand the *appearance* is that Este has been left behind. And if this is the message Roberto has been conveying from the Crown, then resentment can simmer. If he senses a power play where he can nurture and manipulate this resentment for his own gain, he could become...dangerous."

Mikaela's stomach tightened as she recalled Ian's warning weeks back at Tryst. She knew what an organized resistance could mean for the kingdom—and for her eventual rule. The thought of Isabella, her soft lips, and her hands fisting in her hair while they kissed, gnawed at her. Mikaela exhaled and willed herself to remain composed.

"This is important," she said. "We must not get overly comfortable and we must understand what's happening, so it can be resolved before it truly begins. I had shared word some weeks back about intel I received, though I wasn't certain how serious it was."

Eduardo nodded. "I remember, Your Highness," he replied. "As a result of these concerns, we have made Juan aware so he can adjust police protocol as necessary. He may wish to activate a larger presence in and around Este, at least until we have a better understanding of how organized this may be."

Mikaela considered this. Something about Juan being involved didn't sit quite right, but she reassured herself that her uncle was family and understood the importance of their positions. She knew Juan had always been a bit volatile, explosive, and rough, especially when compared to her father's keen strategy and careful planning. She also knew that her father had purposely given Juan his position as general, the head of the Cayo Azul military, as a way for her uncle to have some sort of royal duty and title that matched his personality—and perhaps kept him occupied while he focused on ruling the island as king and the family as elder brother.

Mikaela took a deep breath. "Do you believe Isabella is somehow directly involved?"

"We don't know," Eduardo admitted. "There's a clear link between her and Javier. If Roberto is truly making moves against the Crown and Isabella is tied to the Jimenez family in some way…"

His voice trailed off as her father's face darkened. "…Then you cannot marry her," he finished firmly.

Mikaela nodded, absorbing their words. "My understanding is that Isabella does not want anything to do with Javier Jimenez," she said and then bit back a smile. "Despite his best efforts."

Her father held her gaze. "Be cautious, Mikaela," he said. "You are my heir to the Crown, but you're also my daughter. I know the last two weeks have been sweet, but you must not be reckless either. You are *far* too valuable to risk."

After a long silence, Mikaela took a deep breath. "I understand," she said. "I appreciate the notice. I will not be reckless with my heart, or anything else."

As she left her father's private office, Mikaela felt torn. She had always prided herself on her ability to navigate politics with icy precision while keeping her emotions in check. She wasn't sure how to resolve the sudden dull ache that pressed down on her chest.

I have to see her. Without a second thought, she turned down another hallway directly to Isabella's guest suite. *I need to be near her. I need to know this is real.*

Chapter Seventeen

Isabella grinned as she opened the door at Mikaela's insistent knock. She had a video call with her mother an hour before and had just stepped out of the shower as Mikaela arrived.

"Hi, Princess," Isabella said teasingly as she wrapped her arms around Mikaela's middle and tilted her head up at her. "Finally getting a break today?"

There was something intense and slightly off in Mikaela's energy as she entered the suite. Mikaela sat on a small leather sofa in the corner and crossed one leg over the other. She blinked as she took in the sight of Isabella, fresh from the shower, in a pair of tight black yoga shorts and a thin gray cami.

Isabella felt a bit exposed and wondered if she should've grabbed a pair of sweatpants before answering the door, though Mikaela appeared quite… intrigued.

Mikaela raised an eyebrow. "How has your morning been?"

Isabella shrugged. "Fine," she replied. "I caught up with my mom for a bit. I wasn't sure when I'd see you later, so I finished a quick shower while listening to some music."

Mikaela glanced at the large TV mounted onto the wall, where Isabella was streaming her playlist.

Oh, shit. Perhaps distracted by Mikaela's impromptu visit, Isabella knew the playlist she had started building a day or so ago was a little too obvious.

"All The Best Love Songs?" Mikaela read the title out loud as Isabella felt her cheeks burn. She looked entirely amused. "And who has inspired you to create a playlist like this, filled with all these songs about love?"

Isabella crossed her arms and refused to give in to the embarrassment she knew was heating her very exposed neck. "Oh, you know," she replied flippantly. "Obviously Javier."

The suite went so silent that Isabella was sure she could hear a pin drop. She blinked in surprise at the stricken look that flashed across Mikaela's face, though it appeared she tried to recover herself quickly.

"Oh my God, Mikaela, I'm kidding," Isabella said, confused by her reaction. She hurried to the sofa and curled up next to her. "I'm completely kidding. I'm sorry, I thought you would laugh."

Isabella's heartbeat quickened as Mikaela's arm tightened around her shoulders. "I know," she replied with an exaggerated shrug of her shoulder. "Duh." She let out a small laugh, but Isabella knew it was forced. She was trying too hard to be nonchalant and everything felt weird.

"Hey," Isabella said gently. She cupped Mikaela's face in her right hand. "Are you okay?"

Mikaela searched her gaze for a long moment and then exhaled gently. "There's a lot going on," she said. "But right now, I want to know…" She ran a hand through Isabella's soft. still-damp hair. "*Everything* about you, love."

Isabella leaned in closer. "Okay," she replied easily. "I'll tell you anything you want to know."

This seemed to settle the air. "Good," Mikaela said with a nod. Her face lit up. "Do you want to get out of here?"

"You mean…This room?" Isabella asked.

Mikaela laughed. "Well, that too," she replied. "No, I mean out of *here*. Castillo Blanco. Just for a little bit. I have a final walk-through this afternoon of the new Gran Corazon Resort in City Center, and I would love for you to join me so I can show you one of my favorite places on the entire island."

Isabella was mystified but relieved that whatever intensity Mikaela had stalked in with appeared to have been alleviated for now. "I would love to," she said. "After the walk-through?"

Mikaela nodded. "After the walk-through. But afterward, we can steal some time together privately."

Isabella was awash with anticipation as she nodded and then bit her lip. "Okay," she said. "I'll change clothes."

As she hopped off the sofa toward the bedroom, Isabella could feel Mikaela's dark eyes lingering on her, traveling up her back and her legs, as she sauntered away. The idea of private time with Mikaela and letting her in by showing her somewhere meaningful was intoxicating. Isabella wondered if she should press Mikaela further about whatever it was that bothered her so much when she'd arrived, but the feeling of free-falling into her further, soaking up Mikaela's undivided focus, was too delicious.

I'll dwell on it later. As for right now? I have a date with Mikaela.

❖

An hour later, the energy of City Center surrounded them, alive even during the daytime. As they stepped into the all-glass atrium of the Gran Corazon Resort, upbeat music pulsed from open-air restaurant patios and boutique storefronts nearby and mingled with the relaxing sound of waves tugging at the beachfront.

The expansive entrance to the newly-constructed resort made the sleek marble lobby feel spacious and airy. A smooth row of polished bamboo service desks were already set up with brand-new monitors, telephones, and state-of-the-art laptops, neatly organized and appearing to promise an even greater tourism influx.

Mikaela strode confidently next to Pablo Bustos, the chief project manager from a local City Center architectural firm who had overseen the development alongside the Bangkok-based investment group. Isabella walked along her other side and looked around as she took in the effortless blend of modern luxury and cultural pride. The newly hired general manager of the soon-to-be-opened resort, Miguel Victoriano, flanked the group from the rear and folded his hands politely over his designer black-on-black suit as they walked.

"One of the many things our team is especially proud of, Your Highness, is that beautiful artisan wall molding," Pablo said as he eagerly gestured around the spacious lobby. "All common areas at the Gran Corazon feature this custom wainscot-style molding that adds an element of crispness and luxury."

Mikaela nodded her agreement as Pablo launched into an explanation of the high-tech security features in place throughout the resort. Still, something tugged at the back of her mind as she recalled earlier conversations with her father and Eduardo. *Sixty jobs earmarked for the people of Este.*

"This is beautiful," Mikaela said. She turned in a slow circle as she took in the lobby. "Gran Corazon is going to be a centerpiece and a global luxury travel destination. Excellent work by you and your team, Pablo. This is incredibly impressive."

Pablo flushed as he glanced down at the smudged tablet in his hands. "Thank you, Your Highness," he replied. "It's been an honor to bring this amazing concept to life. If I may, I'd like to add that we are right on track for our scheduled soft opening in four weeks."

Miguel nodded. "My team has already begun the recruitment and training process to ensure a capable staff," he said smoothly. "We have already accepted offers for the roles of head chef, sous chef, vice president of events, and the director of operations, who will eventually be my righthand. The senior leadership team is coming along quite nicely."

"And the non-senior roles?" Mikaela asked.

Miguel opened and then closed his mouth. "Certainly, we expect to have many open roles to fill," he said. "So far, most applicants for our entry-level operations roles have come from City Center as we are focused on those with university education, hospitality experience, and strong customer service backgrounds."

Mikaela met Miguel's eyes and straightened her spine. "University education for entry-level roles? That leaves a lot of Este out, without even so much as the opportunity. There is a noted discrepancy in the highest level of education completed between Este residents and those in City Center. We should be prioritizing the removal of those barriers, Miguel, not supporting them."

Miguel hesitated as he unclasped his hands and wiped his palms along his tailored suit jacket. "We've had fewer qualified applicants from that province, Your Highness."

Mikaela arched an eyebrow. "Fewer perhaps because they haven't been invited?" She looked over the empty lobby once more. "We're in the final development stages of a project that would make transport around the island much more accessible to all. Between the jobs this resort has created and a viable public transport option coming soon, there's no reason we should not be actively recruiting those from Este."

Miguel shifted uncomfortably. "Your Highness, the original resort development plans only allocate sixty jobs to those in Este."

Mikaela chewed the inside of her cheek for a moment and then shook her head. "Consider the allocation plan revised, Miguel. I want twenty percent of the entry-level and mid-tier positions for candidates in Este, and that will require a detailed recruitment strategy. Work with your operations director and, once hired, your vice president of human resources to launch a targeted outreach program. Visit the community center and the local schools. My cousin, Sir Alejandro, oversees our federal nonprofit and grants program. We will bring him in and you can collaborate on a grant that could cover the costs of a weekend hospitality training program to support these hires."

Miguel nodded as he scrawled notes onto a small pad. "This is excellent, Your Highness," he replied excitedly. "We'll start on this right away."

After a few more moments, Mikaela politely bid goodbye to Pablo and Miguel. She turned with an exhale as Isabella's fingers brushed against her own. "I apologize that took longer than expected," Mikaela said. "Now we can get a few moments of privacy and I can show you why the rooftop is one of my favorite places if you still want…"

Her voice trailed off and she blinked at Isabella, who was gazing back at her with a combination of surprise and electric heat that heightened the energy between them.

"I still want," Isabella confirmed teasingly. "That's really cool what you did, you know. Do you really think Alejandro will be able to find the grant money for that new program to come to fruition?"

Mikaela nodded. "We've discussed reallocating a percentage of the funding and reinvesting it into Este. This is the perfect way to do so. I want every Cayo Azulean to know that we are for them, not only a beneficial few."

Isabella slipped her hand into Mikaela's as they took the concrete service stairs to Gran Corazon's impossibly high roof. As the security detail lingered in the lobby, Isabella shook her head ruefully. "You realize you're rewriting the royal playbook on how influence works, right?"

Mikaela smiled as they reached the heavy door to the rooftop. She held it open for Isabella. "Maybe not," she said as she blinked against the sudden bright afternoon sunlight. "Perhaps I'm using it the way it should be used, love."

Chapter Eighteen

The rooftop of the soon-to-be opened resort had been one of Mikaela's favorite private spaces since the hotel was still in its early construction stages. She'd often sneak up to the roof late in the afternoon, after the construction crews had long since clocked out, and enjoyed the privacy of being alone with her thoughts high above the noise of the busy streets below. With the soft opening just weeks away, Mikaela knew she'd have to find another quiet, private spot for a few precious moments alone.

Up where Mikaela and Isabella sat side by side above the rest of the world, it was just the two of them. The smooth concrete of the flat rooftop was cool beneath their legs, as thin, wispy traces of soft white clouds floated across the endless baby-blue sky.

"I come up here a lot," Mikaela said, pushing her shoes in a tumble to the side. The sun was warm on her bare feet as she stretched her legs out before her. "There's something freeing, relaxing even, about having a private space to be alone or to think. Castillo Blanco isn't always the most intimate place to be."

Something unreadable but warm flickered in Isabella's expression as she turned to her. "I never got out to City Center much," she said. "It's kind of fun seeing it from up here."

Mikaela's chest tightened unexpectedly as she watched Isabella's face, bathed in the soft glow of the warm afternoon sun. Something deep within her, primal almost, screamed at her with the urge to claim Isabella, to make her hers and only hers. Her father's warning rang in her mind as she pushed the ache down and instead followed Isabella's gaze toward a man in brightly-colored clothing selling organic frozen fruit bars from a wheeled cart on the corner.

"You'll learn the area," Mikaela said. "It continues to grow quickly. It's a great vibe, you know? Full of excitement and energy, new restaurants and shops taking up residence every day. Our commerce minister, if you haven't met her yet, is a lot of fun. She really believes in what City Center could be." Mikaela took a breath before changing the subject. As fun as City Center was, Mikaela wanted to dig deep into Isabella. She had to know more. "Tell me about Este."

Isabella tilted her chin toward the sky as a small smile played at her lips. "I feel as though *you* probably know more about Este than I do," she replied. "After all, Cayo Azul belongs to you, no?"

Mikaela bit her lip as she studied Isabella and the way the breeze gently tousled her hair over her shoulder. The faint honk of a car horn and distant conversations drifting up from the streets below met the beat of silence between them. "Cayo Azul doesn't belong to me simply because of who my family is or our history on the island," she said as she weighed her words. "It doesn't. This beautiful island we call home belongs to everyone who lives here, everyone who has made it what it is today. From the farmers, to the city planners, to the teachers educating the next generation. I'm just…I mean, I'm just someone whose place in life is to ensure its sovereignty, its strategic growth, and its place within the world."

Isabella turned toward her. "You love it here, don't you?"

Mikaela nodded. "I do. I want to protect our island and ensure it remains a place where people, all our people, feel as though they belong."

Isabella's teasing expression softened into something deeper as she shifted closer. "Sounds to me like you're exactly where you're meant to be, Mikaela."

Mikaela felt a bolt of lightning tingle down her spine at the soft way her name rolled from Isabella's lips.

"As for Este," Isabella continued after a moment. "It's more untamed. People get a reputation for being rougher around the edges, but it comes from a lifetime of self-preservation. They work hard. They watch out for their own."

Mikaela nodded as she considered Isabella's description.

Isabella sighed as she gazed over City Center below. "As beautiful and golden as everything looks from up here, it's hard not to forget that on the other side of the island…"

"What?" Mikaela prodded her gently. "Tell me."

"It's not the same," Isabella finished simply. "Back in Este. The schools are half-staffed, businesses are struggling, the closure of the fish processing factory eliminated so many jobs from the area, and for what? Another resort? That's great, but where will the residents work if they are shut out from opportunity there? People are proud and hardworking, but they're also tired. They need tangible action and opportunity."

Mikaela brushed her thumb along Isabella's hand. "Even if we implement the same job allocation at that resort too, it will take time since they've only begun breaking ground there," she said. "It's not enough, is it?"

Isabella shrugged. “It’s a start,” she replied, her tone belying her doubt. “But many may not even know where or how to apply and even more may be discouraged if they feel they don’t have the training or knowledge to succeed. Something more permanent in Este would be ideal…”

“You mean like a job corps program,” she said. “Something at the community center that offers paid training, mentorship, and educational courses that could relay as college credits. I’ve seen case studies about programs like this being very successful in other countries.”

Isabella leaned her head on Mikaela’s shoulder. “That’s exactly the kind of thing that would make a lasting difference,” she said. “Give the people of Este the tools they need to shape their futures. They’ll know what to do then because they will have hope and see what’s possible.”

Mikaela pressed a kiss to Isabella’s hair. “It could be transformative,” she said, struck by the affection she felt for her. “I will find the resources, identify a lead team, and help them kick off a discovery project. This kind of rooted change could really turn the sentiment in Este.”

They sat in comfortable silence for a moment as an idealistic excitement that Mikaela hadn’t felt in a long time crept through her veins.

“You know, it’s funny you brought me here,” Isabella said as she shifted closer. “I used to sneak onto the roof of my house in Este all the time. At first, my mother would get mad when I’d climb up there. She’d say I was being reckless or that I’d fall and injure myself.” Isabella shrugged. “But as I got older, eventually she’d just bring a blanket, climb up, and sit with me. We never even talked much. We’d just watch the planes from the airport go by in the sky, guess where they were going, or what exciting adventures people were about to embark on. I think she enjoyed being up there with me too.”

“She sounds like a lovely woman.”

“She is,” Isabella murmured. “As I got older and understood that her life had turned out so far from where she probably wanted it, that she never had much to show for how hard she’s worked, it made me really sad. And I promised myself I’d always be there for her, just like she has been for me. My parents are both textbook studies in broken dreams and shattered hopes for the future. They just have different ways of coping, I guess.”

Mikaela watched Isabella with quiet curiosity and then took a deep breath. “I’ve noticed you always talk so lovingly about your mother,” she said. “But you never say much about your father.”

Isabella seemed to still for a moment before she nodded. “That’s true,” she replied as she let out a long breath.

Mikaela patiently waited for Isabella to elaborate and felt that same affection deepen as Isabella appeared to weigh her words.

“My father is an alcoholic,” Isabella finally said. “Always has been, for as long as I can remember. It’s…complicated. And embarrassing at times. He has a temper that flares especially when he’s had too much to drink.

He's never put his hands on me and I've never *seen* him put his hands on my mother, but I have seen occasional bruises on her after the *really* bad episodes. He mainly just yells a lot. Stomps around and slams things. Says mean, nasty things with the intent to inflict hurt."

"I'm so sorry." Mikaela slid her arm around Isabella.

"Those are just the particularly bad times," Isabella said. "Though when he's sober, he's not much better. Mostly quiet and distant, like he just doesn't want to be bothered with anything or anyone." She sighed. "Not even his family. You learn to build your life around it, I guess. I think he selfishly liked the idea of getting my mother pregnant and tying her to him for life, but he had no idea what to do with an actual kid. My mom carried everything, especially after he was kicked out of the armed forces. As for me? I learned early on not to expect too much from him. Eventually I grew detached and shut him out too."

Mikaela swallowed as she fought the urge to pull Isabella onto her lap and hold her close. "Do you miss them? While you're here with me, I mean?"

Isabella turned to face her again. "Of course I miss my mother," she said. "But it feels like a different life there already. Like I was someone else, maybe not completely whole but ready to come into my own."

Mikaela searched her gaze as that familiar ache again settled deep into her chest. "You're still her," she replied after a moment. "You'll always still be her. Just…evolving. And that's okay too."

Isabella shifted closer again. "I like that."

"You know, I think the ultimate freedom comes from letting go," Mikaela said thoughtfully. "Trusting that everything will turn out okay. Letting go of the ideas, the conditioning we all have, the things you *think* you know, and being okay with it. That's freedom."

Isabella raised an eyebrow. "And how many rooftops will you escape to until you're there, Princess?"

Mikaela blinked at the unexpected, albeit rhetorical, question. *Who's going to give in first?* The delicious feeling of anticipation coursed through her again. The air between them grew charged with something unspoken and undeniable.

"You can take control of me however you want, Mikaela," Isabella said, her voice low. "But if you want me to acquiesce to you, to fully submit to you, you need to understand that I'm your safe space. Your rooftop or whatever. And let me in, trust me to take care of you too."

Mikaela couldn't ignore the deep, primal urge to claim Isabella any longer. In a split second, she met Isabella's lips in a kiss that tasted both sweet and desperate as bolts of warmth, tenderness, ownership, and vulnerability blurred between them.

As the kiss deepened and Mikaela felt herself tighten at Isabella's soft tongue in her mouth, City Center and its eclectic energy ten stories below seemed to vanish. Right now, Isabella and the undeniable connection between them was all Mikaela could feel.

A gentle cough and the sound of steps echoing through the concrete stairwell interrupted the steamy, bliss-filled kiss. Mikaela reluctantly pulled away with the knowledge that the lead security guard would be at the rooftop door in less than ten seconds to tell them that it was time to return to Castillo Blanco. Isabella stared back at her in wonder, and Mikaela realized she was just as dizzy.

"Ready, Your Highness?" the security guard said politely.

Mikaela nodded as she stood and helped Isabella to her feet. She tried hard not to stare at her swollen lips or the flushed deep pink that colored every millimeter of her mouth.

Mine. They followed him down the echoing stairwell. *Isabella is mine. I don't care what anyone says. You can't fake a kiss like that.*

CHAPTER NINETEEN

The sleek black Escalade rolled through the tall iron gates of Castillo Blanco and parked directly in front of the familiar main entrance.

As the security guard opened Mikaela's door, another fell into step with him and opened Isabella's door. Mikaela stepped out first. The warm air carried the faint scent of tropical flowers from the gardens, but Mikaela's attention snapped onto the figure waiting inside the front doors.

"Shit," Mikaela muttered under her breath.

Jorge Acevedo stood fidgeting just inside the main entrance as he sweated profusely in his tailored suit and clutched his laptop. His posture screamed *official business* and the way he scanned the front grounds of the castle told Mikaela he was looking for someone specific. More than likely, *her*.

"Who's that?" Isabella asked as she fell into step with her.

"Jorge," Mikaela said with a groan. "He's our very anxious transportation secretary. And he probably wants the final feedback I told him I'd provide on his public bus system data so he can receive official approval from my father and begin strategizing implementation phases."

Isabella smiled. "Should we run past him?"

"Too risky," Mikaela said teasingly. "He's persistent. I told him I'd provide final feedback by tomorrow, but he likes to follow up. A lot." Mikaela grabbed Isabella's hand and tugged her around the side of Castillo Blanco's expansive main building. "Come on. I know a shortcut."

"Of course you do." Isabella said as they ducked behind a row of neatly trimmed hedges lining the side of the building. "I guess you've done this before. In heels, no less."

Mikaela nodded. "Many times," she said. "Follow me."

The easy way in which Isabella gripped Mikaela's hand as she followed was not lost on her. The realization that Isabella's trust in her was deepening made Mikaela tighten her hold on her hand as they slipped through an unmarked door along the side of the building and down a small set of concrete stairs. The hallway between kitchens was quiet and unremarkable, designed for utility and staff—not impressions. Mikaela had memorized every corner of the sprawling estate, leading Isabella as they weaved from one hallway to the next, until they reached the double doors of the main kitchen. The smell of fresh bread and sautéed garlic wafted out, but it appeared otherwise quiet.

"For someone who doesn't know how to work a stove, the kitchen is the last place I'd expect you to hide out," Isabella said as she raised an eyebrow.

Mikaela rolled her eyes. "Very funny. But not quite." She nodded at an industrial-sized service elevator just before the kitchen doors and pushed the call button.

"Wait, *this* is another of your hiding places?" Isabella said incredulously as Mikaela led her inside and the doors rumbled shut.

"It's faster than walking and especially convenient if I don't want to run into anyone taking the usual way through the building." Mikaela pressed the button for the main floor. The elevator hummed as it began its ascent and Isabella glanced at her as she shook her head.

"You're unbelievable," she said, her tone filled with mirth.

"Royal problem-solving at its most basic," Mikaela replied. "Now, so long as I don't have three texts and five emails waiting from Jorge by the time I get home, it'll have been a successful escape."

The service elevator ground to a metallic, groaning stop as they glanced around in confusion. The dim overhead light flickered once but continued to illuminate the large elevator with a yellow glow.

Isabella took a deep breath, all traces of humor gone. She clenched her fists against her sides.

"This…this is fine," Isabella stammered as she looked around. "Right? I'm sure this happens all the time. After all, it's an old service elevator. Someone will eventually notice it's not running. Right?"

Mikaela took a hesitant step closer to Isabella. The natural desire to *touch*, to hold her and comfort her, had been overpowering on the rooftop but was nearly overwhelming in the confined space.

Mikaela swallowed hard. "Of course," she said gently. "This elevator is as old as the castle itself. I give it ten or fifteen minutes at most until Terese or someone else on the kitchen staff notices it's jammed. We'll be okay, Isabella."

Isabella nodded. "Of course." She swallowed hard and glanced down at her phone. "I just…Oh, look at that. No service in the service elevator. How ironic."

"Breathe, Isabella," Mikaela commanded. Isabella glanced up and met her gaze. *She's responding to me. Good. Calm will help her*. "It's just a minor mechanical issue because the elevator is old. We'll be moving again soon."

Mikaela's heart fluttered as Isabella subconsciously stepped closer to her. The deep urge to wrap her arms around her again was all she could think about.

Isabella paused for a moment, as if realizing her proximity to Mikaela in the elevator for the first time. After a moment of hesitation, she instead leaned one shoulder against the wood-paneled back wall. "Quick or not, I've always hated the feeling of being trapped. It's terrifying."

Mikaela's body and brain screamed at her to wrap her arms around Isabella and to reassure and protect her. The large elevator felt small, and Mikaela wondered if she'd ever felt like this before, though she already knew the answer.

I have to be closer to her. The logical part of Mikaela knew there wasn't much she could do to physically be closer to Isabella—after all, they were stuck—but not touching her seemed ridiculous and unnatural.

"Look at me," Mikaela said. As Isabella's gaze found hers, she could see the vulnerability laid bare. Mikaela laced their fingers together as she pulled Isabella into her arms. She could feel her heartbeat pounding against her as she wrapped her arms tight around her. "I know it can feel terrifying. Something unexpected like this. I really, *really* get that. But we're not trapped, okay?" The words tumbled out of Mikaela's mouth, raw and without her usual practiced eloquence. She wasn't even sure if she was talking about the elevator or themselves anymore. "We're just…pausing. Together."

Isabella's arms were surprisingly tight around her, something that would've made Mikaela feel uncomfortable with anyone else. The tenderness that arose instead emphasized her realization.

This is exactly right. This was always meant to be.

Mikaela's words hung in the air as the top of Isabella's head brushed against her cheek. The desire to gently dust a kiss across her temple nearly took Mikaela's breath away as she reveled in how *right* it felt to have Isabella in her arms.

"Together," Isabella repeated, her voice steadier. She blew out a breath that seemed to ease the tension in her shoulders as she relaxed against Mikaela. "You make it sound so easy."

Mikaela rested her chin on top of Isabella's head. "It doesn't have to be hard," she replied. "Besides, we'll get out of this elevator soon. Trust me."

Isabella swallowed hard as she searched Mikaela's eyes. She could feel Isabella's nerves dissolving as she spoke without breaking their gaze.

"I do," she finally said. Her voice was quiet and sure. "Trust you, I mean. I do trust you, Mikaela."

Mikaela wanted so badly to dig further, to know *everything,* and prompt Isabella to continue spilling her soul to her. Instead, she took a deep breath.

Just listen.

After a moment, Isabella glanced at the worn tile floor and then back at her. "Why are you so good at this?"

Mikaela tilted her head. "Good at what?"

"At…At making me forget why I'm afraid. At making me feel seen and completely at ease all the time, like it's simply natural for us—"

Isabella was cut off by the groaning metallic sound of the elevator gears. She looked around as Mikaela tightened her arms around her.

"Maybe because I would do anything to see you be truly happy," Mikaela said.

The raw vulnerability hung between them as Isabella's breath appeared to catch. The calculated moves, the careful planning, and the push and pull of their attraction had deepened into something far more intimate in those quiet moments.

"Mikaela, I think I might be…" Isabella started. A swell of emotion seemed to silence her for a moment as she blinked in surprise. "I think I'm…"

Before she could finish, the gears squealed again as the old elevator shuddered to life. It jerked upward with an unexpected lurch that sent them both stumbling. Mikaela instinctively tightened her arms around Isabella again, steadying them both, as she held her close. The hum of the industrial light above sounded loud and unwelcome as the heavy doors slid open.

Neither spoke as they held onto each other for a beat longer than necessary before untangling themselves from one another. Mikaela's pulse was deafening in her ears as they stepped into the small main floor prep kitchen above the larger kitchen below.

"What on earth were you doing in the service elevator?" Terese chuckled as she bustled past them. "I haven't seen you take that shortcut in a while, but I just knew when I saw it was stuck that it was probably you in there. Sneaking around the castle, eh?"

Mikaela tried to readjust, but the only thought in her mind was the tantalizing fantasy of what exactly Isabella had been about to confess. "And now I'm reminded why I gave up that shortcut a while ago," she replied with what she hoped was light airiness. "I'll let the maintenance and grounds crew know it should be inspected again."

"Already on it, Your Highness," Terese said as she turned her attention to the fresh vegetables on a large wooden cutting board. She picked up a chopping knife. "Don't you worry about a thing. You go on and have some fun now, eh? I've got veggies for the next three days to chop and a salad menu to finish."

"You got it," Mikaela said as she slipped her hand into Isabella's and walked out of the prep kitchen corridor. "Ciao, Terese," Mikaela called over her shoulder. "Thanks for rescuing us."

As they headed in the direction of Isabella's suite, Mikaela could hear Terese's goodbye echoing behind them. With Isabella's hand soft and warm in her own, she couldn't help but feel like it was home.

CHAPTER TWENTY

Later that week, Isabella sat in a dark brown rattan chair and took a sip of her ice water. Tiny beads of cold condensation slid down the tall, frosty glass as a group of Australian tourists walking down the main street of City Center joked loudly nearby. Dayanara sat across the table from her, with her spine straight and her ankles crossed neatly against a leg of her chair. Deep Blue, a popular Cayo Azul restaurant, was located in the heart of City Center. Its white stucco walls were accented by lush greenery, vibrant bougainvillea, and smooth midnight-blue painted wooden shutters that complemented the eatery's open-air design and allowed the ocean breeze to flow through.

One of the tourists, a twenty-something man with sea salt-tangled blond hair, strolled into the restaurant and walked right up to the large rectangular bar. Isabella was aware of his gaze lingering on her and the lascivious expression on his face as he turned twice to look at her again as he waited at the bar. She knew he wanted her to meet his obvious interest as a silent invitation to approach the table and introduce himself.

Dayanara watched his over-the-shoulder glances and then looked directly at Isabella. "Tourists," she said dryly. She cleared her throat. "So, I don't know if I ever asked you, and please let me know if it's too personal. How *do* you identify?"

Isabella was taken aback but had come to understand Dayanara could be blunt at times. After all, she was one of just a handful of people who were closest to Mikaela.

I'd be protective over her too, if I was in her position.

"Um..." Isabella thought for a long moment and gazed out of the open shutters. "I know that what I feel for Mikaela is very, very real."

Dayanara nodded and took a sip of her frozen tropical concoction, its bright blue paper umbrella twirling in the breeze. "Look, I don't doubt that," she said matter-of-factly. "Mikaela is amazing. She definitely has a, uh, *way* with people. Feelings can be very real, but they don't always mean *forever*. Sometimes they're just fun to explore or act on once or twice. But Mikaela truly is one of a kind. You know, I've known her since we were very young. She's always been a person who'd drop everything for someone she cares about. She doesn't love often, but when she does it's *deep* and it's intense. Sometimes too deep, but that's just who she is."

"Has she, um, been in love a lot?" Isabella asked as she swirled her paper straw in her ice water and tried to tamp down the tendril of jealousy that was working its way through her belly.

Dayanara fixed her with a look. "No," she replied. "And I get it, sexuality is fluid, anyone has the ability to fall in love with anyone. But I ask because this is her *life*. This is your life. You may find yourself attracted to Mikaela or crushing on her. But could you look at life with her forever and *not* feel like…something is missing?" Dayanara threw a sidelong glance at the Australian tourist, who was now chatting up the bartender. "I mean, I get it. I'm a straight woman. I think women are beautiful, but…"

Isabella took a deep breath. "I understand what you're asking," she replied, deciding to go with honesty. "And I know what I feel for Mikaela far surpasses what I have ever felt for anyone I've dated before. Of course, I attended the gala as the guest of Javier Jimenez. I suppose you could say he and I casually dated. But it never felt right, at least for me, and that's why I could never fully commit to him. Looking back, I understand why it never felt quite right with *any* man I dated, and there weren't many." Isabella paused. "If there was even the tiniest ounce of me that was interested in him, or mostly straight, I would have jumped at the chance and at his persistence. And now I realize why I couldn't. Everything feels so much more…electric with Mikaela. She's *so* breathtakingly gorgeous. And she's genuine, like how you said she's intense? I feel that too when I'm with her. She feels everything so intensely and…"

Isabella stopped as she blinked at Dayanara's knowing smile. *Oh my God, I'm gushing. To her best friend. Kill me now.*

"You like her," Dayanara said after a slow sip of her drink. "Like, *really* like her, don't you?"

Isabella's cheeks were warm as she picked at the edge of the empty tapas plate closest to her. Translucent shells from the garlic shrimp and a few drops of olive oil were the only evidence left of their lunch.

Isabella sighed. There was no point in pretending anymore. "I think I'm falling for her," she admitted. "It's terrifying. But weirdly, it's also like…"

"The best feeling ever?" Dayanara finished. "I can see it all over your face. And honestly? Mikaela deserves someone who sees her the way you do. She might put up that cool front sometimes, but she *needs* you to feel as intensely about her too."

Isabella bit her lip. "You think so?"

"I know so. Mikaela doesn't just open up to anyone. But I can tell she's different lately. She's happy when she talks about you and her voice is softer, you know? Like...You're someone really important to her and she wants to safeguard you."

Isabella felt a leap of hope deep in her chest as her heart swelled. "I keep telling myself it's too good to be true. I guess I've gotten used to doing that throughout my life, not letting myself get too excited or hopeful. And the easiest way to do that is to not let anyone all the way in. But Mikaela? She sees me so easily. I don't want to mess it up."

"Then don't mess it up," Dayanara said simply, her tone both playful and serious. "Just be real with her. Always. Mikaela needs to know she can trust you too. And if anyone can get her to acknowledge the real love that's right here in front of her, it's you."

Isabella's chest tightened with electric anticipation. *Love. Is that what this is?* The thought felt amazingly freeing.

Dayanara slid her black Prada sunglasses over her nose, and Isabella sensed that Mikaela's friend, a gatekeeper of sorts, was recognizing that she was real. Her subsequent candor felt like an approving nudge forward and Isabella wanted to keep the bond and conversation flowing.

"You said you've known Mikaela since you were children?" she asked.

"Basically forever," Dayanara said with a casual shrug. "At least, that's how it feels. We were four or five years old when my family moved into Castillo Blanco. My mother was hired as her and Alejandro's full-time private teacher. We had a small apartment on the castle grounds and lived there for nearly fifteen years. Mikaela and I hit it off from the very beginning."

"Wow, so you've literally grown up together."

"My dad also worked at Castillo Blanco; he was a sous chef working under Terese for years," Dayanara said. "He passed away unexpectedly when I was eighteen."

"I'm so sorry," Isabella replied. "I can't imagine how hard that must've been."

"Thank you," Dayanara said gently. "It was. My parents were so close to retirement. Now it's just my mom and me down the street, in that beautiful apartment building over there." Dayanara pointed about a block and a half down the sun-soaked street. "One thing I can say with certainty is that the de Medreno family has always taken wonderful care of us. That was especially apparent after my father passed away. They were so kind and concerned about our well-being. In fact, I truly believe, as tragic as it was, it deepened my friendship with Mikaela."

"How so?"

Dayanara shrugged. "I'm not sure what I expected at the time," she said. "We were always good friends, but I understood my place and hers. In my mind, the friendship was always to be centered around the princess and her needs. When my father passed away, she unexpectedly became, like, this *anchor* for me. A rock. She asked me questions and wanted to hear about my memories with him, but she never pushed too hard. We'd sit in her room like any other pair of friends, I'd cry and play songs that reminded me of him, and she'd just listen alongside me next to the speaker."

Isabella considered this. "Why was that surprising to you?"

Dayanara took a deep breath. "Honestly, it was when I understood she was human too," she replied. "And this pedestal I'd placed her on was actually nonexistent in her mind. She saw us as equals, not with this caveat of her being somehow superior to me or anyone else. She understands her role well, but she truly doesn't see herself as better than anyone on Cayo Azul. And it made me love her all the more."

"I can understand that. Mikaela is genuine and I see now that's who she really is, not the result of some polished royal act. It's incredibly sexy."

Isabella's cheeks flushed as she realized she'd actually vocalized the last part and sent up a silent prayer that it didn't completely derail the enjoyable afternoon—and forging bond—with Mikaela's best friend.

Instead, Dayanara threw back her head and laughed. "You got it *bad*," she said. "What the hell are you waiting for? Tell her!"

Isabella shifted nervously. "What, just like that? I mean, this isn't some rom-com where I just blurt out how I'm feeling and everything magically falls into place. This is reality, right?"

Dayanara raised an eyebrow. "Look, we've established that I know Mikaela. Better than most. She's *already* let you in, whether she even realizes it or not. If you tell her how you feel, that will be incredibly powerful."

Isabella swallowed hard. The sun felt hot on the back of her neck and her low ponytail felt like it was sticking to her skin. "You're her best friend," she said. "If it doesn't work out, she'll be fine. She'll still be the princess, jet-set with her BFF, and having scores of women fall over themselves for a chance with her. What if she doesn't feel the same way about me?"

Dayanara scoffed. "Well, for starters, she doesn't even like the jet-set lifestyle," she said. "There's a reason even googling her comes up with minimal information outside her official royal biography. As far as the rest? *Please*, Isabella. Mikaela lights up when you're around. She never stops looking at you. I haven't seen her like this with anyone." She paused for effect and then pursed her lips. "Does that help?"

Isabella blinked as warmth bloomed through her chest. "You mean that?"

"*Yes*," Dayanara laughed. "I want Mikaela to be happy. But if you don't tell her how you're feeling soon, you're both going to end up overthinking it and doing this dance around each other forever."

Isabella considered this. The last month had been incredibly intoxicating, filled with getting to know Mikaela, stealing glances at her, shamelessly flirting and approaching ever closer to the edge of falling. *But now I want more. Am I ready to fall?*

She already knew the answer. "I almost told her earlier this week when we got stuck in the service elevator," Isabella admitted. "But I lost my words and I guess my nerve. There was this moment where it felt like…it was just us. And it was always meant to be us. It was so intense, though, that right away I started pushing it away. What do I even say?"

Dayanara leaned back and shrugged one shoulder. "Just be honest," she said encouragingly. "Tell her everything you told me." She winked at her. "Whether you meant to or not. Be vulnerable. Tell her that you've never felt the way you do about her with anyone. That you *don't* want to push this away anymore because she makes you feel seen and safe and *happy*. That you're falling in love with her."

There was that word again. It sent Isabella's pulse racing, but beneath the nerves there was something else: Excitement. Hope. *Love*.

Isabella met Dayanara's gaze and nodded. "Okay, I'll tell her."

Dayanara clapped her hands together and inadvertently attracted a few puzzled glances from nearby tables. "That's my future unofficial sister-in-law!" she exclaimed. "Now, let's talk about when we're getting together for another girls' afternoon because this has been *perfect*."

CHAPTER TWENTY-ONE

That evening, Isabella lay in her bed and blinked up at the high arched ceiling until it melded with the shadows and angles, blurring her vision in the darkened room. She knew this was the time of night when Castillo Blanco became hauntingly quiet as moonlight spilled through the windows.

With a sigh, she stood and padded across the room to the window nearest her bed. She cracked it open, relishing the rush of warm breeze on her skin, and lay back down. The gentle rustling of palm leaves and the distant crash of waves seeped through the thick silence, but it did nothing to soothe Isabella's restless energy.

I should be tired. After all, I was out with Daya all afternoon. I should be exhausted.

She shifted around under the thick comforter, unable to put out the fire she felt both low in her belly and deep in her chest. There was an ache, an intense longing, and every time she stilled, her mind went directly to one face.

Mikaela.

Isabella tried very hard not to think of the soft way her hair fell over her shoulders or the subtle natural blond highlights that illuminated her dark brown eyes and practically made her sun-kissed skin glow. Isabella swallowed hard as she recalled the intensity that she was sure dove right into her soul, and the way her full lips and delicate cheekbones easily gave way to glances that could bring her to her knees in a heartbeat.

Speaking of being on my knees... Isabella's body tingled as she recalled Mikaela's face and the way she had kissed her on the rooftop, claiming her and leaving heat that still lingered inside.

Isabella sighed and tossed onto her other side as she squeezed her thighs together and tried to will the ache away. It was useless. Desire, longing, and something else coiled inside her and it was insatiable in the still quiet. It wasn't just physical need that was keeping Isabella from falling asleep. As she recalled her earlier conversation with Dayanara, she felt her throat close up as her heart raced.

It's deeper than just physical. I have to be near Mikaela. I need to feel her warmth next to me and around me, and I need it now.

Isabella sat up as she tried to make sense of the torrent of thoughts in her mind. "I can't go to sleep," she muttered. "Not like this."

Her heart pounded as she pulled a tight T-shirt over her head and grabbed the jogger sweatpants folded neatly at the foot of the bed. Isabella's brain was trying to reason with her, but her body already had other ideas. She gently shut the door of her suite behind her as she headed in the only direction that made sense: Mikaela's residence.

Mikaela stood on the rounded deck off her bedroom and breathed in the warm night air that wrapped around her exposed skin like a comforting embrace. The moon was high and bright in the clear, inky-black sky and cast everything around her in a silvery glow.

The breeze tousled her hair as she traced patterns along the marble railing with her fingertips. *I wish I was tracing Isabella's skin instead.* In the private quiet of the dark night, Mikaela allowed herself to delve into the fantasy. Even the thought of Isabella was enough to make something in her chest tighten and her pulse skip in a way that should be unnerving.

But it's not. There's only so long I can keep these emotions in check and compartmentalize how much I want her until it spills over and soaks everything that touches me.

Mikaela swallowed hard as she sat back into the fluffy cream-colored cushions lining the small outdoor sofa. As she gazed unseeing into the distance, the realization settled over her like a warm, all-consuming hug.

I'm falling in love with Isabella. Every day.

Mikaela couldn't pinpoint exactly what it was as the inescapability washed over her. It was everything and everywhere, from the way Isabella's laughter deepened the dimples on either side of her face to the fire Mikaela felt ignite in her veins when Isabella's touch lingered just a beat too long. It was also the way that her absence felt like an aching crack in her heart that she couldn't soothe. She hadn't seen Isabella today and neither of them had checked in with the other via text or phone call. It was unlike them and Mikaela wondered if they both sensed they were standing on the edge of inevitability, as they each waited for the other to acknowledge what was happening between them.

A tiny cloud of uncharacteristic doubt crept along the edge of Mikaela's thoughts. *Or maybe Isabella is realizing she doesn't feel the same. Maybe she doesn't want this.*

"No," Mikaela whispered into the night. "I am Mikaela de Medreno Soliz. It's time I take control of this now."

As Mikaela decided how she would corner Isabella the next day and what she would say—how hard she would kiss her and whether trailing soft kisses along the back of Isabella's neck or down her spine would make her melt into her arms—a soft rustling interrupted her thoughts.

She straightened on the sofa and her breath caught in her throat as she zeroed in on a familiar figure emerging from the shadows. The white glow of the moon caught the shimmer of emotion on Isabella's face as their gazes collided. Mikaela barely had time to process the storm of emotions and her raw, almost desperate expression.

She appeared to hesitate for just a moment before she spoke, her voice low and vulnerable but filled with certainty.

"I can't stop thinking about you, Mikaela."

It took every ounce of Mikaela's willpower not to launch herself down the stairs to swing the front door open. She took a deep breath instead, though it disappeared at the sight of Isabella just centimeters from her.

"Couldn't sleep?" Mikaela said knowingly. Isabella's dark hair was tousled over her shoulders, long and loose, and Mikaela longed to run her tongue along the smooth exposed skin between the hem of her tight T-shirt and the loose low-rise of her sweatpants.

Isabella swallowed hard. "I need you."

Mikaela stepped aside and held the door open just enough for Isabella to slip inside. As she turned to her, Mikaela noticed the fire in her gaze and a certainty that told her Isabella, too, was finally giving in to the inevitability. Mikaela was already wet with anticipation as Isabella took a tentative step closer to her.

"It's crazy, right?" Isabella said. "Just tell me I'm crazy. It's like every moment, every breath, I feel you *all* the time. I feel you in me, around me, and I swear I tried to fight it, Mikaela, but I can't anymore." She took a deep breath. "I can't even sleep. I don't want to fight it. I'm ready."

Mikaela's heart pounded as Isabella reached for her hands. The soft warmth of her fingertips pressing into her palms sent a shiver down Mikaela's spine. "You're not crazy," she replied gently. "Tell me. What are you ready for?"

Isabella straightened. "Ready to be yours. To give myself to you completely. I'm ready to love you the way I've always known I wanted to, the way you need."

A sharp breath escaped Mikaela's lips as she pulled Isabella into her arms, holding her as though she'd disappear if she let go. Isabella melted into her as Mikaela relished the feeling of her burying her face in her neck as she breathed deeply.

"I love you," Mikaela murmured. The words slipped from her lips effortlessly as she realized that Isabella was undeniable—and undeniably hers now.

Isabella lifted her head as she searched Mikaela's face for a moment. With a gentle sigh of surrender, she traced a slow fingertip along Mikaela's lips. "I love you too."

There was no time for pretense or small talk as the air was already charged with consuming, inevitable desire. Mikaela captured Isabella's lips into a searing kiss as Isabella willingly parted her lips to allow Mikaela's tongue entry.

Mikaela wound her hands in Isabella's loose curls as her entire body tightened with possession and intent. She felt Isabella's hands on the small of her back, gripping at her soft cotton camisole and pulling her closer into her, and Mikaela gently pulled Isabella's head back—not enough to hurt her, but enough to command her and ensure she knew who was in charge. Isabella exhaled as Mikaela trailed languid kisses down her exposed neck before stopping abruptly.

Isabella blinked up at her. Mikaela ran her fingertips up the length of Isabella's neck, where her lips had just been burning their claim onto her and traced a teasing path back to the delicate, feminine curve of her jaw.

"Look at you," Mikaela murmured. "Already trembling for me and I haven't even torn your clothes off you yet."

Isabella's breath was shaky as she nodded. Mikaela was torn between wanting to take her time and unravel Isabella completely before making her come fully undone in her arms or impatiently make love to the woman who had consumed her thoughts for weeks.

"This is…" Isabella swallowed hard, "…what you do to me, Mikaela."

Mikaela dragged her short, manicured fingernails down Isabella's sides and just beneath the hem of her T-shirt. Isabella flushed and shifted under her touch, clearly desperate for more.

"You love this, don't you?" Mikaela whispered. "You think you can handle being under my mercy?"

Isabella arched into Mikaela's touch. "Yes," she breathed. "I love it and I want it."

Mikaela rewarded her with a deep kiss as she took her time enjoying Isabella's soft, full lips and exploring her mouth, her tongue, until Isabella was melting against her once more.

"Come with me," Mikaela finally said as her heart beat wildly in her chest. She tugged Isabella's hand as she led her into her bedroom. As they reached the low king-sized bed, Mikaela turned. She backed herself onto the soft, tangled sheets and pulled Isabella facing her into her lap.

"So," Isabella said, her tone belying her anticipation. "You like being in control in bed too."

Mikaela regarded Isabella for a long moment. The moonlight washed over her through the tall windows. "Yes," she finally said. "I do. But don't worry, love. I'll be gentle with you too."

CHAPTER TWENTY-TWO

Isabella was relieved when they made it to Mikaela's bed, because her intensity made her knees go weak. As her heartbeat quickened with the teasing thought of more touch, more intimacy with Mikaela, Isabella understood what her body and heart had tried screaming at her long ago: She *wanted* to submit to Mikaela. There was something incredibly sensual about belonging to her, letting her take charge, and protect her fiercely.

As she straddled Mikaela, their lips and tongues exploring each other once again, Isabella was frustratingly wet. The friction between them was just enough to tease, but she wanted *more*. As their kisses deepened, she ground her hips into Mikaela's and shifted this way and that as she looked for *any* release.

Mikaela laughed against her mouth. "Impatient, love? Don't worry. There will be plenty of time."

Isabella fought the urge to groan as Mikaela's hands slipped under her T-shirt, cupping her breasts as her fingertips found her hardened nipples. Mikaela dipped her head and took a nipple into her warm mouth as she teased it relentlessly with her tongue. The tension was already coiling deep in Isabella as she wound her fists in Mikaela's hair and moaned at the sensations that sent shocks of pleasure straight to her clit. Mikaela kissed across her breasts until she reached Isabella's other nipple, taking it gently between her lips, as it dawned on Isabella that Mikaela was just getting started.

And it's already better than any sex I could have imagined. Mikaela's controlled, expert tongue on her nipples made the pool between her legs grow warmer and wetter. Granted, she had never gone fully all the way with any of the few men she dated, but Isabella had never before found herself already so undone and so ready to cede control.

Isabella's breath hitched as Mikaela bit gently and sent spikes of pleasure and pain rolled into one that danced down her nerves right to her clit.

"Please," Isabella breathed as she slowly rolled her hips on Mikaela again. "I need you."

Mikaela's breath tickled the sensitive shell of Isabella's ear. "I want you to shatter into pieces for me," she murmured. "Let yourself feel everything. Every sensation. I *want* you to feel it."

Mikaela planted a gentle kiss on her lips. "I want to discover you. All of you. Every inch, love. Is that okay?"

Isabella nodded as her body moved against Mikaela's as though it had a mind of its own. "Yes," she replied breathlessly. "I need you, Mikaela. All of you. And I promise you have all of me. I…I belong to you now."

Mikaela's sharp intake of breath was all Isabella needed to hear to know she was falling as hard as she was. "I'm going to start by learning every inch of your neck." Mikaela gently tilted Isabella off her lap and onto her back against the thick pillows. She kissed up and around Isabella's neck, hovering over her, and practically covered her completely. "And I'm going to figure out exactly what—and where—makes you feel so good."

Mikaela's lips across her neck had already brought Isabella deep into an irresistible state of pleasurable submission as she clutched the sheets against her gentle tongue teasing her nipples again.

Isabella blinked just long enough to register the spherical, cream-colored candle on the bedside table. Isabella wasn't even sure when it had been lit or how long its bold orange flame had been licking at the darkness, but her breath caught as Mikaela straightened, straddling her and holding her in place with her long legs.

"Do you trust me?" Mikaela murmured. The candlelight threw shadows across Mikaela's face and Isabella wasn't sure if her gaze looked so dark from the dancing flame or desire or both.

Isabella swallowed hard. Her need outweighed any trepidation. "Yes," she whispered. "Always."

Mikaela tilted the candle just enough for the melted wax pooled around the edge to drip. Isabella watched, transfixed.

The first drop of candle wax landed just below Isabella's collarbone, and she gasped as the quick, hot sting melted away into a cool, thick wetness almost immediately. Droplets continued to rain carefully across the slick skin of her neck and stomach, spreading across her like little twinges of fire that disappeared as quickly as they landed. Isabella's mind was spinning with the exquisite contrasting sensations. Her mouth opened into a breathless moan as Mikaela's thigh ground into her wet center, giving her something to writhe against and the delicious hard friction that she so desperately needed.

Mikaela gently brushed the bits of hardened wax from her, as she kissed and soothed all the places where it had reddened Isabella's skin. Isabella had never felt so undone, so claimed, and so loved. The mingling sensations were intoxicating. Mikaela leaned forward, covering Isabella's body with her own, as she pulled down Isabella's sweatpants and her own tight shorts with one confident hand.

"You're perfect like this," Mikaela said. "Mine."

"Yours," Isabella whispered. Her body trembled as Mikaela gently wiggled herself down until she was between her legs. Mikaela's lips teased along her inner thighs, inside her hips, and millimeters from her wet center. Her hair tickled her legs as one hand gently massaged Isabella's nipple, and it was almost more than she could take.

Isabella took a deep breath as she tried again to shift under Mikaela, who was having none of it. She kept Isabella firmly in place as she pressed her lips to the sensitive skin of her inner thighs, dangerously close to her clit, marking all of Isabella as hers. "Please," Isabella murmured.

Mikaela licked one firm, deliciously languid path directly up and along Isabella's wetness. Her tongue lingered there for a beat as Isabella moaned into the dark.

"Patience, my love," Mikaela murmured against her swollen, sensitive folds. Her tone held both promise and torment. "After all, we have all night. I want you to come slow and hard, so you remember who you belong to now."

Isabella wound her hands in Mikaela's hair as she slowly, tortuously used her tongue to tease her clit and explore her wetness.

"God, you taste…" Mikaela dipped her tongue deep into Isabella and then brought it out, running it along the length of her. "*So* fucking good."

Isabella saw stars and streaks of flashing light behind her eyes as Mikaela gently pushed two fingers into her and steadily pumped them in and out. Her tongue continued to tease and taste her as Isabella arched her hips, pushing herself further into Mikaela's confident mouth.

Mikaela was everywhere and Isabella was hopelessly wet. Everything was soaked as Mikaela's tongue and fingers steadily became faster and firmer. The tension inside Isabella coiled and tightened until she was sure she would break into a thousand pieces. Still, she felt Mikaela protective and sure all around her, giving her incredible pleasure that heightened every sensation. Every nerve ending along her clit was stoked alive as Mikaela's tongue rubbed, massaged, gently sucked, and soothed, and Isabella let the last shred of surrender go as the stars exploded behind her eyes. Waves of pleasure rolled from her as she tightened around and then released Mikaela's fingers over and over again. Her orgasm soaked her, her thighs, and the sheets beneath her, but Isabella couldn't stop herself as she cried out Mikaela's name like a prayer.

Mikaela let Isabella ride out the last of her orgasm before she gently pulled herself up and sucked each of the fingers that had been plunged palm-deep into Isabella just moments before. As Isabella tried to breathe, Mikaela settled next to her and pulled her onto her chest before pressing a slow kiss to her temple and running a languid hand through Isabella's sweat-dampened hair.

"Your pulse," Mikaela said, her lips still resting against Isabella's temple. "It's going so fast."

Isabella nodded as her body hummed with the afterglow. "I…I don't think I've ever…Not like that," she stammered.

Mikaela traced lazy patterns along her spine. "You broke into pieces." Her voice was soft, but still carried an air of confidence and ownership. "Now I put you back together. Over and over and over again."

Isabella lifted her head for a moment. "Come here." She pulled Mikaela into a kiss. "Let me give you that too."

"In time," Mikaela said gently. "Tonight is all about you becoming mine."

Isabella sighed and relaxed against Mikaela as the first bloom of tension tightened inside her again at her casual dominance. "I'm yours."

As Isabella blinked, her mind becoming a clouded trance with the relaxed afterglow of her earth-shattering orgasm, Mikaela's gentle fingers in her hair, and the heat of her skin against her own, she had never meant anything more.

Nearly a week later, Mikaela sat at her desk in her private office at Castillo Blanco. Golden late afternoon sunlight spilled across the smooth cherrywood and the glowing keyboard of her laptop. Her fingers tapped the keys, the rapid typing the only sound in the expansive room, as she scrolled through the rough framework for the Este Job Corps Initiative. Her father had been impressed with the idea and directed her to ensure the initiative got off the ground as soon as possible, for both strategic and altruistic reasons.

Mikaela scanned the detailed slides once more as she skimmed over the objectives and key steps, timelines, funding streams, and potential community partnerships that would all align to make the vision an eventual reality. She had already begun tapping the Royal Council for recommendations on a leadership team that she envisioned would consist of experienced project managers, highly lauded educators, and local community leaders who would work together to connect the people of Este.

A beat of anticipation flooded her at the eventual reality and all it would entail. A state-of-the-art training center alive with purpose and filled with people of all ages perfecting important skills, finding stable work more easily, and having access to better futures with intangible barriers removed. Mikaela fought back a yawn and lifted her long-forgotten smoothie glass. She wrinkled her nose as she glanced at the empty glass and placed it back on its cork coaster.

She turned back to her monitor and bit her lip as the cursor blinked at her expectantly. Somewhere between slide number seven and a projected soft launch date, her mind was slowing down. Her office felt too stark, too empty, and her thoughts were filled with Isabella's face. The small curl of excitement in her chest gave way to an aching desire as she thought of her barefoot in her home and the way she curled her legs around herself as she read or video-chatted with her mother. The magnetic pull that Mikaela always felt with Isabella had only deepened and become even more undeniable, and she recognized with a start that she missed her.

As her focus slipped from the slide deck completely, Mikaela stood resolutely and brushed off her neatly pressed white skinny pants. She had made massive strides on the Este Job Corps Initiative this week. Today, the work could wait. It was incredibly important, but being with Isabella right then was somehow the most essential thing Mikaela needed.

She practically groaned with frustration as her personal cell phone, reserved for select family members and friends, began vibrating loudly across her desk. Mikaela didn't need to look at the screen to know it was her father.

"Papa," she answered warmly as she glanced helplessly at the rapidly setting sun out the glass windows.

"I discussed your initiative with Eduardo and his team this afternoon," her father said without preamble. "I know you understand the urgency behind implementing the beginning phases quickly. Juan and Eduardo have both confirmed brewing unrest in Este that appears to be getting louder. Right now, the sentiment is still subtle, but there has been some quiet organization. As suspected, there is indication that Roberto Jimenez may be doing some rogue campaigning of his own but nothing concrete yet. This is the sort of splintering that can grow quickly and give him backing if the appearance is that we are ignoring it, them."

Mikaela remained standing but leaned back against the edge of her desk as she frowned. "I understand the need for visible action," she said. "The more people see that we are listening and, most importantly, taking action, then we can shift the mood."

"That's precisely why I'm calling. We should plan a press release and public announcement around this initiative to let the people know, even if every detail isn't ironed out just yet. We must show Este they are just as much a priority for us as those in City Center and Santa Julianna. I want to ensure my eventual abdication to you is without discontent and does not provide an easy opportunity for this unrest to spike."

Mikaela tapped her fingers against the edge of her desk. "I've got this under control, Papa," she replied. "I have the core leadership team to take charge of the day-to-day implementation nearly assembled. We'll start small and control what we can control, but we'll make this loud and exciting to ensure Este knows we are investing there too."

"I'm proud of you, Mikaela," her father said. "This could be a big win if this is done right. For Este, for us, the Royal Council, for everybody."

Mikaela smiled despite the sensitivity of the situation and the pressure to ensure this project and so many others in various stages of development were implemented with precise care. As they hung up, she took a deep breath. The weight of knowing she was at a critical moment in Cayo Azul history, one that could either fortify or destroy her family's royal legacy, pressed down between her shoulder blades. A brief beat of uncertainty at the magnitude of the next few years made her pulse race with uncharacteristic nerves but she tamped it down. Right now, there was only one place she wanted to be.

CHAPTER TWENTY-THREE

The evening air inside Mikaela's home was thick with lingering warmth and stifling humidity, all evidence of an impending overnight thunderstorm. Though Cayo Azul was not in an area that often saw hurricanes or fierce tropical storms, occasionally a heavy thunderstorm would work its way across the island from somewhere far away over the ocean. Mikaela loved when these storms would roll through, and tonight was no exception. The windows of her bedroom were cracked just enough to let in the salty, rain-scented air, the sound of crashing waves, and the persistent rustling of palm leaves as the winds picked up speed and ferocity.

As Mikaela absent-mindedly twisted her still-damp post-shower hair into a clip, the distant sound of running water down the hall filled the background. She ran a fingertip along the tiny marks along her collarbone and shoulders from yesterday's escapades in Isabella's guest suite.

The earlier sense of pressure and duty faded as she recalled the way Isabella had worshipped her body and how frustration clouded her gaze as Mikaela gently pulled her back before Isabella's tempting mouth worked its way lower. It wasn't that she didn't want it—*God*, how she wanted it. Instead, Mikaela mused on the years she had spent perfecting poised control and the easy way it unraveled at just the thought of Isabella and the memory of her lips against her skin.

As Mikaela considered going to the kitchen to pour a glass of wine, she glanced at the bathroom door and saw Isabella had left it purposely ajar. The slow, steady sounds of water streaming against Italian tile and the thought of Isabella, naked and warm under the comforting spray, seared through her veins. The wine forgotten, Mikaela marveled at how different she felt—still powerful and composed, but softer too, more connected to the things she had tried to bury, and touched by something deeper and intangible that she had spent years pretending she didn't need.

With that, Mikaela followed the sliver of soft light emanating from the bathroom door and slipped inside. Her grip tightened on the doorknob as she paused at the sight of Isabella, clear through the thick glass shower doors, and drank in the sight of water running in small rivulets down her golden skin and pooling at the soft dimples in her low back. Her dark hair cascaded over one shoulder and droplets rained from its curled tips, sliding down her back, her shoulders, and her breasts, before languidly trailing lower.

"Yes?" Isabella's voice was teasing as she acknowledged Mikaela's presence without opening her eyes against the spray. "You must be enjoying the view."

Mikaela leaned against the doorframe and raised an eyebrow. "Very much so."

Isabella carefully turned the shower off and stepped onto a thick bathmat. As she wrapped a soft towel around herself, Mikaela caught her wrist and pulled her closer. It was just enough to ensure only millimeters remained between them. Isabella met her gaze, biting her bottom lip, a challenge in her expression.

Despite Isabella's attempt to play it cool, Mikaela could feel the pulse in her wrist quicken beneath her touch. She gently ran her fingertips along the insides of Isabella's wrists and leaned forward just another half inch or so, close enough that their lips nearly brushed.

"You should dry off," Mikaela said as she trailed slow circles over Isabella's silky skin.

Isabella pressed the faintest of kisses to Mikaela's jaw before pulling away playfully. "I'll take my time, thanks."

Mikaela blinked. Her gaze never left Isabella's face. *She's testing me.* "Do you need my help or do you want to be punished?"

Isabella stilled for a split second as she took a deep, steadying breath. Mikaela knew she was loving this. "Maybe I want that."

Fine. If Isabella wants to play games, I'll remind her who's in control. Mikaela thought as she watched the flush that bloomed across Isabella's neck. With slow, deliberate movements, she massaged the towel wrapped around Isabella's body over her skin and then pulled it off, leaving Isabella naked, exposed, and oh-so-delectably tempting in the soft glow of the bathroom light.

"Come with me," Mikaela commanded her. Her gaze remained locked onto Isabella with an unwavering intensity. Heat curled low in her stomach as she understood that Isabella loved this and that she wanted Mikaela to pull her in until she surrendered.

And that's exactly what I'll do.

Isabella crossed her arms, her breath coming out in a huff, as she followed Mikaela into her bedroom. The humid, stormy air clung to her heated skin as she tried to ignore her body's response to Mikaela's steady confidence.

"You know, it'd be great if I could have some clothes," she said with both annoyance and anticipation. Part of her felt uncomfortable and exposed, completely naked while Mikaela remained fully dressed.

The hems of Mikaela's fitted black yoga pants dragged lightly along the smooth floor as she entered the bedroom and turned so abruptly that Isabella nearly walked right into her.

The other part of Isabella—the part that made her heart race in her chest—wanted to push Mikaela, own her brattiness, and see just what she would do.

Isabella's breath hitched as Mikaela looked at her with a steady, knowing gleam. She stood still for a moment and allowed Isabella to get lost in her nearness without touching her.

"Get on the bed." Mikaela's voice was edged with a certainty that told Isabella she would own any challenge she threw at her.

The slow burn poured through her, deep in her belly, as she recognized Mikaela's tone and tried to tamp down the heat collecting between her thighs. Isabella glanced at Mikaela's bed and then back at her, hesitating for just a moment, as Mikaela tilted her head, silently challenging her.

Isabella took a deep breath and lay gently against the sheets as a shiver ran down her spine. They were cool on her nude body, but as Mikaela stepped closer the heat between them spiked to nearly tangible levels. Isabella wriggled against the pillows in excitement as she anticipated Mikaela's mouth capturing her own.

And then…nothing. After a long moment, Isabella blinked and found Mikaela still standing over her, close enough that she could feel the heat from her skin.

"Touch yourself," Mikaela murmured, her tone sweet but firm.

"What?" Isabella asked, wondering if she had misheard. "You want me to…"

Mikaela trailed her fingertips down Isabella's jaw before tilting her chin up to ensure their gazes locked. "You heard me," she said softly. "Tell me, what is it you want?"

Isabella tentatively ran her fingers down her chest, over her stomach, and stopped with hesitation a few inches below her belly button. She was wet and Mikaela's teasing seemed entirely unfair. They both knew her own touch was a pale substitute for what she truly craved.

"I…I want *you*," Isabella replied as she realized her voice was very close to a whine. "I want your hands, your mouth, on me."

"Good girl," Mikaela murmured. "I know you do, baby. I know you want me very, *very* badly." She gently ran a fingertip along Isabella's wetness. As Isabella pushed down onto her finger, her body silently begging for more,

Mikaela retracted her touch. "But I want to watch you first. I want to watch you drive yourself crazy trying to achieve the same pleasure you know only I can give you. And if I feel you're sufficiently remorseful, then *maybe* I'll give you what your body so desperately craves."

Isabella shifted against the sheets in frustration. The heat between her legs was relentless. She bit her lip as she explored further with her fingers, dipping them into her warm wetness, and she gasped as they brushed her swollen clit. Isabella pressed more firmly there as her eyes fell closed against the jolts of pleasure that arched her back.

"Open your eyes," Mikaela said. "Look at me."

Isabella obeyed as she met Mikaela's hungry gaze. Her lips parted slightly as Isabella inserted one and then two fingers inside herself. "Imagine your fingers are me instead."

Isabella did as she was told and recalled the way Mikaela's fingers and tongue had claimed her days before. She knew exactly how and where to touch her and…just like that, Isabella deflated slightly as she remembered it was her own fingers that desperately slid in and out of her wet folds.

Mikaela watched her knowingly, leaving no doubt who was in charge. "What's the matter? Not exactly the same?"

Isabella took a deep breath and steeled herself. She imagined Mikaela pressing down onto her and fucking her as their most sensitive areas rubbed together, creating a delicious, wet friction that mercilessly teased the ultra-sensitive nerve endings along their swollen centers.

"I can…God, Mikaela, I can feel you *everywhere*." Isabella's breath came out in quick gasps as she lost herself in the sensations and, in the back of her mind, wondered how she could feel Mikaela so clearly without her touch.

"That's it," Mikaela went on, her voice soothing and calm. She braced herself against the edge of the mattress with one hand. "Keep going." She leaned in and let her lips gently brush Isabella's ear. "You know it feels even better when it's me."

Isabella nodded furiously, her resolve already coming apart at the seams. *Why, oh why, did I think it was a good idea to resist Mikaela?* Isabella felt herself surrendering again as she blinked up at Mikaela. She slid her fingers in and out of herself quickly as she pressed her thumb down in firm circles around her clit. She could feel the tension building inside as a humming warmth washed over her body.

Is she going to make me make myself come? Isabella was frustrated again as she wriggled under her hand and wildly wished that it was as effective, as soothing, as Mikaela.

"What happened, baby?" Mikaela's voice cut through the distant, gentle roll of thunder. "You were so close for a moment." Her hands were closer now and rested along either side of Isabella's arched hips. "What do you need?"

Oh my God, is she going to make me beg? As she met Mikaela's gaze again, she suddenly knew with a delicious twinge of excitement that it was *exactly* what Mikaela was going to make her do.

"You…" Isabella breathed out. "I need *you*, Mikaela. Please."

Mikaela tapped her index finger against her pursed lips in pretend thought. "I don't know," she said. "Poor baby. You're frustrated, yes, but you don't seem quite as undone as I want you to be before I take every inch of your body and let you come."

Isabella groaned, partly in frustration and partly as tiny shocks of pleasure raced through her as she moved her thumb slowly and steadily against herself.

"Mikaela, *please*," Isabella said as her hips arched further into her hand. Untangling her free hand from the sheets, Isabella was desperate now. She cupped her breast and rolled her nipple between her thumb and index finger as she continued to work her clit.

Another moan escaped her throat as the pleasure intensified. Mikaela was *everything*, all she needed to throw herself off the edge and get the release she so desperately needed and she maddeningly, frustratingly, remained just centimeters from her. Mikaela shifted on the bed, pressing her thighs together, as one hand lingered along her lap over the thin fabric of her yoga pants. Her other hand wandered closer to Isabella, and she sensed Mikaela's resolve was splintering.

"*Please*, Mikaela," Isabella breathed. "I want you *so* badly. My love."

With that, Mikaela nodded slowly and satisfactorily. "Yes, baby," she murmured as she kicked off her pants and covered Isabella's naked body with her own. "I'm right here."

Isabella arched her back into Mikaela as she subconsciously spread her thighs to allow her entry. Mikaela pressed her soaked center into Isabella's, her warm wetness drowning her own, as she shifted to find just the right angle. Isabella moaned into the thick air as she ran her nails up and down Mikaela's spine. As soon as Mikaela found *that* precise spot, where their centers pressed together and their clits glided against each other's slick wetness, Isabella dug deeper into her skin as she surrendered to her. Mikaela didn't grimace despite the desperate scratches eagerly seeking purchase, though her eyes fell closed for a brief moment. She blinked as she fucked Isabella slowly and steadily, letting the tension tighten and build.

Isabella wasn't even sure anymore where one of them ended and the other began. Thin, jagged bolts of lightning lit the sky from behind the curtains, illuminating the room in a quick, white glow, and gave Isabella glimpses of Mikaela's face, lost in deep pleasure. Mikaela kissed her deeply and possessively, as the ecstasy spilled in deep rolling waves that soaked

Isabella in her own wetness and Mikaela's. She wound her arms around Mikaela's neck as they rode out the last of their powerful orgasms. Isabella never wanted to let go and, in that moment, she knew she would do *anything* Mikaela asked.

Mikaela wasn't sure what time it was as the thunderstorm crashed around them. All she knew, in her deeply sated state, was that it was late and her thighs were going to be sore tomorrow. Gentle burning tingles tickled her bare back as she shifted against the sheets. A deep boom of thunder shook her house as sheets of rain thrashed down onto the roof. Isabella, still asleep, snuggled closer into her side.

"Mika," she whispered, notes of enchantment and satisfaction coloring her voice as it trailed off into a sleepy sigh.

Mikaela arched an eyebrow and pressed a kiss to Isabella's temple as she considered her longtime nickname. As far back as she could remember, only her closest family and friends occasionally referred to her as Mika. To all others, she was Her Royal Highness Mikaela Sofia de Medreno Soliz, the Princess of Cayo Azul.

Mikaela gently ran her fingertips through Isabella's hair. The idea of actually following through on the marriage agreement felt wildly enticing in the protective dark of the stormy night.

Mika. Isabella's arm tightened around her middle. *I never really thought about it before, but it sounds...strong. Capable.*

As Isabella's breath gently evened against her neck, Mikaela blinked sleepily in the dark as another, more distant clap of thunder rumbled somewhere far away. She decided that, just this once, she was okay with someone new referring to her as Mika.

I will live up to it. For her and all of Cayo Azul. Mika...

CHAPTER TWENTY-FOUR

Hours later, the soft morning light filtered through Mikaela's satin bedroom curtains and cast a pastel glow over the tangled sheets. It was quiet now, with no traces of the fierce thunderstorm that had rocked the island overnight. Isabella's relaxed body intertwined with her own and Mikaela took a deep, satisfied breath as she stirred. She was loathe to move from the warmth of Isabella grounding her in the slow, peaceful moment.

God, how late did we sleep? She felt around on her bedside table for her phone. Mikaela pressed a lazy kiss to Isabella's bare shoulder as she traced slow, absentminded circles down her spine. Isabella sighed as Mikaela finally found her phone.

Before she had a chance to blink at the screen, a loud, unwelcome *bang* pounded at her front door. Mikaela blinked in confusion as the pounding paused and then resumed, this time more insistent. She tensed as she gently moved from beneath Isabella and pulled on her black yoga pants and fitted gray T-shirt from the night before.

Isabella groaned as she flopped onto her back. "Tell whoever it is that they're ruining my morning."

Mikaela sighed as she took a quick glance at the mirror. Her hair was tangled around her shoulders and her lips were slightly swollen from last night's deep, insistent kisses. She padded down the stairs as the pounding continued and yanked open the door in annoyance.

Dayanara stood there, wide-eyed and breathless, as she glanced at Mikaela up and down. "I...You were having sex, weren't you?"

Mikaela blinked at her friend, uncharacteristically frantic, and squinted into the morning light filtering in from behind her. "Not at the *moment*. But, Daya, what is so critical that you're pounding on my door at dawn?"

Dayanara blinked back at her. "It's *nine* o'clock, Mikaela," she said carefully. "You missed the weekly morning meeting with your father and the

Royal Council, but it was so unlike you that I knew something was up. I told them you weren't feeling well to buy you time."

Mikaela nodded, still confused. "Thank you." She mentally kicked herself for oversleeping. Dayanara was right, it *was* highly unlike her, and she wasn't sure if her father would buy the not-feeling-well excuse. "I'll get ready."

As Mikaela turned back, Dayanara gripped her forearm. "There's more," she went on. The low urgency in her voice stopped Mikaela in her tracks. "It's bad, Mika. *Really* bad."

A humming anxiety rose in Mikaela's chest as her stomach dropped. "What is it? I just spoke to my father yesterday evening and everything was fine."

Dayanara swallowed hard. "I can't tell you. You need to come to Castillo Blanco," she said. "Now."

Mikaela heard Isabella pad out of the bedroom behind her. "Daya, of course you can tell me. What—"

Dayanara shook her head emphatically, her mouth set in a grim line. "I wish I could, Mikaela. Trust me, I wish I could give you some sort of warning for what you're about to walk into. But your parents gave me strict instructions not to say a word, and to only get you to Castillo Blanco *stat*. They want to speak to you themselves."

Mikaela blinked as the severity of whatever was happening sunk in. She barely registered Isabella squeezing in under her arm and tilting her head casually toward Mikaela's shoulder.

"Is there anything I can do to help?" Isabella asked. "Surely I can at least make you both a quick breakfast before you go."

Dayanara smiled at her, though it didn't quite seem genuine. "Thank you, I've already eaten," she said politely. "Besides, I was also instructed to ensure you were present too, Isabella."

Isabella wrinkled her nose. "Me?" She glanced between them in confusion.

Dayanara nodded. "You should both get ready," she replied, her tone tinged with…was that sadness that Mikaela detected? A touch of disappointment or resignation? "His Royal Highness King Bartolo and Her Royal Highness Queen Cristina do not like waiting, especially in an emergent situation directly concerning their daughter."

Isabella and Mikaela arrived at Castillo Blanco within the hour, after getting ready in record time while Dayanara waited impatiently in the living room. Mikaela's hand was entwined with Isabella's as they followed Dayanara into her father's private office.

Mikaela blinked in surprise, her unease reaching her pounding temples, as she saw that his private office was uncharacteristically full. Her father sat behind his wide mahogany desk, his fingers bridged together in thought as his gaze locked onto the flat-screen television elegantly mounted in a cabinet on the opposite wall. Eduardo stood behind him and leaned against the wall with his arms crossed in furrowed concentration.

Cristina and Alejandro sat in polished chairs opposite Bartolo's desk, and they both turned to look at Mikaela and Isabella as they slipped into the room, which suddenly felt small and cramped. Mikaela noted the stricken look on Alejandro's face and the glow of the television, which she had long assumed her father used more as office decor than for actual utility.

Mikaela regarded the scene for a moment. "What's going on?"

Dayanara glanced at her mother, who appeared to be considering her words. "There's a coordinated media attack on the family," she said. "Someone is coming for you. For both of you."

Mikaela's stomach dropped as Isabella blinked in shock. "What?"

"I received a call from our PR team an hour ago," her mother went on. "Believe me, we were lucky they even got that much of a tip-off, with how tight-lidded this has been and how much of a bombshell the media is planning to use it as."

Mikaela racked her brain, trying to come up with anything, any angle, that someone could carve up and use against her. "I…I don't understand."

"Seems the military has at least one mole that's working as an informant for the organizing discontent in Este," her father cut in. "This anonymous person went to the press claiming that we have been secretly funneling money from our armed forces to Isabella's family."

Mikaela felt Isabella go taut next to her. "That…That…" she stammered before glancing wide-eyed at Mikaela.

"Explain," Mikaela said.

Her father exhaled sharply. "The person has been secretly working to bolster this resistance for some time," he went on. "We haven't identified them yet, but we will. It appears they've been looking for something, anything, they can latch on to to give credence to their message as they organize. And, well, it appears they found it."

"What does that mean?" Mikaela asked. "We haven't been funneling anything to Isabella's family."

Her father took a deep breath and rubbed a hand over his forehead, an uncharacteristic sign of weariness. Out of the corner of her eye, Mikaela spotted Alejandro as he sighed and pinched the bridge of his nose between his thumb and index finger.

This isn't good.

"Apparently, we have," her father said. He gestured to Eduardo. "My first inclination was to file a lawsuit and have one of our judges place a gag order on this media outlet while we did additional investigating. Unfortunately, we were unable to because Eduardo tracked down significant ETF payments directly from an obscure military account to Fernando Acosta and Araceli Ramon's joint bank account. The military account they originate from is rarely used and, quite frankly, if this hadn't happened we probably never would have looked closely at it. At any rate, the media's report is framing the informant as a whistleblower claiming they were ordered to send payments to Isabella's family as directed by the Crown, and they have the proof." He met Mikaela's gaze. "They're making it seem as though Isabella was *bought*."

There was a beat of heavy, suffocating silence as Mikaela desperately tried to process. Her pulse roared in her ears as she tightened her fingers in Isabella's. "That's impossible," she replied. "That can't be."

"Lucia and I have been in crisis mode with the agency all morning," her mother interjected. "The media is already eating it up and they're running a breaking news interview with Fernando and Araceli in about five minutes."

Isabella shook her head. "No way," she said. "My mother never mentioned any of this and I just spoke with her three days ago. I'll call them right now and fix this. I'll tell them to stay inside, lock their doors and to not, under any circumstances, answer for any reporters. My mother would never agree to a news interview or to doing this to me."

Her mother pursed her lips gently. "It's already done, Isabella," she replied. "The interview was filmed late yesterday afternoon before that storm rolled in. It's already taped and they plan to air it any moment."

Isabella's eyes filled with tears as Mikaela shook her head in confusion. "I still don't understand," she said. "How are they receiving money? When did this start?"

"No one seems to know anything about this," Alejandro said as he looked between Mikaela and Isabella. "Nobody. We've turned over everything we have to Eduardo and our finance minister for investigation. Your parents, myself, the Royal Council? Nobody seems to know how this money is being funneled to Isabella's parents, but it *is*."

"And that means we need to do damage control while we dig deep into this on our end," her mother said.

"Goddammit, where is Juan?" Her father growled. He slammed his open palms onto his desk. "This is a limited access military account that's being used and he's nowhere to be found."

Alejandro nodded. "He may be at the range over at the base. He sometimes likes to start the day with target practice. I'll call him again."

As Alejandro pulled out his phone, Mikaela turned to Isabella and took a slow, deliberate breath. "Love," she said as she searched her eyes. "Tell me this isn't true. Have your parents been accepting money under the guise of payments from the Crown in exchange for…you?"

Isabella's lips parted, but there were no words. Mikaela felt Isabella's fingers curl and tighten around her own as her stomach dropped precipitously. "Isabella, what is going on?"

Mikaela watched as Isabella swallowed hard. Her pulse slammed harder in her ears as the polished floor seemed to tilt and sway beneath her bright red Louboutin heels. "*Tell* me."

Mikaela was acutely aware of everyone watching her and Isabella. She dropped Isabella's hand as if her touch burned.

Just then, a reporter in a tight skirt and blazer spoke from the television set. "Good morning, Cayo Azul." Her voice was like silk. "We're coming to you live with a breaking development regarding our royal family. A scandal is brewing at Castillo Blanco as an armed forces informant tells us that they have been instructed to send payments to a longtime Este family in exchange for their young daughter."

Tears, hot and unfamiliar, burned deep inside Mikaela and blurred the smiling reporter until she was an abstract wave of deep reds and golden browns.

Isabella gasped as footage of her parents, standing on their modest front porch, emerged on the television screen. The reporter continued with a voiceover as the camera zoomed onto Fernando's and Araceli's faces.

"We have an exclusive interview with Fernando Acosta and Araceli Ramon, parents of Isabella Acosta Ramon, the twenty-five-year-old at the center of allegations that the monarchy secretly funneled money from the military to this family. The claims suggest that these hefty payments were made in connection with Isabella's relationship with Princess Mikaela de Medreno Soliz and that an arranged marriage, financially benefitting this family, may be in its planning stages."

Mikaela took a step closer to the television set as she ignored the hand that reached out to grab hers. It may have been Dayanara's, or Alejandro's, or even her mother's, but she couldn't look away from the image of Fernando's and Araceli's tense expressions. Another figure emerged behind them, solemn and uncomfortable, and Mikaela recognized Javier Jimenez.

The reporter sat next to them on a worn lawn chair and smoothed her skirt. "Señor Acosta, Señora Ramon, let's address these allegations directly. Are you receiving money from the royal family?"

Fernando cleared his throat and glanced around. "Yes," he replied after an uncertain moment. "We approved an arrangement with the Crown for financial assistance in exchange for Isabella relocating to Castillo Blanco."

Araceli wiped a tear from her eye. "It was never, *ever* presented as payment for Isabella. That idea is disgusting. Isabella chose to pursue a relationship with the princess of her own free will."

Javier laid a gentle hand on Araceli's shoulder as Mikaela recognized the fake concern that seeped from his stance.

"It cannot be of her own free will when significant financial assistance is presented," Javier said as he looked directly into the camera. "Many of us in Este do not have the resources or the privilege to say no to an arrangement of that nature, particularly when it involves the royal family. The same royal family we are to somehow trust will guide and protect us. I was so concerned when I learned of Isabella's trafficking that I returned home from my university on an excused absence immediately to help her parents, who have been so like my own family for many years."

Isabella's hands were balled into fists as she glared daggers at the television set. "Javi, that *asshole*," she whispered. "Our families were never that close. Get away from my parents."

"And is that what you believe this is?" the reporter asked, eagerly digging deeper. "Trafficking?"

Javier nodded solemnly. "I don't know how else you could define this. It's important we call out the royal family and this elite class to avoid these heinous acts from being swept under the rug. They should understand that you cannot buy love or devotion, no matter how much money, power, or privilege you have."

The reporter nodded. "Can you explain the nature of these payments?"

Araceli wrung her hands nervously. "A…a couple of gentlemen from the police and the armed services arrived at our home," she said. "Our family has…has always had a difficult time making ends meet. Fernando had just arrived home and relayed that he'd been fired from his job as a municipal worker. They…they said that they could help and that we would be taken care of in exchange for Isabella residing at Castillo Blanco for seventy-five days. There were no stipulations or additional expectations. I've spoken to Isabella and video-chatted with her several times…"

The reporter turned to Fernando before Araceli had finished. "Why the secrecy?"

Fernando shrugged and rubbed a hand over the top of his head. "I don't really know, Señora," he replied. "We were told not to speak of it. That it was simply for our cooperation and to never mention it to anyone."

The reporter considered this as she leaned closer. "Was Isabella also aware of these payments?"

Fernando tensed slightly. "She…she knew. We were all told not to say anything. We didn't want to cause problems…"

Mikaela whirled around in shock. She took a deep, uneven breath as her jaw clenched with the fury and betrayal that coursed through her, hot and angry. "You *knew*?"

❖

Her parents' voices echoed in Isabella's mind as she trembled despite the warmth of the room. Her mother had clearly been under duress as she tried her best to present neutral, factual responses to the reporter's probing questions and Javier's own charged comments. In the hurried haste from Mikaela's home to Castillo Blanco, she hadn't even checked her phone since much earlier the day before. She imagined the dozens of missed calls and texts from her mother, apologizing profusely and trying to warn her of what was to come.

So stupid. So, so stupid of me.

She fought the sobs that were building in her chest as she met Mikaela's gaze. "Mikaela, please..." Isabella cursed at the way her voice broke. "I didn't want to keep it from you, I swear. I...I had pushed it to the back of my mind because they told me to never tell you..."

"Right," Mikaela said flatly, ice dripping from her tone. "Secrets are okay then?"

Isabella shook her head. "No! No, I just...Mikaela, I've loved being here with you—"

"Who told you not to say anything about these payments?" Mikaela cut her off sharply, her expression unmoved.

"I don't know," Isabella replied, helpless to stop the tears that had begun free-falling down her cheeks. "The police officer and the man from the military who came to our home. I didn't want my parents to bear the brunt of any hardship if I said anything."

"Isabella," Alejandro said. "If you had told us, we could have addressed this discreetly. We would have done a proactive investigation, extinguished this, and rid the military of whoever there is willing to betray the Crown. We could have nipped this safely and strategically."

Bartolo nodded once. "Exactly," he said. "Now we must deal with the fallout. We..."

His voice trailed off as Mikaela turned and headed straight for the door.

"Mikaela!" Isabella rushed after her and reached for her wrist. "Please, just listen to me, my love. We will figure this out and I'll do whatever it takes..."

Mikaela yanked her arm back and spun to face Isabella. The fire in her eyes stopped her short in her tracks. "You *lied* to me."

"I didn't..." Isabella tried again.

"You *lied* to me," Mikaela repeated, louder this time. "You kept something like that from me?" She took a deep breath. Her hands shook with fury as her wobbling tone betrayed the depth of her devastation. "This entire time, I trusted you. I *fought* for you to be here because I felt something with you that I have *never* felt before in my life from the moment I met you. And this whole time I was letting myself feel *everything* for you, you were here so your parents could get paid?"

Hot tears snaked down Isabella's face. She didn't try to wipe them away as her lips trembled. "Mikaela, I love you."

Mikaela's sharp laugh echoed through Bartolo's office as she raked a hand through her hair. "Right," she replied bitterly. "*Love*? That's not what this is and not what it ever *could* be. Not like this."

Dayanara and Cristina both stood, their movements fluid and graceful as they flanked Mikaela. "My daughter." Cristina's voice was hushed as she placed an arm around Mikaela's shoulders. "Emotions are high right now. I understand you're rightfully upset." She glanced at Dayanara. "Please take her home. Watch over her and let her rest. We'll finalize our strategy and be in touch shortly with more details."

Dayanara nodded as she cleared her throat. "Come on, Mika," she said, her voice filled with empathy and compassion. "Let's go."

Mikaela turned to the door without another word and held her head high as she stormed out. She didn't look back.

CHAPTER TWENTY-FIVE

A few more steps. Mikaela steeled her spine. *A few more and I'll be outside. Then I'll be closer to home.*

Mikaela ignored the flashes of concern across the faces of those she stalked by without a second glance.

"Let's go out the side door." Dayanara's voice was calming as she led Mikaela down a shorter hallway. "It's closer to the path leading to your residence."

Mikaela nodded. *Don't let them see you cry. Don't let* anyone *see you cry. A few more steps and you can shatter. I just have to get there first.* It was all Mikaela could do to control her long strides and not break into an unbalanced and potentially treacherous sprint on her four-inch heels as the sweet view of her personal home emerged in the distance.

Finally.

Mikaela pushed open the door harder than intended and collapsed onto the leather sofa. She sat forward, her elbows on her knees, and rested her head in her balled-up fists. After a long moment, Dayanara set a half-filled glass of amber whiskey in front of her. Tiny square ice cubes clinked against the thick glass as Dayanara nudged it closer to her.

"Mikaela, you have to breathe," she said as she sat next to her. "Drink. Breathe. And, when you're ready, talk to me, Mika, please."

Mikaela exhaled sharply and took a long sip of the whiskey, relishing the rich burn against the back of her throat. Her chest ached as her mind raced through replays of the last hour. Her father explaining the depth of the scandal, Isabella's voice breaking as she pleaded for Mikaela to hear her, the uncomfortable body language of Isabella's parents during the interview. The way Isabella sobbed as Mikaela walked away.

The way she lied this entire time.

Mikaela clenched her jaw as she took another sip of whiskey, slower this time, as her body began to still. "I can't do this," she said. "Daya, I simply can't move forward with this relationship. Or whatever it was, because evidently it was only a relationship in my own mind."

Dayanara placed a hand over Mikaela's tightly-balled fist. "Mika, I know it seems bad—"

"She's only here because her parents are being compensated," Mikaela cut her off. "Because *someone* paid for her family's cooperation." Her throat tightened as Isabella's face flashed through her mind and she forced herself to swallow. "I'm not sure if the worst part is that she *knew* all along and still let me believe this was real or that I…I can't even hate her for this."

Dayanara shook her head. "You shouldn't," she replied gently. "You *know* that's not why she's here."

"Do I?" Mikaela shot back. "I get it. Her mother means the world to her and has worked hard her entire life. Isabella told me how she promised herself she'd always be there for her mom the way that her mom has been there for her. How sad and guilty she feels that Araceli's life never quite panned out the way she probably hoped, after having Isabella so young and then being stuck in a miserable marriage. Of *course* Isabella, being who she is, would jump at the chance to better her parents' fortunes. It's just…it's a *hard* pill to swallow, realizing I meant nothing to her. I was a means to a much brighter end."

Dayanara exhaled and ran a hand through her hair. "Mikaela, you love her."

Mikaela glared at the whiskey glass before her. "I know. And that makes it hurt so much worse." She hated the hot, angry tears as they finally coursed down her cheeks.

"Isabella loves you." Dayanara placed a comforting hand on Mikaela's back. "I know she does, Mika. I wouldn't insist if I didn't truly believe she was head over heels for you. She was *gushing* over you at lunch last week. The way she was talking about you and how she would literally glow anytime I mentioned your name? It wasn't fake."

"She was dutifully playing her part," Mikaela said. She ran the tips of her index fingers along her cheekbones, cursing the flecks of black mascara that stained them. "Besides, my father was very clear about being cautious with her, especially given her involvement with Javier Jimenez and his pendejo father. I won't be with her. Not anymore."

A flash of defeat clouded Dayanara's normally sunny gaze, but a knock at the door made her pause as she opened her mouth to respond. Mikaela's head snapped up as she watched the front door warily.

After a moment, Alejandro stepped inside. His face was tense as he stood in the foyer with his fists casually stuffed into his pockets.

"My father," Alejandro spoke before Mikaela or Dayanara could. His voice was dull with shock and confusion. "He's somehow involved; I know it."

Mikaela blinked. "What?"

Dayanara stood and gestured at the whiskey glass on the coffee table. "Sounds like you could use one of these too, Alejandro."

Alejandro nodded, though his gaze was somewhere far away. "I...I don't understand it," he went on. "I came straight here. He showed up right after you left. He admitted to orchestrating the financial arrangements and it was *him* who pulled the strings to encourage Fernando's firing. Not that he had to do a lot, considering his overall job performance, but it was his nudge that did Fernando in."

"Uncle Juan? Why would he do such a thing?"

Alejandro sunk into an armchair opposite Mikaela and gratefully accepted a half-filled whiskey glass from Dayanara. "I don't know," he finally replied. "I don't think he ever thought it would come to light, hence the obscure military bank account used to transfer the funds. He hadn't anticipated this morning's events and the publicity surrounding it all. Doesn't seem to understand why anyone is upset about the actions he took upon himself to get Isabella here. He claims to have no idea that his trusted lieutenant who helped facilitate everything may be the anonymous informant secretly working with this burgeoning resistance." Alejandro shook his head. "It's a fucking mess, Mikaela. And I can't believe my own father is somehow involved. I wish I knew what the hell he was thinking. Did he think it was somehow helpful? What was he trying to achieve? I just...I have no idea."

Mikaela gripped her glass tightly in both hands. Alejandro sounded so confused and devastated, and her heart went out to him. It wasn't the first time she wondered how Juan could have such an intelligent, keen son while his own brutish nature seemed to frequently handicap him with short-sightedness and emotional impulsivity. "Juan was the only one within the family and the Royal Council who knew anything?"

Alejandro nodded. "That's my understanding, cousin. Well, my father and I suppose Isabella, if you want to consider her family."

Mikaela steeled her gaze as the sharp, unbearable ache in her chest deepened at her name. "I do not."

Alejandro glanced at Dayanara and then back at her. "Mikaela..."

Mikaela let out a slow breath. She felt steadier, but her body felt numb and cold. She had spent years staying away from opportunists. She had long resisted the idea of love but fantasized about the tantalizing prospect that real, true love could be without conditions, pretense, or expectations. She had always hoped that when she *did* let herself fall, it would be far deeper than surface-level. It would be *forever.*

"I already told Daya," Mikaela said. "I can't do this. It's over between Isabella and I. I will not see her again."

Alejandro sipped his whiskey as he furrowed his eyebrows in thought. "There's something more there, Mika. She..." He shook his head. "She isn't pretending. The way she looks at you, Mikaela, she really..."

As memories of holding Isabella close in her arms came flooding back, Mikaela couldn't bear to listen anymore. She curled her legs into her and wrapped her arms tightly around herself desperately trying to ward away the heartbreak that was already splintering her from the inside out. As Mikaela hid her face in her knees, she willed the sob rising in her throat to stop. Instead, her back shuddered as the tears flowed freely. This time, neither Dayanara nor Alejandro argued with her.

Dayanara's arms wrapped around her as she whispered in her ear, but the crush of Isabella's betrayal was nearly suffocating.

"Okay, Mika," Dayanara said. "Let it out. You've got us. We'll help you however you wish to proceed."

Mikaela sniffled and then finally lifted her head and looked at her through her tear-soaked gaze. "I want Isabella to leave."

The following morning, Isabella sat frozen on the edge of the bed in her suite as she stared blankly at the television. She wrapped her arms tightly around herself as the flickering light cast shadows across the room, but she barely registered the '80s sitcom reruns or the canned laughter of the studio audience. Isabella knew somewhere in the back of her mind it was morning, but the idea of drawing open the curtains and soaking in the early white-hot sunshine seemed like an impossible task. She wanted to sit in the darkened room alone as the last twenty-four hours looped in her mind.

Her parents' voices echoed through her brain alongside the buzzing vibrations of her phone as her mother tried to call over and over after the interview had aired. Isabella couldn't bring herself to speak to her. She couldn't bring herself to speak to anyone. There had been no word and no contact from Mikaela or anyone in her inner circle and, though it drove Isabella crazy, she stayed distant too in an effort to allow Mikaela time to process as well. The thought of leaving the suite and facing anyone at Castillo Blanco was tortuous, so she tearfully paced the length of the sitting area as she replayed the day's events until she fell into a fitful sleep.

Isabella took a deep breath. The rumbling in her stomach was an aching reminder that she hadn't eaten since yesterday.

I need to eat something. An idea dawned as she wriggled out of her pajamas and into a cream and navy-blue patterned halter jumpsuit. *Why don't I get something from one of the nearby City Center cafes? After all, I can leave without security detail if I want to. I can still do anything I want.* Isabella stuck her chin out defiantly as she tied her hair up into a high ponytail. *Besides, it might be good to get out of Castillo Blanco for a while. It's not like anyone even cares that I'm here right now anyway.*

As Isabella swept a dusting of bronzer over her face, Mikaela's devastated expression filled her mind. The way she had stepped back and yanked her arm away, as though her touch scalded her. The way her voice had cracked when she demanded to know the truth. Isabella's breath hitched at the memory, but the look on her face when she heard that Isabella knew was the one that cut most deeply.

"You lied to me!" Mikaela's voice zinged across her mind as Isabella fought the lump that settled into the base of her throat.

"Mikaela is gone," Isabella said to her reflection. "All because of a stupid secret I never *wanted* to keep. I let myself get caught up in Mikaela and I ruined it."

Isabella's chest ached with the kind of longing that was deeper than physical; it was the kind that felt like it was tearing right through her heart.

Isabella sniffled as she blinked at her reflection. "The most real thing you've ever had in your life, and you ruined it." She turned away, unable to look at herself any longer. Just as she picked up her phone and a small white leather clutch, ready to escape to City Center for the morning until she could bring herself to return, a sharp knock sounded at the door.

Isabella turned just as the door swung open, and her heart stopped.

Mikaela's dark eyes were blazing and her jaw clenched tightly, which inadvertently pouted her glossed lips. She was positively vibrating with fury as she paused for just a moment before striding into the suite. The heels on her calf-length boots tapped with an angry certainty across the polished hardwood as she glared at Isabella.

Oh my God. Her heart raced with nearly every emotion, including a deep, dark excitement that flooded her core. *She looks like she wants to kiss me or kill me. Or both.*

CHAPTER TWENTY-SIX

"You." Mikaela spat out the word as she stopped just short of Isabella. Before Isabella could respond, Mikaela's arm snaked out as she wrapped her fingers around Isabella's throat.

Isabella stood still as the moment stretched between them. After a beat, Isabella realized that Mikaela wasn't squeezing. In fact, she barely applied any pressure at all. Her palm was firm as her fingers splayed along the delicate curve of Isabella's neck, and she knew Mikaela could feel the rapid pounding of her pulse beneath her touch.

Isabella lifted her chin just slightly as she kept her gaze locked onto Mikaela's. The air was thick and charged with raw emotion, but it was tinged with something *else* too—the *something* they had never been able to control.

Mikaela's thumb traced along the edge of her jaw before she inhaled sharply and yanked her hand away.

"Is this what you wanted, Isabella? Keeping secrets? Lying to my *face*? Making me crazy?" Mikaela swallowed hard and Isabella recognized a split-second flash of…*something*. Whether it was fire or vulnerability, Isabella was overcome with a dark desire to launch herself into Mikaela's arms and kiss her hard, deeply, until she again believed in the depths of her soul that they were real.

Isabella took a step forward as Mikaela turned slightly away. "Mikaela, I didn't lie to you. *Please*. Everything we shared and everything I felt was real."

"Don't." Mikaela cut her off. "At what point were you going to tell me about this arrangement?"

Isabella wasn't sure how to respond. She recognized her confusion by the strict conditions that had been placed on the arrangement, bound by her desire to protect her mother, and so utterly wrapped up in falling for Mikaela that the entire situation had been irresponsibly thrown to the back of her mind.

"Right," Mikaela said tightly. "That's all I needed to know."

"Mikaela, I swear to you that what we have is real. You *know* it is."

"You *knew*." Mikaela shook her head furiously. "You *knew* your family was getting paid and still you insist this is real. What, are you afraid the money is going to stop flowing now that your secret is out?"

Mikaela's words felt like a burning slap across her face. "I never wanted to hurt you," Isabella said.

Mikaela yanked her forward and her body collided against Mikaela's. Isabella tried not to lose herself in the heat of Mikaela's lips just millimeters from her own.

"Mikaela, I'm sorry," Isabella said as she tangled her fingers in the loose waves that swept over Mikaela's shoulders. Her heart pounded in her chest as desire outweighed all other emotions fighting for dominance. She could hear Mikaela's uneven breathing and feel the way her fingers dug into her hips as she held Isabella to her. She recognized how Mikaela appeared to fight between the primal urge to pull Isabella even closer or throw her away.

"Please," Isabella said. "Let me make it better. I'll show you this is real. Let me help fix this."

Just as Isabella was certain she was getting through to Mikaela, the tumultuous heat between them and the acknowledgement of something deeper softening her stony expression, she abruptly pulled back instead.

The loss of Mikaela's warmth felt like a searing rejection that Isabella barely had time to process before Mikaela walked to the door.

"This doesn't change anything," Mikaela said without turning. "We cannot continue this."

With that, she was gone.

Isabella took a deep breath, dazed and left behind in a cloud of Mikaela's sweet-scented perfume, her storm, and her passion. She brushed her fingertips along the tingling skin of her neck where Mikaela had touched her, practically branding her, as she battled with herself.

Isabella barely had time to sit on the edge of the sofa before a much quieter knock sounded at the door.

"Yes?" she called weakly.

"Senorita Acosta Ramon." A younger woman that Isabella recognized as an assistant to Eduardo's chief of staff tentatively cracked the door open. "Her Royal Highness Queen Cristina would like to speak with you."

Isabella swallowed hard as she tried to brush away the last of the trembles Mikaela had left her with. "Thank you," she replied. "When?"

The aide's face was carefully neutral. "Now. Please follow me and I'll take you to her. I believe she's having an early lunch in the garden today."

Isabella's stomach dropped at the unexpected request, but it was mostly resigned defeat that settled deep in her chest as she stood and nodded. "Very well."

I've already faced Mikaela's fire. Might as well walk straight into the den of the lioness.

The back gardens of the palace were quiet under the late morning sunshine. It should have been peaceful, but Isabella's heart was anything but.

"Your Highness," the aide said as she gestured politely at Isabella.

Cristina nodded. "Thank you," she said. "Señorita Acosta Ramon and I will have our lunch here today."

"I will inform the kitchen staff, Your Highness," the aide replied before striding back into Castillo Blanco.

Cristina regarded Isabella carefully, her expression unreadable, as she held her arm out to a chair opposite where she sat across the table. "Please," she said. "Sit. You must be starving."

Isabella sat and folded her hands tightly in her lap. "Thank you," she replied. "I'm fine."

Cristina fixed her with a knowing glance. "One of Terese's chefs informed me that you declined lunch and dinner in your suite yesterday. You must eat something before you begin wasting away."

Isabella sighed. "Thank you," she tried again. "I…I have not had much of an appetite. I know it sounds silly, but I haven't really thought much about eating."

Isabella felt Cristina's curious gaze on her, probing and reading every nuance, every between-the-lines gesture, and she felt oddly exposed. She straightened her spine, sitting up taller, and wondered just how much Cristina was gathering.

"You love Mikaela," Cristina finally said as her gaze bore into Isabella.

Isabella's breath caught in her throat. She had spent so long trying to defend herself and explain everything away, but Cristina had cut right to the heart of what was happening, momentarily stripping away everything else.

Isabella nodded. "I do. I'm completely in love with her."

Cristina sighed as her gaze lingered on a row of hedges somewhere at the edge of the gardens. "I see that." She took a slow sip of lemonade. "I regret not understanding a lot of things sooner."

Isabella nodded but sensed that Cristina wasn't finished.

"Mikaela has always been strong, independent, and incredibly stubborn. There has been something different about her lately. Perhaps something more joyful, *softer*." Cristina glanced at Isabella. "That doesn't come easily for her. It's…rare that she lets herself feel too deeply for another, and I shoulder some of the blame. This life and this responsibility as part of our family… It's a lot. Much more than most people could ever understand. I wanted to protect Mikaela from so much of the bad and so many of the pitfalls from the moment she was born."

Isabella bit her lip. "If I may, you did an excellent job, Your Highness," she replied. "Mikaela is an amazing woman."

Cristina smiled lightly. "She is. Though I sometimes wonder if I became so caught up with trying to protect her that it overlapped into trying to mold her. Of course, Mikaela is her own person. She won't be molded into anyone or anything that she doesn't want to be. It was always easier somehow for Bartolo. He and Mikaela had such a synergy and an easy relationship from the time she was small. They just seem to understand one another. As for me, I always fretted over her and perhaps overprotected her from the pressure we face and the world around us. And though it may have eventually chafed and driven her away from me as she became an adult, I don't regret a single thing about the woman she is today."

The tension Isabella had been holding as she braced herself for whatever was to come began melting away as she nodded again. "Thank you," she replied. "I never, ever want to hurt her."

Cristina looked at her for a long moment, her expression unreadable. "I know."

The quiet hum of nature throughout the gardens stretched between them for a moment before Cristina shifted on the bench, crossing one knee delicately over the other, as she became all business once more.

"Unfortunately, this situation is now much bigger than just the two of you. And also most unfortunately, it's bigger than love. Tell me, what is it you plan to do?"

Isabella blinked, unsure how to answer Cristina's question. "Fight for Mikaela, of course," she said. "Beg her to hear me, to understand. As long as it takes. I won't give up on her."

Cristina clasped her hands in her lap as something close to amusement flickered across her face. "That's very noble of you," she said. "Though I will advise you that *strategy* is of the utmost importance right now. I know emotions are still high and you wish to stay and fight for Mikaela, but I believe the most beneficial thing you can do right now is return to Este."

Isabella's stomach twisted. "Go home?"

"Please understand that I'm speaking to you as a mother and as someone who wants to see Mikaela happy and thriving just as much as you do."

"So…so what will leaving achieve?" Isabella fought the burgeoning lump deep in her throat.

Cristina leaned forward slightly. "Speak to your parents," she said. "Your mother has reached out to nearly every staff member and aide she can find, and she's devastated. Talk with her and find out what truly transpired. You are the only one who really can."

Isabella shook her head. "I'm so mad at them," she replied. "And I don't want to leave Mikaela."

Cristina's expression softened just a fraction. "I understand," she said. "I do. But Mikaela is too hurt right now to hear anything from anyone and this story is explosive. It will not disappear on its own. If you truly want to fix this, not just with Mikaela but in regards to the entire situation, we need answers. And you need the truth from your parents. They are your family."

Isabella's throat tightened. She didn't want to go, but she knew Cristina was right. There was more to it and her parents held some of the missing pieces. Whether she wanted to face them or not, she had to get to the bottom of what was going on in hopes that maybe, just *maybe*, time and distance would help Mikaela see beyond her devastation and remember that she loved her.

But what if she doesn't? What if I leave and that's it? What if... What if I never see Mikaela again?

The thought was nearly too much to bear, but Isabella was pulled from her thoughts as a staff member wheeled a small silver butler's cart alongside the table. He uncovered their salmon salads with a flourish as Cristina politely thanked him.

Isabella took a deep breath. "Okay," she said. "I will go. May I have the afternoon to get my things together and then leave tomorrow morning?"

"Take as much time as you need," she said gently. "Remember, this is not a punishment. This is how we begin to fix things. For yourself. For her."

"Tomorrow then," she said.

Though Isabella understood, it still felt as though her heart was breaking inside her chest.

CHAPTER TWENTY-SEVEN

As the black Escalade deftly navigated the dusty, curving roads into Este, Isabella glanced out the dark tinted windows at the place she had called home for so long. The familiar land was still as rugged, raw, and untamed as she'd left it. Modest, weathered homes and rolling hills of farmland dotted the landscape. The familiar open-air pizza place, no more than a tin-walled shack with a long, splintered wooden bar separating the large brick oven and taps of beer from the narrow road, had its usual crowd of retired men seated in white plastic chairs in a loose semicircle just outside as they shot the breeze and joked with one another.

Farther down, a roadside stall selling fresh fruit and vegetables was being managed by a bored-looking teenager as a small group of kindergarten-age children chased each other in the adjacent field, their high-pitched giggles piercing the thick, humid air.

Este was the same, but it somehow felt different and less familiar. Isabella wondered if it was *her* that was different or if the new charge in the air—buzzing with reckless energy and burgeoning resentment—had always been there and she'd just never noticed it before.

As the Escalade turned left down another road, Isabella blinked at a newly-erected billboard on the corner. The tall, jagged letters were bolder than the propaganda she had seen cropping up around Este prior to her stay at Castillo Blanco and it made her stomach twist. *Resist the Crown*, the billboard implored passersby as its letters streaked against a dark backdrop of raised fists and shadowed faces with black masks. The atmosphere in Este felt sharper and more distrustful.

Roberto is really starting something here.

Before she could ponder it further, the Escalade pulled into the familiar driveway. Her parents' house looked frozen in time as the familiar scent of warm spices hit her senses as soon as the car door was opened for her.

Has it only been six weeks?

The front door swung open as Isabella reached the front porch. She had let her mother know that morning that she was headed home, though she didn't provide many details. There were too many questions she needed answered and too much she had to know first before she felt comfortable spilling her heart.

"Daughter!" Isabella's mother reached her in record time as she pulled her into a tight hug. Tears flowed freely down her face as she inhaled the scent of Isabella's hair and held her arms in her hands as she pulled back for a moment to look at her.

Isabella's throat closed at her mother's trembling fingers and the unabashed relief that washed over her in waves. "Surprise," she said weakly. "I'm home."

Her mother wiped her eyes and then cupped Isabella's face in both hands. "I'm so sorry, my daughter," she said through her tears. "I am so very sorry, my girl. I tried to call you so many times to warn you and let you know what was going on. It all happened so quickly. I didn't want to do it. I didn't want that nosy reporter here."

Isabella swallowed hard as her heart twisted at the pain and fear in her mother's voice. "Why, Mami? Then why?"

Her mother glanced away as shame darkened her gaze. "Come," she replied as she gestured to the kitchen. "I'll tell you everything."

As Isabella sat across the kitchen table from her mother, she glanced around their home. It was strangely quiet.

Her mother pushed a small bowl across the table and eyed her tentatively. "Your favorite snack."

Isabella smiled despite herself as she popped a chunk of dried mango in her mouth. "It still is," she replied. "Thank you."

Her mother glanced somewhere in the distance. "The news crew contacted us out of the blue," she said. "We were paid for the interview. Roberto's group, they encouraged us to talk. Said that the news crew had been contacted by someone from the military, I guess, who has been secretly working with his group, and they would run with the story no matter what. Your father smelled more money and took it."

Isabella's stomach churned. *Of course he did.* "You were manipulated, Mami," she replied tearfully. "Papa too, though I doubt he cares about anything other than the money. Which makes him the perfect person for Roberto and the news crew to manipulate." She shook her head in disgust.

Her mother took a deep breath. "I didn't want to participate, but your father…" her voice trailed off as her lips pressed into a thin line. "As soon as he knew money was involved, he told me he was going to do it with or without me. It all happened so fast. Roberto assured us he would have Javier there to oversee the news crew. I guess, in some way, I thought if I participated then I could help soften the blow, control it, and not let them frame things so badly. Especially if I was truthful."

"Papa sold out our family," Isabella said as white-hot anger sizzled in her veins, fueled by years of damage inflicted by her father. "And he sold *me*, multiple times now, for whatever price was offered to him regardless of later consequences. Javier had his own agenda too, based on his father's political aspirations. He was not there to protect you." She met her mother's gaze. "Where is Papa?"

"He took the money from the interview and left. He hasn't been home since yesterday. You know me, my daughter, I don't mind. I even prefer when he's gone. I just hate that this happened to you. I am so sorry I couldn't stop it, but please understand that I made what I felt was the smartest decision at the time. I thought if I called you right away and kept trying to reach you to warn you, that maybe the palace or someone could do something to stop it from proceeding further."

Isabella's cheeks burned as she remembered exactly why she hadn't been near her phone. "I know. You did the best you could in an impossible situation. I'm sorry this was placed upon you."

Her mother squeezed Isabella's hands in her own. "I should have fought harder. Should have locked your damn father in the bedroom…"

Isabella laughed lightly as she squeezed back. "Ay, Mami," she said gently. "He would have hurt you. I could never live with myself knowing he hurt you while you were protecting me. What's done is done. We can't change it now. And part of me is glad that the whole arrangement is out in the open now." Her throat unexpectedly closed up at the thought of Mikaela. "Well, sort of. I mean, it's better off this way. It would have been worse to marry her with this shadow always lurking in the background."

Her mother's face fell. "I'm sorry, Isabella. I know you love her."

Isabella's breath caught. "You do?"

She nodded matter-of-factly. "From the moment you told me that you two had formed a…connection at the gala, the pieces began falling into place," she replied. "You've never spoken so reverently or so sweetly of anyone before. Certainly not Javier or any of the men you've gone out with in the past, and here you were looking positively dreamy over a woman you had only met that night."

Isabella's face flushed as she glanced down at the table. "It doesn't matter now," she went on with a quick shake of her head. "I've lost her. Mikaela wants nothing to do with me, and I don't blame her. I let her fall for me, knowing this secret was looming in the background. And it was so easy, because I loved her from the moment I saw her. It was so much fun and so exciting to fall in love too, so I ignored it and pushed it away.

I…I got so caught up in her, Mami. And now I've ruined things, probably forever."

Her mother came to Isabella's side and gently brushed a lock of hair behind her ear. "I could see the love you were both developing for each other," she said. "The way you'd talk about her when we had our video calls and you would light up. You had a glow. Even through your quick texts and your phone calls, I could read your tone and hear your voice. You were the happiest you've been since you were much younger."

"I know," she sniffled. "But Mikaela doesn't want anything to do with me. She won't talk to me, won't hear me, won't be near me. She's *so* hurt and I can't get through to her because I'm the one who caused her pain. Mikaela doesn't want me anymore."

Her mother kissed the top of her head and stood with a sigh. "You don't know that yet, my daughter," she replied. "Today has been a lot. This *week* has been a lot already. Let's get you settled so you can rest. You must be mentally exhausted."

Isabella took a deep breath and knew her mother was right. Exhaustion crept into her bones despite it being only midday. The weight of the last few days was finally crushing her as it settled heavily across her shoulders.

She followed her mother down the narrow hallway to her bedroom and felt a wave of relief at the neatly made bed, exactly as she'd left it six weeks before.

Her mother plumped the pillow and smoothed the crisp sheet as her long maxi skirt swirled around her ankles. "This is still your home," she said. "It will always be your home, whenever you need it. It may not be a palace, but it's still a home for you."

Isabella's limbs felt as though they were filled with concrete as she absent-mindedly nudged her suitcases into a corner and collapsed back against the pillow. She wasn't sure where—or what—home was anymore, but right now all she wanted to do was slip into unconsciousness and temporarily forget everything that happened.

Mikaela's father's private office was quiet with the heavy wooden door firmly shut behind them. She sat opposite his large desk while Eduardo sat in the chair next to hers, his head bent as he scanned a neatly-stapled stack of papers.

"There it is," Eduardo said. He pushed the papers across the desk to her father and pointed at a small line item near the center of the page. "An account opened last year in Roberto's name at the central bank, and a large payment funneled directly to Isabella's parents seventy-two hours ago. This wasn't just a random attack on the monarchy's reputation, Your Highness. This was calculated to ensure damage."

Mikaela's stomach dropped as icy tendrils twisted through her veins before solidifying into something cold and angry. She had spent the last days drowning in betrayal, confusion, and disbelief, and had finally begun taking meetings again. Her first one on the calendar was with her father and Eduardo, and she had braced herself as she entered the room thirty minutes before with no indication of what to expect.

Her father exhaled. "And Juan?"

Eduardo hesitated. "We have confirmed from the information uncovered that the payments to Isabella's parents originated from his closest allies," he said as his gaze flicked to Mikaela. "The question is whether this was simply poorly thought out overreach or if there was something more deliberate planned. I would suggest keeping a close eye on him, Your Highness."

Mikaela shook her head slightly. "Wait, we're spying on my uncle now?"

Her father's face remained unreadable. "Eduardo's advice is solid, Mikaela," he replied. "He has served us as our prime minister for nearly ten years now and he has not steered us wrong. It's important to have objectivity to provide perspective and guidance, especially in instances like this where it can be more difficult when…family is involved."

Mikaela swallowed hard. Everything had fallen so wildly off the rails over the last few days. Everything felt all wrong—the deceit, the bombshell revelations, the hard reality that those closest to her—Juan, Isabella—were tangled in this mess in ways she couldn't have anticipated. "I understand. I think."

"We must ensure that no one, family or not, makes reckless decisions that put our dynasty and this kingdom at risk," her father said as Eduardo nodded in agreement.

Mikaela pushed her chair back and stood as she crossed her arms. "Are we done here?"

Her father gave her a long, searching look before motioning for her to sit. "Eduardo, thank you for your diligence in identifying the payment from Roberto's group to Isabella's parents," he said. "If you don't mind, I'd like to speak to my daughter privately for a moment."

Eduardo gathered his laptop and paperwork. "Understood, Your Highness."

As the heavy door shut behind him, her father rapped a gold-plated pen against his desk. "Juan has always been emotionally impulsive," he said. "But I have concerns that this is something that has strengthened within him, particularly in the years since your aunt Eva passed."

Mikaela stilled at the rare mention of Alejandro's mother. "She was lovely," Mikaela said. "What happened was unbelievably tragic."

Her father nodded. "I don't think I ever told you all the details about that night," he replied. "There's things you should be privy to now."

Mikaela blinked in confusion. As far as she knew, Aunt Eva was killed instantly after a tragic, fiery car accident following a celebratory dinner party in Madrid after a week of joint naval exercises between the two countries. Alejandro had been ten years old at the time and Mikaela had just turned twelve. Luckily, neither had been present at the accident.

Her father took a deep breath and leaned back in his chair. "Your uncle Juan was exhilarated after those joint naval exercises," he said. "It was his first real show of success in the years after being named general of our armed services. It helped solidify his support and was a highlight of our mutually beneficial relationship with Spain. He had rented a Ferrari while in Madrid and loved speeding it around."

Mikaela suppressed a smile. "That sounds like Uncle Juan."

"Unfortunately, he had too much to drink at the celebration," he said. "It was a lively night, all pomp and circumstance and excitement. When he got behind the wheel of that Ferrari to drive himself and your aunt Eva back to the hotel, he was driving too fast and too recklessly."

"But...but the other vehicle hit them. It was clear in the footage of the accident. The other driver was even arrested on the scene."

Her father nodded. "Yes, it was technically the other driver at fault," he said. "But if Juan hadn't been tipsy, it was very likely that he could have seen the driver coming sooner and slowed down to minimize or even avoid the accident entirely."

Mikaela sucked in her breath. "I...I didn't know this."

"Not many do," her father replied. "Though Juan couldn't be held legally responsible, I didn't want his reputation irreparably harmed. I ensured the full police report was sealed so the notes about his blood alcohol level would not become public. Only the synopsis, where it's clear the other driver was legally at fault, is publicly available."

He inhaled sharply through his nostrils. "I suppose I thought after the initial shock and tragedy of the accident passed, Juan would take this and grow from it. Instead, I've watched him become more reckless, more hard-headed, and stubborn over the years since. We have tried to encourage him to deal with Eva's passing, but the more I've pushed him privately it seems the harder he doubles down. I will not let him harm this family or our standing."

Mikaela's mind whirled with the revelations. She glanced up. "Does Alejandro know everything?"

"I've never spoken to him personally about this, but Alejandro is incredibly sharp and very keen. I wouldn't be surprised if he's drawn his own conclusions. Thank goodness for that au pair Juan and Eva had hired at the time. She stayed at the hotel with Alejandro so they could attend the dinner party on their own. I think your cousin had a cold, so she had earlier convinced them that he should stay at the hotel to rest rather than attend the evening."

Mikaela nodded as she recalled the tragedy. Her father had been the only one in her immediate family to attend the naval exercises alongside Juan. Still, she remembered the stricken look on her mother's face the next afternoon at Castillo Blanco and the tears that had streaked down her cheeks as she sat in Mikaela's bedroom to break the news. She recalled her father, Juan, Alejandro, and a few staff members returning from Spain a few days later, and the dark shadows on her cousin's face, Aunt Eva conspicuously missing from the returning contingent. The air had been heavy with shock and devastation as they began planning a national funeral and day of mourning.

"I had no idea," Mikaela said.

"You had only just turned twelve," her father said. "You and Alejandro were children. Now, I must proceed strategically here. Your uncle has immense trauma from this event, but he has refused to deal with it for many years. I cannot let him recklessly destroy our family's legacy, unintentionally or…not."

Mikaela nodded. "I understand, Papa."

Her father pressed his lips together and glanced at the door. "With that, you may go if you wish."

Chapter Twenty-eight

That evening, Mikaela sat in the dim glow of her living room surrounded by silence. She had spent the last half hour sitting forward on her sofa as she stared at the half-full tumbler of vodka on the coffee table. She sighed as she swirled the liquid around absent-mindedly. The sun was setting rapidly into the ocean just beyond, and Mikaela knew at some point she'd need to turn on a light or risk tripping over her own feet when she gathered the effort to retire to her bedroom.

Everything had unraveled so quickly, and it was all she could do to stay above the surface, despite the strange feeling of drowning amongst the secrets uncovered and the betrayal all around her. Even after her earlier meeting with her father and Eduardo, Mikaela couldn't decide what hurt more: the fact that Isabella had known all along about the payments to her family or the fact that Mikaela still *wanted* her. She had confronted Isabella days before in her guest suite with the intention of giving her a piece of her mind and instead had fought against every primal urge to throw Isabella onto the bed and have her way with her, still desperate to shut out the world and fall into the fire burning between them.

And then Isabella had left the following day. Mikaela knew it shouldn't bother her; after all, she had pushed for it. She swallowed hard as she considered how everything in the days since had felt emptier and less vibrant.

Get over it. Mikaela let out a slow breath and pressed her fingers to her temples.

An impatient knock at the front door cut through the silence. Mikaela took a sip of her watered-down vodka and ignored it.

Another, louder knock sounded. "I know you're in there," Alejandro called. "You can be a vampire hiding in the dark as much as you want, but we know you're there."

Mikaela groaned and pushed herself off the leather sofa. She had barely cracked the front door open before Alejandro and Dayanara barged in along with an unmistakable mischievous energy.

Alejandro glanced at her as he poured himself a shot of her vodka. "You look like hell."

Mikaela glared at him. "Good," she muttered. "It matches how I feel. Help yourself to a drink."

"Already on it."

"Enough of this," Dayanara cut in as she crossed her arms. "We're going to Tryst tonight."

Mikaela shook her head. "No chance."

Alejandro sighed. "Mika, you've been sulking for days like some tragic, broken figure in a telenovela," he said. "And while that's very on-brand for you, it's time for us to intervene."

Dayanara stepped closer. "You need to get out of your own head for the night," she said. "Get dressed up. Dance. Forget. *Something* other than sitting here drowning in your own misery and half a bottle of Belvedere."

Mikaela hesitated. When Dayanara put it like that, it sounded almost… pathetic. And that was one thing Mikaela de Medreno Soliz was *not.* The thought of sitting in the silence any longer, watching darkness creep across her house, and letting her mind loop over Isabella's face, her arms, her hair, those irresistible dimples, her tanned legs, the way she looked at her all full of fire and passion, the heartbreak—it was unbearable.

"Fine," she practically spat the word as Alejandro and Dayanara exchanged satisfied glances.

"That's the spirit," Dayanara said. "Let's get you ready."

Mikaela wasn't convinced escaping to Tryst would help rid her of the deep hole in her heart.

But at least for a little while I won't have to think.

Exactly two hours later, Mikaela sat at her usual private booth on the upper level of Tryst looking over crowds of bodies writhing and gyrating on the dance floor below. The nightclub was already alive as its colorful lights flashed and music pulsated through a state-of-the-art sound system.

Mikaela had been acutely aware of the intrigued glances as she, Dayanara, and Alejandro strode into Tryst and directly to their private booth, as dark-suited nightclub security stood at attention just beyond the black velvet ropes. She wasn't sure if the throngs of club-goers who turned as she passed recognized her simply for who she was or if there was a higher level of interest because of the current news cycle. A group of twentysomething men turned, openly gawking and elbowing each other through cheeky whispers, while another woman winked and suggestively licked her lips near the bar. Mikaela didn't care about the attention, though she arrived dressed to kill.

Tonight, her confidence would be utilized as a weapon. As she glanced around, Mikaela knew she looked every bit the part she hoped to portray. She had dressed to show herself that she still could, and that she *wasn't* this pathetic woman unable to get out of the cloud that had enveloped her for days.

"I can't decide if this is concerning or amusing." Ian's thick Irish brogue cut into Mikaela's thoughts as she set her empty glass on the table. He glanced between the three of them with mild amusement.

"Definitely edging onto concerning," Dayanara replied as Mikaela quickly drained the crystal-clear liquid from the shot glass he had handed to her. She turned to Ian. "Haven't you seen the news?"

Ian blinked. "Oh, the bullshit story the media is trying to peddle? I haven't paid much attention because this place keeps me plenty busy. Plus, I know who Mikaela is."

Dayanara sighed dramatically. "Not everybody does," she said. "It's a coordinated smear campaign, and with the organization lately in Este? It could have devastating consequences, especially if it gives this movement real legs."

Alejandro cleared his throat as he raised an eyebrow at Mikaela. "You know, drinking yourself into oblivion isn't going to solve anything."

Mikaela laughed sharply. "You're right, dear cousin," she replied. "*Nothing* is going to make this better. Besides, wasn't coming to Tryst your idea?"

"Yeah, but…"

Ian clapped his hands on both their shoulders. "Look, if you're determined to be miserable, Mikaela, at least have *fun* with it." He nodded at the DJ booth across the dance floor. "I have it on good authority, aka *me*, that DJ Kat has had her eye on you for years. Pretty much since she moved here from Toronto and took up unofficial residency at Tryst. And she's due for her break in…" he glanced at his watch. "Oh, exactly two minutes now."

Alejandro and Dayanara exchanged a look as Alejandro shrugged weakly. "I mean, no one is forcing you to marry *this* one," he said.

Mikaela exhaled as she dragged a hand through her hair. She considered leaving, returning home, and locking out the world for the rest of the night. The thought of being alone there now, where every single space in her bedroom and beyond reminded her of Isabella, made her chest pound with a suffocating throbbing.

Instead, Mikaela grabbed another shot from their tray and tossed it back. "Fine," she said with a shrug. "Let's say *hola* to DJ Kat and dance."

Mikaela stood and ducked under the velvet rope before gently squeezing the burly security guard's bicep in thanks as he politely stepped aside for her. DJ Kat took off her headphones and placed them carefully on her soundboard before swinging open the side door of the booth that led to the dance floor. Kat looked at her, intrigue and a question in her green eyes.

"Hey," Mikaela said. "I'm Mikaela."

Kat gripped her outstretched hand tightly. "I know who you are," she replied. "You look"—she looked Mikaela up and down—"absolutely fucking stunning, if you don't mind my saying."

Mikaela forced a smile. "Thanks," she said. "Want to dance?"

Kat nodded as she took a deep breath. "It would be my honor."

As Mikaela followed Kat to the center of the dance floor, the humid air thick with heated bodies pressed against each other, she let Kat lead her further into her arms. Still, she bit her lip as a twinge of *something* sunk in her stomach. Mikaela wondered if she drank enough and lost herself in the music, the vibrancy of Tryst, and the unbridled interest of the punky DJ, it would be enough to stop feeling the twisting ache that Isabella had left in her wake.

As the bass pulsed through her veins as she moved slowly and suggestively against Kat, she tried to register the seductive way Kat's hands found her waist and pulled her closer. She closed her eyes and tried to lose herself in the music while she moved her hips in sultry rhythm. Mikaela felt Kat's face shift closer to hers, her earlobes stretched with dark-colored gauges that caught bursts of the colorful lights from above, and she blinked to find Kat watching her intently. Kat trailed a fingertip down Mikaela's jaw as she gazed at her.

Isabella.

Mikaela swallowed hard. It wasn't Kat's hands that she wanted on her, and it wasn't her voice she wanted murmuring near her ear about how sexy she looked either.

Mikaela tried to feign interest, but she felt hollow. She wanted so badly to drown in this moment and to let someone else's touch erase the phantom of Isabella, but it felt all wrong. Kat's heady scent—a mixture of cologne, whiskey, and the sharp peppermint of her gum—wasn't the soft warmth of Isabella's skin. Frustration curled in Mikaela's chest as she bit her lip again. She was trying to lose herself tonight, but Isabella was still stubbornly there and threaded through every moment.

"God, you look so hot when you bite your lip like that," Kat said close to her ear. "You must really want to drive me crazy."

As Kat pressed closer into her and her hands dipped lower, trailing over her ass, Mikaela swallowed hard. She needed to get out of there.

"When is your break over?" she asked over the music.

Kat glanced over at the booth. "Shit," she replied. "It was over, like, ten minutes ago." She met Mikaela's eyes wistfully. "I'd better get back before the tracks I set to play are done. Can I find you in a few?"

Mikaela nodded as she extricated herself from Kat's arms and hoped her relief wasn't too obvious. "I'm grabbing another drink."

She turned, confidently stepping around sweaty club-goers without a second glance, as she made a beeline for her private booth instead of the bar. The energy of the evening was subsiding quickly. Suddenly, Tryst felt too loud, too hot, and too tightly packed. Mikaela pressed her fingertips to her temples as she finally reached the booth and slipped past the security guards. Her head was buzzing, not just from the alcohol but from everything she had tried to forget tonight. She blinked, the table before her precariously close to appearing as though it was tilting, before meeting Dayanara's concerned face floating a few feet away.

"You okay, Mika?" Dayanara asked.

"I'm ready to go," Mikaela replied, unable to keep the rawness from her voice. "I…I should get home."

"Good choice," she said with an understanding nod. "Alejandro is outside on the roof deck chatting up some woman who caught his eye." She scoffed. "But no matter. I'll let the royal security guards in the car outside know to send another vehicle for him when he's ready to leave. Shall we?"

Mikaela nodded as she hooked her elbow into Dayanara's and they were led out by nightclub security. Mikaela knew that Dayanara understood she wasn't running from Tryst—she was running from the only person she couldn't seem to escape.

Chapter Twenty-nine

Mikaela groaned and threw her arm over her face as the morning sunlight streamed through her bedroom window and stabbed at her temples like a dagger. A bird somewhere in the distance cawed loudly, something Mikaela was sure it was doing just to taunt her. Her stomach roiled as she rolled onto her side, and she wondered if she was starving for something greasy or ready to run into the bathroom and throw up.

"Daya," Mikaela croaked. "Kill me. Just off me right now."

Dayanara perched on the edge of her bed, already dressed for the day, and handed Mikaela a glass of water and two ibuprofen. "No need," she said. "You did a fabulous job of that yourself last night."

Mikaela cracked an eye open and glared at her. She winced as she scooted to sit up in bed and pushed her tangled hair out of her face. *God, I need a shower.* "Never let me drink that much again."

"I *tried* to keep things under control," Dayanara said with a shrug. "You were determined to self-destruct with vodka and bad decisions. Maybe it was too soon for Alejandro and I to drag you to Tryst. We honestly just thought it would be good to get you out of this depressing house for the night."

"It's not depressing," she replied stubbornly. She popped the painkillers and took a long swig of water. "I have an amazing view from that deck."

"You wouldn't know it from the way you've parked yourself on that sofa downstairs anytime you're not in meetings," Dayanara shot back. "Lesson learned, I suppose. Vodka is *not* your friend and maybe just hanging out at my place or at Alejandro's residence would have been smarter than forcing you out to Tryst."

Mikaela groaned again as she flopped back onto her pillows. "I can't decide if I want a big, greasy burrito for breakfast or if it'll make me puke in an hour." She sighed. "At least I made a scene."

"A beautiful one. You were dressed to kill and daring anyone to look twice at you. Oh, and you danced very publicly and *very* suggestively with the DJ before you got all angsty and depressed about Isabella and told me you were ready to leave. I was proud of you for not taking it further with the DJ, though. She would *certainly* have been into it. But I know you would've woken up feeling five hundred times worse than you do now."

Mikaela sighed. "Thanks for looking after me, Daya."

"You know, I'm surprised," Dayanara went on lightly. "For someone who has such control over herself at all times, you were certainly playing the part of someone with a shattered heart last night."

Mikaela glared down at her legs beneath the thick comforter but didn't say anything.

"Keep drinking the water," Dayanara said. "One of Terese's people will be by shortly with menudo and huevos rancheros. Try to eat what you can."

Mikaela took a long sip of water as she sat up further. Her head still throbbed at the base of her skull and along her temples, but her mind was clearer now. As she glanced at Dayanara, something tugged at her. She recalled her conversation with Alejandro about Dayanara and Ian, though it felt so long ago now.

"Can I ask you something?"

Dayanara laughed. "You just did, but sure."

Mikaela ignored her. "I may have been a little drunk, but I remember Ian sitting with us for a while. You two still have feelings for each other. Why won't you try again?"

Dayanara faltered slightly as she glanced down at her hands. "Honestly, Mika? Because Ian's end game has always been to move back to Ireland eventually. It's why we broke things off the first time. He wants to get married and start a family. But he wants to do that in Ireland and settle there, so he can be close to his parents again."

Mikaela waited, sensing there was more.

"And, I mean," Dayanara went on as she rubbed her temples. "If I get back together with him, it's with this knowledge. And that would mean agreeing to move to Ireland. Not right away, but maybe in some months? A year? Ian even told me he would like to bring my mom with us, so she's not here alone."

Mikaela shrugged. "So? That sounds great."

"Don't you understand, Mika? If I move forward with Ian, that means letting go. Of *everything* in Cayo Azul, including you."

"Letting go?" Mikaela asked.

"Mika, I've been your shadow since we were small children. I'm your unofficial lady-in-waiting. I've always been the one helping coordinate your meetings and events, accompanying you everywhere, making sure you don't spiral into royal madness." She laughed. "You know, making sure you don't punch the wrong people..."

Mikaela rolled her eyes good-naturedly. "I *don't* punch people and I am *not* spiraling into royal madness."

"The point is, Mika, I've been by your side for so long. And it's been an amazing ride, like a dream. How many other women our age can say they're best friends with a literal princess and, oh yeah, she's actually a great person too? I don't…I don't know what it means to *not* be your companion every day. That scares me a little."

Mikaela was quiet for a long moment and then reached for her hand. "I love you, but you're *allowed* to be happy, Daya," she said. "Not that I think you're miserable, but I understand that you have your own life too and that our paths may not always be meant to be walked side by side. If you have strong feelings for Ian, I *want* you to choose that. Even if it means living in another country."

"What about you? What if you need me?"

"Daya, we are thirty years old," she replied. "You are the greatest friend I ever could've hoped to have. You're also a grown woman who deserves a life of love and happiness. *And* I am incredibly self-sufficient."

Dayanara scoffed. "Are you, Mika? Here you are, hungover from drinking yourself into oblivion. All because you won't admit your heart is broken and you're wallowing in the refusal to acknowledge that you're deeply in love with Isabella."

Mikaela took a deep breath. *She's right.*

"Okay, fine," she conceded after a moment. "I made some questionable decisions last night, but it's not your burden to carry. We'll always be friends, no matter what. Please don't stay here just because you think you have to or out of some sense of duty. You deserve to fall in love and Ian is a great guy."

Dayanara swallowed hard and shook her head with a chuckle. "Damn it, Mikaela," she said. "Why are you making me emotional when *you're* the hungover one?"

Mikaela laughed. "Maybe heart-to-hearts are easier when my brain is half-functioning."

Dayanara wiped at her face. "You'll have to work on that for Isabella's sake," she replied. "You really think I should go for it with Ian?"

"I *know* you should. That man can't stop looking at you. You'll be married in the Irish countryside before you know it. And, by the way, I'd *better* be your maid of honor."

Dayanara stood as the doorbell rang. Mikaela wrinkled her nose and covered her ears at the high-pitched *ding* that seemed to reverberate extra-loudly through her home.

"The kitchen works fast," Dayanara said teasingly. "One hangover breakfast, coming up."

Mikaela groaned again as she swung her legs over the side of the bed and grimaced as she ran a hand through her tangled hair. "Thanks, Daya," she replied. "I'm taking a quick shower to get last night *off* of me, and then I'll be right down."

Mikaela padded into the bathroom and turned the spray to its hottest setting. Despite the incessant throbbing in her skull and despite *everything* happening, she felt inexplicably lighter. It felt good knowing that, no matter what happened next, her best friend would have love.

The worn porch swing creaked as it swayed gently beneath Isabella and her mother. The morning breeze carried the ever-present scent of jasmine mingled with the ocean, alongside the bold scent of freshly brewed coffee from their kitchen. It had been nearly two weeks since Isabella returned to Este and, for the first time in as long, she felt something close to peace.

It wasn't that she found herself moving on—far from it. Mikaela had been deeply hurt, her heart was guarded, and the road ahead was a blur of uncertainty. In the quiet of this morning, though, Isabella felt steady.

"I know that look," her mother said. She nudged Isabella's bare foot lightly with her own. "You're deep in thought."

Isabella exhaled. "I am," she replied. "I…I think I should try to get in touch with Mikaela. I know I hurt her. And maybe the conversation will be more about closure for both of us, but I love her. I won't just let her go. If she tells me that it's truly over, that she really doesn't feel anything for me anymore, then, well, I guess that will be that. And I'll accept it."

Isabella gazed at the front yard as her brain churned through all the possible scenarios. She had the tugging feeling somewhere deep in her chest that it *wasn't* over, that she and Mikaela belonged to each other. Still, if Mikaela refused her then at least she would know to let go. It would be one of the most difficult things Isabella would do, but she felt stronger than she had. More confident and capable. She was certain she would get through it, no matter how much it shattered her heart.

"Good," her mother said with a nod. "I was wondering when you'd say it out loud."

They sat in a comfortable silence for a moment as the morning washed over them with the weight of unspoken words. Isabella glanced into the distance, and she saw an unmarked military vehicle parked at the front of Roberto's long driveway. The sight piqued her interest before she turned away resolutely. She never intended to speak to either Jimenez man again.

"I don't know if Mikaela will take me back," she said. "But I know how it feels when we're together and when we're apart. When we're apart, it feels like something is, I don't know, *off* as the world goes on around us. Like there's some sort of glitch in the universe and things aren't quite right."

"Perhaps you two truly are one another's soulmates," her mother said. "You love each other very much. Despite Mikaela's hurt feelings and bruised pride, real love isn't something that can be flicked off like a light switch. My guess would be that Mikaela has been going through all the emotions too."

"I feel ready for whatever may be next," Isabella said. "Even if it isn't the outcome I so desperately desire."

Her mother tucked a stray lock of hair behind Isabella's ear. "Love isn't about knowing the outcome," she said gently. "It's about fighting for what really matters, even if it pulls you out of your comfort zone and scares you a little bit."

Isabella blinked. Her mother's advice sounded strangely familiar. A wave of memory crashed over Isabella as she recalled Mikaela telling her that the ultimate freedom came from letting go and trusting that everything would turn out okay. The vivid memory twisted something deep in her chest as she wished again that she could go back to that moment with Mikaela, but there was also a pang of hope.

She was right. They're both right.

"Remember, daughter, you're a fighter too," her mother said. "I have witnessed strength and resilience in you since you were small. Your father's drinking, the tumult between him and I, these are all things that could have scarred you." She glanced down at the mug in her hands. "And perhaps they did. I am so sorry for the things you witnessed and for not leaving him sooner. But this has also given you incredible strength and emotional intelligence, my girl, and for that I am so proud. I see you tapping into that now as you realize how strong you really are."

Isabella let that sink in as she took a sip of her cooled coffee. "Thank you, Mami," she murmured. "Have you heard from Papa?"

Her mother shook her head. "Not since he came home a few days ago. This might be it, Isabella. I plan to speak with a lawyer when I get my next paycheck to understand the process around formally filing for divorce. I know it's unconventional here, but I'm feeling strong too. The interview, the manipulation by Roberto, the damage it has caused you? That's it for me."

"Wow, that's a big decision," she replied. "But I understand. You've stayed with him for so long. I don't think he'll ever expect you to file for divorce. I'm proud of you. You deserve happiness too, Mami."

Her mother wiped an eye with the back of her hand. "Yes, I think I do too, my daughter."

Her father had returned to the house for a day or so and had barely acknowledged Isabella's presence before leaving again with what he claimed was a job opportunity in Santa Julianna. Isabella knew her father well enough to know that an urgent job opportunity that required him leaving quickly almost always meant some sort of gambling involved.

"Would you ever consider coming with me? To Castillo Blanco?"

"No, my daughter," she replied. She squeezed Isabella's hand. "This is my home. Besides, once I file for divorce and kick your no-good papa out once and for all, someone has to stay here to make sure this old shack doesn't collapse."

Isabella nodded, unsure why she wasn't surprised by her mother's response. She understood, though it was tinged by sadness. Her mother had always loved their home, even if the lives inside of it—her own, her father's—hadn't quite gone the way she had hoped. Isabella knew she loved the quiet rhythms of the village she knew so well and the lengthy nursing career she had built for herself.

As for me? I know I belong with Mikaela.

"But you'll always know where to find me," her mother said. "Este is my home. No matter what Roberto and his men are trying to accomplish with the people here. And I am always a video chat or phone call away."

Isabella thought for a long moment about how her heart was now in two places. It longed for Mikaela while it beat in time with the rhythm of Este and the comfort of the modest house where she knew she'd always find her mother, dried mango to snack on, and a cozy bed to sleep in.

Her mother gave Isabella's hand another comforting squeeze. "Don't let Mikaela go without a fierce fight," she said. "I'll be here whenever you need me."

Isabella squeezed back as her heart steadied in her chest. *No matter what, I'll be okay.*

"I won't," she replied. "I'll contact Lucia, the family's executive assistant, and plan to leave tomorrow morning." She glanced nervously at her mother. "Wish me luck."

Her mother fixed her with a look. "You don't need luck," she replied. "Something tells me that Mikaela knows exactly what she's missing. And if her judgment is still clouded by hurt feelings or that pride of hers? Well, then you *show* her exactly what she's missing when you walk out of Castillo Blanco with your head held high and come right back home. Remember, you're a fighter too, my daughter."

CHAPTER THIRTY

The next morning, Isabella stood in the kitchen as her mother busied herself with wiping down the countertops, pushing things this way and that, as she gripped the rag in her hand.

"Mami," Isabella said as she placed a gentle hand on her mother's shoulder. "I'll be back to check on you soon, yes?"

Her mother nodded as she turned and embraced her tightly. "Yes," she said. "You'll text me once you arrive at Castillo Blanco so I know you arrived safely?"

"Of course," Isabella replied. She took a deep breath as she felt quiet resolution settling deep into her bones. Today, she would return to Castillo Blanco, return to Mikaela, and fight for her. The house was still as Isabella and her mother awaited the unmarked black Escalade. "I'm going to take my coffee outside. Want to join me?"

Her mother shook her head as she busied herself with the stovetop. "Don't take too long," she said as Isabella stepped out the back door. "You said Señora Lucia confirmed a car to pick you up at nine, yes?"

"Yes, Mami," Isabella replied. "I want to thoroughly enjoy this last cup. Don't tell anyone you heard it from me, but the coffee at Castillo Blanco just isn't as good as yours."

"There you go, buttering me up," she said, a blush coloring her cheeks. "You'd better drink fast. It's already 8:40."

Isabella stepped further into the fields behind their house She took a deep breath as the early morning sun warmed her face. As she blinked, her gaze fell on something further out in the field, far beyond their overgrown vegetable garden that had long since been neglected.

Isabella's stomach dropped even as she blinked again. She willed herself to focus and correct what her body seemed to already register. Short black hair flapped in the morning breeze, but the person lying in the tall grass didn't move.

Isabella felt sick to her stomach as she walked quickly and then stopped. The sight of her father, motionless in the wild grass, looked almost peaceful.

He passed out, she told herself as her brain rapid-fired every possible conclusion at her—except the one that all her senses seemed to already understand.

Isabella swallowed hard and started walking toward him again. "Papa?"

Her heartbeat thudded in her chest when he didn't move. Isabella's pace quickened into a sprint. "Papa?"

Isabella slowed again as she approached. The coffee mug dropped from her hands as the truth hit her hard and all at once. Her father's body was too still and his clothes were rumpled and streaked with dried dirt. The stench of old alcohol permeated the air around him as Isabella sank to the ground. Wet dirt stained the knees of her white skinny jeans as she brushed a hand over his sallow cheek. He was unresponsive and cold to the touch.

"You have to get up *now. Now*. Mami is going to be livid that you passed out cold here in the fields."

Isabella's hands shook uncontrollably as she reached out once more. She pressed her fingertips to his neck as she desperately searched for the pulse she already knew wasn't there.

"Oh my God," Isabella breathed as she pulled her hand back as if stung. "Oh my God, he's dead." Her voice sounded foreign in her ears as her mind scrambled for any explanation. Had he fallen? Had his heart given out? Did he drink himself so far into alcohol poisoning that his weakened body had finally given in?

Had someone helped him along?

Isabella desperately wanted to feel *something*, anything, but instead the hollow shock spread through her as it icily extinguished the grief, the anger, and the disbelief that all fought within her. The breeze rustled through the grass again as a bird circled overhead, blocking out the sun.

Isabella scrambled to stand as the realization that she would have to tell her mother twisted deep inside her stomach. "Oh my God," she repeated again as she forced herself to breathe.

"Isabella?" A familiar male voice in the distance called out in concern. "Is everything okay?"

Isabella squinted in the direction of the voice to see Roberto ambling toward her from the edge of where his property met theirs.

"I'm glad to see you back home," Roberto went on. His voice was eerily calm and not quite friendly. "I can't imagine what you must have been going through at the hands of the de Medrenos and their depravity." He smiled at her, but it didn't reach his eyes. "Javi will be happy to know I ran into you out here, but I'm afraid he's got his eye on another young lady at his university these days."

Roberto approached as white-hot anger seeped into Isabella's veins and fueled the shock that already pooled there.

"What are you doing in the dirt?" Roberto asked as he squinted towards her. "Those white pants are filthy. Tell me, did the de Medrenos dress you up and give you an entirely new wardrobe to fit the role of the princess's forced wife?"

A sinister thought struck Isabella as she recalled the unmarked military vehicle she had spied in his driveway earlier. *What if Roberto hurt my father? What if he's coming to finish the job and hurt me now?*

Isabella looked around wildly as panic took over and the initial shock collapsed into pure fight or flight. "Police!" she screamed as loudly as she could. "Call the police, *now*!"

Roberto looked confused as he held up his hands in a calming gesture. "What's going on?"

Isabella kept screaming as Roberto's footfalls grew closer. The last thing she was vaguely aware of, as her limbs felt like molasses and a kaleidoscope of green swirled around her, was her mother sprinting from the house.

"What's going on?" her mother shouted as she waved her phone in her hand. "Isabella? I'm calling the police!"

Isabella wasn't sure if the loud gasp was her mother's, Roberto's, or her own as she collapsed onto the rich earth. The last thing she was aware of was the soft grass tickling her arms as everything went black.

Chapter Thirty-one

Mikaela sighed and blinked at the color-coded spreadsheet on her laptop. Budgets were one of her least favorite aspects of royal business, though the initial budget proposal for the Transportation Department's public bus system project in collaboration with the royal family was an essential piece to moving the project forward.

Though Mikaela hoped to finish her review that evening, the numbers and formulas swam before her. The faint scent of garlic and scratch-made flour tortillas floated beneath the door of her study in Castillo Blanco, and her stomach growled as she wondered when she had eaten last.

She drummed her fingertips on the polished desk and glanced up as the heavy door cracked open, both annoyed and grateful for the intrusion.

"Mikaela." Her mother's head poked through the doorway. "Your father and I would like to speak with you. Please join me in his private study."

Mikaela wrinkled her nose as her mother shut the door behind her. The last few times she had been called to her father's study for a private conversation had led to awful revelations and unwelcome surprises. She stood and followed her mother down the hallway.

"Come in," her father called from the slightly ajar door of his study. Mikaela frowned as she sat in a chair opposite her father's imposing desk.

Late afternoon sun poured through a tall window behind him and illuminated the solemn expressions on her parents' faces. Mikaela's stomach sank as she sensed this private conversation would again fall into the *not good* category.

She hesitated for just a moment as she glanced between their faces. "What's going on?"

They exchanged a glance, the kind Mikaela had understood since she was a child meant that they were pretty much speaking telepathically. She felt a deep swell of longing as she wondered if she'd ever be with someone that long, and love someone that much, that they could speak with only fleeting glances. Isabella's smile, highlighting her deep dimples and sculpted cheekbones, flashed through Mikaela's mind as she shifted uncomfortably on the chair.

As if on cue, her father cleared his throat. "I know it's late in the day and you've been throwing yourself into your work," he said. "We received word from Este a short while ago. Fernando Acosta, Isabella's father, was found dead this morning."

Mikaela froze. She wasn't sure what news she had been expecting, but the death of Isabella's father was not it.

"What?"

"His body was discovered in a field behind their home, on the edge of the Acosta Ramon property," her mother continued. "Lucia has spoken directly with the coroner, and he has already ruled it heart failure. Unfortunately, it appears to be a clear-cut case of organ failure brought on by years of alcoholism. There was no foul play."

Mikaela's pulse roared in her ears as the questions ricocheted through her mind. "Fernando is *dead*?"

Her mother nodded. "Yes, Mikaela. I know it must feel as though the hits keep coming…"

Mikaela stared at the corner of her father's desk as she ran a hand through her hair. The news was too sudden and too final to fully process. Despite the resentment she felt toward the man for the way he had used Isabella and sold out his daughter—and her relationship—for financial gain, it wasn't how she imagined things ending.

"And Isabella?" Mikaela asked.

Her mother's lips set into a thin line as she looked at her hands clasped in her lap. "Most unfortunately, we received word from Este's police chief that it was Isabella who found him. She fainted but has since been resting."

Mikaela inhaled sharply as a pang of *something* tightened her chest. Her father's study felt small and the late afternoon air felt almost too thick to breathe as she imagined the pain and complicated feelings that Isabella must be navigating.

"Oh my God," Mikaela breathed. "I…I…"

"There's more, Mikaela," her mother said. "Isabella was planning to return today. She wanted to talk to you, and I was going to encourage you to listen. To hear what she wished to say. Anyone at all can plainly see that you haven't been yourself since she left. I believe she was hoping to reconcile, or at least request that you hear her out."

"Isabella was coming back?" She repeated. "To…to fight for us? Even after everything that happened?"

Her mother nodded solemnly. "Yes. And now, this." She spread her hands across her lap helplessly. "Of course, she's still in Este…"

Mikaela tuned her mother out as her fingers tightened on the arms of the chair. The feeling of being gut-punched was nearly overwhelming. All the anger she'd held, the pain of betrayal and hurt helping to build impenetrable walls, crumbled under the weight of this news.

"Mikaela," her father said. "Put everything else aside for now. In this moment, Isabella needs you. Go to her."

Mikaela nodded as she stood. Her mind was already made up. "Yes," she replied. "I need to be with her. I'll get a car to Este right now."

As she turned toward the door, her mother's voice stopped her once more.

"Mikaela," she said. "Be gentle with her. Isabella is not just grieving her father and the complicated relationship they may have had. She's also grieving any last chance he would've had to make things right with her. Go easy."

Mikaela nodded as she turned from the study. As she grabbed her laptop and made a beeline for her private residence, unsure how long she would be gone, the news repeated itself in her mind. Fernando was dead. It was deemed heart failure. No foul play was involved. Still, one sentence burned hotter than the rest:

Isabella was planning to return today.

Mikaela's heart felt as though it was slamming against her ribcage as she tossed a few essentials into a black leather Dior messenger bag.

Isabella had been coming back. For me.

The weight of it all hit Mikaela as she glanced out the front door at the familiar headlights pulling up the driveway, with one of the security guards ready to chauffeur her into Este.

I spent nights drowning in heartbreak, in betrayal, and self-pity. But through it all, I wanted *Isabella. I ached for her.* Now, through the shock of this news, Mikaela felt the urgency to find Isabella coursing through her veins as she hopped onto the cool leather backseat of the familiar black Escalade.

Mikaela recalled the anger from their last encounter. The fire still lingered, burning deep inside her, as she remembered how Isabella felt tangled up with her. Heat crept between her thighs as she recalled every inch of Isabella—how she tasted, how she *yielded* under her, how she kissed her just as deeply and fiercely.

Mikaela typed out a text message on her phone to Dayanara:

I was so silly to think I could ever forget her. How foolish to push her away, to think that what we have could be severed so easily.

Her phone trilled with Dayanara's reply:

No shit! It's about time. I just heard the news. Where are u?

Mikaela took a deep breath, typing quickly, and then jabbed the send button.

On my way to Este.

She swallowed hard as her chest filled with the knowledge of just how much she *wanted* Isabella and how much she had *always* wanted Isabella. Knowing that she was hurting, all Mikaela ached to do was take Isabella into her arms, soothe her pain, and remind her exactly where she belonged.

Mikaela glanced down at her phone as one last reply from Dayanara appeared:

Yes! You go, girl. Get to her as fast as you can.

Once I do, I'm going to pull her into my arms and never let go again.

It was time for her to fight for Isabella too.

Chapter Thirty-two

As the Escalade neared the driveway of Isabella's family home, Mikaela's pulse thumped loudly in her ears.

The moment the security guard eased the Escalade into park, Mikaela slammed the door and sprinted up the grassy yard toward the front porch. She knew someone, probably Dayanara or Lucia, would have contacted Isabella ahead of time to let her know that she was on her way, but her heartbeat still pounded wildly against her chest as she stepped onto the porch.

No turning back now.

Before she could raise her hand to knock, the front door swung open. Mikaela drank in the sight of Isabella. Her red-rimmed eyes were wide with shock and her lips parted slightly as though she wasn't sure if Mikaela was real.

Isabella's hair had been swept up into a casual bun and Mikaela longed to brush the loose strands framing her face behind her ear. Her white skinny jeans were hopelessly stained at the knees with dark mud, her pink cami clung to her tanned curves like a second skin, and Mikaela was sure she had never seen a more perfect woman in her life.

"You're really here," Isabella whispered in awe.

Mikaela didn't waste another second. Though her intent was to close the distance between them, cup Isabella's face in her hands, and kiss her senselessly, Mikaela surprised even herself as she fell to her knees.

Isabella froze as she took in the sight of Mikaela, who appeared to be fighting back tears. It was all she could do to keep from diving into Mikaela, right in front of her looking like an absolute fucking goddess.

"Please," Mikaela murmured as she gazed back at her. She clasped Isabella's hands in her own and stroked her fingertips. "Please come back to me, Isabella."

Isabella felt the swell of emotion deep in her belly and she was surprised at how her body reacted before she even had time to process Mikaela's words. She fell to her knees.

Isabella cupped Mikaela's tear-streaked face between her hands and kissed her full lips. "Always," she replied. "I will always come back to you, Mikaela. Never will I ever leave you again. I will be your wife. And you will be our queen."

Mikaela took a deep, shaky breath as they stood together. Isabella couldn't help but marvel at Mikaela's deep vulnerability. For all her cool confidence, royal training, and poised unflappability, Isabella knew she was seeing a side that very few were privileged—and trusted—enough to witness.

Their lips crashed together in a desperate, dizzying kiss that was filled with everything that had been unsaid. Isabella clutched at Mikaela's shirt as the kiss deepened and grew more urgent.

Mikaela pressed Isabella backward into the house and pushed the door shut behind them without breaking the kiss. The world outside and all the things they were battling didn't exist—just the heat between them and the feverish way that Isabella clung to Mikaela. She wasn't sure if she was trembling from grief, need, desire, something deeper, or a culmination of everything, but Mikaela held her steady as Isabella pulled back just enough to take a deep breath.

"I love you," Isabella choked out. She cursed the way her voice broke so easily. "I love you forever, Mikaela."

Mikaela gripped her waist and rested her forehead against Isabella's. "I know," she murmured fiercely. "I know, cariño. I love you too."

Isabella let out a shuddering breath as she tangled her fingers in Mikaela's hair and desperately tried to re-memorize the feeling of her. "I thought I'd lost you."

Mikaela shook her head and pressed a kiss to Isabella's temple, then her jaw, and finally the spot just behind her ear. "Never," she murmured against her skin. "I won't let you go again."

Isabella exhaled as she melted into Mikaela. The kiss was slower this time, and deeper. Isabella's hands slid just under the hem of Mikaela's shirt as she reveled in the silky warmth of her skin.

This is where we belong. Together. No more doubts, no more secrets, no more walls. Just us.

❖

"My mom," Isabella whispered as she playfully bit down on Mikaela's bottom lip. "She's in the shower and will be out soon. We…we should go to my bedroom."

Mikaela stepped back as she took a deep breath, her gaze locked onto Isabella's. "There is nothing I would love more," she said. "But I'd like to meet your mother. I…I'm sorry, I should have shared my condolences first; I just saw you and—"

Isabella cut Mikaela off with a gentle kiss. "I know. I felt it too, the second I opened the door and saw you standing there. You're everything I want, Mikaela. *Everything*."

Mikaela wrapped her arms around Isabella again. "I'd like to talk with your mom," she said. "And of course the Crown will help in any way with… arrangements or anything your family needs. Perhaps we could take your mom to dinner, if she's up for it."

The sound of a throat clearing made both Mikaela and Isabella turn expectantly. Isabella's mother padded from the narrow hallway, her wet hair in a clip, as she absent-mindedly finished pushing dangly jade-colored earrings through her earlobes. "Now, why would we go out to dinner when you have the best cook in Este right here, if I do say so myself?"

"It's nice to meet you, Señora Ramon," Mikaela said. "I'm so sorry for your loss. Please, I wouldn't want you to cook tonight."

She fixed Mikaela with a slightly bemused look as Isabella glanced down at her bare feet. "Just let her cook," Isabella whispered. "It's a thing with her. She loves it. It gives her something to focus on. Really, nothing beats one of Araceli Ramon's home cooked meals."

"If I may, Your Highness," her mother said hesitantly. "In our shared culture, cooking is more than just survival. It's in our blood and our stories. This is how we show love and how we honor the memories and strength of our ancestors."

Mikaela listened intently as she considered her words. It had been so long since she dove deep into Cayo Azulean culture and what it really meant; she had been so wrapped up in royal life, her duties to the Crown, and the desire to push Cayo Azul into a lucrative future.

Maybe in all of that, I've lost sight of what it really means to be Cayo Azulean.

"Can I give you a hug?" she asked, her arms already outstretched and her feet only two steps from Mikaela. "I'd like to get to know you, Your Highness."

Mikaela startled, leaning awkwardly into her warm embrace, and then relaxed as she wrapped her into a tight hug. "Of course," she replied. "Thank you. Please, call me Mikaela."

As Araceli led them to the kitchen table, she puttered around the kitchen and took a few ingredients from the pantry, a few pots and utensils from nearby cabinets, and continued. "You know, my mother taught me to cook when I was a girl. She used to say that a well-cooked meal is a prayer. Not in the religious sense, but rather a way of saying I see you. I care for you. You are safe here and you are home."

She glanced at Mikaela over the countertop as her hand hovered above a ripe tomato. "That's why I've always cooked for Isabella," she said. "And why I'm cooking for you tonight. Food for us isn't just food. You know that. It's trust. It's love. It's family."

Mikaela swallowed hard.

"Besides, it gives me something to do." Isabella's mother waved a hand. "The kitchen is my solace. I know it's nothing compared to what you're used to at the castle, but it's the love in the food that matters, eh? And that's something I can say I'm very proud of. *Almost* as proud as I am of my Isabella."

Isabella rolled her eyes dramatically at Mikaela, but she didn't miss the flush that colored her cheeks. Mikaela thought of Isabella and how deeply ingrained the Cayo Azulean culture was in her, and in Este. She thought of how Isabella always closed her eyes for just a split second at the first bite of something good, when she thought no one was looking. She thought of how she *felt* everything so deeply, so similarly to her, even when she tried to hide it. Mikaela wanted to lean over the table and kiss Isabella again, but instead pressed her palms together over her crossed legs.

"All right, Mami," Isabella said. "Can I help you with anything?"

She turned to Mikaela, an amused question in her gaze. "*What*?" She mouthed at her.

Mikaela sensed too late that she was staring as Araceli waved her hand again. "No, no, no," she replied. "The pozole rojo will take a couple of hours. I'll get some fresh salsa together and chips for you both to eat in the meantime. Perhaps you'd like to show Princess Mik…er, *Mikaela* around the house. The priest won't be back until tomorrow morning to confirm all final arrangements, and I don't think any more neighbors will be dropping by. The evening should be quiet for us now."

Mikaela stood abruptly as she followed Isabella. She squeezed Araceli's hand. "Again, I am so sorry for your loss, Señora," she said. "And thank you. For everything. For letting me be here. For trusting me with Isabella."

Araceli squeezed back as she shot Mikaela a knowing look. "I knew you'd come around," she replied. "Perhaps not literally and certainly not under these circumstances, but I'm glad you're here, Mikaela. Just don't let Isabella go hungry," she teased her. "And don't leave her heart empty either. Please. Because she is *my* heart."

Mikaela nodded as she understood the weight of what she was promising to Isabella's mother. "I won't," she replied. "Her heart will always be safe with me." She perked up. "Though perhaps you can share some of your recipes with me. I can't promise they'll turn out as good, but I can try."

Isabella padded back into the kitchen as she overheard Mikaela's last sentence. "You? Cook?" She raised an eyebrow at her incredulously. "Mika, that's a lovely sentiment, but you barely know how to turn on a stove." She giggled. "*I'll* stick to cooking Mami's recipes for us, yes?"

As they laughed and Mikaela followed her toward the bedrooms, Isabella slipped her hand into Mikaela's and turned. "Don't change anything about yourself, love," she murmured. "You're perfect. Even if you're hopeless when it comes to food."

Chapter Thirty-three

As the evening stretched into nighttime, the rich, savory scent of Araceli's pozole rojo wafted through the small house, and the air between Isabella and Mikaela was thick with heat and desire. It was all Mikaela could do to keep herself from pouncing as Isabella led her into her bedroom, closing the door behind them, and patted the space on the mattress next to her.

Mikaela gazed at her for a long moment before kissing Isabella with slow, all-consuming purpose. A thrill shot up her spine as Isabella yielded beneath her, parting her lips to allow Mikaela's tongue entry, and arched herself further into her trailing, exploring fingertips. The sheets tangled around them as they took their time rediscovering, seeking, and claiming as each touch silently promised *forever*.

"Mikaela," Isabella panted as she sunk further into the pillows. "I want you so bad. *Everywhere*. I've dreamt about this moment and how hard you make me co—"

The sharp chime of Mikaela's phone was an unwelcome intrusion as Mikaela groaned against her skin. She had just finished tracing the curve of Isabella's collarbone with her lips and was working toward her neck as it chimed again, more insistently.

"Ignore it," Isabella murmured as her fingers tightened on Mikaela's hips.

Mikaela reached blindly toward the nightstand for her phone. *God, how I want to.*

As she blinked at the small screen, a photo of her mother on the deck of a yacht off the coast of Santorini a few summers ago flashed back at her.

Mikaela sighed as she flopped back against the bed. "It's my mother," she replied. "Probably checking in."

As Mikaela accepted the video call, she saw that her black shirt was rumpled and her lips were practically swollen from Isabella's slow, deep kisses.

Cristina's sharp, ever-composed face filled the screen. "Mikaela," she said and then her gaze narrowed slightly. "Am I, uh, *interrupting* something?"

Mikaela ran a hand through her messy hair as she tried in vain to appear poised. "Nothing really."

She felt Isabella stifle a giggle as she laid her head on Mikaela's stomach, out of view of the phone's camera, and lazily traced patterns along her thighs.

Her mother didn't look convinced but took a deep breath. "And how is Isabella doing?"

Mikaela wasn't sure why she was surprised. It wasn't like her mother was *heartless*, she was just more so typically...uninterested in dissecting tough emotions.

Perhaps she actually took a liking to Isabella.

She glanced down at Isabella and idly ran her fingertips through a lock of soft hair that had fallen from her loose bun. "She's doing well," Mikaela said. "As you can imagine, it's been a lot, but she's happy that I'm here."

Isabella turned slightly and gave a silent nod in sweet confirmation as she continued tracing her fingers along her legs.

"I'm glad to hear that," her mother replied. "I must brief you on the latest intel. As you know, there have been a lot of moving pieces happening at once as we stay in front of the original story in the media. Now word has begun to get out, which we knew it would, about Fernando's unexpected death."

Mikaela glanced down at Isabella as her fingertips stilled. They both carefully sat up as Mikaela pointed to the hallway to let her know she'd finish the video call there.

The last thing Isabella needs right now is to hear the down and dirty details of her father's death. She looked once more over her shoulder as she slipped out of the bedroom. *No matter how much of an ass he was.*

"The optics of Fernando's death are so far *very* bad, Mikaela," her mother said.

Mikaela tensed as she leaned against the rough stucco wall. "What does that mean?"

Her mother exhaled. "There are already awful rumors floating around, originating in Este of course, that our family had him killed as a result of the interview. And that *you* may have orchestrated this as revenge."

Mikaela's heart pounded as anger and panic flooded her veins. "That's *ridiculous—*"

"Of course I know that," her mother cut in. "But, as you know, public perception and our people's *trust* in us is everything. Your father has personally dispatched a team of intelligence officers to officially open an investigation into this resistance movement, since Juan has been dragging his feet on doing so. They are using this discord to their advantage and they are moving quickly."

Mikaela glared at her mother through the screen. "Oh, that's rich, considering Uncle Juan was the one who orchestrated the grand plan of paying Isabella's family. He's just as much to blame for practically gift-wrapping this for them to use against us, and I do *not* make that accusation lightly."

Her mother sighed. "I understand that your father and Eduardo are handling that," she replied. "Now is not the time for more fracturing within our family. That's exactly what this resistance wants, and every splinter we give them will only weaken us and fortify their organizers."

Mikaela's hand clenched into a fist. "I came here to be with Isabella in her time of need and to fix what had been broken between us," she said. "Now the outside world wants to drag us right back into this chaos that we did not create."

Her mother frowned as she adjusted the position of her phone. "I will not allow you to be *anyone's* pawn, Mikaela. Please know that plainclothes security has been deployed throughout Este for the length of your stay as a proactive precaution. Though I do urge you and Isabella to return to Castillo Blanco as soon as Fernando is put to rest."

Mikaela nodded reluctantly. "Luckily, Araceli and Isabella requested a private service for family only, given the scrutiny," she replied. "That means no curious residents and no Roberto or Javier Jimenez. No one except Araceli, Isabella, myself and some of their extended family."

"That's good," her mother said. "I also wanted to make you aware that an official protest has been organized in City Center in the coming months. Of course, this is being organized by Roberto's group so I am glad he will not be at Fernando's services. He cannot be trusted, certainly not in proximity to you. Until the intelligence team gathers every detail possible to allow us to understand our options and whether we can legally impeach him from the mayoral council, we cannot yet act."

"A protest?" Mikaela repeated incredulously. In her lifetime, she had never heard of such a thing on Cayo Azul. "This is our *home*. Our island. It is in our *blood*."

"We're already ahead of it. Eduardo and Juan have been working with the police force to ensure they are on standby when this happens. We cannot disallow the right to protest, Mikaela. But we must be realistic and acknowledge this as both uncharted territory for Cayo Azul and a clear sign of serious unrest."

The pit in Mikaela's stomach grew as she considered the ramifications of this growing resistance. It was time to show strength and unity, and to quell the discontent before it spiraled out of their control. "We'll be back after the funeral."

"Good." Her mother nodded. "For now, be mindful of being in Este. You are protected and, in addition to the plainclothes security, there are also royal guards taking shifts in an unmarked trailer parked a few yards from the Acosta Ramon property. Mikaela, just…just please be careful."

As the call ended, the heavy silence in the hallway felt deafening. Mikaela slipped back into the bedroom and tossed her phone onto the nightstand before flopping back onto the bed.

"Unbelievable," she muttered.

Isabella squeezed her hand tightly.

"Whatever is going on, we'll face it together," Isabella murmured as she curled into Mikaela and gently kissed her collarbone. "But for now, what can we do?" Isabella stretched next to her and Mikaela's breath slowed at the feeling of her skin brushing against her own. "Except help each other forget, even for a little while." Isabella took a deep breath. "Please." The last word fell as a whisper from her lips. The fire in her expression pleaded with Mikaela to take her and to let them both lose themselves in one another.

Mikaela sat up on her elbows, cupped Isabella's face with one hand, and kissed her deeply. After a long moment, Isabella pulled away.

"On second thought, I do need a shower," she said suggestively.

Mikaela blinked at her. "Now?"

Isabella stood from the bed and reached down with both hands to pull Mikaela up. "You could use a shower too, right?" She leaned close, her breath tickling Mikaela's ear.

"But…but…" Mikaela glanced at the closed door and bit her lip. It had been a long time since she'd had to worry about being caught by someone's parent, and she felt a bond forming with Araceli that she didn't want to risk. "What about your mother?"

Isabella gave her a knowing look. "She won't disturb us. She has a lot on her mind right now and I know she wishes to also allow us privacy this evening."

Mikaela raised an eyebrow, torn. It would be humiliating to have Araceli find them, but the thought of Isabella, soft and naked, under the wet spray…

Isabella grinned as she turned and slipped out the bedroom door. She loosened her bun and let her hair cascade down her back. "If you'd rather rest, of course, you can do that too. But if you change your mind, you know where to find me…"

She's teasing me and she knows it. And I like it. Time to remind Isabella exactly who she belongs to.

Mikaela followed her into the bathroom as Isabella turned on the spray and carefully undressed. As she stepped into the steaming shower, the wet haze curled through the small bathroom as the mirror fogged and the air temperature spiked. Mikaela undressed as she followed Isabella in and gasped at the delicious feeling of warm water cascading down their bodies.

Mikaela positioned herself behind Isabella, her body pressed firmly against her own, and squirted liquid soap into her hands as she casually explored Isabella's body. She glided her fingertips slowly and deliberately over the slick curves and soft skin she knew so well.

"You know you're still mine," Mikaela murmured against the shell of Isabella's ear. She kissed her neck as she felt Isabella shiver under her touch. She brushed her fingertips against Isabella's nipples and she casually circled them, relishing how hard they became under her touch. As she teased Isabella's nipples beneath her fingers, she enjoyed the way Isabella's breath hitched and she leaned back further into her hold.

"You know I am." Isabella's head fell back against Mikaela's shoulder. "You feel so good."

Mikaela teased the tip of her tongue along Isabella's neck as she savored her trembling body, already so excited, and the way her wet skin glided against her own. "I need to hear it," she said in a low voice. She dipped one hand lower along Isabella's flushed skin, as she continued teasing her sensitive nipple with the other. "Tell me you're still mine."

Isabella let out a soft, unsteady breath. "I…I need you to *take* me so badly, Mikaela."

She pinched Isabella's nipple, just enough to give her a split-second shock that she knew echoed through her body, before continuing her light, controlled teasing. She stepped back and gently turned Isabella so she was facing her, enjoying her little groan of frustration at the sudden loss of contact.

"Say it properly," Mikaela replied firmly. She took in the sight of Isabella, naked, wet, flushed, and already *so* ready for her. Her gaze finally settled onto Isabella's face through the steamy mist surrounding them.

Isabella didn't break their gaze. "I'm yours, Mikaela. Always."

Fire and desire flared in Mikaela's chest as she buried a hand in Isabella's wet hair and rewarded her with a deep kiss. She filled Isabella's ready mouth with her tongue as she continued kissing her. Isabella's fingernails clawed into her back as she desperately pressed herself into Mikaela again.

Mikaela couldn't stop her moan as Isabella's wet nipples rubbed against her own and sent white-hot streaks of pleasure straight between her thighs. She understood her dominance when it came to Isabella wasn't exactly about control—it was about *knowing*. She knew exactly how to unravel Isabella and how to push her to the edge until she was trembling, begging, desperate for something only Mikaela could give to her so perfectly, and it was then that Mikaela would pull her back or let her fall.

And *God*, how she wanted Isabella to fall every time, so she could catch her, claim her surrender, soothe her, protect her, and pick her right back up into her arms.

As the hot water coursed over them, Mikaela knelt until she was level with Isabella's slick folds. She was swollen with desire and she could smell Isabella's scent, even as rivulets of water traced paths down her stomach, her thighs, and her legs.

With the water beating against her back, simultaneously burning and soothing the spots where Isabella's nails had already made their marks, Mikaela gently pulled one of Isabella's legs over her shoulder. Isabella leaned hard against the corner of the shower as her palms splayed against the smooth tiles and sought grip somewhere, anywhere, until her hands found their way into Mikaela's hair.

Mikaela ran her tongue along the full length of Isabella's folds and relished the gasp she elicited. She gently plunged two, then three fingers into her as she lapped at her clit. She wasn't going to show her body any mercy tonight; it had been too long and she wanted to *feel* Isabella's inner walls tighten and explode against her fingers. She wanted to lick Isabella's desire from her own lips, taste every drop of her orgasm on her tongue, and hear her moan her name between ragged breaths.

As Mikaela curled her fingers inside Isabella and gently opened her lips over her hard, swollen bud, Isabella angled herself harder and deeper into her mouth. Mikaela teased Isabella, finding her clit over and over again. Each time she felt Isabella start to tighten around her fingers, she would slide her tongue away, instead running the length of her clit from the top of her hood to the opening where her fingers pulsed in and out.

All Mikaela could feel was steam swirling around her and wet mist intermingled with Isabella's desire dripping down her face. Each time she slid her tongue away, Isabella would groan in frustration, trembling, and shift this way and that as she tried to force Mikaela's tongue back to *that* spot. Mikaela was overcome with the raw, breathless *need* to be closer, to draw out Isabella's orgasm for as long as she could in order to fully relish her surrendering against her.

Mikaela gently stroked her fingers in and out of Isabella as she reached up with her other hand to tease her slick, already-sensitive nipple between her fingertips. Isabella moaned, pushing against Mikaela's mouth, as she found her clit again, teasing and roaming with firm, sure confidence.

Mikaela knew the tension coiled deep within Isabella was too much as the sensations overrode everything else. Suddenly, Isabella was bucking, pulsing against her lips, her tongue, and her face, her hands wound tightly in Mikaela's hair, as her inner walls shuddered over and over again against her fingers.

Isabella slumped against Mikaela as the still-running water cascaded over them. Mikaela wrapped her arms around her and pressed lingering kisses up Isabella's stomach, her chest, her arms, and finally to her lips as she stood.

"I love you," Mikaela murmured against her damp skin.

Isabella sighed as she melted further into her. "I love you too."

Mikaela turned off the water and the rhythmic drizzling faded into oblivion. "I'm not sure if that's the type of shower you had in mind…"

Isabella threw her head back and laughed as she wrapped a towel around herself and handed one to Mikaela. "That is *exactly* the kind of shower I had in mind," she said as she ran a hand through her wet hair. "This has been the craziest, most insane day with the biggest highs…and the most unexpected lows." Isabella appeared to shake it off as she shot Mikaela a look. "And it's not over yet. I'm going back to the bedroom, I'm going to lie on the bed, and you're going to ride my face just like I practically lost my mind right now riding yours."

The tight heat between Mikaela's legs, along with the tantalizing thought of Isabella's tongue on her, was nearly too much to bear.

Even as exhaustion finally settled in much later that night, the stark reality of everything going on clouded around the edges of their satisfactory bliss. As Isabella faded into sleep on her chest, Mikaela kept her arms tight around her. From now on, she was unwilling to surrender even an inch of space between them.

CHAPTER THIRTY-FOUR

Two days later, Fernando had finally been laid to rest. The day had begun early at the funeral home, where Araceli and Isabella accepted members of their extended family who had traveled from Spain and other parts of Cayo Azul to pay their respects. Araceli, Isabella, Mikaela, and some of their extended family walked solemnly behind Fernando's casket, led by the local priest, in a small procession down the dusty street to the local cemetery. Several royal guards flanked the procession to ensure Mikaela's safety among the curious onlookers who had gathered at the edges of the street.

Though Mikaela wanted to support Isabella and Araceli during this time, she was acutely aware of the simmering undercurrent surrounding them and fought the urge to look over her shoulder, through the intricate black lace of her mantilla, for Roberto or one of his men to shout something at them from afar. Aside from a few curious stares, some respectfully bowed heads, and a group of older women who crossed themselves as the procession passed, she was grateful that the most public-facing part of the services was quiet and uneventful.

Mikaela blinked at the tall iron cemetery gates a few yards ahead.

It's almost over. The thought had just filled her with something akin to relief as movement in her periphery caught her eye. There was a ripple, almost too small to notice, as a weathered older man on the outskirts of the curious onlookers began darting in and out of the throngs of people.

His wiry gray hair was matted to his temples as he pressed what appeared to be flyers into the onlookers' hands from a sheaf of paper clutched against his chest. Mikaela watched with rising suspicion as they glanced down at the paper and back at him as murmurs began to buzz along the narrow street.

At that moment, the man glanced up toward the procession and Mikaela felt an uncharacteristic knot of discomfort in her stomach as his stare locked onto her.

There's no possible way he could know who I am. I'm partially covered by my mantilla and I'm surrounded by security and Isabella's family.

"Join us!" the man shouted as he rushed toward the funeral procession. "Know the truth about your government or this"—he gestured at the polished casket—"this will continue. Let them hear your voice!"

Gasps echoed down the street as the royal security team intercepted him before he could shove his flyers into the hands of the small group of funeral-goers.

"I don't think so, brother," one of the guards said as he gripped the man's upper arms tightly. "Not today."

"Fight!" the man shouted as two more guards rushed to help the first. "How can you call me brother? You are with *them*." He tried to lift his arm to point at the procession, but the security guard's grip was too tight. "The Crown, desperate to cover up a mess at the expense of us! Fight, people of Este! We cannot trust those in power."

As the security guards roughly shoved and pulled the man away and down a nearby alley, the remaining papers fluttered to the chipped cobblestone in their wake. The scuffle of the security guards' polished boots down the alley and the echoing shouts of the man as he was placed under arrest pounded in Mikaela's temples.

"Are you okay, my love?" Isabella interlaced her fingers in Mikaela's, squeezing tightly.

Mikaela nodded as she glanced down at a lone flyer that had drifted to the curb before the cemetery gates. The bold black ink was smeared, but the large words printed across the flyer were clear:

Question everything. Demand better. Take back the power.

The Crown cannot be trusted.

Beneath, details of an "Este Town Hall" were shared, urging residents to gather and join the movement. Even as the procession continued into the cemetery, the words on the flyer burned into Mikaela's brain as her chest tightened. It felt as though ice was running through her veins as she processed that Este was now taking boldly to the streets.

Mikaela swallowed hard, willing herself to focus on the final part of Fernando's funeral, but the ice in her veins had coalesced into a tiny pulse of warning that beat in time with her heart. Urgency rose in her chest as she understood this was something that could no longer be pushed aside.

We'll return to Castillo Blanco first thing tomorrow morning. The storm within her quelled as she felt Isabella's fingers still firmly interlocked in her own. *I will fix this and bring our people together.*

❖

The house was silent as they arrived later that evening, the sudden stillness welcome after a day of distraction, activity, and tradition as Fernando was laid to rest. Araceli carefully lit a tall white candle depicting el virgen de Guadalupe in the living room window.

"I haven't lit this candle in a long time," she said. "Not since my own mother passed. But I have lit it every night since Fernando passed to ask for her intercession. Fernando would get so angry when I would pray on behalf of him."

The candle flickered across the small living room as long shadows danced over the walls and the scent of salt from the ocean breeze drifted through the open kitchen window.

Isabella sat at the kitchen table. "He didn't understand, Mami," she replied. "Too much had happened and he had too much anger and resentment. I believe…" she swallowed hard. "I *have* to believe he's at peace now."

Mikaela sat beside Isabella and hoped her hand on the small of her back was a gentle, steady sign of reassurance. She recalled her mother's advice as she left Castillo Blanco. *Just listen. Isabella isn't just mourning her father; she's mourning any chance, no matter how small, they could have had to repair their relationship.*

The weight of all the complicated emotions hung heavy in the air as Araceli gazed out the living room window for a long moment. "He was a hard man to love. I had planned to leave. In fact, I was sure I was going to this time. But, my God, that didn't mean I wanted him to *die.*" She took another deep breath. "I did love him once. We were so young. It was practically another lifetime."

Isabella blinked and pressed her hands to the table. "Mami…"

Araceli turned quietly. "He made so many mistakes. I don't think he ever understood exactly how much they cost him. Not until it was too late anyway. I wish you could have remembered him before, my daughter. You were so small when he turned to alcohol after being discharged from the military. I never told you why, did I?"

Isabella shook her head as discomfort bloomed in Mikaela's chest, the strange feeling of her uncle's oversight of the military somehow ruining Isabella's father causing a bolt of guilt, however unfounded, to slice through her.

"He joined the military in hopes of achieving a better life for us," Araceli said. "For you. You were just a baby, and we struggled with the rising costs you still see today. He was about to return to Este on a short leave and I had called him crying because we didn't have any diapers. I tried to sew cloth diapers for you to save money, but they never quite worked." Araceli glanced affectionately at Isabella. "Your skin was so sensitive and you always soaked through them so quickly. It was still another week until he expected his stipend, so he and another young father in his battalion snuck out late one night. They had a detailed plan, and they stole boxes of diapers from a grocery store in Santa Julianna. They almost got away with it too." Araceli glanced wistfully at the flickering candle. "But they did get caught. Unfortunately, the rules within the armed services are very clear, no room for interpretation. He was removed and dishonorably discharged. I wish you could've had the opportunity to know him before. He wasn't so bad then."

Isabella looked away as a tear slipped down her cheek. "I never knew," she said. "After everything he did, after the lies, the instability, the deals he made, I wish I could just hate him. It would make all of this so much easier. But I can't and I don't think I ever will. Instead, it just leaves a lot of sadness."

Mikaela leaned closer to Isabella. "You shouldn't hate him," she said. She brushed her hand against Isabella's wrist. "Even though your relationship was complicated, I know you don't really want to have hate in your heart. He was still your father and knowing what he sacrificed shows that he loved you very much. Besides, letting hate fester changes you at your core. And I know so many people who love you for exactly who you are, Isabella."

Isabella's lips parted, but there were no words as she tried to blink back the tears that spilled down her cheeks.

Araceli sat at the table and took Isabella's hand. "You don't have to forgive him," she said. "He made many selfish choices. But you don't have to carry those choices either. You have an entire life ahead of you, my daughter. It's all yours to make of it what you wish."

Isabella took a deep breath as she appeared to steady herself. "I need you to know something," she said as she turned to Mikaela.

Mikaela nodded, waiting.

"My mom and I have spoken many times since I've been here," she said, her voice firm despite the emotion trembling just below the surface. "About the payments. We want to return the money that has been given to us. Well, minus whatever my father spent already. It never felt right to accept the arrangement, and it was never right to keep it from you either. I know this doesn't make it okay, but I've been sick over the situation since everything happened. I *never* wanted it, Mikaela, and I would have fallen in love with you no matter what. I know…I know nothing could've stopped that from happening. And I *know* I'm meant to be part of your life."

Mikaela's heart twisted deep in her chest as she held Isabella's gaze. "I know too."

"You do?"

Mikaela nodded as she squeezed her hand. "I do now." She swallowed hard. "There's no need to return the money that has been provided. The de Medreno family honors their commitments, even if, um, we may not have been aware of this one. Going forward, we must stop the payments from the current account because it is tied to our armed services." Mikaela met

Araceli's eyes. "However, we will figure out a way to ensure you are taken care of, Araceli. I'll speak to my father."

Araceli shook her head. "I don't think Fernando ever thought about what would happen once the truth came out about that arrangement," she replied. "He never cared to, and that was always the problem. Act first, consequences later. Even when it meant causing pain for Isabella or myself. You're not obligated to take care of me, Mikaela. My concern is and always has been my daughter."

Isabella's mother stood and moved into the kitchen. "I promise you," Mikaela said, her voice steady. "I will take care of Isabella, now and forever."

"I know you will," she replied. "But you don't just take care of someone you love, Mikaela. You *fight* for them. You put in the work. And you trust them to do the same."

Mikaela considered this. Deep down, she knew Araceli was right.

Isabella let out a quiet giggle. "You're giving Mikaela a lot of wisdom, Mami," she said. "In fact, I'd say you like her, don't you?"

Araceli gave them both a knowing look as she turned back to the stove. "You both need to eat," she replied matter-of-factly. "I'm making something simple so you can go to bed with something warm in your bellies, and I don't want to hear any protests."

"You don't have to fuss over us, Mami."

Araceli poured a generous dollop of olive oil into a pan. "I do when you've barely eaten all day." She turned to Mikaela and dropped a gentle kiss on the top of her head. "And you too, daughter. Let's get one last home-cooked meal in you before you both leave tomorrow."

Mikaela blinked in brief surprise. She couldn't suppress the affection she felt at Araceli's casual tenderness and reference to her as daughter.

As Isabella's mother moved quickly and expertly around the stove, ingredients sizzling to life in the pan, Mikaela wrapped her arm around Isabella and enjoyed the comforting warmth of her head casually on her shoulder.

Who would've thought I'd miss being here in Este just a little bit?

Chapter Thirty-five

Isabella curled against Mikaela on the small sofa angled along the back of her semi-circular white marble balcony. Over Isabella's T-shirt, Mikaela's fingers idly traced patterns along her ribcage as they watched the magnificent sunset that had begun over the ocean.

Isabella was surprised at the reception she received upon returning to Castillo Blanco with Mikaela earlier that afternoon. The security guards eagerly waved them through, and other staff members—from the chefs, housekeepers and grounds crew to even the members of Eduardo's staff that had always been so kind to her—welcomed her back with warm hugs and excited well wishes. Even Alejandro emerged from his private office to wrap an arm around her shoulder.

"Castillo Blanco is far too dull without you," he told her teasingly. "And between you and I, Mikaela *definitely* needs you around. But don't tell her I said that."

Isabella laughed and waved as he promised to see her around soon before ducking back into his office. Still, through it all, it was Mikaela who made it the most real—from the way her hand would confidently find hers as they walked through the castle to the way her gaze never left her face.

As they finally returned to Mikaela's home, with all of Isabella's favorites set out for dinner on the kitchen table as a special welcome back from Terese, she felt for the first time that Castillo Blanco was becoming a home to her too.

"So how many others stayed in my guest suite while I was away?" Isabella teased her as she stroked Mikaela's knuckles. She noted with amusement that the dark maroon polish over her short fingernails was as impeccable as ever. "I hope they were at least tidy. Speaking of that, I should get my luggage over there before it gets too dark. I'm certainly not going to take one of the security guards off duty just to carry my things."

Mikaela glanced at her before she met Isabella's lips in a lingering kiss. As she savored the taste and feel of Mikaela, it occurred to her that she had said something. She blinked and pulled back just slightly.

"What?" Isabella asked as her mind struggled to keep up. After all, it wasn't her fault that kissing Mikaela felt like being sent to an entirely different and totally blissful dimension.

"Stay here," Mikaela murmured against her lips again. "With me. In the house."

Isabella let out a soft laugh as her heart hammered against her chest. "You sure about that, love? No more guest suite?"

Mikaela smiled as she pulled her in again. "Positive," she replied. "After all, I want you to marry me."

Isabella turned to face her in surprise. She brushed her hand along Mikaela's jaw and gently turned her face to her own. "*What*?"

The corners of Mikaela's lips curved up as she studied Isabella's reaction. "You heard me, love."

Isabella sat up straighter. "You're really asking me? You want to get married?"

Mikaela's expression softened into something slightly vulnerable as she held Isabella's gaze. "There's nothing else I want more in this world than to marry you and make you mine forever."

Isabella opened her mouth and then closed it as she pulled Mikaela in for a kiss. She melted further into her, tangling her fingers in her hair, as she held her tightly.

"Is that a yes?" Mikaela whispered against her lips. "I have a ring, I promise. I'll get it from my mother so it can be official. So *we* can be official."

Isabella flopped against the low back of the sofa as something raw and unguarded broke open inside her. "Yes," she said. "Of course that's a yes."

"Good," Mikaela said as she exhaled. She brought Isabella's knuckles to her lips and pressed a lingering kiss to her fingertips. "Now you'll be mine. Forever."

The moment felt electric, and Isabella brushed her lips against the soft skin just below Mikaela's ear as the evening breeze swept across the deck.

"And you're mine."

As the first few days back at Castillo Blanco blurred into a week, Mikaela began to ramp her royal duties back up. She headed casually to her parents' private dining room. She hadn't joined them for breakfast since she had returned to Castillo Blanco with Isabella, but she knew their morning routine like clockwork.

The familiar clink of fine china and the faint rustle of newspaper pages were comfortingly familiar as she pushed open the heavy oak door and sat at the long mahogany dining table. Her father was seated in his usual place at the far head of the table as he casually scanned the business section of the Cayo Azul newspaper. Her mother was seated at the opposite head of the table as she carefully sliced into her egg white and spinach omelet. Their quiet conversation paused as they both turned to Mikaela, with amusement and mild surprise flickering in their expressions.

"Good morning, Mikaela," her mother said. "It's nice to see you. You haven't joined us for breakfast in quite some time."

Her father threw a disarming look at her mother as he took a long sip of hot coffee. "Love, you know she's been taking breakfast at home with Isabella. There's nothing wrong with that. After all, they are in love and newly reunited. Look how much she smiles these days." Mikaela blushed as he gestured at her.

"Isabella and I are engaged," she said casually, as she willed her unshakable confidence to not waver at her parents' looks of quiet surprise. She carefully crossed one leg over the other and picked an invisible piece of lint from her tailored beige pants.

Her mother's teaspoon hovered just above the wide rim of her latte mug as she blinked. "I'm assuming you didn't elaborately get down on one knee," she finally replied as she arched an eyebrow.

Mikaela smiled. "No need," she said. "She said yes anyway."

Her father shook his head as he set the newspaper down. Mikaela sensed the same quiet acceptance that he always gave her when he knew that her mind was unchangeable. "Congratulations, my daughter," he said as he rubbed his chin in thought. "I thought we'd have another conversation after the seventy-five days. Though you have never learned to wait for permission, have you?"

"Not when I am already certain what I want," Mikaela replied as she lifted her chin slightly. A beat of silence stretched between them and Mikaela sighed. "If you had told me weeks ago that this whole idea to find a spouse would actually be successful and that I would fall in love, I would've thought you were crazy. I *did* think you were both crazy. But honestly, Papa? I love Isabella in a way that feels almost like breathing. It's so natural and instinctive, and it's impossible to stop. I tried, and it felt like my heart had been torn out." Mikaela took a deep breath. "She is who I want to marry."

Her father opened and then closed his mouth. He nodded and cleared his throat as Mikaela wondered if he had expected that level of passion from her.

"Then congratulations, my daughter," he said warmly as he placed a hand over hers for a moment.

Her mother's faint nod of acknowledgement wasn't overly sentimental, but Mikaela didn't expect it to be. She sensed her underlying acceptance, as her mother raised her latte mug in a silent toast. What mattered was that she had their approval and that Isabella would officially become a member of their family.

The dining room door opened and Alejandro poked his head in.

"Good morning," he said. "Eduardo sent me an urgent text asking if we have thirty minutes for him at eight."

Her father glanced at his phone. "It'll be eight o'clock in five minutes," he grumbled. "Does he need all of us?"

Alejandro nodded. "I believe he has an update from the intelligence team on the official investigation into the resistance movement," he replied. "He'd like a private meeting as soon as possible to relay his findings. He did mention it was time-sensitive, as it involves the international community."

Her father nodded. "Very well." He shrugged into the tailored suit jacket that had been neatly folded over an empty chair. "Mikaela, this means you too."

Mikaela fell into step with them to a nearby council chamber. Mikaela sat coolly near the head of the table and crossed her arms as Eduardo, always composed in his crisp navy suit, hurried into the room from the other end of the long hallway.

The council chamber wall nearest the door was tastefully decorated with thick-framed antique tapestries and dark oak shelves. A large presentation screen was carefully hung on the opposite wall and, in between, the long table was set with a sleek black speaker and conference phone in the middle.

Eduardo took a deep breath as he sat and handed a bound dossier to her father.

"What was so urgent that you had to send my nephew to interrupt my breakfast?" he asked as he flipped through the sheaf of papers. "Human Rights International? What is this?"

Eduardo leaned forward slightly. "We've been monitoring discussions that the resistance movement has been having online," he said. "The payment arrangements and the interview with the Acosta-Ramon family has driven attention to Cayo Azul by some of our neighboring governments. Most of it has just been curious so far, perhaps mildly concerned, but the sentiment overall is that the de Medreno family rules Cayo Azul and will continue to do so."

Her father nodded. "Of course."

Eduardo sat back. "However, Fernando Acosta's unexpected death has raised discussion within some of the international human rights organizations, particularly Human Rights International. I am increasingly concerned that they may consider launching a formal investigation into the financial payments made to Isabella's family."

Mikaela stiffened. "An investigation?"

Her father exhaled sharply as he rubbed his temple. "Has there been an official announcement yet?"

Eduardo shook his head. "As of now, nothing has been announced. The whispers, however, are concerning. This is not the kind of international attention we want to garner, no matter how small. If Human Rights International proceeds, the simple fact that our government is under scrutiny could be damaging. Even though *I* know and *we* know there is nothing nefarious to hide, the optics here are dangerous, particularly as we hope to continue partnering on investment and development from abroad."

Alejandro folded his arms. "If Human Rights International investigates, the resistance will use this to their advantage. Even when they come away from their investigation with the understanding that no wrongdoing has been committed and no laws have been broken, the court of public opinion can be far different."

Mikaela clenched her jaw. "We are all aware that Uncle Juan orchestrated these payments," she said. "Do we have an official reason as to why?"

Her father and Eduardo exchanged glances.

"We must consider that our enemies will use this against us and will likely push for an investigation," Eduardo said. "And I cannot stress enough that an international investigation into human rights abuses, regardless of merit, would bring a level of global scrutiny that we can't afford."

Her father's expression darkened. "The last thing we need is foreign organizations questioning our governance." He tossed the dossier onto the table with a loud thump. "This has never happened in the history of Cayo Azul, and it certainly will not start now. If this escalates, it could embolden the resistance in ways we haven't yet experienced."

Mikaela glanced at Alejandro, who stared miserably at the table and chewed the inside of his cheek in thought.

"What do we do?" she finally asked.

"My recommendation is that we get ahead of it," Eduardo said. "Isabella's return to Castillo Blanco was an important step. Her presence here signals stability and, most importantly, consent. We must counter any false allegations before they gain traction and emphasize the coroner's published findings after Fernando's autopsy. Lastly, we must ensure Juan remains contained. His reckless decision-making helped put us in this position and it's imperative this doesn't happen again."

Mikaela exhaled as her mind spun. She had fought to reclaim Isabella and make things right. Getting married was now more important than ever—both as a sign of their love and commitment and as a signal to the rest of the world. She glanced at Alejandro, his face dark, and she felt a wave of sympathy for him.

"Alejandro," her father said. "This conversation must not be relayed to your father. I am not certain yet what repercussions he may face as a result of his involvement, but it's important that *I* relay them to him privately. Of course you understand the politics here."

Alejandro nodded. "Yes. His actions were reckless, thoughtless, and set this chain of events in motion. I…" He took a deep breath. "I understand there must be consequences."

As the meeting dragged on and the discussion turned to facts and talking points that should be packaged into official messaging, the weight of it all pressed heavily on Mikaela's shoulders.

At long last, Alejandro excused himself for another meeting on the latest and better-than-expected economic forecast. He left the room and a brief, knowing silence fell over the chamber. She drummed her fingertips on her thigh.

"You look like you have something you wish to say," her father said. "I know this is a delicate subject for us all. It's never easy when tough decisions must be made regarding family."

"Alejandro deserves to know what the repercussions for Juan will be," Mikaela said. "He has always been more of a brother to me than a cousin. I know and *you* know that he is loyal, wildly intelligent and, most importantly, he has integrity. He has never compromised doing the right thing. You must be transparent with him. If he's inadvertently shut out, he may question why. It will fracture our family further."

Her father rubbed his jaw as he considered her words. His thoughtful gaze flickered for just a split second with something she couldn't remember ever seeing in her father: hesitation.

"Of course I want to be transparent with Alejandro," he finally said. "It's not easy to tell a young man that his father has done something egregious and must be punished, especially when this young man and his father are family. I have looked out for Juan throughout our lives. Perhaps the duty I felt as his older brother to protect him, to mentor him, only served to further enable him after so many years. Regardless, Alejandro will struggle with the sense of duty, of responsibility to the Crown, alongside the sense of family. After all, Juan is his father. He's the only parent he's had since he was a boy."

Eduardo leaned back in his chair. "I agree with Her Royal Highness," he said. "It's better that Alejandro hears it from you. He understands that Juan's choices were his own, but he must see that there are consequences for his actions. If I may, you and Alejandro have always had a close bond. Talking about this with him and taking him further under your wing may serve to strengthen that bond. Shutting him out could have the opposite effect and lead to splintering, to Her Royal Highness's point."

Mikaela studied her father closely. For as long as she could recall, her father was a man who ruled with fairness and certainty, with decisions based on strategy and a keen ability to anticipate the long-term. As she looked at him, his broad shoulders hunched in thought and his strong, towering frame was beginning to thin with age, she swallowed hard. Her father was not getting younger, and the bold silver dusting the neatly clipped hair around his temples and the slight bags beneath his dark, calculating gaze emphasized his exhaustion as he readied himself to soon pass the throne.

For the first time, Mikaela felt something stir in her chest that she recognized as doubt. She didn't doubt her father's ability to rule and lead, his strength, his intelligence, or even his deep love for *her*; it was a small, unsure curl of doubt in her own ability to lead with what felt like everything stacked against her—including her own uncle.

"You both are right," her father finally said. "Juan will not be happy with the repercussions. I don't want to risk losing Alejandro too, though I don't want him to feel as though he must choose loyalty between his father or the family as a whole." He inhaled deeply. "I know my brother. It is not a conversation I'm looking forward to having with him."

From the moment Mikaela was old enough to understand her duty as the princess of Cayo Azul and the weight of the de Medreno name, she knew that the throne one day would be hers. She wondered why she had never before reflected on the enormous pressure that would accompany it when that day finally came.

And it's coming sooner than later.

Eduardo tapped his pen on the table. "That's good," he said. "Alejandro deserves to hear it from you, even if it's a tough conversation."

More importantly, am I truly ready for all of this? The thought flashed across Mikaela's mind and unsettled her as a cold hollowness spread through her chest.

"I'll talk to Alejandro," her father said. "Soon."

Mikaela nodded, but her mind was elsewhere. The uncomfortable trickle of doubt had opened up to difficult reflections that she had never before considered. For the first time, her royal duty of succeeding the throne upon her father's eventual abdication felt frightening, filled with pressure, betrayal, and a growing number of citizens who wanted to see the Crown removed from power.

For the first time, Mikaela wasn't sure if she could live up to the lifelong expectations.

CHAPTER THIRTY-SIX

The pool party fundraiser hosted alongside the official soft launch opening for the Gran Corazon Resort was in full swing by the time Mikaela, Isabella, Alejandro, Dayanara, and Ian arrived at the luxurious rooftop pool. Gran Corazon had received plenty of attention by international travel blogs and luxury publications for the beautifully constructed infinity pool that seemed to spill right into the glittering skyline.

The five of them had arrived together after being dropped off by their security detail and their presence drew attention as they bypassed the launch party downstairs and stepped into the fundraiser surrounded by a pulsing blend of Latin beats and house music. It had been nearly a week since Eduardo had shared his findings about Human Rights International and this fundraiser had been a prime opportunity for a public show of strength and unity, given the number of photographers snapping away at the short red carpet that had been set out in Gran Corazon's expansive lobby thirty floors below.

Isabella kept her hand firmly locked into Mikaela's as they walked to a private roped-off cabana that had been reserved for their party. Her straight, dark ponytail tousled lightly in the breeze as she glanced, unguarded, at the curious faces appraising her.

Alejandro, ever the charmer, nodded in acknowledgement at the occasional familiar face in the crowd while Ian and Dayanara, hand in hand, exuded casual confidence.

As they sat on comfortable white chaises inside the cabana, Mikaela felt her cheeks flush as she noticed Isabella was biting her lower lip and staring at her.

"What?" she asked.

Isabella shook her head and blushed. "I don't know how anyone could possibly think I'd be here against my will. I mean, *look* at you. I'll gladly be your captive prisoner any day."

"You being here means a lot," Mikaela said as she ducked her head and felt uncharacteristically shy under Isabella's gaze. "This environmental nonprofit does great work anyway, but your presence with me is especially meaningful as we try to contain the damage as much as possible from everything going on."

Alejandro snickered as he joined them and handed them each a flute of champagne. "Wow, way to be romantic, Mika. You're here at a beautiful event filled with gorgeous people, including your own *stunning* fiancée, and all you can think about is the PR side of it." He took a short sip from his own flute. "Word of advice from your cousin? Up your romance game."

Mikaela rolled her eyes as Isabella suppressed a giggle. "Up *yours*, Alejandro," she retorted as he and Isabella laughed harder. "I *am* much more romantic than you think."

Alejandro glanced at Isabella. "Is that true?"

Isabella paused for a moment, pretending to ponder, and then met Mikaela's eyes. "Well, I *am* the one who agreed to spend seventy-five days at Castillo Blanco," she replied teasingly. "Though that was entirely my own choice."

Mikaela's mouth fell open. "You don't think I'm romantic?"

Isabella shrugged one shoulder. "I didn't say that!" she exclaimed. "I think you're…you."

Alejandro was nearly doubled over as he shook his finger at Mikaela. "Now *that* was Isabella's really nice way of saying you need to up your romance game. Perhaps our Mikaela is so used to women falling at her feet that she's forgotten what it's like to *work* for it."

Alejandro paused his teasing long enough to wave at someone through the open door of the cabana. "Oh, there's my buddy Matteo!" he exclaimed. "We went to university in Madrid together. You might know of his dad, actually," he turned to Isabella. "Since you're a *futbol* fan and all. Have you heard of Gabriel Velez?"

Isabella's mouth dropped open. "Gabriel Velez? Of *course* I have. What futbol fan hasn't? I don't care what anyone says, he's still one of the old-school GOATs of the field."

Alejandro chuckled. "Come on," he said. "You'll love Matteo. He's almost as good as his father, but don't tell him I said that. It'll go to his head." He nodded at Mikaela. "I'm stealing your girl for a second, Mika."

Mikaela met Isabella's pleading expression and bit back a laugh as she excitedly mouthed to her *Gabriel Velez!*

"Fine," Mikaela replied as she waved a hand. "I should go mingle."

As Isabella took off excitedly with Alejandro, Mikaela looked around the cabana and saw that Ian and Dayanara had slipped away too. She spotted them side by side at the bar chatting casually with a well-known City Center arts and culture philanthropist and his wife.

With her champagne flute in hand, Mikaela walked casually around the tiled edge of the infinity pool to the clear glass barrier overlooking the island below. She took a deep, steadying breath as she took in the vibrant energy and twinkling lights that surrounded her.

Her fingers tightened around the razor-thin edge of the barrier as she exhaled. She had spent her life knowing exactly who she thought she was and what she thought her future would be. In the wake of everything—the scandal, the betrayals, the clarity of the throne's burden—Mikaela was no longer sure that she could lead as well and as valiantly as her father.

"Your Highness, wonderful to see you." Miguel Victoriano interrupted her thoughts as she turned expectantly. "I'm thrilled you were able to make the time to attend our opening party. You know, you inspired the idea to have a fundraiser piggyback off the event. A way to do some good while celebrating the opening of this incredible resort."

Mikaela beamed. "Thank you," she replied. "That's fantastic to hear."

Miguel nodded eagerly. "I must tell you, we've already seen incredible progress since reallocating more of our open roles to the people of Este. The hospitality training classes have been full and the hires that have officially started since completing the training are exceeding expectations. They're eager, hardworking, and proud to take care of their families. This will truly change lives in Este, Your Highness."

"I'm so glad," she replied. "We must understand that these jobs are more than just numbers. They're lifelines, and the people of Este deserve equal opportunity and dignity. If it helps them and the Gran Corazon, then we've succeeded."

Miguel glanced over as Alejandro leaned against the glass barrier next to her. His expression was friendly and contemplative as he sipped his champagne.

"Sir Alejandro!" Miguel nodded in eager greeting. "I don't want to keep you from enjoying this beautiful night by talking business. Please, let me know personally if there's anything your party needs."

As Mikaela turned toward Alejandro, he gestured toward the cabana. "Isabella is deep in futbol discussion with Matteo," he said. "Don't worry, Miss Protector, she's safe. Matteo would be lucky to get a girl like Isabella, but he's very aware of who she is and who she's *with*."

Mikaela smiled, her gaze still on the island before her.

"I met with your father yesterday," Alejandro said. "There will be an official rebuke against my father and the officers involved in the payments to Isabella's family. I believe one will be dishonorably discharged from the armed services and stripped of his titles and recognitions. If my father makes another egregious mistake or if he's found to have knowledge of his lieutenant colluding with the resistance, he too will be removed as general of the armed services and stripped of any official royal duties and titles."

Mikaela studied him under her lashes as she took a slow sip of her champagne. Alejandro sounded resigned and understanding, though he rolled his shoulders as if trying to shake off the weight of the situation.

"And how do you feel about that?"

Alejandro sighed as he glanced down at his champagne flute. "Conflicted, Mika," he said. "After all, he's my father. Despite everything, I have to believe he's always looked out for us, for me. Tried to protect us in his own obtuse way. I think." He glanced at the horizon, contemplative. "You know, I never quite understood him. He's my father, right? You'd think we'd have this close bond, but we never really have. I think he always wanted to push me to be more like him. You know, rough. *Machismo*. And he'd get frustrated when I just…wasn't." Alejandro shrugged. "I think he even thought I was gay for a long time." He fixed Mikaela with a rueful look. "But you've got that covered for the family. And anyway, I always knew I liked women. You don't have to be a certain way to be straight or gay. But after a while, I think he just threw his hands up and gave up. I've tried to connect with him too, to build that father-son bond over the years, but we're just…different."

Without a word, Mikaela wrapped her arm around his waist as they gazed at the island before them in a companionable moment of reflection.

"I also know that actions have consequences, and I see the terrible position he's put the Crown in with his inexplicable decision-making," Alejandro said. "I agree with your father's strategy. People, especially those in positions of power, must take responsibility for their actions. Even Juan de Medreno Soliz."

Mikaela nodded as pride bloomed in her chest at his level-headed ability to see all sides.

Alejandro is my most trusted ally and he should take on a larger political role. The thought struck Mikaela like lightning, and she wondered why she had never seen it before. He had her father's patience, his intelligence and acumen, and his uncanny ability to inspire trust among all Cayo Azuleans and even abroad. Like her father, Alejandro was always able to see the long-term strategy and make wise decisions fairly and objectively. If she was to eventually rule Cayo Azul, she wanted to do so with her trusted cousin as an integral part of her advisory council.

"You should consider taking on a larger political role," Mikaela said, the words out of her mouth before she could rethink them. "You should talk to my father about what may fit best. Do you think you'd be ready for something like that, Alejandro?"

Alejandro blinked in surprise. "Thanks, Mikaela," he replied, sounding genuinely touched. "I'll give it some thought, but I'll talk with your father if you're okay with it."

Mikaela nodded as she finished the last of her champagne. "Of course," she replied. "I think you're ready for it."

A look of determination flashed across his face and Mikaela recognized the same resolve she'd seen in her father throughout her life. "Okay," he said with a nod. "I think so too."

Before Mikaela could ponder her swirling thoughts further, Isabella appeared at her side. She was flushed and breathless from the tantalizing combination of exhilaration and French champagne as she slid an arm around Mikaela's waist and pressed a quick kiss to her cheek.

"You should come dance with me," Isabella murmured.

Mikaela arched an eyebrow as she let herself be tugged toward a neon-flashing dance floor beneath rows of twinkling lights.

Alejandro chuckled as he lifted his champagne flute in a silent toast. "Have fun, cousin," he called after her. "Don't forget you deserve to enjoy yourself too."

Mikaela glanced back at him, but the moment that Isabella pulled her onto the dance floor, the rest of the world seemed to blur around them. The air was thick with humidity, the warm press of bodies, and the lingering scents of salt and expensive perfume. Through it all, Mikaela's gaze remained fixed on Isabella as she swayed in time with the deep pulse of the music.

Isabella turned as she pressed her back into Mikaela's front and wrapped her arms around her, guiding them to rest low on her waist. Isabella rolled her hips against Mikaela in time with the beat as she teased and melded her body against hers.

Mikaela leaned in as her lips brushed Isabella's shoulder and relished the slight shudder she felt from her. The beat vibrated between them, but their rhythm remained slow, deliberate, and fiery.

Isabella turned and wrapped her arms loosely around Mikaela's neck. Neon flashes from the dance floor reflected in her gaze as the dimples in both cheeks deepened with her flushed grin. Mikaela was acutely aware that their lips were just a breath apart, and she wondered if it would be too much to kiss Isabella right there in front of everyone on the dance floor.

"Take me back to your house," Isabella said into Mikaela's ear, her voice thick with need.

Mikaela exhaled sharply as she felt her cool control weakening with every second that Isabella danced seductively in her arms. She knew then that she couldn't care less about the party or ensuring they were "seen." She just wanted to be home, making slow, sensual love to Isabella.

"Let's go, love," Mikaela said as she took Isabella's hand and led her toward the exit. Right now, it was only them.

CHAPTER THIRTY-SEVEN

Isabella blinked as soft morning light streamed over the deck and through the glass doors into Mikaela's bedroom. She rolled over as she relished the delicious stretch down her shoulders and spine. Mikaela's side of the bed was cool and empty. The sheets were smooth beneath her fingertips and the bedroom was still as Isabella glanced around blearily. She knew Mikaela likely had royal business to attend to and hadn't wanted to wake her, especially since their love-making had taken them into the early morning hours. Still, Isabella missed Mikaela's warmth.

She gently traced the cool silk-encased pillow where Mikaela had slept. They had a lunch meeting later with Cristina and the vice president of events at the PR agency to begin wedding planning, though Isabella hoped to get a quick shower, a video chat with her mom, and a late morning walk in before.

Isabella swung her bare legs over the side of the bed and pulled her discarded swimsuit cover-up from the floor. She shrugged it on over the T-shirt and underwear she'd fallen asleep in. As she cranked the shower to its hottest setting, she sniffed the air. *Coffee*. Despite not being a big coffee drinker herself, Mikaela had ordered an espresso machine days ago and had started a fresh pot for her before she left.

It's the little things. Isabella stepped into the shower and closed the glass door behind her. She took a deep breath and enjoyed the hot spray on her skin as it massaged her muscles.

Alejandro was wrong last night. Mikaela can *be sweet and romantic.* Isabella blinked against the spray. The steamy water did nothing to minimize the shiver that ran down her spine at the tantalizing thoughts of Mikaela.

As Isabella wrapped a fluffy white robe around herself and ran her fingers through her damp, towel-dried hair, she propped her phone against a stack of books on the living room coffee table. She sunk into the plush leather sofa and took a sip of coffee as the video call connected. The screen flickered for a moment before her mother's warm, familiar face greeted her.

"Daughter!" her mother exclaimed. Isabella could see that her mother was seated at the kitchen table. Sunlight streamed through the worn lace curtains as patterns danced over her forehead, and she could hear the soft hum of a radio in the background.

She looks so much lighter. Happier.

"You're glowing," her mother said with a knowing wag of her finger. "Castillo Blanco must be treating you very well. I would expect nothing less for my beautiful daughter."

Warmth spread through Isabella's chest at her mother's evident happiness. She tucked her legs beneath her and cradled her mug in her hands. "It is," she said with a nod. "Everyone has been wonderful. More than wonderful, really. I'm glad we've been able to chat regularly. I miss you, you know. Plus, I never know when you're going to be on shift at the hospital these days."

Her mother clucked her tongue. "You know, I've been able to cut down my hours? I told Mikaela not to worry about that stipend, but she insisted. Apparently, it *is* somewhat normal so long as it's not done in secrecy or under duress. At least that's what I've been told. I'll admit it has been nice to not work so many hours, but if you think I'm going to just quit my nursing career and live my life doing nothing but sitting around here and getting chubby…"

Isabella laughed. She knew that Mikaela's family had added her mother to the royal books, with a modest monthly stipend to cover "living expenses" as an extended member of the de Medreno family—a transparent and legal way to ensure she was taken care of.

"I'm glad you don't have to work so hard, Mami, but I would never dream of asking you to quit your job."

"What do you have planned today?" her mother asked.

Isabella took a deep breath. "Wedding planning officially kicks off," she replied. "We're meeting with the leader of their events team and I suppose we'll get a theme, a location, perhaps colors and basics planned."

Her mother gasped. "Already? My goodness! Tell me everything."

Isabella launched into the plans for the meeting as her mother listened intently, nodding, and occasionally murmuring her agreement or shaking her head.

After a few minutes, Isabella paused. "You know, I'd love for you to be part of this planning, Mami," she said. "I always envisioned you being a big part of whatever wedding I had, and that's no different now. Once we have this first meeting finished, I would really love for you to be involved."

"Oh, this is a fancy royal wedding," she said. "I'm sure they don't want some old lady from Este getting involved in all those details. I can't even imagine the things that Her Royal Highness Queen Cristina might want included."

Isabella fixed her mother with a look. "Queen Cristina does have a tendency to…steamroll," she replied. "But somehow even *I* think she would be a little intimidated by a tough, unfiltered nurse from Este."

After the lighthearted moment, her mother's expression softened into something more thoughtful. "Isabella," she said hesitantly, "I have a serious question for you. Please answer it honestly. No matter your response, I'll love and support you."

Isabella blinked, caught off guard. "Well, that's one way to lead up to your question, Mami."

Her mother took a deep breath. "Are you *sure* about this? Getting married?"

"Of course," Isabella replied. "I love Mikaela."

"I know you do," she said gently. "There isn't a part of me that doubts that, or that she loves you. But you know that marriage is a commitment *forever*, Isabella. It is not just love; it's choosing that person every single day through good and bad. You know Cayo Azul is not like the States, we are not like so many countries in the EU, where divorce is much more accepted. Here, we have always believed in its sanctity, whether it consists of a man and a woman, two women, two men, or any two people. And you, my daughter, have been through so much. I don't want you to enter this marriage feeling forced or wishing you had more time to know Mikaela first."

"I know what you're asking, Mami," she said. "And I understand that marriage is a sacred commitment. But when it comes to Mikaela, I've never been more sure of anything."

Her mother studied her for a moment through the camera and then let out a soft chuckle. "I remember when you were a little girl, you were so stubborn," she said. "When you decided you wanted something, nothing could change your mind. When you turned twelve and the boys started saying you couldn't play futbol with them anymore, you practiced night and day. You were so good on your school team that, after a while, they couldn't help but invite you and a few of the other girls to play in their weekend pickup games. And you'd beat them all every time." Her expression turned wistful. "I miss that stubborn little girl and that bratty teenager. They never tell you how short the years really are, despite the days being so long sometimes. But, most of all, I'm so proud of the woman you are."

"Thank you, Mami."

"You know, I see that same stubborn look in you now," she said. "And I see how sure you are too."

"Because I *know*," Isabella said. "Mikaela is my present and my future."

Her mother beamed with pride. "Then I am happy for you, my daughter. Truly. You and Mikaela are two pieces of the same puzzle. I'd be honored to help with the wedding planning."

Isabella laughed. "Castillo Blanco isn't going to know what hits it!"

"Perhaps it could use a little shaking up," she replied good-naturedly. "Now, tell me what you're thinking for a dress…"

Later that morning, Isabella had slipped into a pair of lightweight, loose black yoga pants, a comfortable fitted white tank top, and a pair of black-and-white Nike walking shoes. She slipped her earbuds into her ears.

The grounds of Castillo Blanco were especially peaceful in the mornings. The air was still crisp and tinged with the faint scents of salt and jasmine, and it was quiet enough to hear the leaves rustling in the breeze and the occasional crash of waves in the distance. Isabella knew that as morning rolled into lunchtime, Castillo Blanco would begin to buzz with more energy.

The upbeat pop song on Isabella's playlist was loud in her ears as her feet pounded firmly against the grass. She swung her arms a bit, hoping to infuse more of a workout into her power walk, and paused to do a couple of stretching lunges as she reached the valley of a rolling hill. Isabella stepped up the gentle hill as she nodded in time with the song.

It was then that she saw her. In the distance across the grounds, Mikaela sat perched atop Luna. Her spine was straight and they were silhouetted against the golden sun as she gazed out into the distance at something unseen. Isabella swallowed hard at the sight and removed one earbud with trembling fingers. The upbeat song faded away and everything was still.

Mikaela was dressed in her riding gear and the wind tousled her golden hair as she sat atop Luna with effortless command. Isabella lingered on the slope from a distance as she drank in the sight of Mikaela looking both untouchable and breathtakingly fierce. Isabella couldn't help but marvel at the way she held herself and the way the morning light danced over her features and painted her profile in shades of rosy amber. In that moment, it gave the air of something ancient and noble, like a conquistador surveying her land or a warrior queen lost in thought before something momentous was to happen.

Mikaela was the quintessential portrait of power and nobility, as if the history of her ancestors was woven into her very being. Isabella felt her heart clench with something so achingly deep and profound that she had to remind herself to breathe.

Mikaela's gaze remained locked on the horizon for another moment before she glanced down and gently prodded Luna forward into a light trot.

They moved perfectly in sync, as if they were one, as their shapes grew smaller toward the stable.

I love her.

It wasn't just a simple thought of admiration fueled by lust; it was an undeniable truth that emanated from Isabella's core and flooded her veins. The force of that knowledge was strong, as unshakable as the ocean tides, and Isabella stood rooted to her spot as she gazed in the direction that Mikaela and Luna had long since disappeared in.

Despite the steadily increasing temperature, Isabella shivered as she thought of the warmth beneath Mikaela's self-imposed armor, the way that intense, contemplative gaze softened each time their gazes locked, and how Mikaela whispered her name against her ear last night.

That fierce, enigmatic woman is mine. Isabella put her earbud back into her ear. She broke into a light jog back down the grassy slope, as her heart pounded not from the mild workout but from something intangible.

And soon, we will belong to each other in every way. Am *I truly ready for this? To be married?*

Her mind traveled over the sight of Mikaela just now, gorgeous and regal in contemplation atop Luna, and then she recalled the espresso machine with a half pot of coffee still warm atop the glossy marble countertops.

Isabella had never been more certain. *I am.*

Chapter Thirty-eight

The lunchtime meeting took place in one of Castillo Blanco's larger and more sunlit conference rooms. Despite the business-focused atmosphere of the conference room, the gathering felt intimate and friendly as Isabella, Mikaela, Cristina, Lucia, the agency's vice president of events, and the vice president's executive assistant casually mingled over lunch before launching into planning and details.

Mikaela leaned over and spoke low, out of earshot from the rest of the room. "What are your must-haves for the wedding?"

Isabella thought for a moment. "I think we should ensure Cayo Azul culture is represented," she said. "It's an important nod to our heritage."

Mikaela nodded. "I agree. We'll emphasize that to the events team. They're based in London, so they may require guidance."

"I spoke to my mother earlier," Isabella said. "She's looking forward to having a role in planning. I told her I wanted her to be involved too. She would be perfect for guiding the team on the intricacies of Cayo Azulean culture and I know she would be proud to do so."

Mikaela nodded. "That's perfect. I look forward to welcoming her for the dress selection soon. The tailor will take her measurements that afternoon, though some of the mother of the bride dress options may be easy for our seamstress to alter right then. I believe my mother was coordinating with the designers' assistants to see which weekend works best for them to present their gowns. Unless there are any others you love, I think we've narrowed it down to Balenciaga, Vivienne Westwood, and Versace." Mikaela rolled her eyes. "Not my favorite, but my mother was married in Versace, so she's clinging to this dream that I will be too."

Isabella blinked. Part of her was unsure why she was shocked—Mikaela was royalty, after all. She bit back her naive assumption that they would simply rent out a City Center atelier for the afternoon to try on dresses.

Of course that's not how royalty does things. The designers come to them with custom couture.

She took a deep breath, as a wave of reminder at just how different they were crashed over her. She took a sip of ice water and shook the thought away.

"Really, the ceremony, the dresses, none of that matters so much as the person I'm marrying," Isabella said. She held Mikaela's gaze for a moment. "As long as it's representative of *us* and we're not trying too hard to be something we're not, I'll be happy." She wrinkled her nose. "I mean, I think of those huge, quaint, super stuffy and formal European royal weddings and I don't want that to be ours."

"No way," Mikaela said as she ran a confident hand through her hair. "There will be select European dignitaries and politicians in attendance, I'm sure. But maybe it's an opportunity to highlight the magic and the beauty of Cayo Azul to them, rather than incorporate things that just aren't us."

Isabella nodded. "I know you mentioned one of your father's last big goals before abdicating was entry into the EU," she said. "Perhaps we can show them some of the best and most wonderful things about our rich history and culture, starting with our strong commitment to the marriage bond."

Mikaela shifted in her seat and glanced down at her plate. "Right."

The shift wasn't lost on Isabella. "Hey," she murmured, taking Mikaela's hand in hers. "It'll be great no matter what. All I really care about is marrying *you*. I love you."

Mikaela met her gaze. "I love you too."

Though her voice held its usual confidence, Isabella couldn't help but wonder if the brief flicker across Mikaela's face—surely it couldn't be doubt?—was something to be concerned about or if she was simply being paranoid after her earlier conversation with her mother.

Isabella didn't have time to dwell. The vice president of events, a tall, intimidating woman with an impeccably smooth platinum blond up-do, delicate gold hoop earrings, and bright red lipstick, approached eagerly. She bent her knee in a curtsy as she nodded at Mikaela.

"Your Royal Highness, it's a pleasure to see you again," she spoke. Her London accent was impossibly posh. "It's been at least a year, hasn't it?"

Mikaela stood and stuck out her hand. "Please, you know you can call me Mikaela," she replied. "I'm glad you could be here in person as we prepare for this momentous occasion. Speaking of, I'd like to introduce my fiancée. This is Isabella Acosta Ramon."

Isabella smiled in greeting and followed Mikaela's lead as she too stood and offered her hand.

"Isabella, Amelia Wilson is the vice president of events at Motion Agency," Mikaela said. "They have been our exclusive and trusted public relations partner for many years. My mother and Lucia primarily coordinate with Amelia on the events side, though she has a full team of wonderful certified professionals working under her."

"It's a pleasure to meet you," Isabella said.

"The pleasure is all mine," Amelia replied. "Congratulations to you both on this exciting event. I know I speak for all of Motion when I say we can't wait to help you plan the wedding of your dreams. Rest assured, my team is here for anything and *everything* you may need during this process. In fact, you may also be in occasional contact with my EA, Blythe." She gestured to the other woman, who stepped to her side. "Blythe manages much of our administrative functions and keeps everyone's calendars running smoothly."

"Very nice to meet you," Isabella said.

Amelia and Blythe sat across the table from Cristina, Lucia, Mikaela, and Isabella as they settled into event planning mode.

"Let's get down to it, shall we?" Amelia flipped through an elegant, leather-bound portfolio as her bright red acrylic nails skimmed over the thick cardstock pages. "My team and I have prepared several concepts based on centuries of royal tradition. The first and most obvious option is a grand castle wedding right here at Castillo Blanco, in line with previous royal unions on Cayo Azul. We could host the ceremony in the Great Hall or perhaps even in front of the castle, at the head of that beautiful front pool and fountain. The reception could then be in the ballroom, which would leave plenty of room for people to mingle and celebrate your union."

With a gentle flick of her wrist, Amelia turned the portfolio so it faced them and pointed out pages of detailed sketches. Isabella raised an eyebrow at the grandeur of it all—the gilded all-white floral arrangements, the long white silk-covered banquet tables neatly set with fine china for hundreds, and waiters in tailcoat tuxedos.

Mikaela chewed her bottom lip in thought before confidently shaking her head. "No," she said. "That's not us."

Amelia nodded smoothly, unfazed, as she flipped through the large book to another section. "Alternatively, a cathedral wedding at the iconic Santa Julianna Catholic Church could be timeless. A quite sacred experience, with the full weight of Cayo Azul behind it. I like the idea of having soft pink lighting throughout. It would really enhance the natural beauty of the stained-glass windows."

Isabella gazed at the sketches of Santa Julianna's familiar tower and spires as she considered the idea of a church wedding.

"If I may," Cristina cut in as she raised her palm. "Santa Julianna does not currently administer same-sex weddings. Now, I know the archbishop well and I'm certain he would make an exception for Mikaela and Isabella if Bartolo or I were to make a personal request."

Mikaela shook her head. "That's the last thing we need right now," she said. "If word got out that you or Papa made a special request for the church to do something typically out of their realm, the optics across the island would be very negative. The resistance is already working hard to convince

Cayo Azuleans that we're out of touch, privileged elites. This would play right into the narrative they wish to drive."

Cristina opened and then closed her mouth. "I want you to have the wedding you want to have."

Mikaela turned to meet Isabella's eyes. "We'd like to keep it as small and intimate as possible," she said. "Simple. As private as we can hope for. Meaningful. And deeply appreciative of our beautiful heritage. Am I missing anything, my love?"

Isabella couldn't help but smile back. "The beach," she said as the idea began to take hold. "Maybe we could do it there."

Amelia straightened with excitement. "Of course! Though it *would* be unconventional for a royal wedding."

"The beach would be an excellent location," Mikaela said. "I agree with my fiancée. I like it."

Cristina, who had been watching closely, nodded. "Unconventional, surely," she said. "But when has my daughter ever been conventional? Playa del Sol in Santa Julianna would be perfect. It's off the main road, so securing the location and building a protected perimeter on the day of should be easier. There's a line of thick trees leading out to white sand. It's quiet. It's intimate."

Amelia and Blythe quickly adjusted, their fingers flying over their laptop keyboards as Amelia began brainstorming ideas for an elegant, intimate beachside ceremony.

Nearly an hour had gone by before Amelia sat back in her chair, satisfied. She looked around the table expectantly.

"What are your thoughts?" she asked. "We've got twinkling string lights woven through the tree line leading up to the beach, which will have white silk canopies set up covering rows of high-backed white silk chairs. And what could be more romantic than the ocean and the sounds of the waves as your backdrop? Once we have an official headcount, my team can sketch out a more accurate representation of how those seating arrangements will look. In the meantime, Blythe will take measurements at Playa del Sol before we return to London tomorrow night so we know exactly the space we have to work with."

Isabella sighed, already envisioning the ceremony. The salty breeze, the sand beneath their bare feet, Mikaela standing before her with that intense gaze…

Mikaela's fingers brushed against hers beneath the table. "Isabella?" she asked.

Isabella's cheeks flushed at the faces around the table looking back at her expectantly. "Sorry, I…I must have missed that," she replied lamely.

Mikaela grinned. "Does it sound like we're in a good place with the wedding basics and location settled?"

Isabella nodded. "Yes," she said. "This feels right."

Mikaela's fingertips drifted beneath the table from Isabella's hand to her thigh and lingered there in a slow, deliberate touch. "Then it's decided," she said. "Playa del Sol and an intimate beach wedding."

Cristina nodded. "A royal wedding by the sea." She smoothed her long skirt over her crossed legs. "It does suit you."

As the meeting ended, Isabella tried not to think about Mikaela's gentle touch on her thigh and instead forced herself to start considering the finer details of the ceremony.

The most critical decisions have already been made.

It won't be a spectacle of power or tradition; it will be ours. *Most importantly, we've chosen each other.*

Late that night, Mikaela lay on her side in bed, propped up on one elbow, as she watched Isabella sleep soundly beneath the crisp white sheets. Another quick but ferocious storm raged outside, as heavy sheets of rain pounded against the roof and occasional claps of thunder sounded like they were splitting the sky in two. Mikaela felt something tighten deep in her chest. The torrent of emotions and anxiety she had been fighting around the swirling fears, doubts, and second-guessing her readiness for the throne coursed through her as a stinging reminder that no matter how hard she tried to ignore them, those feelings didn't magically disappear.

Isabella loves my strength and ability to lead Mikaela thought as she bit her lip. *She accepted an engagement from a princess, soon to take over the throne and lead Cayo Azul into the future. Not from someone wondering if she wants it at all. It could make her question our entire future.*

Mikaela watched as Isabella's shoulders gently rose and fell with her breath as her expression appeared peaceful and completely at ease, the latter of which Mikaela envied. The terror of the unknown, of a massive change, of accepting the throne and failing everyone around her clawed at Mikaela as her gaze drifted over Isabella's face. She carefully brushed a strand of hair from Isabella's cheek. Even in her sleep, Isabella sighed happily and leaned into Mikaela's touch.

I know she loves me Mikaela thought with a hard swallow. *But Isabella is expecting a princess, not someone who is doubting her ability to lead now that the throne is a near future inevitability. Here I am, standing on the edge of something I've spent my life preparing for and, for once, I'm paralyzed.*

Mikaela exhaled as she lay back down and blinked at the sturdy wooden beams arched across the high ceiling. The weight of these thoughts and of the potential for her parents' deep disappointment felt crushing. She surprised even herself as a single tear snaked down her cheek.

If I say it out loud, then it's real. The fear tightened her chest as another tear followed the first. For her entire life, Mikaela had assumed and expected that she would fall in line like she was brought up to do. But confiding her sudden fear to Isabella meant it was no longer something she could ignore and hope would go away.

I have to confide in her before the wedding Mikaela told herself firmly. *Isabella deserves to know exactly what and who she is marrying, so she can decide for herself if my indecision on the throne is a dealbreaker for her and if she sees me differently. If so, then she can call it off before we're locked into life together.*

Before Mikaela knew it, the tears were falling silently down her face at the crippling thought of disappointing everyone in her life. The guilt at not being truthful with Isabella before they were married was even worse. She wasn't sure when she finally drifted to sleep, her eyelids heavy from the tears, but the anxiety remained a tugging constant in the background, in time with the beating raindrops and the gusting wind, even as she slept.

CHAPTER THIRTY-NINE

Isabella stepped out of the steam-filled glass shower and wrapped a soft gray towel around herself as she padded into the bedroom. Mikaela's house was quiet and, as she glanced onto the balcony, she spotted her stretched in a plush lounge chair, one toned arm and an oversized Prada sun hat slung carelessly over her face.

Isabella stilled as she drank in the sight. It was rare to see Mikaela so relaxed, so completely unguarded, and she wanted to savor the moment and memorize exactly how the golden sunlight danced over her profile and brightened the shimmery blonde in her hair.

God, she's gorgeous Isabella thought, as her heart twisted with an ache that she knew she had never felt for anyone before. She dressed quickly, the tight, dark olive breeches and tall brown riding boots unfamiliar, as she pulled a simple white T-shirt over her head.

With one last lingering glance at Mikaela and the effortless way her long, dark eyelashes rested against her cheeks, Isabella stepped onto the sunny balcony. She almost hated to wake her, but she smiled at the surprise she had planned. Isabella crawled onto the lounge chair next to Mikaela and pressed a kiss to her bare shoulder, feeling the slow stretch of muscles beneath her lips.

"Baby," Mikaela mumbled sleepily. "I fell asleep. Is this how you plan to wake me every day when we're married?"

"Maybe," Isabella teased as she lazily trailed her fingertips down Mikaela's stomach. "But this afternoon, I have something even better planned."

Mikaela finally blinked as she wrinkled her nose in confusion. "Better than this? I don't know."

Isabella rolled her eyes as she grinned. "Well, we don't want to be late," she went on. "And you definitely can't do this in your pajamas, so you'll need to get dressed. Come on, we're going on an adventure."

Mikaela groaned as she sat up. "An adventure?" She repeated and then paused. "Wait, why are you dressed like an equestrian?"

Isabella straddled Mikaela's waist and leaned down so her lips ghosted over her ear. "An adventure I know you can't deny. One word: horses."

Mikaela sat up further, awake now. "Did you say horses?"

"I did," Isabella confirmed. She ran a playful hand through Mikaela's tousled hair. "I can sense there has been a lot weighing on your mind lately, so I planned a private ride for us through the forest in Santa Julianna. Secluded. Just us, the horses, and the trail, which security has blocked off until this evening. Someone from the grounds crew is transporting Luna and one of the other horses." Mikaela just stared at her, her expression unreadable. "I know how much you love horseback riding," she finished. "And Luna. I thought you might enjoy it."

After a long, still moment, a real, genuine smile lit across Mikaela's face and Isabella's chest panged with the familiar ache that she had come to realize was love.

"You planned this for me?" Mikaela asked incredulously.

Isabella glanced down, unsure why she felt shy. "Of course I did," she said lightly. She brushed her lips over Mikaela's cheek. "You're always doing things for others. I wanted to do something for *you*. I want you to know I *listen* when you tell me things, even the things you think are mundane and even the things you don't share. I always want to show you love, Mika."

Mikaela opened and then closed her mouth as she traced her fingertips along Isabella's jaw. "I…I think you might make me cry." Her voice sounded stunned at that realization, though no tears glimmered in her gaze.

Isabella raised an eyebrow. "I wouldn't *hate* that, you know," she replied gently. "I mean, as long as they were happy tears and not Isabella-you-broke-my-heart-tears. It's okay to let down your guard around me, Mikaela. I'm your safe spot. I'm going to be your *wife*. Just promise me you'll trust me enough to not feel as though you have to protect yourself even with me, okay?"

Mikaela looked at her for a long moment, a beat of uncertainty flickering in her gaze, before she leaned forward to nip Isabella's bottom lip playfully. "I love you," she said. "I can't wait to go riding. Thank you."

Isabella felt a pang of frustration at Mikaela's obvious reticence to be fully vulnerable with her, but she shook it away and instead wrapped her arms around Mikaela's neck. "Better get dressed," she replied as she kissed her lips once more. "Your riding clothes are on the bed, baby."

Mikaela shook her head ruefully as she pushed herself off the lounge chair, the blanket she'd been napping beneath trailing behind her. Deep satisfaction settled into Isabella's chest as Mikaela retreated into the bedroom.

Today. Today I will get Mikaela to open up to me once and for all.

❖

The heady smell of damp earth mingled with the light floral scent of wild orchids danced along the cool forest breeze as Mikaela rhythmically guided Luna along the narrow dirt trail. The clop of her hooves sounded softer against the thick, mossy ground and the air outside felt at least fifteen degrees cooler, thanks to the shade from the emerald canopy high above. Isabella stole another glance at Mikaela and was mesmerized as she watched her lean forward and gently pat Luna's neck.

"I still can't believe you planned this," Mikaela's voice was low and contemplative as she looked around in the closest Isabella had ever seen her to wonderment. The sound of a distant waterfall and the occasional chirp from tropical birds circling high above surrounded them, and Isabella sensed Mikaela relax. "I don't know what it is about riding," she said as she tossed her hair confidently over her shoulder. "I just feel like I can *breathe*, you know?"

Isabella nodded and then glanced down in surprise as her own horse, a stocky white mare, splashed through a puddle. "Hey, lady!" She exclaimed. "Next time go around!"

"I don't think she understands you, my love," Mikaela said teasingly. "Though you *can* loosen your grip on the reins and gently guide her around the puddle next time. Besides, a little muddy water never hurt anyone." She arched an eyebrow. "It just means you'll have to take another shower and this time I can watch."

Isabella laughed as they continued farther down the trail. "Touché," she replied. "I don't know about a loose grip though. What if she, like, sees a butterfly and takes off?"

Mikaela patted Luna's neck again. "Trained horses usually only go faster if you give them a nudge. Like this."

Mikaela gently dug the heels of her polished black riding boots just beneath Luna's ribcage. The horse's pace quickened into a light gallop as Mikaela's delighted laughter echoed off the towering trees. They rode farther ahead and then slowed to a stop, turning expectantly.

"Hey, wait up!" Isabella called as she and her horse plodded toward them. "No way this old mare and I are doing a full speed run through the forest."

They continued on, as a trickle of water alongside the trail opened up into a rocky, crystal-clear creek. The gentle rush of water was soothing as they slowed into a relaxed side-by-side ride.

"Do you ever feel like people expect marriage to be this big, grand thing all the time?" Isabella mused. "With, like, constant passion, grand gestures, and sweeping romance?"

Mikaela's expression was teasing. "Is that your way of telling me you want that?"

Isabella laughed. "*No*, Mikaela, that's my way of saying I *don't* need that," she replied. "I feel like that would become exhausting. Once the excitement settles, what will you be left with? Nothing, if it's all surface-level fun. I just want our marriage to be something…" she trailed off as she thought. "*Real*. Steady. Knowing that at the end of every day no matter what happens, we get to come home to each other. I mean, sweeping romance is nice," she said. "But a real soul connection? That's *everything*."

Mikaela was quiet for a moment, though Isabella was certain she had seen a rare flash of vulnerability. "That's exactly how I feel," she said. "But I've never known how to say it. Honestly? I just want marriage to feel like an endless sleepover with my best friend. With plenty of amazing sex throughout, of course."

Isabella blinked in surprise and flushed as Mikaela quickened Luna's pace. "*Mikaela*," she exclaimed. "I never expected you to say something like that. I…I love this." She paused as her horse finally caught back up to Luna. "Does this forever sleepover mean we'll stay up all night telling secrets in the dark?"

Mikaela raised an eyebrow. "We already do that."

"True," Isabella said. "Does this mean you'll steal the blankets *every* night?"

Mikaela scoffed in mock outrage. "That's *you*, love!"

"No way," Isabella said as she absentmindedly ran her fingers through the base of her horse's mane. The mare seemed to grudgingly accept this for a moment before shaking her hand off her neck.

"You wrapped yourself up like a burrito last night and left me with the corner of the sheet," Mikaela said and then sighed dramatically. "After all those amazing orgasms I give you too."

Isabella gasped through her laughter. "I would *never* do that to the love of my life!"

Mikaela fixed her with a look. "You did."

Isabella leaned over and gently kissed Mikaela's lips. "Fine. Maybe you're right," she conceded. "But I'll always make it up to you."

Mikaela took a deep breath as she leaned further across Luna into the kiss. "You mean that?" She asked. "I'm the love of your life?"

Isabella held her gaze for a moment. "Yes," she said. "I can't wait to marry you."

On the other side of the clearing, a thin waterfall trickled into a shallow pool of clear water.

Mikaela laughed and it made Isabella's heart pound faster. "You have no idea how stunningly beautiful you look up there."

Isabella swallowed hard as warmth flooded her. "Are you flirting with me, Your Royal Highness?" She asked teasingly.

Mikaela arched an eyebrow. "Is it working?"

Isabella tapped her chin and pretended to think for a moment. "Um, maybe a little."

Mikaela glanced at her knowingly as she dismounted her horse and secured the reins loosely around a nearby tree. She wrapped one arm around Isabella's waist as she helped her off her horse and then secured her reins around a tree next to hers.

"This water is gorgeous," Mikaela said as she perched on a flat, grassy patch at the edge of the shallow pool and unzipped her riding boots. She dipped her bare feet into the clear water as she tossed her boots and socks to the side.

Isabella settled next to Mikaela and followed suit. "It's beautiful out here," she agreed as she looked around. She took a deep breath at the magical splendor of it all.

After a moment, she stole a glance at Mikaela and felt her breath catch at the soft smile ghosting over her lips and the slow way she blinked as a beam of sunlight passed over her face. Without thinking, Isabella gently clasped Mikaela's fingers.

"Mika," she said. "I need you to talk to me. Please."

Isabella felt Mikaela tense slightly as her spine straightened and her jaw set. "What do you mean?" she asked, though the way she kept her gaze trained on the shallow pool before them told Isabella she already knew.

"You know what I mean," Isabella said. "Something is going on with you. Don't you know that I can *feel* it, my love? I already know when something is not right or when your energy is off. You've been...different. And I've been waiting, trying to give you space and time, but *please*, Mika. Let me in. Whatever is going on, you don't have to carry it alone."

Mikaela inhaled sharply as the forest seemed to still around them. For a long moment, Isabella was sure that Mikaela would deflect and brush her off with a kiss or change of subject. "You know," Isabella said. "I get it. I understand that you're the one who will lead this marriage and you're the final decision-maker and you like...being the more dominant one," Isabella blushed as she recalled their lovemaking. "And I *like* you being in control. A *lot*. It's unbelievably sexy. But that doesn't mean you don't *talk* to me and treat me as your partner. I know you've had this wall up your whole life and I understand why, but you don't have to protect yourself around me. I just..." Isabella sighed. "I hope one day you can learn to let me in."

Mikaela swallowed hard and kept her steely gaze straight ahead. "I don't know if I'm ready for the throne. I'm scared and I'm not certain I'm ready to lead."

The soft, barely audible confession hung between them in the cool forest air.

"Okay," Isabella said after a beat. Isabella wasn't sure what she felt in that moment. She wasn't shocked and she wasn't reeling. She imagined the pressure that Mikaela must have been feeling, weighed down with doubt and fear of disappointing those who held her to high expectations.

That's all of Cayo Azul. The magnitude of everything Mikaela had been born into came into sharp focus.

"Tell me what you're feeling. I want to listen," Isabella said.

Mikaela met her steady gaze. "I…don't know if I'll ever be ready for the throne," she said, an uncharacteristic tremble in her voice. "Now that my father's abdication will be sooner rather than later, I feel crippled by this sudden *fear*. Lately, it feels like I'll never be able to lead as well as my father has and there is so much depending on my ability to navigate unrest, unite our people, root out betrayal within. If I make any mistakes or fail even the tiniest bit, it could be detrimental for *everyone*. My family. Our people. You."

Isabella squeezed Mikaela's hand. "That's a lot to carry."

After a moment, Mikaela let go of her hand and instead idly dragged her fingertips through the water as she appeared to consider her response. "I don't know what the right solution is," she said. "And that's terrifying. I do know that people can turn against one another at any moment, even family, when power and money are involved. Every day, I feel the weight of this impending royal duty pressing down on me and lately…" She took a deep breath. "It's been crushing."

Mikaela stared at the water before them. "Ironically, the reason I agreed to allow my parents to pressure me into getting married right away was to prove that I was prepared for the throne, ready to step into a more visible leadership role, and to transition to the next ruler of Cayo Azul. It seemed so easy when it was just a far-off eventuality."

"You are an amazing leader," Isabella said. "I've seen it firsthand. After all, this is in your blood. Thank you for finally telling me what's been on your mind and your heart, my love. Do you think your parents will be upset that you feel this way?"

"They'd probably disown me and exile me as far away as possible, like Japan or something."

Isabella scoffed. "Mikaela, they would never!"

Mikaela stood, her hands on her hips, as she paced the grassy patch near the water. "And what if they did? You don't understand. My parents' expectations for me do not allow for doubt or fear of the future."

Isabella hastily stood and faced her. "Then…Then fucking *konnichiwa*, Mikaela!" She threw her hands up in frustration. "I guess we get exiled, live in a tiny apartment in Japan, and…and bake bread or something for a living!"

"Bake bread?" she said. "You…you'd still marry me?"

Isabella rushed forward and closed the short gap between them as she wrapped her arms around Mikaela's waist and pressed herself against her. "You know what breaks my heart?" she asked. "That you even have to ask that. I love you more than anything, Mikaela. I don't care if you're the queen one day or simply Mikaela de Medreno Soliz who can't cook a thing, because every version of you is *mine* and I belong to *you* no matter what."

Isabella was sure she had never before felt the fierce tenderness that pounded through her chest as Mikaela's trembling fingers gently brushed away a tear that tracked down her face.

Mikaela closed the millimeters between them as she met Isabella's lips. The kiss was hungry, raw, and mixed with the salt of what Isabella thought were her own tears.

As she reached up to cup Mikaela's face in both her hands, she realized her cheeks were wet too. She kissed her deeply and desperately, as Mikaela reclaimed her lips, her mouth, and her neck over and over again.

"I'm so sorry you've been going through this alone," Isabella mumbled against Mikaela's lips after a long moment. "Never again, my love. Promise you'll always let me in."

Mikaela nodded as her lips brushed Isabella's ear. "I promise."

Isabella pulled back. "You are amazing." She held her gaze. "You are a badass, and there is no one in this world more fit to lead Cayo Azul into our future than you. I will always support you and I will never stop believing in you, Mikaela."

Mikaela crushed her lips against Isabella's again in a dizzying kiss as her fingertips wandered along her spine.

Isabella blinked up at the splinters of sky visible through the deep green canopy overhead. "Shit," she finally said with a laugh. "The sun is going down."

Mikaela looked puzzled. "So?"

Isabella gestured to their horses, who swished their tails in the cool breeze. "Our trail ride should have been over thirty minutes ago," she replied and then glanced at her mare with a good-natured shake of her head. "As much as my horse and I have forged this, shall we say, very *shaky* bond, we'd better head back because the trail is only closed for us until the evening."

Mikaela quickly turned toward the horses to untie their reins from the trees. As she mounted Luna, Isabella couldn't help but recognize something different and more relaxed in her gaze.

She's finally at ease. Her pulse seemed to skip a beat as the realization warmed her all the way to her core.

Mikaela carefully nudged Luna into a quick canter down the soft dirt trail. "Guess you'd better learn how to gallop," she called teasingly over her shoulder.

CHAPTER FORTY

Three days after returning from Santa Julianna, Mikaela sat confidently in the largest Royal Council chamber between her father and Alejandro. Eduardo and several other council members sat opposite them, including Arturo Benitez, their director of IT and cybersecurity.

"Please summarize your findings, Señor Benitez," Alejandro said as he gestured at Arturo's laptop.

Arturo cleared his throat. "My team uncovered a string of encrypted text messages using an international app between Jose Barrientos, Juan's trusted lieutenant, and a close associate of Roberto Jimenez," he said. "These indicated that not only was money changing hands from the resistance to Señor Barrientos in exchange for classified information and presumably an alliance, but that Juan has been empowering this movement."

Eduardo shook his head. "Unconscionable."

Her father's face was stone. "Unforgivable. Even if unintentional, Juan should have known better. He should have been smarter. I have repeated these words more times than I care to count over the course of our lives, but this time he has caused incomparable damage to our government and to the de Medreno legacy." He paused. "And Jose was immediately discharged from all military duties and arrested for collusion against the government, yes?"

Eduardo paged through a manila folder of paperwork. "He sits in jail at the military base now. My understanding is that he's been very open with investigators so far and willing to talk," he said. "Though he will unfortunately face a lengthy jail sentence either way. His cooperation though will be helpful to us as we navigate this unrest and resolve it in a way that ensures everyone is satisfied."

Mikaela folded her hands over her lap. "How did Juan react to this information and his official rebuke?"

"As expected, Juan reacted with considerable anger," her father replied as he rubbed his chin wearily. "His temper flared and he left Castillo Blanco in a state of disarray. He has not returned in five days and he's not answering my calls right now. As we all know Juan's personality, it is usually best to let him have a cooling off period. I have requested that no one else on the Royal Council reach out to him at this time, particularly until we have more answers."

"We have learned that he has temporarily withdrawn to the military base," Alejandro said. "Which makes sense, as he's always fancied that as his domain on Cayo Azul." He turned to Mikaela. "We have a united front here. It also sounds as though, from Eduardo's update, that we'll finally be getting ahead of this unrest if Jose is cooperative and willing to talk."

Eduardo leaned forward, his brow furrowed. "Despite Señor Barrientos being discovered as a traitor, Juan's influence within the military and our armed services is significant," he said thoughtfully. "Is there reason to be concerned that this could be cause for any fracturing or disruption between the Crown and these integral parts of Cayo Azul?"

A murmur of concern rippled through the chamber as Alejandro looked at each of them resolutely. "I confronted my father about his behavior and defended our collective decision. He well understands that he's already on precarious standing within the royal family and any further missteps will result in considerable personal and legal trouble for him."

Mikaela took a measured breath and felt a surge of pride as she nodded at Alejandro. He appeared confident, at ease, and unafraid to assert his integrity, despite the risks and the complicated familial bonds. "Thank you for the detailed update," she said. "Arturo, thank you for this investigative work. Without it, we would not have understood the inroads that this resistance has made, particularly in reaching those who may be influential and, unfortunately, swayed by money. While I am saddened to hear that a lieutenant in our own military would turn against us, my hope is that his knowledge can be used to resolve this situation with the resistance in a peaceful manner where, as Eduardo stated, everyone feels satisfied. My stance has always been and continues to be that learning and long-term peace is extracted from this situation."

Alejandro nodded. "I agree with Her Royal Highness."

Her father tapped his hand on the table. "Yes," he said with a nod. "Peace must be the answer. Juan's departure from Castillo Blanco, while unsettling, means that we all must remain vigilant to ensure the Crown remains stable as we work toward resolution. Let us all work together as one to uphold the integrity of our kingdom."

Mikaela felt a renewed sense of determination alongside a wave of apprehension flood through her as the meeting adjourned and the council members filtered out of the chamber.

As she stood, her father beckoned to her. "Mikaela, a private word, please," he said. "There is something I want to share."

Mikaela's body tensed, but she sat back in her chair. "Go on," she replied.

"I have given it a lot of thought and careful consideration," he said. "I suspect Juan orchestrated the payments to help facilitate and spark the growing unrest and to selfishly serve his own agenda."

Mikaela's mind raced as she considered her father's words. "He believes I would be easier to manipulate as ruler of Cayo Azul?"

"Yes," he replied after a moment. "By forcing unrest during your ascension to the throne, Juan could use that instability and transitory period to solidify and even expand his power over key areas of the kingdom. He knows there would be an adjustment period before you fully establish yourself as the new leader, allowing him to promise Roberto and his men certain benefits by colluding together now. *Particularly* if you're taking the throne through an unprecedented period of unrest on the island. He also knows you have no reason not to trust him, so you likely would not push back on him anyway."

"You're saying he wanted me on the throne," Mikaela said. "Not out of loyalty or any sort of familial *love*, but because he saw it as an advantageous opportunity for himself."

Her father nodded. "Of course Juan has not admitted as much himself," he replied. "But I've known him his entire life. The timing, the sudden interest in your affairs, the secrecy of the payments, the questionable interaction with those involved in the resistance. Juan is a man who has always loved control over others and if he was never to have the throne himself, then the next best option would naturally be to manipulate the person who does—to his own advantage." He took a deep breath. "And I will *never* allow you to be manipulated that way, family or not. If we cannot trust Juan as part of the Crown, then he must be eliminated."

Mikaela glanced at her father in surprise, but he held up a hand. "In theory, of course," he went on. "As Alejandro mentioned, Juan well understands that one more misstep, dependent on the results of our investigation, will spell considerable trouble. That means he would be stripped of his royal titles and authority and instead be provided a small stipend to live as a private citizen. Now, I know his ego and I know he would likely choose to relocate himself elsewhere rather than stay in Cayo Azul as a private citizen. We *will* weed out and remove betrayal at its roots to ensure your smooth transition."

Mikaela straightened in her chair. "I understand."

Am I truly cut out for this? Disgust simmered low in her stomach as her uncle's face flashed in her mind. She felt a beat of empathy for the person that perhaps he was before losing her aunt, but Mikaela shook it away. *He made these choices. If this is what the throne does to people, making them bitter, manipulative, angry, and willing to betray anyone to get what they want, then am I really ready for this?*

As she and her father stood, Mikaela stole a glance at his face. He already appeared tired and a crop of wrinkles lined his forehead as he raised an eyebrow at her.

"How are you feeling, my daughter?" he asked as they fell into step together. "It's not too much, is it? You know Alejandro, the rest of the Royal Council, and I are here to help you, Mikaela."

Mikaela's throat tightened and she blinked rapidly a few times, glad that they were walking side by side so her father couldn't see her face. "No, of course not, Papa."

"I know it's not," he said. "You've always been my strong, tough daughter. You will be an excellent leader, and we'll ensure no one will enter this transition period with their own agendas."

As her father veered off toward his private office, Mikaela stopped short in the hallway as she bit her lip. Guilt flooded her at her father's obvious confidence in her ability and readiness to lead. She realized the only place she wanted to be at that moment was with Isabella; a slightly jarring thought as Mikaela understood just how under her skin she'd gotten.

With a deep, steadying breath, Mikaela turned down the hallway toward Castillo Blanco's main entrance as she smiled to herself. She knew exactly where she was going.

Chapter Forty-one

As Mikaela approached her house, she glanced up at the giggles emanating from the open windows. She recognized the soft, melodic sound of Isabella's laughter mingled with Dayanara's distinct chuckling. She opened the door and paused in the foyer and gazed at Isabella, sitting barefoot and cross-legged on the loveseat with a small bowl of salad in her hands, and Dayanara, who was stretched comfortably across the sofa as she rested her head in one hand and shook her head good-naturedly at whatever Isabella had said.

Mikaela took a deep breath as Isabella and Dayanara looked up expectantly from the living room. *I'm glad that my fiancée and my best friend are getting along like longtime besties.*

Isabella's eyes sparkled as she unfolded herself and rose gracefully. "Mikaela! You're back sooner than expected."

Dayanara stood. "Don't worry, we got a *lot* done for the wedding," she chimed in. "Two hours video-conferencing here with the agency. But, as you know, we're having to move fast with this. Though we were excited to loop in Isabella's mom this time so she could take part in the planning."

"I had no idea that Daya was so good at event planning!" Isabella exclaimed. "She was so helpful with getting some of the details settled."

Dayanara blushed. "I may have helped Her Royal Highness Queen Cristina and Señora Lucia with more than a few events in my time."

"Lovely," Mikaela said. "Not only are you besties with my fiancée, but my future mother-in-law too."

Dayanara rolled her eyes. "Oh, *that's* why you're back early," she said knowingly. "You're having one of *those* days."

Mikaela fixed her with a glare. "What days?"

Dayanara and Isabella exchanged a look, and Mikaela couldn't help but feel they were in on a joke that she wasn't part of. "You know," Dayanara said. "One of those days where you pretend like everything is fine..."

"...When it's definitely *not*." Isabella chimed in.

Dayanara nodded. "But you don't want to *admit* that not everything is fine..."

Isabella blew out her breath and lifted her chin as she held Mikaela's gaze. "...Because you don't want to appear as though you can't handle it all or that you're stressed..."

"...Or overwhelmed," Dayanara supplied helpfully.

Mikaela arched an eyebrow as she looked between her fiancée and her best friend. "How..." She took a deep breath and tried again. "What..."

Dayanara's lips twitched as she gathered her purse and laptop. "I should be going anyway," she said. "Ian and I have dinner plans in City Center."

"That's exciting," Isabella replied as she embraced Dayanara. "Tell Ian we said hello. Have fun with your Irishman."

Dayanara stepped onto the porch and glanced over her shoulder. "Always," she replied with a wink and then fixed Mikaela with a look. "You're welcome, by the way, for helping your fiancée finalize some of the small but very important details of your wedding."

Mikaela opened her mouth, but Dayanara was already halfway down the walkway as her thumbs flitted over her phone.

As the front door closed, an intimate silence enveloped the house. Isabella closed the distance between them and wrapped her arms around Mikaela's waist. "Hey," she whispered as she traced a finger over Mikaela's bottom lip. "You know you're always my priority."

Mikaela claimed Isabella's lips in a slow, deep kiss. A shiver snaked down her spine as Isabella's hand threaded through her hair and a soft sigh escaped her lips.

Breaking the kiss for just a moment, Mikaela trailed a path along Isabella's jaw to the spot just below her ear. "Let me reemphasize how much you mean to me," she murmured.

Isabella tilted her head to give Mikaela better access. "I'm yours," she whispered, her voice laced with anticipation.

Mikaela guided Isabella to the plush leather loveseat where she'd sat just moments before. Mikaela gazed at the woman beneath her, from the eager rise and fall of her chest and the flush that crept across her neck to the splash of pink across her full lips after those deep kisses.

With deliberate slowness, Mikaela kissed and teased down Isabella's body. She gently nipped at the sensitive areas just beneath her ribs and inside her hips. She brushed her fingertips over her soft skin, trying to memorize every inch.

Isabella unfastened the first two buttons of Mikaela's shirt as her hands explored lower and her fingertips teased Mikaela's nipples. A surge of warm, electric pleasure filled Mikaela as she tugged down Isabella's lightweight black linen pants, eager to taste her and feel her gliding against her tongue as her body tensed and her orgasm built.

Isabella groaned in frustration as Mikaela moved lower, her hands no longer able to reach her breasts. "How is it possible that every moment with you feels like the first?" she asked breathlessly.

Mikaela glanced up. "You are my everything," she said as she pressed a kiss to Isabella's inner thigh.

Isabella was already glistening for her, her folds swollen and wet, as Mikaela teased her tongue gently over and around her clit. It was only after Isabella's moan that Mikaela remembered the living room windows were still wide open. She looked down at Isabella, wet and *so* ready. *Too late*.

Mikaela dipped one finger, then two, into Isabella, who sighed in pleasure. "The windows are open, love," she murmured as she bent her fingers to brush against the spot inside Isabella that she knew drove her crazy.

"Oh *God*," Isabella breathed. "You feel so good, Mikaela. I don't know if I can be quiet."

Mikaela slid her fingers through Isabella's slick wetness again and again, her core tightening at her little gasps of pleasure, and planted open-mouthed kisses along her inner thighs and over her folds. Her lips and chin were already soaked in Isabella's sweet pleasure as she smiled against her sensitive skin. "Try, baby. Shhh."

Mikaela's breath danced over Isabella's clit as she arched her hips further into her. "Okay," Isabella said after a moment. "I'll try."

"Good girl," Mikaela murmured as she rewarded her with a third finger inside. After a moment of Isabella riding her fingers, her hips sliding up and down over them as the heat between them grew, Mikaela couldn't wait any longer. She opened her lips against Isabella's swollen clit, as she trailed her tongue the length of her. She massaged and gently sucked the area that she knew would send Isabella over the edge. As she worked her with her tongue, she continued a steady rhythm with her fingers, teasing and pushing her further into Mikaela's mouth from the inside.

Mikaela knew exactly when Isabella was about to come. Her walls tightened around her fingers as she tried to stifle her moans, biting hard on her bottom lip to muffle her cries, before a surge of wetness coated Mikaela's fingers and lips in Isabella's intense pleasure. As her orgasm coursed through her, Isabella arched off the soft leather and pulled Mikaela up. She wrapped her arms around her neck and buried her face in Mikaela's shoulder as she bit down hard on her collarbone to stifle her cries.

Mikaela didn't flinch at the bite, though she knew it would leave a mark. She held Isabella, breathless, for a long moment and then brushed a lock of hair from her face. "I love you," she said as she gently kissed her pounding temple. "And in just a few weeks, we will be married as one."

Isabella blinked. "You have my heart, Mikaela," she said, dazed. "Always. I love you."

After another long moment of sated silence, the gentle afternoon breeze and the call of a tropical bird from the open windows as the only background noise, Isabella trailed her fingertips down the length of Mikaela's rumpled silk skirt. "And I'm going to show you just how much I adore you," she said. "Though perhaps we should go upstairs, because I'm not certain *you* will be able to stay quiet."

Mikaela opened and then closed her mouth before she stood and let Isabella lead them to the stairs. It was only then that she remembered with a smile that she hadn't even taken off her heels yet.

CHAPTER FORTY-TWO

Later that week, Isabella glanced at Mikaela from her shade on a cushioned chaise. Mikaela leaned against the edge of her private pool, her tanned arms stretched along the smooth tile, as droplets of water sparkled against her skin. Isabella sensed that she had still been somewhat distracted around the impending ascension to the throne, though her fear of disappointing her parents seemed to keep her mostly paralyzed as she continued with her duties as though nothing else was on her mind.

Heat emanated from Mikaela's wet body as Isabella traced a droplet's lazy path down her collarbone with her fingertip. "How was your day, love? You're finally back before dinner."

Mikaela took a slow, steadying breath. "It was good, thank you," she replied. "I just…" She watched Isabella's fingertips along her collarbone. "There appears to be evidence that my uncle had knowledge of his lieutenant's collusion with the resistance. My own uncle, who has known me since I was born. I thought I was prepared for my eventual ascension to the throne, but knowing that someone in my own family sees me just as a strategic pawn to manipulate for his own gain is a gutting betrayal." She glanced at the horizon in contemplation. "I wonder if I'm enough for this. To withstand betrayals from those closest. To lead. To build upon my family's legacy. To bring together citizens who are divided and angry and struggling while others live lives of luxury."

"You are the most capable person I know," Isabella said gently. "What is it that makes you fear accepting the throne?"

Mikaela tilted her head as she considered it. "What if I fail the island?" A quiet moment passed between them as the world seemed to settle into the weight of her soft words. "What if I fail my family? I love this island." She took a deep breath. "Even if some of it doesn't love me back right now. It's my home. And it deserves the *best* leader for all. I'm not certain anymore that I can be who Cayo Azul needs me to be."

Isabella watched Mikaela's face as she spoke, her fierce determination and passion always so evident in her expression as she sat on the edge of the chaise.

Isabella slid closer as she wrapped her arms around Mikaela's waist and brushed her lips along her jaw. "Mikaela," she murmured. "You *are* exactly who this island needs. You're thoughtful, you listen, and you care more than anyone I've seen. You have every quality that an incredible leader must have. And a badass one too."

"A badass?" She shook her head ruefully.

Isabella cupped Mikaela's face in both hands as she brushed her thumbs along her soft skin. "Yes," she said as she pressed her forehead to Mikaela's. "I know the pressure you feel is tremendous. I can't pretend to know what it's like, but I know it's not easy. People see how powerful you are, and that's why they are testing you now. I'm proud of you, my love. For being reflective and self-aware and *willing* to be vulnerable, instead of driven by ego. You know I am bound to you forever. I will always support you and remind you what a brilliant, gorgeous, and extremely capable badass you are. And, oh yeah, you also make everyone around you feel like they matter. You are *everything* Cayo Azul needs to heal and grow into the future."

Mikaela let out a short breath. "You're not worried I'll mess it all up?"

"Never," Isabella replied with certainty. She gently met Mikaela's lips with her own. "Because someone beautiful told me once that real freedom lies in letting go. You will always be a de Medreno, it's in your blood. I *know* you, Mikaela. You will use your voice, your savvy, your leadership, and your intelligence to do amazing things for this island. And if you ever have moments of self-doubt, remember that I believe in you. Always. I'll remind you ten thousand times so you never forget."

Mikaela threaded her fingers in Isabella's thoughtfully. "You make it all sound so simple."

"Because it is. You were born for this. And you will never be doing it alone."

She leaned in to rest her chin on Mikaela's shoulder as Mikaela brought Isabella's fingertips to her lips. The afternoon sun was warm against her back, and Mikaela's hands soothed her skin beneath its golden rays.

"I'll talk with my parents next week," she said. "I want to speak to them openly and honestly. I want to have a clear succession plan in place. I..." She took a deep breath. "I want to feel confident in who I am again and see myself the way you do, my love."

Isabella kissed her softly, slowly, and sure. "No matter what, I'm with you always."

❖

The east wing of Castillo Blanco was still as Mikaela stepped into her father's private office the following week. It was past dinner time and getting later, with most of the royal attendants and staff having already departed for the evening. Isabella had left early that morning for Este, accompanied by a small security detail, to spend the day with Araceli. Mikaela knew she was due back to Castillo Blanco soon and looked forward to getting this conversation over with. She glanced at her parents, who waited calmly and expectantly as the setting sun streamed in through the tall windows and cast a warm, solemn red glow across the polished chairs and shining floor.

Her father sat at his wide mahogany desk, his posture relaxed, as he leaned back in his chair and nodded at Mikaela in greeting. Her mother sat nearby with her hands folded casually in her lap. There was a quiet intensity in her mother's energy and Mikaela wondered if she somehow sensed the seriousness of the conversation that was about to take place.

As Mikaela sat comfortably in another chair opposite her father's desk, her heart thudded in her chest. She felt otherwise calm, steady, and self-assured as she looked between her parents confidently.

"Is everything all right, Mikaela?" her father asked. "When you requested a private sit-down with us both after hours, I understood there must be something urgent you'd like to relay."

Mikaela nodded. "Thank you for meeting with me later than usual," she said and then took a deep breath. "I have been giving the future a great deal of thought and consideration. I do feel our island is at a critical crossroads, where it's moving rapidly into a lucrative future while a third of the population is inadvertently being left behind. Given the political infighting and the betrayal we've uncovered from within, we need someone adept, sure, and diplomatic to bridge these gaps."

Her father's brow furrowed as he stroked his jaw while considering her words. "Do you feel as though you aren't ready to lead?" he asked after a moment. "Have I been putting too much pressure on you?"

Mikaela met her father's eyes. "No, Papa, it isn't that you've been pressuring me," she replied. "I certainly know how to manage pressure and expectations. I have been doing that my whole life. I have been questioning lately if I am the right person to lead the next generations of Cayo Azuleans into the island's future."

The silence that followed was sharp as a look of disbelief flashed across her father's face. "What are you talking about?" he asked as his voice grew louder. "Mikaela, we have been preparing you for this your entire life. The Royal Council sees your impeccable leadership and expertise. They have long been in unanimous agreement that you will be our next queen. Your whole life has been designed for this succession!"

"This isn't about what my entire life has been designed for," Mikaela interrupted firmly. "I never had a choice in that. This is about what is right for the people of Cayo Azul and for our family's legacy. I am not scared to lead. I am not caving to pressure. For once, I am being completely honest with myself. I don't want to fail you or our people."

Her father scraped his chair back and stood tall. "Is this because of Juan?" he barked. "Has he approached you or said anything to you? If my brother has manipulated you in any way to question your leadership…" His fists balled up at his sides.

"No," Mikaela cut in. "Besides, Uncle Juan is the last person I would be fearful of or intimidated by. I know his personality and I've known men like him; they're brash and all ego and talk. I have all the confidence in the world handling Juan."

He sat back in his chair. "Then what? The resistance? Are you concerned about a rebellion? I know it has seemed as though there's been a microscope on you lately, but you must understand that this is politics, Mikaela. Opposition will look for any way, any *in*, to bolster their cause and cripple the other. These things ebb and flow, and you saw the final report released last week from Human Rights International. *No* findings of any wrongdoing, as we knew they would conclude. You've been in these meetings. You've personally spearheaded so much recent progress. Your public bus system project is set to kick off early next year. You know that there is infighting among the resistance now as Roberto Jimenez and two others vie to lead this movement. Eduardo's team has been in communication with the other two and it appears as though we are close to reaching a common ground."

Mikaela opened her mouth, but her father continued as he slammed a hand on his desk. "This is not a reason to question everything you have prepared your life for! You are my heir, my daughter, Mikaela. You are stronger than that!"

"Papa, stop!" Mikaela stood and held her father's gaze steadily across the desk. "This is *me*. I'm not running away and I am not afraid. I am far stronger than you know, and that is unfortunate because I always believed that you recognized my strength. The only thing I *am* afraid of is taking on a role in which I will somehow fail our family and our people, particularly during this sensitive political time."

She glanced at the tall window and blinked at the setting sun rays filtering through the thick glass. "This is my home and Cayo Azul runs through my blood. One thing that will never change is my promise to protect this island. And that is exactly what I am doing by putting aside my ego. I need to know, deep in my soul, that I am ready."

Her father stared at her for a long moment as the vein along his left temple throbbed. Mikaela felt the stubborn, invisible clash of wills tugging between them.

Who will blink first?

"If I may," her mother's quiet, composed voice tinkled through the charged air like a calming bell and Mikaela suddenly remembered she was in the room too. "I'd like to address this. You two are so very similar, so stubborn at times and dominant. Let me add a voice of reason before this devolves into an emotional shouting match."

They turned to her in mild confusion as she rose gracefully from her seat and tucked a strand of hair behind Mikaela's ear.

"You have always belonged to the world in one way or another," her mother said gently. "I knew that would be the case from the moment your father and I found out we were pregnant. We struggled to bring you into this world, you know. For whatever reason, becoming pregnant was difficult for us. When we found out we were having you, we were overjoyed. Still, I always knew in our position, in our roles, you were never going to have a traditionally normal life. There would always be people looking, strangers clamoring for you, expectations to uphold. But…" Mikaela felt a twist of surprise in her chest at the tears that filled her eyes. "You were *mine* first. My baby. My little girl. And all I have ever wanted is to protect you from a world that takes too much if you're too kind. You may have grown up thinking I was overbearing and perhaps I was. But I was willing to be that to shield you from as much of the negative, the evil, and the heart-wrenching that I could."

Mikaela felt her throat tighten as her mother stepped closer and brushed a cool hand along her cheek. "Truth be told, I am surprised but relieved that you're being so open and discussing this with us, Mikaela," she said. "Because it means you are putting ego aside and being selfless. I trust the succession is something you would never take lightly. I commend you for being reflective and truly understanding the weight of who you were born to be."

Mikaela let out a breath as her mother pulled her into a soft, grounding hug. "I was afraid you were going to tell us you were already rethinking your engagement," she said good-naturedly. "I thought you would push calling it off, despite the wedding invitations already being sent."

Mikaela shook her head. "Of course not," she replied. "I understand the sacred bond of marriage means that we are bound to each other for life. I'm so glad that it's Isabella." Emotion softened her voice as Isabella's face flashed through her mind.

Her mother nodded. "Good. I've taken quite a liking to Isabella. Have you spoken to her about your conflicting feelings?"

Mikaela nodded. "Yes," she replied. "It felt only right to ensure she knew everything that was weighing on my heart before we married."

"And she doesn't mind?" her mother asked as she arched an eyebrow and sat back down.

Mikaela shook her head again. "No," she said. "She loves me."

Her father was quiet as he watched their exchange. "We always raised you to think for yourself," he said. "And I can't be upset that you are. We will draft a detailed succession plan, my daughter. One in which you feel confident and sure as our island's next leader. You will not be thrown into this alone."

The room seemed to lighten. For the first time in Mikaela's life, it felt as though she was finally pushing through the layers of cool poise and healing the parts of herself that she knew she needed to face in order to be the best possible leader. *Isabella believes in me. So do my parents. Maybe I* am *ready.*

Her father scratched his chin. "Perhaps you can help me draft a three-year succession plan," he continued. "One we will work on together, and then officially present to the Royal Council. I want to ensure alignment and that you feel fully prepared—"

An urgent knock on the heavy wooden door cut him off as he looked up sharply.

Eduardo opened the door, his face stricken. "Your Royal Highness, I apologize for the intrusion," he said. "There's a situation outside Castillo Blanco. The scheduled protest by the resistance has turned violent. We need to get to one of the chambers *now*."

CHAPTER FORTY-THREE

Mikaela's heart dropped as she hurried through the quiet hallway between her parents, with Eduardo leading the way.

"What's going on?" she asked. "The protest that was scheduled weeks ago?"

"Yes," Eduardo replied as he ushered them into one of the larger chambers. Several members of the Royal Council sat around the long conference table, their expressions dark and concerned.

"The supporters of the resistance gathered peacefully, but…" Eduardo glanced at her father. "Juan gave an order to deploy the full force of the military two hours ago. He circumvented standard protocol to obtain Royal Council clearance before doing so and did not attempt to let anyone know."

Her father's face turned hard and furious. "He *what*?"

All the inroads we were making. All the diplomacy, all the trust-building, gone in an instant. Once again, because of Uncle Juan.

"We do know that it escalated incredibly fast," Eduardo said. "I have confirmed that live rounds were fired into the air and tear gas has been deployed. The crowds began retaliating. Throwing stones, shouting, pushing, and shoving. Castillo Blanco is on emergency lockdown, but it's a chaotic scene outside the gates right now. Security is attempting to disperse the crowds, but they're far outnumbered. I have personally demanded that the armed forces stand down immediately, but there is confusion as this is opposite to the order they were given from Juan."

Mikaela clenched her fists in her lap. "How many are injured?"

"No confirmed numbers yet. Unfortunately, emergency services are encountering access issues due to the sheer amount of people and military in the streets right now. It also appears that Juan ordered barricades, probably to make mass detainment of the protestors easier."

Her mother covered her mouth, but the horror was clear on her face. Her father paced the chamber and turned to one of the windows as he appeared to think.

"He's completely lost control," Mikaela said. "Or he wanted this to happen. Either way, it's unforgivable."

Her father looked at her over his shoulder and shook his head. "He's trying to provoke and show strength through force. He wants to emphasize his authority. He's felt backed into a corner since his official rebuke and investigation, and his solution has always been to punch back harder. He thinks blood in the streets will portray strength, decisiveness. Strike a sense of *fear* into anyone who goes against him." He took a deep breath and raked a hand over his head. "It goes without saying that this is not how we've ever operated, not when our monarchy is built on fairness, integrity, leadership, and peace."

"This protest may have been manipulated to create this outcome," Eduardo said. "This response was designed to stoke terror among our people."

An icy-cold tingle of dread rose from Mikaela's stomach and clenched around her chest as realization hit her. "*Shit*," she exclaimed. "Isabella. She's supposed to be returning now from visiting her mother. Oh my God." She stood. "Oh my *God*, her car is likely caught in the chaos outside."

Mikaela's blood pulsed like ice through her veins. Somewhere in the back of her mind, she could hear her father interjecting something about royal protocol and risk, but she didn't turn. Something primal twisted inside her at the thought of Isabella being overwhelmed by crowds of shouting people, sirens, flying debris, and riot shields.

"If Isabella's car is caught in this and they realize it's part of the royal fleet, it will be targeted," Mikaela said. "They could hurt Isabella."

Eduardo pressed his phone to his ear. "Yes, I need eyes on Isabella's car," he barked to someone on the other end. "She's in one of the Escalades. We need to locate the vehicle and divert it away from the riot. If it's already there, we need an immediate protective boundary around the car so it can turn around and we can bring it through the service road around the back of Castillo Blanco. I want at least six guards waiting at the back for her."

Mikaela stood motionless at the chamber door for a moment and then crossed her arms over her chest. "Thank you, Eduardo."

He nodded once. "We're on it, Your Royal Highness," he replied and then pressed his phone to his ear. "She what?"

Eduardo swallowed hard before looking at Mikaela. "The Escalade was spotted near the main square. The crowd turned. She's caught in it right now, but we have a plan…"

Mikaela tuned Eduardo out as she tried to reel in the storm raging inside her. Her body felt tight all over and her head pounded. She trusted their security team implicitly, though a sliver of doubt stabbed at her as she wondered if she could trust the military under Juan's command.

The echo of Isabella's words by the pool lingered in her mind and stoked the sparks of a fire flickering deep in her chest. *A brilliant, gorgeous, and extremely capable badass.*

She straightened and set her shoulders. The time to show up and prove her fiancée right was now. "I'm going to get her," she said. "I'll be right back."

Mikaela wasn't sure if her mom calling her name was a throbbing echo in her head or if she was really shouting after her, but she didn't look back. Gone were the weeks of self-doubt and questioning. The weight of nerves, pressure, and paralyzed indecision began to melt into the fire she recognized as it sharpened into something primal, something ancient from generations of ancestors before her whose impenetrable strength seemed to fortify her all at once.

A handful of security guards milled around the doors, their black boots heavy against the sleek floor as they positioned themselves. The loud static of their walkie-talkies was harsh and unwelcome in the otherwise quiet corridor, but Mikaela was focused only on Isabella's safe return to her.

Mikaela knew somewhere at the back of her mind that she wasn't just Bartolo de Medreno Soliz's daughter anymore. She wasn't just the heiress to the throne. She was the next leader of Cayo Azul, and today she would command.

"Your Royal Highness, Castillo Blanco is on lockdown," a security guard spoke as he reached for her arm. Mikaela didn't stop as she pulled her arm away defiantly and pushed open one of the heavy back doors. "Princess, you must go to the Royal Council chamber. It's dangerous!"

Mikaela turned and fixed him with a stare. "My fiancée is out there," she replied. "Dangerous is leaving her there. Isabella is *mine* to protect. The people, *all* people of Cayo Azul, are mine to protect. I will not sit behind castle walls while they bleed in the streets. And if I must walk through this riot myself to bring my fiancée to safety, I will do exactly that."

The security guard's mouth dropped open. "Princess, you cannot leave," he tried again. "Rest assured that our team is out there and we're working alongside the police..."

I am *a badass. And it's time for me to lead.*

Mikaela walked out the doors without a backward glance. She didn't stop and she didn't hear the security guards sprinting behind her for protection as she continued purposefully down the long gravel drive that cut through the isolated back of the castle grounds.

Nothing is going to take Isabella away from me. Not without first going through me.

Isabella's mind raced as she folded her hands tightly in her lap in the cool leather back seat of the Escalade. The security guard in the driver's seat gripped the wheel so tightly that his knuckles were nearly translucent as his eyes darted nervously back and forth through the fog and across the crowds of people, police, and military. Her second guard, sitting in the passenger's seat, pressed his phone to his ear as he tried to describe the scene to someone on the other end.

The main square was chaotic. Shouts and screams rose above ragged shadows and quick, bright flashes. Protestors were standing atop parked vehicles, smashing windshields, and pushing against heavily armed military men who shouted and shoved at them.

"We'll get through, señorita," the driver spoke, glancing at her in the rearview mirror nervously. "Horatio has been in nonstop contact with the lead security team at the castle." He nodded at the security guard in the passenger's seat. "We will get you home safely."

Isabella had been just about to nod, a brief swell of relief flashing through her, when a large rock clanged against the back windshield. She jumped at the loud crash as a few more rocks were hurled toward the back doors and side mirrors of the Escalade. She twisted in her seat, blinking through the dark-tinted windows, as a protestor sprinted down the street before being blindside body-slammed into the curb by a military man with a riot shield.

Isabella jumped and bit back a shriek at the hard impact before forcing her gaze away and out her own window. She froze as it landed on two familiar men tucked in a narrow alley.

Of course Roberto Jimenez is here. Sowing chaos and yet standing untouched watching everything he set in motion come to a head.

Isabella saw a taller man next to Roberto and blinked once, twice. It couldn't be. Was that *Juan de Medreno Soliz*? Roberto gestured rapidly and Juan, beneath his dark sunglasses, simply nodded as he ran a hand through his shaggy hair and turned away from the street.

Isabella's stomach twisted as cold realization dawned on her. The Royal Council's suspicions were correct. This was controlled, orchestrated *strategy* designed to stoke flames and Juan—Mikaela's own uncle—was a traitor who had teamed up with Roberto for his own selfish power grab. Isabella reached for her phone and hoped she had enough battery left to get a quick text to Mikaela. Panic and unease crawled beneath her skin as the driver shouted something and slammed his fist on the horn as two protestors pounded on the hood of the Escalade.

The next few minutes happened so quickly that Isabella was sure she was dreaming. Security guards that she recognized from Castillo Blanco marched through the street, their rifles balanced against their broad shoulders. Isabella's mouth went dry and her heart thumped in her chest as she saw who the guards had formed a human shield around. Mikaela, tall, poised, and every bit the absolute fucking goddess that Isabella knew she was, stepped confidently through the smoke, the noise, and the chaos. Somehow, she was protected from it all around her as her posture and gaze radiated strength and focus. Her dark blond hair glinted in shards of evening light that cut through the haze and then her gaze was on Isabella's car, as though nothing else around them mattered.

In moments, security guards surrounded the Escalade, pushing the mob back and shouting orders to the police and armed forces as they directed the car down the street. Isabella glanced around in wonder as the car was guided through the riot, around the square, and then eventually to a nondescript gravel road. Clouds of gray dust rose from beneath the Escalade's large tires as it rumbled up the path and was flagged through the iron gates around the far back of Castillo Blanco.

Horatio jumped out of the passenger's seat before the engine even fully shut off and opened the back door. Isabella stepped out carefully. She turned at the sound of heels on gravel just as Mikaela's confident strides turned into an uncharacteristic sprint as the stunned security guards shielding her looked on.

Mikaela pulled Isabella into her arms without a word. Isabella melted into her, the physical connection sparking something through her veins. Mikaela closed her eyes before Isabella buried her face into her shoulder. She sighed as Mikaela threaded a hand in Isabella's hair and held her tightly. Her heart rattled wildly against her chest and then slowed as Mikaela gently brushed her lips against her temple.

"You're safe," she whispered. "I promise. It's okay."

"I'm okay." Isabella pulled back just enough to meet Mikaela's gaze. "I'm fine, my love. I'm right here." She blinked as realization hit. "But wait, Mikaela, what were you doing out in that chaos? That's dangerous for you! Isn't Castillo Blanco on lockdown?"

A security guard from Mikaela's contingent reached them and took a deep breath as he glanced around the grounds. "Great question, señorita," he said flatly. "The princess broke emergency protocol and put herself in immense danger during a rapidly evolving and uncontrolled situation. It's imperative that we return you both to the Royal Council chamber immediately."

Isabella bit her lip and then turned to Mikaela. "I have to tell you something," she said. "I need to tell you and your parents what I saw, but you're not going to like it."

Chapter Forty-four

Mikaela knew she had broken every rule when it came to emergency royal protocol. She knew it was irresponsible, but she didn't care. In that moment, it didn't matter who was watching or could see them, or if the press had their cameras and drones trained on the grounds of Castillo Blanco. All she cared about was the woman in her arms.

Let them look. Let them see how much Isabella means to me.

As they fell into step surrounded tightly by the security team and let themselves be escorted inside, Mikaela laced her fingers in Isabella's. She vowed that nothing—and no one—would ever come between them.

As they entered the room after Isabella had relayed what she saw, Mikaela lifted her chin as she surveyed the tense scene. A live Google Map of the island was projected from someone's laptop onto a screen on the far wall and members of the Royal Council spoke in low, urgent tones as their fingers flew over their tablets. Her father was seated at the head of the large table as he rested his chin in his hand.

Alejandro stood as relief flickered across his face at the sight of them, though Mikaela recognized something darkly intense and furious warring in his expression.

"Is she okay?" Alejandro asked. His hair was damp and he looked casual in a pair of dark denim jeans and a white cable-knit sweater. "I had just gotten out of the shower at home and was preparing to finish work when I got word of the riot and the lockdown. I came as quickly as I could."

"I'm okay," Isabella said. "Mikaela and the security team knew exactly what to do."

Alejandro sat heavily and slammed his palm against the table. "This has gone too far," he said. "My father turned the military onto our own people. On innocent civilians gathered to peacefully protest. To collaborate with Roberto Jimenez, a leader of the resistance movement working directly against the Crown? How could he do something so treasonous? He's supposed to be family."

Mikaela's father cleared his throat. "Alejandro…"

Alejandro slammed his hand onto the table again and then raked it through his hair. "He doesn't get to hide behind his status or rank anymore," he said. "He has never honored the importance of his position and has always put only himself first. Enough is enough." His voice shook with anger. He resolutely met the king's concerned gaze. "Give the order, Uncle. I'll go to the base myself and personally arrest him."

The chamber went silent as Mikaela's breath caught at the gravity of Alejandro's words. Isabella squeezed her hand, gently grounding her, as her father and Eduardo exchanged glances.

"We can't escalate further until we understand the chain of command on the ground," Eduardo said. "I know this is a difficult and unprecedented situation, but we need more proof of Juan's involvement and a warrant first."

Alejandro nodded. "We can get a warrant immediately," he said. "My father has broken a countless number of laws today. He's crossed loyalties and there's no coming back from that. I know it and you know it. We all do."

A guard stepped into the chamber and whispered something to one of Eduardo's senior aides. He crossed the room and murmured the update.

"The military has stood down," Eduardo said. "Just minutes ago. The lieutenant on-site acquiesced to my order on behalf of King Bartolo rather than continue with the onslaught under Juan's command. Evidently, many soldiers refused to act further after seeing civilians become injured. They have pulled back and the police are now carefully working to disperse the crowds."

A collective sigh of relief seemed to lift over the chamber as Mikaela's father raised an eyebrow in disbelief.

"They refused Juan's order?" he asked. "And placed priority on ours over his?"

Eduardo nodded. "Yes, Your Royal Highness. It appears, though he has loyalties within the armed forces and perhaps an alliance with the resistance, his control is not as iron-tight as he seems to think. Ultimately, the armed forces are loyal to the Crown which, until very recently, included Juan."

Alejandro tapped his knuckles on the table in thought. "Then the time to act is now," he said. "Every moment that we wait is another moment that the monarchy appears to be aligned with this deliberate destruction of trust and sowing of fear. My father and the resistance will use that to their advantage. We must prepare the warrant for his arrest. If we delay, it will give him time to strategize."

"We'll need to coordinate with the judiciary wing immediately," Mikaela's father replied. "Eduardo, please reach out to Señor Campos. As chief judge of Cayo Azul's judiciary network, we'll need to involve him right away. In fact, I would bet he's waiting for our call right about now."

Alejandro looked expectantly at Mikaela's father. "Yes, Alejandro," he finally said with a nod. "Tonight, we must prepare and ensure an air-tight strategy is in place to understand the depth of Juan's betrayal and to begin making things right with our people. We will place him under arrest at dawn."

He cleared his throat. "Are you sure…"

Alejandro nodded. "Yes," he replied evenly. "I will present the warrant alongside a contingent from the police and place him under arrest myself."

Mikaela glanced at her cousin and then back at her father as she straightened her spine. "I'm going with you, Alejandro," she said. "We will do this together. He will then have to face the Royal Council and the consequences of his selfish actions. We will stand together."

The Royal Council appeared relieved and emboldened by the assertive leadership of Mikaela and Alejandro—their future.

Her father sat back in his chair and drummed his fingers on the thick upholstered arms. "We must prepare a statement to be released after his arrest," he said. "Tonight will be long. We have footage to review, people to interview, social media to monitor, statements to draft, and many critical decisions to make in a short amount of time. I suggest we call the kitchen and get the coffee started now. We'll need it."

As Mikaela slid into her seat at the table between her father and Alejandro, she pressed Isabella's fingertips to her lips. "Get some rest, love," she said. "The lockdown should be lifted as soon as security has completed their final sweep across the grounds. They'll escort you to the house and I'll send for Daya to join you. The next days will be busy, but your safety is most important to me."

Isabella nodded and Mikaela desperately wished she was returning home with Isabella. She craved to wrap her arms around her and hold her tightly as they fell asleep safely wound around one another in a tangle of limbs and soft skin. Instead, clarity and duty flooded her and gently numbed the aching pang in her chest. She looked up from the table long enough to watch the back of Isabella disappear, surrounded by security, into the hallway.

Mikaela sat back in her chair after a moment, confident that Isabella was now safe. She no longer felt burdened by indecision or paralyzed by pressure or doubts. This wasn't just about the throne anymore. This was about justice, their people, and protecting the ones she loved most.

The first threads of dawn unfurled over the vast sea as gentle waves rippled and foamed against the empty sand. Mikaela and Alejandro approached the wide concrete steps of the Santa Julianna Catholic Church as their security guard idled in the Escalade parked behind the tall, imposing structure. The centuries-old building was a breathtaking testament to Spanish architecture, from its weathered limestone and tall wrought-iron gates to the intricate carvings of tropical motifs and solemn, devoted saints that adorned the exterior around its large wooden double doors.

The drive from Cayo Azul's state-of-the-art military base into Santa Julianna had been quiet, with only the sounds of the night air whooshing through the cracked car windows and the soft purr of the engine surrounding them.

Juan had been formally taken into custody before a barricade of news crews, journalists, and a small throng of protestors. He stood tall as he shook his hair off his neck and was guided into the waiting police car. A scowl darkened his face, but he refused to acknowledge Mikaela and Alejandro. He didn't speak to them nor did he look in their direction as he was led away from the base in silver handcuffs. For all the bravado and show of force, Juan's arrest was oddly anticlimactic, quick, and quiet.

As they entered the still sanctuary of the church, Mikaela stole a glance at her cousin. They were waiting to meet with the clergy for an urgent damage control conversation, where they intended to assure them of the monarchy's devotion to the people of Cayo Azul and ensure their continued backing as the Royal Council began steps to fix what Juan had nearly destroyed in mere hours.

"Thank you, Alejandro." Mikaela's voice was soft in the large church.

Alejandro glanced back at her. "For what?"

"For your bravery," Mikaela said. "For standing together in the face of dangerous agendas within our own family." She placed her hand on Alejandro's strong forearm. "For standing up to him."

Alejandro watched the rows of votive candles that flickered beneath colorful stained-glass depictions of saints and martyrs. "I wasn't sure how it would feel," he replied. "I suppose I thought I'd feel triumphant that justice had been served. And I do. Though there is part of me that feels…heavy. Let down."

"You're still his son," Mikaela said gently.

Alejandro exhaled. "And Uncle Bartolo is our king," he said. "He is a phenomenal king to all. And you're our soon-to-be queen."

Mikaela didn't respond. She took a few steps and sank into one of the old wooden pews as she ran a hand through her hair. Alejandro sat beside her.

At long last, Mikaela took a breath. "You know, I spent the last several weeks wondering if I was ready for this," she said. "The pressure. The politics. Those who only wish to serve their own interests."

Alejandro shook his head. "You have been preparing for years for this succession," he said. "I know things are challenging now, but you're leading us through it as we speak. The resistance may have targeted you because it was easy, or rather, my *father* made it easy. But the vast majority of people on this island love you, Mikaela. As we make things right, find compromise, and maintain peace, you'll see that our people still believe in this family."

"Of course they do," Mikaela replied. "And they will continue to because I know in my heart now that I am ready. Ready to fight for Cayo Azul and make us whole again."

Alejandro glanced at her and smiled. "You *are* ready to lead," he said. "I can see it. My loyalty is to you, always."

"I know it is." Mikaela squeezed Alejandro's warm hand. "Likewise, mine is to you. *Always*. And that's why this is so easy. Like it was meant to be, huh, cousin? I've been pushing you to take on more royal responsibilities. You have achieved so much in such a short amount of time. You have the strength and fortitude, the clarity and integrity, the brilliant mind, and most importantly you have the heart to help me lead Cayo Azul into the next several generations. I want you to be my senior-most advisor, my right-hand."

Alejandro searched her face as he exhaled. "Are you...Are you certain?"

"I've never been more sure of anything," Mikaela replied. "Except making Isabella mine, of course."

The early dawn sunlight peeked through tall stained-glass windows and poured muted splashes of light pink, yellow, and red across the scarred wooden floor. Mikaela couldn't help but get the sense that it truly was a new day on Cayo Azul. There was significant work to be done, but her chest bloomed with confidence that they would get there. The sounds of footsteps from a narrow hallway behind the sanctuary meant the meeting with the local clergy was about to begin.

Alejandro nodded as he tightened his grip around her hand. A senior clergy member approached the altar with a nod as the golden embroidery on his white robes caught the dazzling morning sun.

"Then I would be honored," he said. "As it was meant to be, as you say."

CHAPTER FORTY-FIVE

The house was quiet when Mikaela finally returned from Santa Julianna a couple of hours later. Outwardly at least, there were no signs indicating all that had happened in such a short amount of time, and Mikaela was relieved. Her body ached with exhaustion and she was physically, emotionally, and mentally drained.

She closed the front door behind her and tossed her wrinkled blazer onto the arm of the leather sofa. The air conditioning was cool against her bare arms and shoulders, and she debated falling into bed in the thin black camisole and skinny pants she had been wearing for nearly twenty-four hours. Mikaela had just finished unzipping and kicking her heeled boots off when soft footsteps rushed down the stairs.

Mikaela glanced up expectantly as Isabella appeared breathless in the foyer. Her sleepy expression dissolved into relief, though her eyes were wide with cautious concern.

She was still in her pajamas. She glanced over Isabella's smooth tanned legs, her dark blue cotton hot pants and an oversized white I Heart New York T-shirt that Mikaela recognized as one of her own, purchased as a silly joke the last time she was in New York City.

"My love," Isabella breathed expectantly, her dimples deepening.

Mikaela felt every ounce of exhaustion settle into her as she opened her arms. Isabella rushed into her and hugged her tightly as Mikaela pressed her face into Isabella's hair and inhaled the familiar, grounding scent of her almond and blackberry shampoo.

"You're okay," Isabella said. "I've been so worried about you." She pulled back for a moment and cupped Mikaela's face in both hands as she looked at her with concern. "Are you hurt?"

"No," Mikaela replied. "Just tired. Everything is done. For now. Juan was arrested and taken into custody. Our public works department is cleaning up everything left behind from the riot. All peaceful protestors taken into custody have been released." She yawned and quickly threw her hand over her mouth. "I am ready to lead."

Isabella's gaze softened as she smoothed a lock of Mikaela's hair. "You already are."

Mikaela said nothing at first. Instead, she leaned closer and gently kissed Isabella's cheeks, then her jaw, then her lips. She teased a slow, sure trail down Isabella's neck and then back to her lips. She finally pulled back and met her gaze. Isabella looked back at her with love as she laced her fingers in Mikaela's.

"You did it," Isabella said. "You did everything you needed to do and everything you *could* do right now. Let me take care of you."

Mikaela let herself be led up the stairs and down the hallway to the bedroom as Isabella explained that Dayanara had left just moments before for an all-attendant and staff meeting at Castillo Blanco to update and reassure everyone after last night's events. She collapsed into bed as Isabella wriggled beneath the sheets next to her. Her fingers and lips trailed slow, relaxed paths across Mikaela's shoulders and collarbone.

"I'm so proud of you," Isabella whispered. "You remained true to yourself and rediscovered the strength that was within you all along."

Mikaela brushed her thumb along Isabella's jaw and then pulled her on top of her, surprising even herself at her desire after having not slept all night. "I'd do it again a thousand times," she replied. "You *are* my strength, Isabella."

As Isabella hovered above her and leaned down for a kiss, her dark hair falling into a curtain around them, Mikaela caught Isabella's wrists knowingly. Her grip was firm and tender as she pushed herself up against the pillows and pulled Isabella to her, kissing her slowly and possessively, as she took her time exploring her mouth.

"You're mine," Mikaela whispered against her ear before nibbling roughly at the sensitive pulse point on her neck. "I need to feel you and remind you who exactly you belong to, my love."

Isabella's breath caught as her fingers curled into Mikaela's sides. "I already know," she said simply as she tilted her head to give her better access.

Mikaela shifted them and pressed Isabella into the rumpled sheets as she trailed kisses down her neck. "Good," she replied. "I want you to feel it in the depths of your heart." She slid her hands up the subtle curve of Isabella's thighs before slipping beneath the hem of her borrowed T-shirt, deliberately taking her time. "Every kiss, every touch, every time you come for me, I am claiming you again and again. You're mine," Mikaela repeated. "First. Always."

Isabella nodded, already breathless with anticipation, as her body arched in surrender beneath her touch. She pressed her thigh firmly between Isabella's legs as she trailed her lips leisurely up her stomach to her breasts.

Her nipples were pink and already hard as Mikaela lavished attention on one and brushed teasing, featherlight touches across the other with her fingertips.

As Isabella moaned beneath her and pressed down on her thigh, desperately seeking heated friction, her nails dug into Mikaela's bare shoulders. "I'm yours," she said. "I will always belong to you, Mikaela."

"I love you," Mikaela whispered as Isabella planted a soft kiss along her jaw.

"And I love the way you make sure I never forget it." Isabella grinned wryly at her. "You know, for someone that hasn't slept in over twenty-four hours, you have a lot of energy."

"Rest is overrated."

As soon as the last syllable was off her lips, Mikaela closed her eyes against the pillow and Isabella's warm body wrapped around her. Within seconds, she fell into a deep, exhausted, and overdue sleep.

CHAPTER FORTY-SIX

A few weeks later, Isabella stood before the large mirror in Mikaela's bedroom. She took a steadying breath as she studied everything the makeup artist had done over the last forty-five minutes, from expertly highlighting the angles and contours of her face to emphasizing her eyelashes and lips.

Around her, the house buzzed with energy. Event planners and royal attendants fluttered about as they paraded in and out of the bedroom, the living room, and even the bathroom. While Mikaela had given Isabella her home to prepare for their wedding, she and Cristina had rented the penthouse floor of one of the nearby City Center resorts for their own preparations. It felt strange not seeing Mikaela for two entire days, though her own mother had stayed with her and the days had been filled from sunrise to nighttime with pre-wedding activities and appointments. She and Mikaela had granted one sit-down interview together with the local Cayo Azul news station at the behest of the PR agency and, though Isabella was nervous for her first official interview, she surprised even herself at her composure and poise while answering questions and graciously thanking them for their congratulations.

Isabella briefly wondered if Javier's head had exploded when he saw the interview, though a gentle knock on the bedroom door pulled her from her reverie.

"Come in," she called.

Her mother, dressed in a long rose-gold gown with intricately beaded fabric that elegantly crossed over her shoulders and bodice, entered. Isabella's mouth dropped open. Her mother looked ten years younger with subtle makeup sweeping her face and her dark hair pulled into a smooth updo.

"Mami, you look radiant," Isabella said as she caught the faintest crinkle of bashfulness in her mother's expression.

"Not too bad for an old lady from Este, eh?" She struck a playful pose. "How are you feeling? It will be time soon, daughter."

Isabella's heartbeat quickened as she smoothed the silky fabric of her form-fitting open-back black dress. The train grazed the floor around her bare feet and her long black lace mantilla trailed nearly half a foot behind her. It was set firmly in place in her hair with a tall, ornately carved white peineta that perfectly matched the color of the creamy orange blossom petals woven through her hair as her loose curls cascaded down her back.

Her mind wandered to the ceremony awaiting her on the private stretch of Playa del Sol and the moment when her life would officially become joined with Mikaela's under the vast blue island sky. She thought of Mikaela and wondered what she was thinking and how she was feeling at that exact moment, and if her heart was pounding as fast as her own.

Probably not. She's always perfectly in control.

"I'm feeling good, Mami," Isabella said. "I am ready."

Isabella closed her eyes for a moment as she thought again of Mikaela, the soft sand beneath their feet, her loving, intense gaze, her golden dark blond hair, and the sacred union in which they were about to enter. As she took a deep breath and blinked, a profound sense of happiness and the same calm anticipation she'd felt after the gala—when she and Mikaela barely knew each other—filled and warmed her.

"You are so beautiful," her mother whispered. Isabella met her gaze in the mirror and recognized tears on her mother's cheeks. "Remember, the path that you and Mikaela walk now and forever is one of love and unity." She placed her hands on Isabella's shoulders. "These orange blossoms are meant to represent joy, happiness, and good fortune for your future. Embrace each moment together, daughter. Though these little moments may seem insignificant, they are the threads that will weave the tapestry of your shared journey."

Isabella took a deep breath and inhaled the light scent of the orange blossoms adorning her hair. Their subtle fragrance was a reminder of the generations of Cayo Azulean brides who had stood where she now stood, facing forever, as their hearts lit with hope, devotion, and love.

"Thank you," Isabella said. "We will honor each other forever."

Her mother pressed a tender kiss to her cheek and gently adjusted her mantilla. "Mikaela's heart will skip a beat when she sees you," she said. "Remember, embrace these moments."

Isabella opened her mouth, but a knock at the door cut her off. The door creaked open and Dayanara slipped in. Her sleeveless apricot-white A-line dress twirled around her knees as she placed a Louis Vuitton backpack on the bed.

"Do you know how hard it is to support *two* brides?" she announced with a chuckle. "I spent all morning at the penthouse running around for Her Royal Highness Queen Cristina and Mikaela and then hurried over here to see if you needed anything." Dayanara glanced up from where she perched at the edge of the bed. "And, *damn*, Isabella," she let out a low whistle. "You look…*stunning*. Mikaela isn't going to know what hit her."

Isabella shook her head. "I think we're okay, Daya," she replied. "But thank you. I just…" she looked around. "…Need to find my shoes, I guess."

Dayanara grabbed a pair of black Versace slingback pumps from the floor. "These?"

Isabella nodded in relief as Dayanara handed them to her and leaned in with a conspiratorial whisper. "Just think, after today you get to boss Mikaela around for the rest of your lives." She laughed. "She might like to *think* she's in charge, but, well, we all know she would be lost without you."

Isabella's heart swelled. "I love her. More than I ever thought I could love another. I can't wait to marry her."

"I'll check to see if the car has arrived yet," her mother said. "I imagine we'll leave very soon."

"Mami," Isabella called, unsure if she heard her as she disappeared down the hallway. A moment later, her mother returned and glanced at her.

"Yes?" she asked.

Isabella swallowed hard, unsure why she was overcome with emotion. "I just… You've always been the most wonderful woman I've ever known."

Her mother was still for a moment and then turned as she wiped away a tear. "Thank you," she replied after a moment and then sniffled once. "I love you. Now you'd better get those shoes on, because I think I see the car pulling up the drive right now."

Isabella glanced out the bedroom window at the bright sunlight and deep green palm leaves rustling outside. She knew it would be a matter of minutes until one of the event planners or royal staff would let them know it was time to leave. Despite the warm, balmy temperature, a shiver of anticipation raced up Isabella's spine at all that awaited her.

Like clockwork, she heard an event planner hurry up the stairs and confirm into her phone that the car had arrived outside and they would be exiting now.

As Isabella carefully buckled one shoe and Dayanara leaned down to buckle the other, an exhilarating, intoxicating reminder crept into her mind.

Today is the day that I become Mikaela's forever.

Mikaela stood inside a large white tent, decorated with twinkling white string lights and bouquets of orange blossoms, as her toes sank into the warm sand. She took a slow, steadying breath as she glanced once more into the full-length mirror. Her black off-the-shoulder gown danced over the white sand around her. The custom lace pattern of her sleeves matched the lace pattern of her mantilla, which gently hung to her shoulders and fluttered in the breeze from the large fans set up throughout her family's private tent. Her hair had been styled into an intricate plait that combined a half-up, half-down style into a long, sophisticated braid. Large, rectangular diamonds glittered along the tall peineta beneath her mantilla and sparkled in the sunlight that filtered between the loosely tied entrance to the tent.

Alejandro, handsome as ever in his custom black tuxedo, sat casually at the edge of a white sectional sofa as he posed into his phone for few pre-ceremony selfies.

Mikaela rolled her eyes good-naturedly at him as she turned and smoothed a tiny wrinkle from the wrist of his tailored jacket. As she faced back to the mirror, her parents stepped behind her and flanked either side in elegant unison.

"Beautiful, eh?" her father said.

Mikaela turned to her parents. "It's everything we imagined and more," she replied. "Thank you, Papa."

She meant it. A custom-built white marble arch, adorned with flowing Italian linens and vibrant orange blossoms, stood tall and just yards before the tide. A simple marble altar stood beneath the arch and faced covered, open-air rows of tall, white chairs that had been custom-upholstered with soft mulberry silk and the de Medreno family crest across the high backs.

The sandy aisle was bordered by thin eight-foot lanterns, their flickering flames illuminating the path in a golden glow, and twinkling white string lights had been strung throughout the beach. The trees bordering the sand, the white silk canopies covering the rows of chairs, the arch and altar, and even the royal family's private tent were all beautifully decorated with the small, warm lights.

When combined with the serene sounds of the waves and the rustle of palm fronds in the gentle island breeze, Mikaela admitted that it felt like walking into a dream. It was intimate, it was elegant, it was deeply rooted in Cayo Azulean heritage, and it was beautiful, as her father said.

"It is," he said. He met Mikaela's gaze. "But I meant *you.* You are the picture of elegance and royalty, my daughter. But today, I…I must admit I'm struggling to be anything more than a father standing beside his daughter, about to walk with her into her future and her forever."

Mikaela blinked at the uncharacteristic emotion in her father's voice. *There's something…different about him today. Less king, more…*Papa*?* She wondered if the significance of everything they had endured together, everything that was about to change, and his targeted abdication date in just under three years was weighing on him.

"Please don't be worried about anything," she said. "The Royal Council was very much aligned on the succession plan we drafted. I'm ready."

"I am not worried, my daughter," he replied. "Mikaela, you have shown more honor and strength in these last weeks than most leaders display in a lifetime. You've made hard choices. You've supported our people and you've protected this family, even against our own blood wishing to do harm to the Crown. Even before, your commitment to Cayo Azul and our family never wavered. I am sorry, my daughter, for questioning your strength. I have always known who you are."

Mikaela grasped her father's hand in hers. "Thank you, Papa. That means everything to me."

"I placed you next in line for the throne before you were even born," he said as he glanced at their interlocked hands and then at Mikaela. "I saw you as my purpose, my legacy, and sometimes forgot to see you as my *daughter*." He swallowed once. "I realize now that I already have those things. And I am so proud of the legacy you have brought this family and of the woman you are."

Her mother placed a gentle hand on his back. "I think what your papa is trying to tell you is that we are so very proud of you, Mikaela."

Mikaela opened her mouth to reply as her mother waved a hand. "Though I'm not certain *I* would have selected the beach wedding," she said. "Sand is so very…*uncomfortable* to work with. And you really need a special type of couture that can withstand…"

Her father chuckled as he leaned over and pressed a kiss to her mouth, temporarily quieting her. "Let's leave it at that, love." The corners of his dark eyes crinkled playfully. "This is Mikaela's and Isabella's wedding and it will be beautiful."

"You and Isabella are now bound for life," her mother said. "She becomes our daughter too. I must say you made an *excellent* choice."

Mikaela leaned in and hugged both her parents. Though they both seemed startled for a beat at the sudden affection, they wrapped their arms around her and held her for a long moment. The music shifted outside the tent as the orchestra seated neatly just behind the rows of guests launched into a slower tune.

Alejandro wandered over as he adjusted the cufflink on his left wrist. "You know, I was fully prepared to have Dayanara help me drag you here if you tried to run at the last minute," he joked. His face softened as he leaned in to hug Mikaela. "But somehow I knew you wouldn't. As soon as you met Isabella, I had a feeling we'd be standing here eventually."

Mikaela playfully nudged him. "Enjoy it now, cousin," she said. "You're the last one to be married off."

Alejandro shook his head good-naturedly. "I'm so proud of you, Mika. You ready for this?"

The strings of the orchestra faded and then swelled into the first notes of the processional as a hushed silence fell over the guests seated outside. Mikaela felt her heart pounding in her chest out of sheer anticipation as she glanced toward the entrance to the tent.

In just a few minutes, Isabella will walk toward me, toward our future as one. Heat tingled below her gown as she thought of Isabella binding herself to her forever and the consummation that would take place later, after they were left alone and the festivities had wrapped.

Mikaela gave a short nod. "Yes."

As if on cue, Amelia walked purposefully into the tent. "Your Royal Highness, it's time!" She tapped her discreet black headset once. "We'll have you line up along the right side. Isabella will come from the left. Sir Alejandro, we'll have you and Señora Ramon proceed from each side first."

Alejandro nodded as he carefully ran a hand over his dark hair.

"Then we'll have a brief pause," Amelia said as she gestured to Mikaela's parents. "The attendants will stand as His Royal Highness King Bartolo and Her Royal Highness Queen Cristina will lead. As we practiced, you will both stand by the altar and receive one of the brides. Her Royal Highness Princess Mikaela will proceed from the right as Señorita Acosta Ramon will proceed from the left. King Bartolo, you will receive Princess Mikaela. Queen Cristina, you will receive Isabella. Once they are joined at the altar, you may take your seats in the front row."

Her father gave a steady nod as her mother smoothed her sky-blue caped crepe gown. "Very well," she said. Her matching pillbox hat and the elegant lace that gently shaded her face remained perfectly in place. "I believe we're ready."

Alejandro clapped a hand on Mikaela's back before dropping it to his side. She squeezed his hand one last time before stepping aside so he could be first in the processional line at Amelia's hurried *go*.

It was time.

Chapter Forty-seven

As the elegant processional music seamlessly transitioned to a traditional rendition of "Here Comes the Bride," Mikaela barely registered Amelia's expectant expression as she waved her around the tent. She stepped across the warm sand, her pulse quickening, as she trained her gaze above and away from the sea of expectant faces she knew waited around the corner.

"You're up," Amelia whispered. "Remember, not too fast. One step each second." She craned her neck, squinting against the sun, and then smiled broadly. "Oh, there she is," she breathed. "She's beautiful."

Amelia turned back to Mikaela and patted her arm. "And *go*!"

As Mikaela stepped into the sandy aisle, she felt the full weight of the moment settle low in her stomach. She felt rows of reverent eyes on her as she clasped the bouquet of flowers in her hands tighter. Mikaela glanced at the front row, where many of the Royal Council and their plus-ones sat, and her gaze landed on Alejandro.

His face was brimming with pride and—were those tears in her strong cousin's dark eyes? Mikaela averted her gaze as she swallowed hard.

Don't cry. Don't cry. Definitely don't look at Alejandro again.

She glanced at the altar, where her parents stood regally, the picture of royal sophistication and pride. Their expressions were warm and their hands were clasped together in a show of dignified unity and strength. Her father smiled expectantly, holding her gaze, as he broke royal protocol for just a split second to mouth *love you*.

Mikaela felt her throat tighten and the pressure pushing inside her chest.

Don't cry. You're royalty. No tears. You're Mikaela de Medreno Soliz.

And then her gaze landed on Isabella. Walking toward her from the opposite side of the horizontal aisle between the front row of chairs and the wide arch, Isabella moved with radiant grace. The hem of her dress whispered over the white sand as her long mantilla trailed behind her. Orange blossom petals decorated her dark curls and her dimples flashed across her face as her gaze found Mikaela's. At that moment, Isabella's face lit up.

Mikaela felt as though the air had been taken from her lungs. Everything else seemed to disappear in a blur around her as she became acutely aware only of the woman before her, who walked toward her now: Isabella, who had unraveled her defenses, challenged her, softened her, believed in her, and loved her with her entire heart.

As Mikaela and Isabella reached the altar together, her father gently clasped her hands while her mother opened her arms to embrace Isabella. Only after her hands were in her father's firm, warm grip did Mikaela realize her fingers were trembling.

After a moment, her parents solemnly stepped back as Isabella's hands found Mikaela's. With just millimeters between them now, Isabella held her gaze.

"My love," she murmured as she gently brushed away a tear on Mikaela's cheek. "You're crying."

Shit. Mikaela hadn't even felt the tears falling down her face. "You're so beautiful, Isabella."

Her father's deep voice boomed across the sand as he spoke steadily. "Welcome, friends," he called. "Today, we gather not just to honor a sacred marriage union between my daughter, Her Royal Highness Princess Mikaela de Medreno Soliz, and her bride, but to welcome the forging of new and expanded leadership, bound by honor and loyalty."

He turned as he bowed slightly to gently kiss Mikaela's hand and then held out his elbow to her mother as they took their seats in the front row. After they sat, the rest of the guests followed suit and sat respectfully. The priest stood to take his place behind the altar.

"Thank you, Your Royal Highness," the priest said. "Today, we celebrate the extraordinary union of Her Royal Highness Princess Mikaela de Medreno Soliz and Isabella Acosta Ramon. We will begin with the handfasting ceremony, a deeply symbolic ritual with roots right here in Cayo Azul. Your Royal Highness, your hand please."

Mikaela took a deep breath as she held her right hand over the altar. Thick navy blue and burnt orange cords dyed in the colors of the Cayo Azulean flag lay neatly across the cool marble.

"Thank you," the priest said as he looked expectantly at Isabella. "Señorita, your hand please."

Isabella remained facing Mikaela as she placed her left hand over the altar. Mikaela recognized a swell of emotion across Isabella's face as the priest joined their hands together. She entwined her fingers in Isabella's on the altar, squeezing them in reassurance, as the priest began carefully wrapping their joined hands with the first cord.

"This ancient ritual symbolizes the binding of these two lives," the priest said. "As I connect these cords around the hands of Her Royal Highness Princess Mikaela de Medreno Soliz and Isabella Acosta Ramon, we bind their souls beyond the limitations of space and time." He began wrapping the second cord around their hands. "Each loop around their joined hands represents the vows they will make to each other, the official joining of their lives as one, and the intertwining of their destinies."

Mikaela swallowed hard as she held Isabella's gaze. Isabella lifted her chin slightly and stepped closer to her.

"Señorita Acosta Ramon, do you arrive here willingly, with an open heart, to share your life and your soul with Her Royal Highness?"

Isabella didn't take her eyes off Mikaela. "I do." She nodded. "I always have," she murmured under her breath so only Mikaela could hear.

Mikaela tightened her fingers in Isabella's beneath the cords as the priest turned to her. "Your Royal Highness, do you arrive here willingly, with an open heart, ready to honor and cherish Isabella forever?"

Mikaela swallowed the lump that rose in her throat as she nodded. "I do," she said.

The priest picked up the final cord. "At this time and as I wrap the final cord in the handfasting ceremony, you may exchange your vows."

Isabella cleared her throat nervously. "Mikaela," she said and then took a deep breath. "I fell in love with you from the moment I saw you. I love the way you look at me and I love your heart, the way it beats so fiercely for the people you love. I know you've always believed that you have to be strong and that holding love at arm's length is something that protects you. But Mikaela, my love, you never have to be strong alone again. I vow to be your safe place, your rooftop, your reassurance, and your grounding. I vow to love you *because* of all your complexities, not in spite of. I will always remind you that softness is not weakness and that you can be strong *and* worthy of deep love that asks for nothing but you in return. I vow to spend the rest of my days showing you that love is something to be lived. I want to live it with you now, and in all my lifetimes. Forever."

The ceremony seemed to still as the guests appeared stunned into a quiet silence. Even the priest looked up as he continued looping the final cord around their hands.

"Isabella," Mikaela said after a moment. "You have been the most unexpected and precious gift in my life. When I say that, I mean that you've shown me that love isn't something to be feared. It *is* a gift. And you, my love, are the greatest gift my life has given me. I vow to choose you in every lifetime and every reality. I vow to honor your heart and your dreams, and to never allow the weight of the world to dull the smoldering fire we've built between us. I will always fight for you, listen to you, and hold you close. I will love you fiercely and tenderly until the very end and then beyond. You told me once that you didn't need grand gestures. But, Isabella, please know that loving you is the grandest thing I will ever be privileged enough to do. And I promise to do it forever. I will love you for eternity."

The priest gently dipped their corded hands in a shallow rose quartz bowl of sea water, representing cleansing and good fortune.

After a moment, he stood back. "Congratulations," he said. "You are now joined together as one."

The priest raised their joined hands to the ceremony guests. "I present to you Her Royal Highness Princess Mikaela de Medreno Soliz and her wife, Her Royal Highness Isabella de Medreno Soliz." The rows of guests stood and bowed their heads in respect and reverence.

Mikaela felt breathless as realization hit her. *We did it.*

She felt giddy with excitement as she and Isabella turned to the rows of guests and waved with their free hands. Despite being symbolically bound with Isabella, their hands still clasped together beneath the thick, wet cords as droplets of warm sea water trailed down their wrists, Mikaela had never felt so free.

The beachside reception had reached its energy-filled crescendo as the fiery Cayo Azul sunset lit the sky in bold reds and deep pinks while rough waves crashed against the sand.

I have to give Amelia credit. Isabella looked around. *I wasn't sure about so many of those string lights, but they really look beautiful at dusk.* The tiny twinkling lights swayed gently in the breeze as she walked through the celebration, stopping momentarily to graciously accept congratulations from Arturo Benitez and his wife.

She had long since changed from her wedding dress into a simple, sophisticated ivory one-shoulder sleeveless jumpsuit, though the velvety-smooth orange blossom petals were still woven through her loose curls.

Conversation and upbeat cumbia drifted over the sand as guests danced and drinks flowed from the bleached bamboo bar that had been constructed alongside covered tables overflowing with fresh paella and sizzling fajita skewers near the tree line. The elegant string orchestra had long since been replaced with a wide DJ booth as Latin music pulsed from tall speakers.

It was casual by royal celebration standards but, as Isabella glanced around at the energy and excitement that surrounded her, she sensed that guests were truly living in the moment and sharing in their joy. *And that's most important of all. This is a night to remember forever.*

Isabella laughed as she spotted her mother, who was dancing cumbia at the center of the lively crowd with Ian. He blushed as he struggled to keep up.

"I know," Dayanara said with a sigh as she appeared next to her. "I'm going to have to teach him how to dance, aren't I?"

Isabella wrapped her arms around herself as she took a deep breath, grounding herself in the joy that was tonight. All she could feel beneath her pounding heart was the lingering warmth of Mikaela's touch and the firm squeeze of her fingertips beneath the binds, the promise in her vows, and the absolute certainty that she had just married the love of her life.

"He'll learn," Isabella replied after a moment. A bead of sweat trickled down Ian's temple. "Look how cute he looks trying. Just be patient."

I'm married. Isabella was sure she was about to burst with lightheaded, giddy exuberance. *To Mikaela.*

"You look completely lovesick," Dayanara said as she nudged her shoulder and then took a sip of her frosty mojito.

The king and queen had made their discreet exit just moments before through a private, highly secured separate path to their waiting Escalade. Alejandro wandered over, his hands casually in his tuxedo pants pockets, with his friend Matteo. Matteo took a long swig from his Dos Equis and nodded in greeting as they joined them.

"I *am* completely lovesick," Isabella said as she grabbed a glass of champagne from a passing waiter.

"Good," Alejandro said. "That's exactly how you should feel on your wedding night. By the way, where *is* Mikaela? I need to make sure I tell her that if she ever makes you cry, she'll have to answer to me. After all, you're officially family."

Matteo snorted. "Yeah, I'm sure Mikaela is terrified."

"Hey, I can be scrappy when I need to be!" Alejandro punched Matteo's arm good-naturedly. "Anyway, who's ready for a wedding shot?" He looked around expectantly. "Patron, anyone?"

Dayanara wrinkled her nose as Isabella shook her head quickly. Warmth bloomed through her as she took in the moments around her, from Dayanara casually sipping her drink and her mother rolling her hips and stepping in time with the beat on the dance floor to Alejandro and Matteo arguing over the best tequila brand.

This is perfect. Still, something tugged at her with a pull deep in her chest as she turned and scanned the throngs of people throughout the reception. After a few moments, her gaze landed on *her*.

Mikaela stood poised and ever-cool near one of the sparkling granite-topped pub tables scattered along the bar, near the seemingly endless piles of food. She threw her head back and laughed at something Eduardo's wife, Ximena, said as the wife and twenty-something daughter of the Danish prime minister nodded along with them. The thin straps of her cropped ivory camisole practically glowed against her tanned shoulders and her high-rise ivory wide-leg pants teased just enough of her toned upper abs in between.

Isabella bit her lip as desire and deep affection flooded her veins. Mikaela's expression was soft as she tilted her head to listen to an anecdote the Danish prime minister's wife was animatedly regaling them with. Isabella's heart twisted so achingly as she gazed at Mikaela, effortlessly at ease, that she barely registered her feet moving through the sand over the overwhelming pang of *want*.

She didn't pause until she was next to Mikaela. She turned expectantly as she met Isabella's eyes. Without hesitation, Isabella reached for Mikaela, curling her fingers around her waist, and pulled her in for a kiss.

Isabella's heart pounded in her chest as Mikaela's lips met her own. The kiss was slow, deep, and intoxicating and Isabella could taste the sweet champagne on Mikaela's lips. The loud music, the sounds of people chatting, and the entire reception around her fell away as Isabella felt a slow, smoldering heat gathering between her thighs.

Mikaela's hands slid around her waist, pulling her closer and anchoring her to the warmth of her skin, before she gently rested her forehead against Isabella's for a moment.

After a breathless beat, Mikaela arched an eyebrow. "Miss me already?"

"Always," Isabella said. She pressed another kiss, softer this time, to Mikaela's lips as the celebration carried on all around them. As the last strokes of bold color faded into a dazzling, rich navy blue above, Isabella sighed happily. There was no better feeling than the infinite certainty of forever with Mikaela de Medreno Soliz.

Chapter Forty-eight

Hours later, long after the last guests had stumbled into private cars from the beach and the tall lanterns had been extinguished, Isabella stepped into the private elevator to the penthouse at City Center's trendy Solmare Resort and Spa. The long ride to the sixteenth floor was a quiet contrast to their loud, vibrant reception party.

She stole a glance across the polished marble as Mikaela leaned casually against the carved wood railing. The bottoms of her ivory pants were still dusted with sand and strands of hair had since fallen from her elaborate plait and framed her face, as she met Isabella's eyes with an infuriatingly knowing glance.

"Something on your mind, my wife?" Mikaela said as she tilted her head teasingly.

Isabella flushed at the word—*wife*—before quickly recovering. "I'm just enjoying the view." She brushed an imaginary speck of sand from Mikaela's shoulder, as her fingers lingered a beat longer than necessary. "It's a very nice one. In fact, I don't think elevators make me feel claustrophobic anymore."

Mikaela laughed as she caught Isabella's wrist and pressed a slow, deliberate kiss to the soft skin at her pulse point. "Flirting with me already? We haven't even made it to the penthouse yet."

Isabella arched an eyebrow. "You're my wife," she said. "I intend to flirt with you for the rest of my life."

Mikaela's full lips curved into a slow smile as the elevator doors slid open. She gently released Isabella's wrist as she pushed herself from the railing. "Careful, cariño," she murmured. "You might get exactly what you're asking for."

The penthouse was dimly lit, though floor-to-ceiling windows framed the dark expanse of ocean and rippling waves that shimmered under the white-glow of moonlight. Thick, plush carpet was soft beneath Isabella's feet and the scent of fresh orchids drifted from bouquets that had been strategically placed throughout the large living area. A bottle of Dom Perignon chilled in a silver ice bucket near the television anchored firmly to the wall, but neither of them reached for the Waterford crystal champagne glasses placed neatly next to the bucket.

Mikaela turned to Isabella as the door shut with a soft *click* behind them. Isabella's heart was in her throat as the charged moment lingered. The room felt hot and electric as Mikaela backed her up against the wall and pressed their bodies together. Her lips found the curve of Isabella's throat, teasing her there slowly and deliberately. Isabella slid her hands beneath the hem of Mikaela's cropped camisole and pulled it up until she could yank it over her head and toss it to the floor.

"I've been waiting all night for this," Mikaela said against Isabella's neck. Her fingertips were already dragging the delicate zipper of her jumpsuit down inch by inch as Isabella shivered against the cool air conditioning and arched into her touch.

"Then don't make me wait any longer." Isabella met Mikaela's lips and kissed her deeply.

They kissed their way to the massive king-sized bed as Isabella pushed Mikaela roughly onto the thick comforter. Mikaela reached up, eager to pull her onto her, but Isabella paused. She felt practically feral in that moment, desperate to claim Mikaela's body first, as she raised an eyebrow at her.

"I know you're craving to top me right now," Isabella whispered as she leaned down, her breath against Mikaela's ear. "But right now, you belong to me."

Mikaela's expression was dark with desire, but she didn't argue. Isabella crawled over her, letting her jumpsuit fall to the floor, and gently held Mikaela's wrists over her head as she nibbled and teased her neck, the hollows of her collarbones, and the sensitive skin around her throat. Mikaela shifted beneath her as their breasts brushed against each other, and a low moan escaped her at the delicious skin-on-skin feeling.

Mikaela sat up on her elbows and then shifted into a seated position as she held Isabella tightly to her. Isabella realized she was straddling Mikaela and her fingertips had traveled between her thighs. Mikaela's fingers were the only thing between them as she massaged against them both. Tiny jolts of pleasure exploded between her legs as she cupped Mikaela's face in both hands and kissed her again.

"How do you manage to top me, even when you're on the bottom?" Isabella asked breathlessly.

Mikaela's fingers continued working in the tight, soaked space between their intertwined thighs. "Never doubt me, love," she said.

Isabella pushed her hips further onto Mikaela's fingers as they stroked faster and electrified her, building the steady heat through her core. Isabella could feel Mikaela's heart pounding against her own chest as her fingers pleasured them both and it was no longer distinguishable whose wetness belonged to whom.

As the pressure continued to spike between her legs, Isabella cupped Mikaela's breasts in her hands as she gently pinched and rolled her nipples through her fingertips. Mikaela tipped her head back against the sensations, before abruptly pausing and extracting her soaked hand from between them.

Isabella groaned in frustration, missing the contact, as she watched Mikaela. "Are you okay, my love?"

Mikaela nodded as she scooted back on the bed and gently flexed her wrist. "I want us to come together," she replied, her voice thick with passion.

Isabella blinked. "I'm almost there," she said, slightly confused.

Mikaela gracefully leaned over to the dark wood table next to the bed, all effortless beauty and relaxed, languid movements despite Isabella's hungry gaze on her.

She pulled a thin double-ended soft silicone dildo from the drawer. Dark desire and a teasing question danced over her face as she trailed one end over Isabella's stomach. "Remember when I said I wanted to fuck you every way imaginable?"

Isabella swallowed hard as she nodded and her eyes widened at the vibrating toy between them. A surge of *want* flooded her veins, extinguishing her nerves, as she bit her lip. "My love, you should know," she said. "I…I have never actually had intercourse like that with a man before. Which probably isn't surprising to know now, but…" She raised an eyebrow at the toy. "I may be a virgin to this type of sex."

Mikaela leaned in and captured Isabella's lips in a searing, passionate kiss. "I had no idea," she said after a moment as she gently ran a hand through Isabella's hair. She paused as an orange blossom petal drifted to the comforter. "Then we don't have to do this. Only if and when you tell me you're ready."

Isabella's pulse throbbed in time with the aching, wet desire between her thighs as she brushed her fingertips along Mikaela's cheekbone. "I want to," she replied confidently. "I'm ready. I want to do this with you."

Mikaela searched her face for a moment. "Are you sure?"

Isabella swallowed hard again. The nerves electrified her and melded right into the searing pleasure that pulsed through her. "Yes," she replied. "Will it hurt?"

Mikaela twirled the ends of Isabella's hair around her finger. "It might," she said. "I will be gentle with you. If you don't come this time, it's okay, my love. I'll see to it that you do through…other ways." Her gaze dropped to Isabella's soaked center as she licked her lips suggestively.

Isabella nodded as she let Mikaela guide her onto the bed, her back sinking into the soft pillows, and relaxed against her gentle caresses over her thighs. She arched further into her touch as Mikaela's tongue teased her nipples, practically setting her skin ablaze as desire flooded her. Mikaela's fingers were gentle as they massaged featherlight caresses around her clit. Isabella squirmed against the bed, lifting her hips from the sheets, as she desperately searched for firmer friction.

Mikaela continued to worship her breasts, kissing every inch of heated skin, and dropping soft kisses across her nipples. Isabella dug her nails into Mikaela's shoulders as she felt herself unraveling beneath her. She threw her head back against the pillow and moaned with pleasure as Mikaela's fingers slipped between her soaked folds.

"Always so insatiable," Mikaela teased.

"You do this to me," Isabella said. She didn't care that her voice was very close to a whine or that she was positively throbbing against Mikaela's fingers and mouth. "Every time," she breathed. "I can't think about anything else."

Mikaela carefully positioned one end of the dildo just outside of Isabella's wet entrance and gently replaced her fingers with the soft tip. "Does this feel okay, love?" she asked, stifling a moan as she positioned the opposite tip just inside her. "Are you all right?"

Isabella bit her lip at the strange but not entirely unwelcome sensation. She was too wet, too unraveled, to know yet if there was pain. She took in the sight of Mikaela, her hips hovering over her and her lips just millimeters from her own, and wondered for a brief moment if she might come before Mikaela had even fully entered her.

"Yes," she breathed. "I want it. Fuck me, Mikaela. *Please*. I want you, my love."

Mikaela pressed a tiny button at the center of the double-ended toy as quiet, subtle vibrations filled the air. She pushed the rest of the dildo into herself first, her long eyelashes falling closed as it vibrated into her, and then gently pumped her hips to guide the other side into Isabella.

Isabella gasped as she stretched over it, her wetness helping it glide through her easily, though the momentary shock and discomfort gave way to tightly coiling pleasure. As Mikaela moved expertly, the dildo slowly slid in and out of Isabella and the gentle vibrations pulsed irresistibly around her clit.

After a few moments, Isabella was moving in time as her hips arched and sought *more*. The more she moved, the longer and deeper Mikaela's breathy moans became. As Mikaela moved, Isabella was rewarded with soft vibrating pulses that teased her clit and left her desperate for more. The realization that they were fucking each other at the same time was almost enough to make Isabella shatter right then and there, and she wound her fingers in Mikaela's hair.

"I'm close," she panted. "*Really* close. Everything you do…it feels *so* good, Mikaela."

Mikaela leaned down to kiss her again and thrust into Isabella, and then it was too late. She felt herself tightening around the toy and arched her back into Mikaela's fingertips as they brushed across her nipples. Isabella cried out as the vibrations pulsed and pleasure exploded through her.

As Isabella rode out her orgasm, she sensed Mikaela coil and still against her. She knew Mikaela's orgasm was spilling over and rippling through her too, and she arched herself further into her to press the gentle vibrations deeper into her swollen folds.

By the time they lay tangled in the sheets, breathless, sated, and their bodies slick with sweat, dawn was just beginning to light the horizon. Isabella turned her head as she pressed a slow, lazy kiss to Mikaela's shoulder and ran her hands down the planes and valleys of her back.

Mikaela shivered against her as she blinked and fixed Isabella with a sleepy but *so* satisfied smile.

"I guess this means we've consummated our marriage," Isabella murmured as she wrapped the cool sheet around her. "Though I don't think there was any concern about that."

Mikaela laughed as she tightened her arm around Isabella's middle. "We might need to make sure. You know, just in case."

Isabella snuggled deeper into the pillow and buried her face in Mikaela's neck. "You're falling asleep, love," she said gently. "But there's always time when we wake up. And when we shower. After lunch. Before dinner. On that gorgeous balcony overlooking the ocean. Um, when and where else…" Isabella's voice trailed off as she yawned.

Mikaela giggled again as her eyes drifted shut. "I told you you're insatiable."

Isabella gave a little sigh of happiness as her fingers intertwined in Mikaela's. "For you?" She replied as she felt herself drop into a deep, satisfying sleep. "Always."

Chapter Forty-nine

Six weeks later, Isabella sat anxiously on a high-backed chair among the row that had been set behind a large wooden podium. Castillo Blanco's front courtyard buzzed with excitement and energy as the long line of camerapeople and reporters jockeyed for position behind horizontal barriers and throngs of security. Amelia Wilson and a full contingent from the agency flocked around the simple black stage that had been set up at the head of the courtyard, just outside the grand ballroom. Isabella didn't recognize most of them, though Dayanara had told her many of them handled the royal family's media relations.

There was an electric, intoxicating feeling of hope and renewal that permeated the courtyard as thousands of local citizens attending the press conference began collecting around the stage with interest and buzzing anticipation. The announcement about the upcoming change in succession—still just under three years away—was officially released the morning before and the Royal Council had scheduled this press conference as a rare public state of the union. Isabella looked around from her seat as Cristina was escorted to her chair next to her and closest to the podium. On Isabella's other side, Alejandro and a few key members of the Royal Council took their seats down the row.

She hadn't seen Mikaela since much earlier that morning and she knew that she was busy preparing herself for this rare public moment. There was hair and makeup to do, extensive talking points to review with the media relations team, and official photos to take with her family and the Royal Council.

As Isabella surreptitiously glanced around, hoping to catch a glimpse of Mikaela, a reverent hush washed over the sea of people crowding the courtyard. She stood and clasped her hands respectfully in front of her, along with the others who were seated behind the podium.

Bartolo stepped from behind the long navy-blue curtain at the back of the stage and surveyed the courtyard with a regal smile. Though age had softened some of the edges around his face, he still looked every bit the long-reigning king as he waved to the crowd. The intricate golden embroidery and silver royal insignia decorating his collared navy-blue military coat shimmered beneath the morning sunlight. He waved again and nodded in acknowledgement of the cheers and applause. His spotless white gloves and neatly pressed navy-blue suit pants were immaculate as he stood tall at the podium.

Isabella snuck a glance at Cristina, who gazed at Bartolo adoringly as she stood with her hands over her heart. Her navy-blue Monique Lhullier button-up dress matched Bartolo's uniform perfectly. Isabella's heart pounded in her chest as she understood just how deeply Mikaela's parents embodied royalty.

"My people," Bartolo began, his voice deep and sure, as the crowd quieted. "Beloved Cayo Azuleans. I have stood before you many times, during moments of challenge and triumph." He scanned the crowd. "For generations, the Crown has been a symbol of strong leadership, of lineage, and duty to *you*, the people of Cayo Azul. Today, we know that it is not always heritage alone that determines leadership, nor title or tradition. It is wisdom, compassion, and the courage to listen and serve in the face of it all. Today, I am proud to present my daughter, Mikaela de Medreno Soliz, as the future of Cayo Azul. Your next sovereign leader, who has proven herself worthy through her actions and integrity. She stood by me and our people during the most difficult hours of our reign. She protects our people, desires to bridge gaps and unite, and she stood up to our own blood in defense of what is just. I am elated that soon she will lead you, who matter most."

Cheers broke out through the crowd, growing stronger and then fading into the soft breeze. Bartolo's face was filled with pride as he glanced somewhere to his right toward where Isabella knew Mikaela was waiting to speak.

"It is with great pride and the utmost faith in the generations to come on this island that I formally present to you your next sovereign leader, Mikaela de Medreno Soliz." Bartolo stepped back from the podium as applause surged through the crowd. As the camerapeople elbowed into one another for the perfect shot, Mikaela approached the podium regally.

Mikaela's smile was cool and poised as her gaze swept over the crowd, surveying the momentous scene before her. Isabella felt her mouth drop open slightly as she reminded herself to breathe. The sea breeze teased a few strands of dark blond hair across Mikaela's cheek as she stood in her short-sleeved navy-blue Armani dress and black slingback heels. Isabella shifted in her seat as she noticed the way the fabric hugged Mikaela's body in all the right places and the soft morning glow of sunlight kissed her golden skin.

Isabella imagined herself kissing Mikaela's soft, full lips and then reminded herself that there were cameras all around to catch every detail of the stage.

The last thing I need is for my lovestruck face to be shared around the world. But then again, let them understand that I have always been here of my own accord. Let them see how much she means to me.

Mikaela stood, her posture strong as she waved to the crowd while they cheered and applauded her. After a moment, she nodded at the crowd, her gaze unwavering.

"Thank you," she said, her voice rich with emotion. "The beloved people of Cayo Azul, I have always loved you and I have always loved our island. Today, I stand before you not because of who I am, but because I was called to something greater. Throughout the years, I have seen what power without purpose can do. What entitlement and abuse of status can lead to. I've watched people close to me make grave mistakes. But I've also seen resilience and I am inspired by *your* courage, the courage of all who are the heart of Cayo Azul. I do not take this duty with ease. I take it with humility and as a leader who listens, who evolves, and who desires our island to be an equitable home for everyone. Already, our monarchy has shown that we do not silence dissent but instead invite it to the table to work together. As a result, we are proud to introduce Cayo Azul's first public transportation system, designed to support accessibility across the island. We are also honored to spearhead the creation of a program based in Este that will provide expert training, education, professional certification tracks, and guaranteed employment in our rapidly growing hospitality sector as well as our public works. Though it will be some time before I officially take the throne, I promise you now and always that I will lead with strength, empathy, and with each and every one of you alongside me."

Isabella looked out over the vast crowd as they cheered loudly, the camerapeople falling over themselves as they clicked dozens of photos, and she recognized the hope that lit the faces of thousands of citizens.

"This is not the beginning of *my* chapter, it's the beginning of *our* future." Mikaela raised her fist in the air. "The Crown will not be a barrier between the people and continued progress and development, but a bridge to deliver our beautiful island further into its most promising future. We will leave no one behind. I will give everything to this purpose."

The crowd thundered with applause, whistles, and cheers. Isabella blinked at an elderly woman moved to tears as she leaned heavily against a middle-aged man she presumed to be her son. She looked back at the podium as the crowd swelled into louder cheers as Bartolo stepped forward and took Mikaela's hand before raising it in the air.

Mikaela waved to the crowd again as they cheered and applauded them.

Isabella's chest ached with something deep and intangible as she watched Mikaela, firm and confident, with reverence.

That's my wife up there. Not the royal, not the public figure. My *Mikaela. The one who makes me shatter in her arms and kisses me like I was always meant to be hers.*

"My daughter accepts this responsibility," Bartolo said with a nod. "Now, we unify. We grow. We move forward, together."

His last few words were drowned out by the echoing cheers and booming applause that reverberated all around. Isabella's eyes stung with hot tears, a combination of the moving emotion of the moment and deep longing for Mikaela coursing through her veins so fiercely that it stole her breath all over again.

I am so hopelessly in love with her. She couldn't seem to look away from her, the way she carried herself, or each imperceptible detail. *This gorgeous, complicated, cool, wildly intelligent, and fearless woman who never backs down, even when it has meant doing the hardest work of all—being vulnerable.*

Mikaela turned her head slightly and their gazes locked across the stage for just a brief heartbeat. The raucous applause, loud cheers, and even the gentle breeze all but faded as her dark eyes burned into Isabella. Her heart pounded, but in the blink of an eye, Bartolo and Mikaela were escorted from the stage. The security team fanned out as they began the long work of dispersing the energized crowd.

As Isabella waited for Amelia's signal for their row to stand and exit at the other side of the stage, she knew she had finally seen all of Mikaela too in that brief split second: The woman she fell for, the person she married and bound herself to forever, and the future they would shape for the island they loved.

I am all hers. And she's mine.

Chapter Fifty

Six months later

The ballroom at Castillo Blanco was filled with the sounds of laughter, the gentle clink of champagne glasses, and an energetic flamenco band playing upbeat tunes in the far corner of the large open space. The warm light from the crystal chandeliers above mingled with bright sunlight streaming through tall open windows, as the scents of jasmine, bougainvillea, and sea salt gently breezed through.

Mikaela glanced at the large golden banner that was strung across the front of the ballroom. It was decorated with whimsical sparkling green shamrocks and white hearts around the words *Congratulations, Ian and Dayanara.*

Long buffet-style tables of tapas and a few Irish specialties lined the adjacent wall as people mingled and sat casually at the round, white-covered tables across the ballroom.

Her mood turned bittersweet as Alejandro, Dayanara, and Ian approached, all smiles as they joined her. *This is the perfect send-off for her. Dayanara deserves every bit of this and more.*

Her best friend was positively glowing as the large square diamond on her ring finger glinted in the bright light. "Mikaela, I can't believe you even had the kitchen staff include corned beef, cabbage, and boxty with the buffet!"

"It's some of the best I've had," Ian added. "I mean it. They really knocked the traditional Irish favorites out of the park. It's been a long time since I've enjoyed boxty."

Dayanara giggled. "Believe me, we appreciate it," she said. "Especially after my weak attempt at Irish soda bread. Here I am, thinking I'm doing something really charming, until it came out like a hockey puck."

Mikaela laughed as Isabella sidled to her side from where she had been chatting with Ximena Rodriguez near one of the tables. Mikaela rested her hand gently on Isabella's back, a subtle show of ownership, as her fingertips burned lightly but possessively along the soft skin beneath her gray silk knit T-shirt—just enough so it was clear to everyone in attendance who Isabella belonged to.

"Ian pretended to like it," Dayanara said as she gazed up at him adoringly. "But seeing the look on his face as he tried to choke it down was possibly more distressing than the bread itself."

Ian took an innocent sip from his champagne flute. "In my defense, I was trying to be a supportive fiancé. But yes, I did fear for the thousands of dollars of orthodontic work my parents invested in my mouth gone in an instant."

"You're a good man, my friend," Alejandro said jovially. "I can confirm that life with Mikaela and Dayanara is mostly smiling through culinary disasters."

"Speak for yourself, cousin," Mikaela countered teasingly. "I could learn to cook if I wanted to. I've just chosen to outsource it because…well, I mean, who can compete with Terese and the amazing kitchen staff assembled here?"

Isabella leaned closer into Mikaela. "You tried to make grilled cheese and you nearly burned down your pool kitchen."

Mikaela arched an eyebrow as she leaned in. "And you still married me afterward, so I'd say it ended well."

Dayanara shook her head ruefully. "Can you two *not* shamelessly flirt for one afternoon? After all, this *is* my engagement and farewell party."

"We can multitask," Isabella replied innocently as she blinked behind her sip of champagne.

"You'll miss it," Alejandro said as he winked at Dayanara. "Though probably not as much as we'll miss you."

"I will, actually," Dayanara replied wistfully. "All of it. All the days and evenings at Mikaela's house, the constant adventures, nights out at Tryst." Her voice trailed off, and then she cleared her throat. "So, how's the succession plan going, Princess?"

Mikaela smiled. "It's been great. Working with my father and the Royal Council in this way has re-energized me. The official launch of the Este jobs program is next month. I'm so excited to be there personally for the event."

"Yeah, if you and Isabella ever emerge from your house," Dayanara joked. "You two barely leave the bedroom during your free hours."

Alejandro clapped his hands over his ears and wrinkled his nose. "Oh my God, I don't want to hear that. Mikaela will always be a de Medreno Soliz and that means royalty will always be in her blood." He shook his head. "And that also means she'll *always* be my cousin, so I don't want to think about just how much they're enjoying being newlyweds."

Isabella's cheeks flushed, though Mikaela rolled her eyes. "Maybe it's time for you to start looking for a wife, Alejandro," she said. "Let me remind you once again that you're the only one left to be married off."

Alejandro shook his head. "I'll need a drink for that." He gestured toward the bar near the long buffet tables. "Though it appears, after all was said and done, it worked out well for *you*."

Mikaela glanced at Isabella and caught her knowing gaze. Her dimples deepened as she brushed a kiss over Mikaela's cheek. "Yes," she finally said after a moment. "It did."

As Alejandro headed to the bar with Ian in tow, a quiet silence fell over them. Dayanara met Mikaela's gaze softly. "Thank you for this, Mika," she said. "This is the best send-off I could have imagined."

Isabella wrapped her arm around Mikaela's waist and gently squeezed. "I'm going to run to the restroom." She glanced knowingly between them. "I'll be back."

As Isabella walked toward the bathrooms and was intercepted by an excited hug from Dayanara's mother, Mikaela felt a lump form in her throat that she tried to swallow.

"Of course, Daya," she said. "It's the very least I could do, after all that you've done for me." She took a deep breath. "Let's sit outside for a moment."

The humid air outside Castillo Blanco was thick with the scent and sounds of the ocean nearby as afternoon light bathed the neatly trimmed deep-green grass in a soft yellow haze. Mikaela perched on the top step of the left-side marble staircase just outside the main entrance.

"I'm going to miss you, you know," Mikaela said as she absent-mindedly trailed her fingers along the polished top stair. "I'm happy for you and Ian, but I'll miss seeing you all the time. I remember how you told me that you weren't sure what your life would look like without it revolving around being my lady-in-waiting. But, really, I think *I* am more unsure what *my* life will look like without having the best friend I've ever had nearby."

"I'm going to miss you too," Dayanara replied. "Should I begin practicing my curtsy for when I visit once you're officially queen?"

"Only if you want me to laugh so hard that I trip and fall on my face walking into the castle."

Dayanara sighed playfully. "Fair," she conceded. "As hilarious as you tripping over your ridiculous collection of heels would be, I don't want to see my best friend injured." She glanced at Mikaela. "I must say, you look very regal these days. Not that you aren't *always* the picture of devastatingly beautiful and put-together, but you look settled. Poised. Ready to take on the world."

Mikaela laughed. "Careful," she replied. "All that hyping up might go right to my head. Even if you *would* tease me if I tripped."

"God forbid." Dayanara raised an eyebrow. "Although I think the real reason you're glowing has less to do with politics and more to do with that absolute goddess you're married to."

Mikaela felt her cheeks flush. "As if."

"Right. Too late." Dayanara playfully nudged her arm. "You're hopeless, Mika. You're so in love." She gazed at the marble fountain beyond the stairs. "I've never seen it on you like this before. You light up when you talk about her, you know. I love it."

Mikaela glanced down at her wedding ring and idly twisted it around her finger. "She might have gotten into my heart."

Dayanara let out a loud hoot. "*Might* have? Sure, Mikaela. You're soft now. You know that, right?"

"Maybe a little softer." Mikaela ran a hand through her hair. "I'm still me. Just me with…clarified priorities, including that absolute goddess you mentioned."

"I'm proud of you," Dayanara said after a moment. "You chose your own path and understand what's right for our island, and you're still crushing it. Everything worked out exactly as it should."

Mikaela was touched as her longtime best friend's sincerity settled over her like a comforting blanket. "Thank you, Daya," she said. "I always knew the ultimate freedom was in letting go and letting myself feel. I just had to take my own advice too."

Mikaela's phone pinged with a text message. She glanced down and sighed. "All right," she said as she stood. "Alejandro and Ian are wondering where we disappeared to. We'd better get back inside."

Dayanara stood with her and took a deep, shaky breath. "I'm going to miss you, future queen." She embraced Mikaela. They hugged tightly for a long moment as hot, happy tears snaked down Dayanara's cheeks. "Damn it, you're making me cry," she laughed through the tears. "I didn't want to cry until at least after the cake. Terese told me she personally baked her scratch-made lemon poppyseed cake that I have been obsessed with for *years* and I will not ruin that spiritual experience with tears."

Mikaela tightened her arms around her before stepping back. She swiped at her own cheeks with the heels of her palms. "I'm so happy for you and your mother, and this new chapter," she said. "And I can't wait to be an auntie once you and Ian start making those babies. You must make sure they grow up knowing their Spanish too. And don't think just because you're all the way in Ireland I won't be there to spoil them rotten."

Dayanara shook her head as they stepped back inside the ballroom. "We'll see," she said. "Babies are still a long way away. But…deal."

As they glanced toward the bar and spotted Alejandro and Ian making their way back with fresh flutes of champagne, Dayanara embraced Mikaela one more time. "Thank you again, Mika," she said. "For the lifetime of friendship and adventure. Remember, don't be afraid of Isabella."

Mikaela scoffed. "I am certainly not afraid of my wife, or anyone for that matter."

Dayanara fixed her with a look. "You know what I mean. You two were meant for one another. Don't be afraid of all that she is to you. Anyone can see how in love with you she is. It's okay to let down your guard and allow your vulnerability to shine through sometimes. *Especially* when you have your soulmate right there and ready to love you forever."

Mikaela glanced across the ballroom as her gaze found Isabella. Her energy was contagious, and her dimples and sparkling brown eyes made the aching pang in Mikaela's chest deepen as she watched her greet one of Eduardo's senior-most aides. Her dark, silky hair fell over her shoulders as she casually crossed her arms, all sweet focus and attentiveness on the lighthearted conversation with the older woman.

"It's okay to let her see all of you too," Dayanara said. "And to love her forever right back. I know you do."

"You're right," she said. "I promise I will."

As if on cue, Isabella glanced in their direction and her eyes locked with Mikaela's. Mikaela felt an electric tingle run down her spine as Isabella's smile deepened just slightly and she held her gaze a split second longer than necessary.

"Oh no, the tears have started flowing!" Ian's joking brogue boomed as he and Alejandro rejoined them. "We should have taken bets."

"I'm glad we didn't," Alejandro said. "I thought for sure the tears would come *after* the cake."

Dayanara threw her hands up. "See!" she exclaimed to Mikaela. She turned to Alejandro. "I'll have you know your cousin started it."

Alejandro nodded good-naturedly. "Sounds about right. She only pretends to be innocent most of the time."

They laughed, the genuine kind that lingered and warmed after a lifetime of friendship, memories, and comfortable familiarity.

Just then, the flamenco band started another song and partygoers migrated to the dance floor. Isabella rejoined moments later and leaned into Mikaela. In that moment it was just the five of them surrounded by love, joy, and happiness. *Family.*

EPILOGUE

Nearly a month later, the house buzzed with a soft, excited energy as the early morning sun glinted brightly through the palm trees. Soft Spanish ballads floated into the living area from a speaker in the kitchen as Isabella took a sip of her agua fresca, the ice cubes clinking neatly against her crystal tumbler. She grinned as her mother's expectant face filled her phone.

"Hello, my daughter!" she called cheerfully. She dotted lipstick over her mouth and waved into the camera. "How are you? How is Mikaela?"

"We're well, Mami," Isabella replied. "Did I, uh, catch you at a busy time?"

Her mother shook her head. "No," she said lightly. "You know I'm never too busy for you. I'm getting ready to go out to dinner. Some of the other nurses at the hospital do a monthly dinner and bingo night at that seafood restaurant down the street from the medical campus. They have been asking me to join them for years and, well, this time I decided why not." She shrugged, suddenly shy.

Isabella couldn't recall the last time her mother had attended a social event aside from their wedding, and her evident happiness and newfound sense of freedom inexplicably made her feel lighter too.

"That's great, Mami," Isabella said sincerely. "You'll have to tell me all about it. Don't get into too much trouble, yes?"

She clucked her tongue playfully. "I've worked with these ladies for years, Isabella," she said. "They ask how you're doing, but they're very respectful and they don't ask invasive questions. Now, mess with their bingo game and that's another thing entirely…"

Isabella listened as her mother went on. She sensed a shadow from her left and glanced up, smiling, as she recognized Mikaela's presence.

Mikaela sat next to her on the chaise and waved into the camera. "Hello, Araceli!" she called.

"Daughter!" She greeted her cheerfully. "So nice to see you too. Are you ready for your honeymoon at long last?"

In just a few hours, Isabella and Mikaela would board the royal family's private plane to Tuscany, where they would spend a few days. After, they would travel to Sicily, where a private luxury yacht awaited to take them across the glittering Mediterranean to Malta. For now, the schedule was flexible enough to allow them to take their time and be fully immersed in one another.

"I'm glad that my father pretty much demanded that Isabella and I take this honeymoon," Mikaela said. "Once we're back, I'll continue to hit the ground running as we work through the succession plan. It'll be beautiful to spend a few uninterrupted weeks with Isabella first."

"Good." Isabella's mother nodded. "Because this..." she gestured at them through the camera. "This is what matters. You both deserve this time away together. Take this pause, be selfish with each other, and get lost in one another. Everything else will fall into place as it should."

Isabella glanced at Mikaela. "And don't forget, your birthday will fall on this trip," she said before turning to her mother. "I don't think she has any idea what she wants to do yet to ring in thirty-one."

As the conversation shifted to other topics, from the cities in Italy they hoped to visit and sailing routes to Malta to whether Mikaela could truly relax for longer than two hours, Isabella's mother smiled knowingly.

"You'll both come back different," she said. "Not because of where you go, but because of what you'll have the space to feel. You're each other's home now. Remember, Mikaela, the world will try to pull at you sometimes but you're strong. Be sure to protect this and cherish it."

Mikaela nodded in understanding. "I plan to," she replied confidently. "Always. Right now at least, the world can wait."

She glanced at the keepsake shadow box neatly placed on a decorative accent table in the living room. The colorful cords that had bound her hand with Isabella's at the wedding, its knots still loosely tied, were arranged in the shadow box alongside one of their professionally-taken black-and-white wedding photos. Isabella laced her fingers in Mikaela's as her mother dabbed at her eyes.

"Don't forget to text me pictures," she said. "Isabella, my daughter, it's clear you've found your place. She's right there to guide you."

The conversation continued a few minutes more before they waved good-bye to the camera and the video call ended. Mikaela shifted as she wrapped her arms around Isabella from behind.

"So, we're really doing this, huh?" she said, her breath tickling the shell of Isabella's ear.

"We are." Isabella twisted in her arms to kiss her. "Whatever comes next, I want all of it with you."

As Isabella's sultry promise warmed Mikaela through her core, she realized their beginning was only starting to unfold before them.

For the first time, I know exactly who I am and who I will be. Mikaela tangled a hand in the ends of Isabella's hair and met her lips again. *I know who I want beside me, and she's already here.*

FIN

About the Author

Midwest-based Lissandra Rowe likes spicy sapphic stories driven by deeply sensual and well-rounded characters, richly descriptive settings, and emotionally charged plots. She's never met (or written!) an ice queen she didn't love and enjoys reading all types of stories authentically representative of our community.

When she's not planning her next novel or diving deep into new characters, Lissandra works in communications, content strategy, and copywriting. She lives with her family, dogs, and entirely too many pairs of shoes and has an intricately crafted playlist for everything.

Books Available from Bold Strokes Books

Hurricane Season Hustle by Greg Herren. Scotty must catch the killer to protect his nearest and dearest, before they strike again. (978-1-63679-882-0)

Royal Rush: 75 Days to Fall in Love by Lissandra Rowe. When a royal matchmaking scheme leads to a chance encounter with Isabella Acosta-Ramon, a slow burn sparks that neither can deny. (978-1-63679-965-0)

The Moon to Me by Ana Hartnett. Sometimes it takes traveling thousands of miles to discover what's been yours all along. (978-1-63679-918-6)

To Love Violets for Their Thorns by Rachel Sullivan. Forced to face the heartbreak they never quite got over, Elly and Sonia must decide: breathe fresh life into an old love or try again with someone new? (978-1-63679-928-5)

Virtually Perfect by Melissa Sky. If your AI flirts better, listens harder, and never ghosts you…does that count as love? (979-8-90035-005-9)

Brooke Takes Queen by Alaina Erdell. Brooke Staley faces personal and professional upheaval when Elizabeth Bettancourt, the emotionally scarred new owner of the resort she works for, considers selling. (978-1-63679-886-8)

Coda by Anna Gram. Parker is intriguing, magnetic, impossible to ignore—and completely wrong for Hannah. But sometimes love's melody refuses to end. (978-1-63679-926-1)

Secrets Under the Junipers by Suzie Clarke. Who killed Hallie Lynn Peeples? Cecilia McConnel needs to know. Bitsy Hanover holds the key. Can love uncover secrets? (978-1-63679-845-5)

The Debutante Dilemma by Jane Walsh. Two debutantes are engaged to wealthy and titled brothers…but discover they only have eyes for each other. (978-1-63679-896-7)

The Love Book by Gun Brooke. When literary agent Rowan Cross receives an anonymous manuscript that deeply resonates with her, Verity realizes she has accidentally sent her own manuscript, complete with her very real feelings for her boss! (978-1-63679-850-9)

Traveling Toward Forever by Erin Dutton. When almost-strangers take a road trip through America's national parks, love may be the final destination. (978-1-63679-894-3)

Beautiful Things by Emma L McGeown. A warmhearted romance of missed chances, undeniable chemistry, and a stubborn love that maybe, just maybe, can find its way back. (978-1-63679-934-6)

Love Takes a Village by Karis Walsh. As Lena Preiss struggles to manage a busy restaurant in the Bavarian Christmas village of Leavenworth, Washington, chocolatier Devin Meyer brings an unexpected richness into her life, along with her delicious desserts. (978-1-63679-902-5)

Secrets of the Heart by Jenny Frame. When a beautiful stranger starts asking questions about Nikki Sharkey, head of an infamous crime syndicate, Nikki will stop at nothing to protect her daughter Isla. (978-1-63679-653-6)

Talon and the Songbird by Julia Underwood. In a world where survival depends on strategic alliances, Makayla and Talon must navigate not only complex politics but also the dangerous territory of their hearts. (978-1-63679-970-4)

The Great Popcorn Romance by Georgia Beers. Opposites attract, and Riley Shaw stands no chance of resisting Hannah Kramer's magnetic pull. But opposites know just how to drive each other crazy… (978-1-63679-910-0)

Three Blissful Days by Dena Blake. Kendall Jackson attempts to make her ex regret dumping her by announcing she's dating beautiful park ranger Ivy Patterson. But there's nothing fake about how attracted Ivy is to Kendall. (978-1-63679-707-6)

Chasing Her Scent by MJ Williamz. When Sheridan Rousseau walks into Lisette Mouton's charming little bookstore in Quebec City, she unknowingly holds the key to a mysterious box hidden in a secret room. (978-1-63679-900-1)

Heart's Run by D. Jackson Leigh. Hoping to recover an escaped racing mare, stock transporter Tobie Mason locks horns with local wild horse advocate Maggie Wilkes. (978-1-63679-825-7)

Scandalous by Kris Bryant. When a Hollywood actress trades places with her twin sister, everyone's in an uproar about getting duped, but Lindsay's more concerned about finding out which twin she made out with. (978-1-63679-874-5)

The Art of Love by Ali Vali. When Mimi and Bianca both set their sights on Jolly, sparks fly, loyalties are tested, and hearts collide as they navigate the unpredictable nature of their hearts (978-1-63679-719-9)

The Other Side of Forever by Kel McCord. Will Kenzie and Rachel be able to make love work when Rachel's cozy suburban dream feels like Kenzie's worst nightmare? (978-1-63679-812-7)

The Secrets of Rhydian Hill by Ronica Black. A doctor in need of a new start. A woman running from a killer. A love story that could end in tragedy. (978-1-63679-880-6)

Feeling Lucky by Krystina Rivers. What happens when, despite suddenly having enough money to buy almost anything, Lucy and Tanner start to discover that maybe all they need is each other? (978-1-63679-876-9)

Iceberg by Gun Brooke. When Lady Arabella hires Zandra, she never expects to find love, especially not as a disaster looms on the horizon. (978-1-63679-908-7)

It Happened One Semester by Aurora Rey. After a Pride night hookup, can eager new Assistant Professor Hudson Greene and Dean of Advising Callie Shaw overcome the odds and ace falling in love? (978-1-63679-814-1)

It's Kind of a Bad Idea by Sarah G. Levine. What happens when an emotionally unavailable serial dater meets the one woman she can't help but fall for—who happens to be the one woman who told her not to? (978-1-63679-920-9)

Thankful for You by Tagan Shepard. Everyone deserves to find their person, maybe Karen has finally found hers? (978-1-63679-884-4)

What Happens on Location by Nan Campbell. How can Helen produce a successful movie when its director is the woman responsible for the demise of her marriage? (978-1-63679-904-9)

When Love Comes Around by Radclyffe and Ronica Black. Can Maya Sanchez and Nolan Wright trust each other enough to build something real, or will the past tear them apart? (978-1-63679-930-8)

BOLD STROKES BOOKS
Bold Strokes Books
Quality and Diversity in LGBTQ Literature